THE CITY BAKER'S
GUIDE TO
COUNTRY LIVING

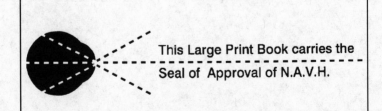

This Large Print Book carries the
Seal of Approval of N.A.V.H.

THE CITY BAKER'S GUIDE TO COUNTRY LIVING

LOUISE MILLER

THORNDIKE PRESS
A part of Gale, Cengage Learning

GALE
CENGAGE Learning®

Farmington Hills, Mich • San Francisco • New York • Waterville, Maine
Meriden, Conn • Mason, Ohio • Chicago

GALE
CENGAGE Learning®

Thorndike Press® Large Print Core.
The text of this Large Print edition is unabridged.
Other aspects of the book may vary from the original edition.
Set in 16 pt. Plantin.

LIBRARY OF CONGRESS CATALOGING-IN-PUBLICATION DATA

Names: Miller, Louise (Chef), author.
Title: The city baker's guide to country living / by Louise Miller.
Description: Waterville, Maine : Thorndike Press, A part of Gale, Cengage Learning, 2016. | Thorndike press large print core
Identifiers: LCCN 2016034986| ISBN 9781410492722 (hardback) | ISBN 1410492729 (hardcover)
Subjects: LCSH: Women cooks—Vermont—Fiction. | Women—Vermont—Fiction. | Man-woman relationships—Vermont—Fiction. | Romance fiction. | Large type books. | BISAC: FICTION / Contemporary Women. | FICTION / Romance / Contemporary.
Classification: LCC PS3613.I5436 C58 2016 | DDC 813/.6—dc23
LC record available at https://lccn.loc.gov/2016034986

Published in 2016 by arrangement with Pamela Dorman Books/Viking, an imprint of Penguin Publishing Group, a division of Penguin Random House LLC

Printed in Mexico
1 2 3 4 5 6 7 20 19 18 17 16

For Elizabeth

Chapter One
SEPTEMBER

The night I lit the Emerson Club on fire had been perfect for making meringue. I had been worrying about the humidity all week, but that night dry, cool air drifted in through an open window. It was the 150th anniversary of the club, and Jameson Whitaker, the club's president, had requested pistachio baked Alaska for the occasion. Since he asked while he was still lying on top of me, under the Italian linen sheets of bedroom 8, I agreed to it — even though I was fairly certain that baked Alaska would not have been on the menu in 1873. But Jamie was a sucker for a spectacle, and his favorite thing on earth was pistachio ice cream, which his wife wouldn't let him eat at home.

I added sugar to the egg whites, a spoonful at a time. As they whipped up into a glossy cloud of white, I leaned a soft hip against my butcher-block worktable and surveyed the kitchen. Now, I've wielded my rolling pin in trendy city restaurants, macrobiotic catering companies, and hotels both grand and not so grand. You would think a Boston Brahmin private club like the Emerson, with its dim lights, starched linen, and brass-studded leather chairs, would have a deluxe kitchen. But no matter what the dining room (or what we in the business call the front of the house) looks like — even if we're talking duct-taped Naugahyde benches hugging tin-rimmed Formica tables — the back of the house, the kitchen, is always the same: a sea of stainless steel. Tables, bowls, freezer all gleaming in a cold gray. Whisks and spoons hanging in orderly rows. A mixer with a hook the size of my arm bent to beat bread dough. It's comforting. No matter how many times I changed jobs, I could always count on the kitchen: the order, the predictability, everything familiar and in its place.

I was swirling the last slope of meringue across the layers of ice cream and cake when I heard the champagne corks pop in the neighboring Jefferson Room. Glen, the GM, sprinted into the kitchen.

"Almost ready, chef?"

I held out my sticky fingers. "Hand me that blowtorch." The blue flame swept across the meringue, leaving a burned trail of sugar in its wake.

A swell of baritone voices thundered through the swinging door, pounding the Emerson Club anthem into the kitchen.

"That's our cue," Glen said.

I ran my fingers through my freshly dyed curls. I had gone with purple this week. Manic Panic Electric Amethyst, to be exact. Not historically accurate for a chef in the nineteenth century, but it's not like I was a guest.

With my thumb across the lip of the bottle, I doused the confection with 150-proof rum and hoisted up the tray. "Light me on fire."

Glen lit a match and carefully set the flame to the pool of rum in the hollowed-out eggshell tucked into the top. In a flash, the flame caught hold and spread across the waves of meringue. Glen raced in front of me, holding open the doors. I stepped into the room to the last notes of the anthem. The crowd burst into applause.

The tray must have weighed forty pounds. Silver is heavy, and they don't call it pound cake for nothing, never mind the ten gallons of pistachio ice cream. But I stretched my mouth wide into a smile and walked about the room, squeezing between the closely set tables and standing with the members as they snapped pictures. The flames were dying down but not quite out. Jamie stood at the back of the room, by the floor-length windows, his arm wrapped tightly around his wife's waist. Their children were by their side, miniatures of their parents, one in a dark suit, the other in a crinoline dress. A light sweat broke out across my brow. How strange that the flames were getting smaller but I was growing hotter by the second. The room was crowded. Members were packed in small groups on every inch of carpet. Somewhere, I knew Glen was counting heads and mumbling to himself about maximum capacity. I elbowed my way through, my biceps straining as I carried the tray above my head, trying to avoid catching anyone's gown on fire. The club treasurer put his arm around my waist, his palm resting lower on my hip than was respectable. "One for the newsletter," he said. My smile widened. I tightened my grip on the tray. Jamie looked over at me then, his eyes vacant, skimming over and then past me. He whispered in his wife's ear. She laughed, glancing in my direction. It was the last thing I saw before the tray slipped from my fingers and hit the floor.

After the abrupt end of my shift, I stopped

by my apartment just long enough to stuff some clothes into a canvas bag and pick up Salty, my chunky Irish wolfhound mix. I drove north for three hours, fueled by the desire to be called "hon," blasting the heater to dry my sprinkler-soaked hair, which was sticking to the back of my neck like seaweed. Salty, who just barely fit in the backseat, pressed his cold nose to my ear and sniffed. The scent of burned velvet clung to my skin. A slow-motion video of those last moments in the Jefferson Room played over and over in my head. A tablecloth had caught fire first. It might not have been so bad if it hadn't been the tablecloth under the four-foot ice sculpture of a squirrel sitting upright with an acorn in its outstretched paw. The flames caused the squirrel to melt rapidly. When its arm snapped off, the sculpture tipped over, taking the table with it. A wave of oysters, clams, and shrimp flew into the panicked crowd before hitting the floor. The flames caught the edge of one of the antique velvet curtains, which ignited like flambéed cherries. And that's when the sprinkler system kicked in.

At the sign for exit 17, I pulled off the highway and into the glowing parking lot of the F&G truck stop. Inside, I lingered by the hostess stand, watching dozens of pies rotate in their glass display case: sweet potato, maple walnut, banana cream. A waitress in a pastel uniform seated me in a corner booth away from a table of rowdy truckers, but even from across the room their gruff laughter felt comforting. My dad would bring me to the F&G for lunch whenever he let me tag along on his delivery route from Boston to the Canadian border — mostly just on school vacations, or if I needed a mental-health day. The last time I had been there with him was to celebrate having passed my driver's exam. I leaned my head back against the booth, staring at the tractor-trailer wallpaper, yellow with grease, age, and smoke.

Half an hour later, I forked the last piece of pie into my mouth, chocolate pudding thick on my tongue. The waitress refilled my coffee mug and grabbed my debit card and check. I dug around in my purse, pulled out my cell phone, and, sliding down low in the booth, dialed my best friend Hannah's number.

"Hrmph?" Hannah groaned into the phone.

"Hann, it's Livvy. I'm at the F&G." I scanned the dining room. No truckers were giving me the "get off your cell phone" glare.

"What flavor did you get?" Hannah

12

paused. "Livvy, what time is it?"

"Black bottom."

The waitress's lace-trimmed apron filled my view. I looked up to see her mouth set in a rigid line.

"Just a sec," I mouthed.

"Declined," she said, waving my card in the air before slapping it on the table.

"Livvy, are you still there?"

"Sorry, Hann." I pawed through my messenger bag and pulled a couple of crumpled dollar bills out of the bottom. "Listen, can I come over? In about an hour? For a few days?"

Hannah made a clucking sound. "Bring me a piece of key lime."

My black Wayfarers could block out the beams of sunlight that stabbed at my eyes like little paring knives but they couldn't block out the smells. Earth, onions and herbs, and the pungent aroma of goats and ground coffee challenged my ability to keep last night's piece of black-bottom pie in its place. I wasn't hung over, exactly. That fine line between still drunk and sobering up was more accurate. Hannah had woken me at seven, despite the fact that I had arrived at her house at one thirty in the morning. She met me at the door bleary-eyed, traded the bottle of Jack Daniel's that she kept solely for my visits for the key lime, and went wordlessly back to bed. I opted to watch Vermont Public Access — a repeat of a sheep-shearing contest — while polishing off a tumbler or two. But today was Saturday, farmer's market day, and Hannah insisted on arriving before it opened.

The Guthrie Farmer's Market was held every Saturday from eight in the morning till one p.m. in the high-school parking lot. Four aisles of white tents stretched across the pavement. By the entrance, between tents, an elderly man dressed in hunting gear scratched out dance tunes on a fiddle.

Hannah was on a mission. She headed straight for a display of sunflowers, walking as fast as a person can without breaking into a run. I took a slow meander through the tents in search of coffee, Salty in tow. Ceramicists hefted thickly glazed mugs. A pair of knitters, needles clicking, turned the heels of socks. A wood carver stood whittling away at a scene of a black bear and her cubs in the pine trees.

Hannah, clutching a bouquet of sunflowers to her chest like she had just won the Mrs. Coventry County pageant, found me in an herbalist's tent, rubbing lavender-scented lotion into my palms. I leaned over to her. "They should name this Eau de Grandmother."

She looked over my shoulder at the herbalist to make sure he hadn't heard me. We strolled from tent to tent, Hannah filling up her wicker basket with vegetables. "Are you okay?" she asked. "You look pale."

I sighed. Arriving at work before dawn and finishing after the sun went down did give me a vampirish hue. Hannah, however, still had a healthy summer glow. I was pretty sure the Clinique counter had something to do with it. I slipped the tips of my fingers underneath my sunglasses and rubbed my eyes. "I'm fine."

"Honey, spill it. Why are you here?"

I leaned my head on her shoulder. "Because you're my oldest, dearest friend in the world and I missed you?" Hannah was the one person I could always count on. She was the kind of friend who showed up when you were too depressed to get off the couch and would proceed to clean your apartment and return your overdue library books before sautéing you a pile of vegetables for dinner.

"And you drove all the way up here in the middle of the night? In your work uniform? You were here five weeks ago."

"How about I was desperate for a piece of

15

pie and ended up at the F&G, and it seemed like a shame not to visit when I was so close to Guthrie?"

Hannah looked at me with practiced patience. "I've known you long enough to know that after your shift you crave beer and French fries, not pie."

I glanced down at my hands. They were veiny, like my grandmother's.

"I may have caused a small fire at work."

"Oh my goodness. Was anyone hurt?"

I thought of Jamie's wife. She had on an exact replica of the dress Ginger Rogers wore in *Top Hat,* the white one with all the feathers. "No, no. Not hurt. Just wet."

"Jesus, Liv. Do you think you'll be fired? Could the guy you're seeing help?"

Hannah knew I was seeing someone from the Emerson, but when she pressed for details I just told her it wasn't serious. She wouldn't have approved of the fact that, at sixty-four, Jamie was exactly twice my age. Plus the fact that he was married. "No one ever really gets fired from the Emerson," I said as I nervously ripped the husks and silk off random ears of corn. "More like encouraged to 'take a break.' "

She scanned the parking lot. After a few moments she linked her arm in mine. "Let's go see if there are any sticky buns left.

They're award-winning."

The deeper we elbowed our way into the mass of hungry townsfolk, the harder my head began to pound. My stomach did a little shift as the smell of manure-caked work boots reached my nostrils. I really should never drink whiskey.

"Uh, Hann? I'm going to have to sit this one out. Get me something greasy."

Hannah wrinkled her nose. "How can you eat grease with a hangover?"

"It's healing," I said as I headed out of the fray.

The fresh air was delicious. I found a quiet spot under a tree on the edge of the parking lot and plopped myself down, leaning my back against the rough bark. Salty sniffed at the grass, turned around three times, then finally lay down beside me, stretching his legs out in front of him.

It seemed like the whole town was at the market that day, and half of it was in the sticky-bun line. Hannah had explained that the market was the only time the farmers ever saw one another during the harvest. Between customers they traded seeds and service, exchanged news of crops and births, and gossiped. Apparently, the rest of the townspeople were there to do the same. I watched a tall, slight man unloading wooden crates of apples, plaid shirtsleeves rolled up to the elbow. Sharp-nosed and thin-lipped, with dark eyes framed by black plastic eyeglasses, haircut and shave long overdue. He felt familiar. Then I realized I was remembering a man in a Walker Evans photograph taken during the Dust Bowl.

I scanned the crowd for Hannah and found her speaking to an older woman with her hands on her hips whose sky blue cardigan hugged her narrow shoulders. She frowned. Hannah patted her arm and pointed to me, her expression cheerful. The woman looked over and studied me, her lips pursed.

My cell phone, which I had jammed in my back pocket out of habit, vibrated. Here in the mountains my cell service was spotty at best — six missed calls. I felt like I had swallowed a biscuit whole.

"Livvy," Jamie shout-whispered on my voice mail, "Where are you? I'm worried. Call me."

"Olivia, it's Glen. Just making sure you're okay. The club is going to be closed for a couple days at least while they assess the damage. The fire marshal has a few questions. Call me on my cell."

"We're having trouble lighting the grill, chef." It was one of the prep cooks. "We thought you could help us start the fire." Howls of laughter in the background before the message clicked off.

Hannah's perfectly French-manicured toes appeared in my line of vision. I pressed the off button and threw the phone into my bag. When I looked up, a cinnamon roll the size of a hubcap had replaced Hannah's face. Creamy white glaze glistened on the curls of pastry.

"Here you go," Hannah said, handing me the sticky bun.

I tore off a hunk and popped it into my mouth, chewing gratefully.

Hannah took a dainty bite. "Hmmmm, I haven't had this much sugar in months." She slipped the pastry into a waxed bag, then licked her fingers. Hannah will tell you that she counts carbs, but I know the depth of her sweet tooth. She reached into her purse, pulled out a cloth napkin and wiped her fingers, then drew her skirt around her legs and sat down next to me. "So, how long were you planning on staying?"

I eyed her sideways. "Not sure. Are you worried I'll still be here when Jonathan comes back from the conference?" Hannah's husband and I have agreed to disagree on just about everything. It upsets her sense of equilibrium to have us both in the same room.

"No, no. You can stay as long as you like, you know that. Besides, he isn't due back for a few more days. No, I was just wondering if you could stay until at least Monday night."

"Well, sure. Believe me, I'm in no hurry to get back to Boston."

"Good. I just need to see when she's available." Hannah reached into her purse and pulled out the wax pastry bag. She twisted off a large chunk of roll and shoved it in her mouth.

"See when who is available?"

"The woman I was talking to in the sticky-bun line, Margaret Hurley. She's the owner of this fantastic inn. She told me that she had to let her baker go, and I mentioned you, about your experience and the awards you've won, and she seemed really interested."

"Hannah," I said, trying to come up with the most polite way to say, *There's no way in hell.* "I can't really see myself —"

"Listen, I know it sounds like a big step, but I think you would love the place. It's called the Sugar Maple."

20

I looked out over the rows of tents. Vermont. Full time. "Don't get me wrong, you know I like visiting you and all, but . . . I'm not sure exactly what I would do here."

"You'd do exactly what you do in Boston — bake. Only when you get off work it will be pretty, peaceful Vermont instead of loud, ugly Boston."

I narrowed my eyes at her. Sure, I complained about living in the city all the time, but it felt like she was making fun of my little brother.

"What I mean is, what do you really have in Boston? No house, no family, no boyfriend — not really, I mean . . ."

"Jeez, Hann, don't hold anything back." I lifted my hands in surrender. At the mention of Jamie, my mind had flashed to the night before, the way he'd looked through me before I started the fire, like I was just another one of the help. "Besides — where would I live? God knows I can't live under the same roof as your husband."

Hannah snorted. "I'm pretty sure the position comes with housing — the last baker lived at the inn." She glanced at me hopefully. "I'd be right down the road. We could hang out all the time. It would be like college all over again." Hannah was referring to the one semester I had gone to state school, before dropping out to go on tour with the Dead Darlings.

I thought about my rejected debit card at the F&G. If the Emerson did indeed decide to have me "take a break," I would be out of a job and, with all the back rent I already owed my landlord, a place to live. Salty wouldn't be too happy about living in the station wagon. "I might consider it."

"I'll call her when we get back. Just go look at the place." She beamed at me, looking satisfied, as though she had done her good deed for the day. Off the hook. "You're gonna love it."

Following Hannah's directions, I arrived at the Sugar Maple Inn shortly before ten a.m. on Monday. It was a beautiful drive from Hannah's house in town, up a long winding dirt road. The landscape changed from tidy painted ladies to sprawling farmhouses to abandoned trailers covered so thickly with bittersweet vine that only the rusted cars in the front yard would tell you someone once lived there. Then, as the houses dropped away altogether, leaving only the dirt road canopied with oaks and maples, I thought I must be lost. Who would want to stay at an inn so far from town? But as I reached the crest of the mountain road, the trees opened up and, as if I were passing from night into day, the world became all green grass against the bluest sky. To my left was the Sugar Maple itself, a bright yellow farmhouse with attached barn, surrounded by huge clumps of zinnias in pinks and reds, faces turned toward the sun. Morning glories, now dozing for the day, climbed up the side of the barn. Rocking chairs were lined up on the porch. The front yard was scattered with garden benches and sleeping cats. To my right was a wooden rail fence, and beyond it a ridge of mountains with the steeple-dotted valley below.

I walked up the flagstone path and hesitated at the front door, nervously picking Salty's dog hair off my chef's coat. Hannah had offered to lend me something, but since I am a size twelve to her six, I had politely declined. I reached for the brass maple leaf on the green door and gave a knock. Margaret swung the door open, eyed me, and then looked at her watch.

"You're five minutes late," she said, blocking my view.

"Are you sure?" I had checked my cell phone before I left the car.

Margaret made a little huffing sound. "Well, you might as well come in." She stepped aside slightly as I entered the foyer.

I followed her slender frame, trim in a navy jacket, down the hallway. I tried to glance at the pictures that lined the walls, but she moved too quickly. Despite her pace, her silver bun stayed perfectly in place. We entered a sitting room, couches and chairs in mismatched florals arranged casually for easy conversation. Margaret led me to a small table by a window and gestured for me to sit down.

"So, Mrs. Doyle tells me you're a baker." Her papery hands sat neatly folded in her lap.

"Yes. My name is Olivia Rawlings. I'm the pastry chef at the Emerson Club. . . ."

"Yes, I can read that on your coat."

I looked down at my left breast. Stupid coat.

Margaret cleared her throat. "Now, how long have you been baking?"

"For twelve years. Since I graduated from the CIA."

"You learned to bake from the government?" She scowled.

"No, no, it's a culinary school in New York."

Margaret looked out the window. "Yes, well then. Tell me, what's your specialty?"

"My specialty?"

"What do you make best?" She said this

louder and more slowly, as if she thought I was hard of hearing or from a foreign country.

I thought for a moment. "Well, *Chocolate Gourmand* magazine requested my recipe for a blood orange and sour cherry napoleon last year. And I was nominated for a James Beard Award for —"

"We're a simple place, Miss Rawlings. Nothing too fancy here." She leaned forward, hands on the table. "Can you bake a good pie?"

"Pie?" I lifted my eyebrows.

"Yes, you know, a flaky crust with filling inside."

I suppressed the urge to roll my eyes. "Well, of course I can bake a pie. An excellent one." I leaned back in my chair.

"How's your apple?" She leaned back as well. The hands went back into her lap.

"I've received many compliments on my apple pie." I felt like we were playing high-stakes poker.

"Would you be willing to bake one now?" she asked calmly.

"Right now?" I did not succeed in hiding my irritation.

"Yes. Why not? Don't need a recipe, do you?"

"You want me to bake an apple pie right

now." Being asked to test-bake in a kitchen was a normal part of the hiring process for a chef's position, but not on the day of the interview.

"Well, not this very second." Margaret stood. "I have to make a few calls first. I'll have one of the girls bring you a cup of coffee." She walked away at her fast clip, calling out, "Sarah . . ."

"Don't you want to see my résumé?" I called after her, waving the sheet of paper. She had already turned the corner and was gone.

A young woman with straight blond hair appeared with a tray. She placed in front of me a dainty teacup and saucer, filled to the brim with steaming black coffee.

"Thanks." I glanced up at her. "Hey, is she always like this?"

Sarah looked over her shoulder. "Pretty much. But she's decent to work for." She shrugged. "I've been here for over two years. The tips are good. And the rest of the staff is more laid back." She gave me a quick smile and walked back toward the kitchen.

This was surely the strangest interview I had ever been on. I was used to being courted, not trying to convince someone I could do the simplest of tasks. It looked like Hannah was wrong about Margaret's interest. A wave of relief washed over me. It would be easier not to get the job than it would have been to explain to Hannah why I couldn't move this far away from . . . everything, without hurting her feelings.

I waited for what felt like hours, making a mental list of chefs who might hire me, before abandoning my teacup and wandering around the inn in search of Mrs. Hurley. I found Sarah toward the back of the house, folding napkins in the dining room. The room was small, dressed in cream tablecloths and tarnished silver candlesticks, elegant in a Miss Havisham kind of way.

"I think I may have been abandoned," I said lightly.

"Sorry. There was a problem with one of the guest rooms. She should be back soon."

"Mind if I look around the kitchen?"

"Not at all. It's through that door."

I pushed through a swinging door at the far side of the dining room. It opened onto a room that broke all the rules of kitchen-dom. It looked just like a farmhouse kitchen, with a yellow tin ceiling and wide maple plank floors, but it appeared to have been stretched and pulled like taffy to accommodate the eight-burner stove top and the walk-in refrigerator.

I set my bag down on an enamel-topped

wooden table. It was a regular kitchen table, sitting on stacks of Nancy Drew mysteries to make it a respectable height for chopping. I wondered how this place ever passed inspection. The table sat in the middle of the room, close to the cast-iron range. I crept about, grabbing tools that I would need for pie baking as I went. Even they seemed odd, like something you would find at a church sale, not in a restaurant supply catalog. The rolling pin was the heavy kind with ball bearings — the type I pictured cartoon housewives using on the heads of their husbands. The measuring cups were glass with painted pictures of roosters on them. I found a beautiful old pair of copper scissors and a set of tin measuring spoons so worn the fractions were unreadable. The pantry still served as a pantry, although the shelves were dwarfed by industrial-sized cans of baking powder and cling peaches. In there I found an old stand mixer, complete with its original bowl of iridescent glass, which I hauled out and placed on the table. The one thing I couldn't find was flour. I kept searching, opening drawers and bins.

Next to the pantry there was a small door. I pushed it open, hoping it was another storage area, and was greeted by darkness. I waved my hand in the air, searching for a cord. My fingers touched something silky and soft as I walked deeper into the stuffy room. A tickle of fabric brushed against my skin like feathers. When my hand found the light cord, I pulled on it and blinked. From the ceiling hung ribbons. Hundreds of them, all blue, their pointed tips swaying gently. They extended the entire length of the ceiling, each one emblazoned in gold with the same words: *Coventry County Fair — First Place.* In a large wooden display case hung larger ribbons, the heads fat with extra loops of fabric like the petals of a sunflower. These ribbons were all blue as well, with the exception of the last three. Those ribbons were red. From somewhere in the inn I heard Margaret's voice, followed by another, this one more cheerful. I clicked off the light and slipped out of the room, easing the door closed behind me.

The kitchen door swung open, and a plump, snowy-haired woman bounded into the room.

"Hello, dear. You must be Olivia!" She grabbed my hand and shook it firmly. "I'm Maggie's friend Dorothy. You can call me Dotty."

Dotty was the opposite of Margaret in

every way but age. She was rounded in the shoulders, with thin wavy hair that hung down her back in a loose braid. Everything about her seemed fluid.

Margaret marched in behind her, carrying a crate of apples, and eyed the collection of tools on the enameled-topped table. "Making yourself at home?"

"Just thought I would get familiar with the kitchen, you know, *while I waited.*"

Margaret ignored me and started digging through the crate of apples.

"So, what do we have here, Dotty?"

"Let's see. McIntosh, Cortland, Spartan, Northern Spy, Crispin, and Golden Delicious."

Margaret turned to me. "Will that do?"

Suddenly all eyes were on me. "Sure, thank you." I felt self-conscious and began to rifle through the crate, sniffing at the apples in what I hoped was a gesture of appreciation.

"Well, let's get going, then." Margaret grasped the backs of two rocking chairs and dragged them across the kitchen.

Showtime.

I took what was obviously my place on the opposite side of the table from the two rocking chairs. "So, do you want me to talk about what I'm doing, like I'm teaching a class?"

"We know how to bake an apple pie, Miss Rawlings," Margaret said sharply as she gathered the ingredients I hadn't been able to find. "We're here to see if you do."

Margaret and Dotty settled into their chairs as I took stock. Along with the flour and a tin of salt, she had left an apron made of green gingham with tiny white lambs dancing across the fabric. This I tied around my waist, feeling a little embarrassed. God, if the boys in the Emerson Club kitchen could see me now, I would never hear the end of it. Flustered, I pulled the stand mixer toward me and removed the bowl. "Any requests?" I asked. "Crumb? Pour-through? Double crust?"

Margaret rocked, her feet firmly planted on the floor. "Whatever is your best."

Remembering Margaret's "nothing too fancy" comment from earlier, I decided double crust seemed safest. I dipped a measuring cup into the flour and swept across the top with my finger, enjoying the cool silkiness. Slipping my finger underneath its wax wrapper, I eased the butter free and began chopping it into small chunks.

Margaret clucked. "Not shortening?"

31

"I use a combination," I said. The butter was tacky against the steel of the knife. I reached for the tin of Crisco.

"My mother always used all shortening, but I couldn't stand the taste," said Dotty, nodding in agreement.

"If you want to use all shortening, the trick is to baste the crust with butter afterward," I offered, plopping the fat onto the flour and starting the mixture spinning. After I added the ice water, I took the lump of dough into my hands, folded it over onto itself, and mashed it into a flattened disc. After laying the dough to rest in the walkin, I dug through the crate of apples, settling on a mix of McIntosh and Cortland, with a couple of Crispin for good measure.

Margaret eyed the Macs. "Those'll turn to mush."

"Only the Macs will, but they add flavor." I dug into the skin of an apple with a small paring knife. Margaret stood up and put the kettle on to boil.

"How's Henry today?" I heard her ask. I was about to say, "Who's Henry?" when Dotty responded.

"About the same." She rocked a little faster, her fingers gripping the armrests.

The kettle whistled a sharp trill. I started at the sound. Margaret shook her head, muttered, "Jumpy girl" under her breath, and poured the boiling water into two delicate cups.

"Martin helping out?"

"Hmm. He's looking after the pickers and leading the hayrides through the sugar bush on the weekends." Dotty's gray orthopedic shoes lifted off the ground. She looked like a schoolgirl on a swing.

"He must be happy to be home, after all this time."

"You know how he is. I'm lucky if I hear him speak twice in one day. But I'm glad to have all of my boys in one place."

The women talked on in short clips, as if they had their own language. I gleaned bits of information about the town. The apple crop had been especially good; Jane White's granddaughter had announced her engagement (this news was delivered with an eye roll); someone named Judith had run off with a dairy-goat farmer, leaving her husband with two children and bales full of unspun wool.

I reached for the large knife and chopped the apples into thick slices. I looked beyond the women and out the kitchen windows as I worked. An expanse of lawn stretched out and uphill, where a line of crab apples stood, heavy with fruit. I caught myself thinking about what it would look like as the sun rose, the grass glinting with dew and frost. I tossed the pile of apple slices into a cast-iron pan with a couple of pats of butter and turned on the flame. The cinnamon scent of the McIntoshes mingled with the tang of the melting butter, reminding me of my old neighbor Mary's kitchen, where I wove my first lattice crust.

"What on earth are you doing that for?" Margaret asked, her sharp voice cutting through my daydream.

"It'll take some of the water out of the apples — keeps them from shrinking in the pie, and the filling will be thicker." I couldn't believe how defensive I sounded. But if she was such an expert, why was I here?

Margaret turned back to Dotty. They resumed rocking, taking sips of tea as they gossiped.

I pulled the dough from the walk-in and began to hammer it with my rolling pin. After sweetening the apples in the pan, I piled the heaping mass in the pastry-lined pie plate, slipped the top crust over them, and tucked in the edges like a child's blanket at nap time. After crimping the edges with machinelike marks, I sliced little vents in the top and placed the pie in the oven.

"Well, there you have it." I wiped my hands briskly on the apron. "Any questions?" I looked over at the two women. Dotty was dozing, her mouth slightly open. Margaret stood up and inclined her head toward the door.

"She needs her rest," Margaret explained as we returned to the dining room. "Might as well show you around the place while the pie's baking."

Margaret led me swiftly through the inn. The downstairs housed the dining room, entry hall, and kitchen, along with Margaret's living quarters, which she declined to show me with a dismissive wave. Upstairs were the guest rooms, twelve in all, with shared baths at the ends of the halls. I followed Margaret back through the kitchen. She skipped the room with the ribbons, opening a door opposite it.

"Here are the baker's quarters. They come with the job." I breathed a sigh of relief that the job came with housing, until I peeked into the tiny bedroom. It had just enough room for a twin bed, a small painted dresser, and a nightstand. "You can share my bathroom down the hall." I tried to imagine my blue sparkly nail polish next to her tub of Noxzema.

"That's nice of you, but I have a large-ish dog, and I don't think he could turn around in this room."

Margaret frowned. "No, a dog wouldn't do. Especially not so near the kitchen." She tapped her fingertips against her thigh, apparently debating something. "There is one other option. Put on your coat."

We walked up the hill through the crab apples, bees humming among the fallen fruit. Beyond the orchard we turned left, out of sight of the farmhouse. There in front of us stood a tiny house, square and trim, with a dainty front porch, complete with a bench and a wooden rocker. The walls were lined with windows, so you could see straight through the cabin, up into the maple trees beyond. There was a brick chimney and on the roof a cupola, its windows framed with metal shutters.

"Well," Margaret said. "This is the sugar-house. My husband, Brian, winterized it years ago. Needed a place to do his carving." She banged her arm against the green front door and it flew open. A plume of sawdust sprang up at our entrance. In the center of the room stood a wood-burning stove, with a long metal pan attached, held up by stacks of bricks. An enamel sink hugged the corner next to a large wooden workbench, and there was a tiny oven in that ocher color no one had used since the 1960s. It was bigger than any apartment I had ever lived in, with plenty of space for a futon and lots of bookshelves. I wondered which window faced east. I stepped around the stove to the back of the cabin while Margaret stood in the open door. A claw-foot bathtub, a little rusty around the drain, sat behind the wood-burning stove. I imagined soaking in the tub, the woodstove blazing, looking out the back windows and into the sugar bush.

"He said he needed a place to think," Margaret said. She rubbed her hands together against the cold. "Didn't like to be at the inn during the busy season." It was obvious no one had used the cabin for a long time, and I wondered how long it had been since Margaret's husband had passed away. I was about to ask but, seeing the tight ridge of her shoulders, thought better of it. "You'd have to clean it out yourself," she said finally, turning to leave. "And you'd have to stay someplace else when the sap's running. I'm intending to sugar this spring." Margaret paused in the doorway, her back to me. "It's a year commitment."

"I'll take it," I said, my voice urgent, surprising both of us.

"Yes, well. Let's see how the pie turned out first."

I followed Margaret out of the dusty cabin and closed the green door to what I had already begun to think of as home.

CHAPTER TWO
OCTOBER

Muffins, coffee cakes, and scones should be ready for the guests by 8 a.m. We need ten loaves of bread for the dining room, your choice, but half should be white and the other whole grain. And make four desserts, at least one chocolate. We have reservations for twenty people so far. First one is at 5 p.m. — M

I wiped a stray curl out of my eyes with my forearm, careful not to touch my face with my flour-caked hand. My first day at the Sugar Maple and I was already in the weeds. On top of its not looking like a professional kitchen, it wasn't behaving like one either. My morning had been like an endless bad first date. Sure, that oven looked handsome in its dark black cast iron, but as I dug around I found the inside gritty with burned breadcrumbs and discovered the hard way that it liked to turn itself off from time to time. That burner that looked so calm and steady reared its ugly temper when I turned my back — flames doubling in size and turning an innocently simmering raspberry sauce into a sticky, blackened mass in a matter of seconds. And there I was, on my second batch of blueberry muffins of the morning, the first ones crusty on the outside, raw and oozing on the inside, feeling like it was my first day of cooking school. I popped the pans into the oven, turned the temperature down another twenty-five degrees, and hoped for the best.

It had taken Margaret three days to call and offer me the position. I imagined it took one day to contemplate the pie and to have her friends and neighbors taste it; one day to contemplate me; and one, I suspected, just to be stubborn. I had stayed on at Hannah's despite her husband Jonathan's return from his conference. He was a family doctor but lent his expertise to drug companies, which paid him thousands of dollars to give a talk about some drug he had never tried. For Hannah's sake, I tried to keep the words *conflict of interest* and *evil power of the pharmaceutical industry* from tumbling out of my mouth, but it wasn't easy. Just when I had decided I was better off returning to Boston, Glen had called to tell me not to rush back, since the club would be closed for a few weeks while they replaced the carpet and repainted, and that "we should talk" when I got back into town.

That's when I got Margaret's call. She informed me that the pie had been "fine" and that if I was interested, I could start my trial run after I had given proper notice to my current employer. Not wanting to explain that my current place of employment was closed for business due to my having set it on fire, I agreed that two weeks from Monday would be doable. I made one trip back down to Boston to pack up the few personal belongings I kept in my little furnished apartment. Then I slipped the keys into my landlord's mailbox so he would know that I wasn't coming back.

I stood by the sink, running the tap marked "hot" over the tender underside of my wrist, waiting for the temperature to rise. Out the window two fawns gently nibbled crab apples in the fog. Fawns! At the Emerson the view from my window had been of another building, where a lawyer spent most of his day leaning out the window so he could smoke without leaving his office. When the water was warm enough for a baby to bathe in, I measured out a quart and poured it into a large earthenware bowl.

The fresh yeast dissolved as I stirred it in with my fingers. I added flour, one cup at a time, until the mixture turned from liquid to solid, from shapeless batter into something I could grasp, hold onto, push and mold into form. I had just scraped the last bit of dough out of the bowl and onto the cool enameled surface of my workbench when a clean-cut man walked into the kitchen, two stacked milk crates in his gray-work-gloved hands.

"Morning," he said as he walked by me and into the walk-in. "You must be the new girl," he said, pulling off his gloves and removing his baseball cap to reveal dark brown hair cut like a fifties TV show dad's. "I'm Tom." He offered me his hand. I smiled and stuck out mine. We both looked at my hand, thick and sticky with dough. It looked like I was wearing a mitten.

"Yes. Olivia Rawlings." I began to rub my hands together, trying to find skin. "But please, call me Livvy."

Tom toyed with the zipper of his woolen red and black plaid jacket and looked around the kitchen. "Milk, heavy cream, and buttermilk."

"That's great, thank you." I stood, waiting. "Do you have anything you need me to sign?"

"Nope." Tom looked around the kitchen. "She usually leaves a check."

"Oh." The timer on the stove buzzed like an angry wasp. "She didn't mention anything about it." Flipping the switch, I made a quick study of the kitchen. No bulletin board, no clipboard near the telephone. Not even a scrap of paper. The scent of browning butter began to fill my nostrils. I pulled on quilted elbow-length oven mitts and opened the oven door, saying a silent prayer to Saint Honoré. The muffins *looked* cooked. I stuck a wooden skewer into one in the center of the pan. It came out clean. "Thank you," I sighed.

"For what?" Tom looked confused.

"Oh. For being so patient." I had almost forgotten he was there. "So," I said, not sure what to do next. He didn't appear to be in a hurry. "Would you like a cup of coffee while I look for it?" I asked, waving my hand in display model fashion. "I have fresh muffins."

Tom pulled up a stool. "I take it black."

Town or country, coffee and something sweet could usually smooth out any problem with a deliveryman. I poured coffee into a mug, placed a blueberry muffin on a plate, and set them in front of him. As he ate, I opened drawers and cabinets and looked in the pie safe, over by the coffee pot near the door to the dining room. Like I said, first date.

"I'm so sorry. Margaret must have forgotten. I'll have her give you a call when she gets in."

Tom took another sip of his coffee.

Why wouldn't he leave? I took the ball of bread dough back into my hands and began to knead feverishly, pushing the dough away, then folding it back. "So," I said, trying to look both professional and busy. "Dairy farmer?"

"Mmm-hmm."

I peeked up at him. He was picking the bits of muffin stuck to the paper liner. I nodded toward the tray. "Help yourself."

He studied the pan for a long moment before choosing the muffin with the most blueberries. "That's some outfit you're wearing."

I was dressed in my usual work attire — white, boxy chef's coat, black and gray pin-striped pants, black clogs. I looked up to give him my best raised eyebrow. "It's just a chef's coat." I don't know why I felt the need to explain this to him.

"From Boston, I hear."

"That's right," I said, working the dough into a soft, round ball and placing it gently in a buttered bowl.

"All the chefs in Boston have purple hair?"

"Only the best ones."

Tom grunted. "Seems like a long way to come for a little job like this one."

"It's not that far, really," I said, running a tea towel under the faucet to dampen it and draping it over the bowl. "And besides, it's not like I'm commuting."

Tom stood. I thought he was leaving, but he plodded across the kitchen to refill his coffee cup.

"Plan on staying long?" he asked as he settled himself back onto the stool. I had to stop myself from asking him the same question.

"That will be up to Margaret, I suppose."

Tom popped the bottom of the muffin into his mouth.

"It true you're the reason Jeff Rutland over in Lyndonville left his wife?"

My hand knocked over a measuring cup of water, causing a small wave. Streams of water ran toward the edge of the table, mixing with the flour, creating a pasty mess. "I'm sorry?"

"I heard you and Jeff Rutland were a thing."

"Well, I did stop in Lyndonville for gas. Was he the tall one? With the beard? Or the

45

stout one who wears a trucker hat?"

Tom coughed out a couple of muffin crumbs.

I squatted down to mop the floor. "Of course, there was also that man at the feed store, where I stopped by, you know, to *browse.*"

Tom crossed his arms across his belly, like he had just finished a large meal. "That's where he works. He owns the feed store, in fact. A good catch if he weren't . . ."

I leaned my forehead against the leg of the table and studied the Nancy Drew under the foot. *The Message in the Hollow Oak.* "Okay," I said, standing, "for one thing, I've been here officially for how long? Maybe thirty-six hours, tops. How on earth would I have time to have a . . . *thing* with Jeff Rutland? And who did you hear this from, anyway?"

Tom shrugged. "Around. At White's?" The White Market was the only supermarket for thirty miles.

At least now I knew where to get the local gossip. It's always good to stay informed. "I'm afraid the mystery behind the break-up of Jeff Rutland's marriage remains a mystery. It wasn't me. I'm not sleeping with anyone's husband, by the way." *At least not anymore,* I thought to myself. "Do me a huge favor and go tell that to the cashier girl at White's. And the butcher. And all the stock boys. Whoever you think will make the news travel fastest."

Sarah, the young waitress I had met on the day of my interview, came into the kitchen.

"Hey, I was hoping it was you," she said warmly as she pulled off a red down jacket. "Margaret interviewed a few others, but I knew she liked you best. Hey, Tom," she added.

"How could you tell? Did she scowl at the others longer?"

Tom stood and zipped his jacket, his mission apparently completed for the day. "See you girls soon," he said, tipping his baseball hat as he walked toward the front.

"No, she pretty much scowls at everyone the same amount." Sarah gathered her long blond hair and pulled it back into a high, tight ponytail. "It was funny. That afternoon you were here, after she and Dotty had tasted your pie and she'd driven Dotty back to her house, I found her alone in the kitchen eating another piece. She never does that."

"Eats seconds?"

"Eats desserts. She can't stand them." Sarah buttoned up her black vest and pinned a bright orange shellacked maple leaf the size of my fist onto her lapel. "So I knew you must have gotten the job."

While the bread dough rose I worked on my desserts for the dinner guests: a flourless chocolate torte that was more confection than cake; grape-nut custard with vanilla bean and freshly grated nutmeg; lemon mousse made with lemon curd lightened by billowy piles of whipped egg whites and cream, topped with crème chantilly and a candied ginger lace cookie; and, of course, an apple pie. I wanted to see if I could catch Margaret in the act.

The kitchen was eerily quiet. Sarah explained that since the inn served only a continental breakfast and no lunch, the dinner crew didn't trickle in till three p.m., an hour after I was scheduled to leave. I hadn't realized how much I liked the chaotic bustle of a busy kitchen until I spent hours with no one to talk to at the Sugar Maple. Margaret surprised me by not showing up until I was scrubbing dried chocolate off the enamel tabletop and waiting for my last loaves of bread to come out of the oven. I had had nightmarish visions of her sitting in that rocking chair every day, watching me work — like the play *No Exit,* but with cookie dough — but even that would have been better than spending the day alone. With a sharp nod of her head she walked past me and into the little office, closing the door behind her. I wrote out the evening's dessert menu on a guest check pad, then yanked at the strings of my apron.

"So, was everything to your liking?"

I jumped. Margaret had suddenly appeared before me, arms folded in front of her chest.

"Yes, of course. Kitchens are all basically the same," I said, eyeing the books holding up my table. "Still getting used to the ovens and stuff, but breakfast went out on time. Here's what I made for dessert." I slid the list across the enamel. Margaret scanned the paper, then tucked the pad into a pocket of her cardigan. It was dark gray this time, with pearl buttons. I swear, she must have robbed a Talbots. "The dairy deliveryman came by with a shipment and was looking for his check, but I couldn't find one."

"Tom Carrigan knows very well I pay him at the end of the month. Check, indeed." Margaret frowned and began to wipe at a bit of flour that I had missed on the table. "You didn't give him anything to eat, did you?"

I folded my apron and placed it on the

49

table. "Just a muffin."

"That man's going to go blind from diabetes." She shook her head. "Sniffing around like a stray dog looking for scraps."

"Well," I said, pulling the elastic out of my hair, "I made some sketches of how I'd like the desserts to be plated."

"I think Alfred can manage on his own."

I had yet to meet the elusive Chef Alfred, who had somehow escaped being a part of the hiring process.

"But he won't know where to put the sauces," I said, trying to sound calm. I was used to having complete creative control. Hell, I was used to working every night and plating the desserts myself.

"I'm assuming the sauces go on the dessert?"

"Yes." *This is Vermont,* I reminded myself. *No one from the* Times *is going to show up tonight with a photographer.* "If you don't need me for anything else?"

"No, that's fine."

"Great." I grabbed my purse, a beaten-up old canvas bag left over from my bike courier days, and headed out the kitchen door.

"Miss Rawlings?" Margaret called. "Speaking of stray dogs, could you please remove yours from my sitting room?"

I stopped and turned around, a weak grin on my face. "Salty? In the sitting room?"

"On my best love seat."

I opened my mouth to apologize, but by the time I could take a breath she had turned on her heel and disappeared back into the office.

I swung open the door into the dining room and hurried to the front of the house. Sure enough, I found Salty stretched out on the floral love seat closest to the fireplace. He thumped his tail loudly at the sight of me, his long, spotted tongue hanging casually out the side of his mouth in the warmth of the fire.

"Come on, Salt," I called, tapping the side of my thigh. He took a long stretch like Superman flying, gracefully slid his long body onto the ground, and loped ahead of me, his claws tapping on the wood floor.

I walked into the apple orchard. The ground was thick with fallen fruit, bright red and gleaming against the green grass, and the air was heavy with the heady scent of rotting apples. My clogs slipped on the pulpy ground, and I made a mental note to buy sturdier shoes to walk to work in. It was funny to think of the walk through the apple orchard as my commute. In Boston, my walk to the Emerson had included a jaunt through both the Public Garden and the Common. Despite the lush beauty of the willow trees, there was no mistaking the parks for the country. Even at dawn there were always people there — junkies asleep on benches; tiny, elderly Chinese women practicing tai chi by the ponds and gathering ginkgo seeds; and the club kids, with their jet-black hair and ripped tights, still drunk and giggling, stumbling and smoking as they headed to catch the first train back to their apartments for a little sleep before school.

Salty and I stopped at the cabin just long enough for me to trade my chef's coat and clogs for a purple fleece jacket and a pair of Converse low-tops before heading out. The maple grove beyond the sugarhouse was burning with color. An old carriage road curved through the trees, the path trimmed with glowing golden ferns, their long bodies stretched back and bent. Salty ran with abandon, stopping short to catch a scent on a tree stump, pricking up his ears and running off again while squirrels squawked their panicked warnings to one another from the branches above. Occasionally the wind would rustle through the branches, sending red leaves to fall gently at my feet. I walked until the maples thinned and blended with oaks and pines.

I had been walking uphill for some time when I came to a clearing. A rolling field stretched before me, with recently shorn hay, spiraled like jelly rolls, dotting the landscape. Halfway down the field there was a small shed with a tin roof and in the distance a white farmhouse dwarfed by a red barn, complete with a big vegetable garden and acres of apple trees and evergreens. It looked like the plastic Fisher-Price farm my dad had given me one Christmas. I wondered if a cow would moo when I walked into the barn.

I lay down on the grass in the sun. Puffs of white clouds moved smoothly across the deepening blue sky. Salty emerged from the woods a minute later and was pawing at the grass beside my head when I heard the unmistakable scratch of a bow being drawn across fiddle strings. The sound was faint at first, the tentative pull of horsehair on metal. But I could picture fingertips twisting the little fine-tuners in the silence that followed. Then the notes of "Angeline the Baker" rang out across the field. Next came "June Apple," then "Little Sadie," old-time classics. I lay back down, tapping the rhythm with my feet and hands against the grass, watching the occasional hawk or crow soar by. As dusk began to creep in over the farmhouse, the tunes slowed down. The music must have been coming from the little toolshed, but it sounded as if the trees themselves were playing. When the last note ended, all I could hear was the whistle of swallows' wings cutting through the sky.

I was three trees deep onto the carriage trail when I heard it. Long, slow notes in a minor key dragged across the lower strings. I leaned against a thin pine and slid back down to the ground. The drone of a double stop — two strings being played together. I didn't recognize the tune, although it felt as familiar to me as my own skin. My body grew still; not a single cell wanted to miss a note. The tune wound back to the beginning again and again, each round more mournful than the last. Salty sat down next to me, aimed his snout up to the sky, and began howling. The music stopped abruptly. I leaped to my feet.

"Shhh, Salty, quit it!" I grabbed him by the collar and turned back into the woods, the darkness surrounding us. I strode ahead, but Old Salt kept stopping and staring back over his shoulder toward the clearing.

Back in the sugarhouse, after I fed Salty

some kibble and warmed my hands on a cup of tea, I dragged out the black cardboard case that I had stashed under the futon. I flicked the latches and opened it for the first time in sixteen years. The banjo was out of tune, its strings dusty from years of neglect. I rubbed them with the cuff of my sleeve. My father had bought it back in the sixties, before I was born, and had kept it in pristine condition. The rim and neck were carved out of parchment-pale maple. An abalone inlay of pinecones danced down the fingerboard. Milky mother-of-pearl tuning pegs dotted the top. The wooden tone ring gave it a deep, quiet voice, like the hoot of a great horned owl. Only the head revealed how often he had played it, a dark, shiny stain under the strings where his frailing hand had worn into the clean, white surface. My left hand stretched into the chords he had taught me, the memory of them stored in my muscles, and with my right I began to strum, searching for the notes of that lonesome tune.

The Friday night after my first week working at the Sugar Maple I took the back road from the inn into town to meet Hannah, wanting an excuse to drive closer to the neighboring farm and hoping to hear the fiddler again. But when I drove by the long dirt drive to the little farm, the only living creatures I saw were two dairy goats, who eyed me with cold curiosity. Halfway down the mountain the shoulder widened and three cars, with their headlights still on, had pulled over on the side of the road. With a loud buzz, my cell phone sprang to life, and a moment later I heard the three sharp beeps, like an accusation, letting me know I had a new voice mail. A cell service hotspot. I gripped the steering wheel and pressed my foot on the gas before any more calls could come through.

The blue and yellow neon sign on the roof of the Black Bear Tavern lit up the dirt parking lot, which was packed with pickup trucks. Two bear statues, cut roughly with a chain saw, guarded a windowless door like library lions. As I pushed my way into the bar, the scents of spilled beer, cooking oil, and stale cigarette smoke greeted me. I found Hannah hunched over a table toward the back, wiping off the last patron's crumbs with a paper napkin.

"I hope this is what you had in mind when you asked to see 'local color,' " she said as I slid in.

"It's perfect." I had been craving a night

like this, someplace dark and anonymous, away from the formality of the inn. Across from us was a long wooden bar, every stool taken by a man with a broad back sheathed in flannel. The bar was tended by an older guy with a thick red beard and a sweatshirt with a picture of wolves howling stretched over his belly. Above him hung the mounted heads of moose, deer, and elk. They looked down at the drinkers like Saint Francis and the Virgin Mother giving their blessing.

"I've only been here a couple of times," she said, dipping a napkin into her water glass and scrubbing at a sticky spot on the table. "It's not Jonathan's kind of place."

"Well, thanks for slumming it with me. I've spent this whole week in only three places — the inn, the sugarhouse, and the woods."

"The woods?" Hannah was trying hard not to laugh. I could tell by the way she pressed her lips together. "You're becoming quite the Vermonter already."

I threw a balled-up napkin at her. "I have to find something to do with my time now that you've lured me out of the city."

At the far end of the room an elegant-looking man with a long blond ponytail and a white shirt tucked into neatly pressed jeans was tuning a stand-up bass.

"Ooh, you didn't tell me they have music here."

"Only on Friday nights," said the waitress, who appeared just then. "Can I get you girls something to drink?"

Hannah ordered a glass of grapefruit juice and I ordered a whiskey. The bar was quickly filling up. Some women were trickling in with boyfriends and husbands, while others arrived in packs, giggling and flirting with the bartender.

"You'll settle in soon. Have you met Alfred yet? He's an amazing chef. And isn't Margaret sweet?" Hannah took a long sip of juice, avoiding my eyes.

"Sweet?" I raised my eyebrows. "Have you ever bitten into a raw cranberry?"

"She's just a little stern. Wait till you get to know her."

"If I ever do. I've only seen her for a total of twenty minutes this week, and all she does is ignore me or take a little jab." I took a long sip of my drink. "I don't know, Hann. A year is sounding a little long."

"You stayed at the Emerson for three."

"Yes, but the Emerson was . . ."

"Exhausting?"

"Stimulating." I drained my glass. "And Boston might not be New York, but it has lots of things going on."

"Things you could never attend, because you were always at work."

"Yes, but . . ."

"Don't even think about it. You made a promise."

"A promise isn't a binding contract."

"In Guthrie it is." Hannah twisted her wedding ring around her finger. "You have to stay."

"What's up with her, anyway?"

"Margaret?"

I watched Hannah take a sip of her drink. "And what's up with the juice? The last time I saw you drinking juice you had taken up jogging. And I am not going jogging with you. Don't even ask."

"Would you ladies like anything to eat?" The waitress was back. Hannah ordered chicken soup and a side salad. I ordered the grilled cheese with French fries, along with another whiskey and a beer chaser.

"I should be asking you the same thing."

"I'm not drinking juice." I held up the whiskey glass. "See, nothing to worry about."

Hannah smirked. "I wasn't worried. But you should keep an eye on the drinking."

"We're in a bar."

"People notice things around here. Believe me. I'm just saying."

I rolled my eyes. "Anyway, have you seen her office? There's like, a million ribbons hanging from the ceiling —"

The crackle of a microphone sputtering to life interrupted my thoughts. The bar was packed. All the tables were full, and the spillover crowd stood in small groups laughing and talking. It seemed as if everyone knew one another, like at a high school reunion. Two other men about the same age had joined the bass player. One was dressed in a navy blue mechanic's jumpsuit with the name *Harold* embroidered on the breast pocket. He was carrying a mandolin case. The other I recognized as Tom Carrigan, the dairy farmer. Tonight he looked sharp in a blue dress shirt under a black vest, guitar slung over his shoulder.

The waitress put our plates down and disappeared into the crowd before I could ask after our drinks. I was scanning the room for her teased-up hair when I saw the bar door open. In stepped the man from the apple stand at the farmer's market. He was dressed in jeans and a white button-down shirt under a thick knitted sweater in a shade of blue that reminded me of the sky at dusk.

"Liv," Hannah said.

"Hey, Martin," Tom called from the stage.

"Want to join us?"

Martin waved, but didn't stop before he reached the bar, sliding onto a vacated stool at the end. Next to him stood a full-grown stuffed black bear, emitting a silent growl.

"Livvy."

I wouldn't have described him as handsome, but he looked like something you would admire in nature — like a fox or a hawk — something that would stare you straight in the eye before disappearing into the woods.

"Livvy! Where are you?"

"Oh. Sorry." I turned my attention back to Hannah. "What were you saying?"

The waitress set down three cardboard coasters and put down my beer and two glasses of whiskey.

"I only ordered one," I said.

The waitress jutted her chin toward the stage. "One's from Tom."

I raised my glass toward the stage, then knocked it back in one swallow.

Hannah craned her neck. "Who were you staring at? And who's buying you drinks?"

"Oh, just Tom, the dairy guy. In the band. Are they any good? I wonder if they're going to start playing soon."

"Livvy, I'm trying to tell you something."

And as if on cue, the man wearing the

jumpsuit, Harold, stepped up to the mike and said, "Evening, everybody! We're the Beagles! Your local all-Eagles cover band!" And with that the band broke into a blue-grassy version of "Peaceful Easy Feeling."

"What is it?" I shouted across the table.

Hannah looked over at the band, her eyes narrow. "I'm pregnant," she shouted back.

"What?" I jumped up, scooted next to Hannah on her side of the booth, and threw my arms around her neck. "That's great news!"

Hannah leaned her head against mine. "It's still early — only a little more than a month. We're not telling anyone officially until the beginning of the second trimester."

"My lips are sealed. I can't wait to be Auntie Mame!"

Hannah punched me in the arm. "Now can you see why I was so excited about you and the Sugar Maple? It's perfect that you're here!"

I looked at Hannah sideways. "I'm not exactly experienced in the motherhood department."

"I don't need help with the mothering part, it's just . . ." Hannah looked over her shoulder before leaning toward me. "It's Jonathan's mother. She's a total control freak. I need someone on my side."

Hannah, despite her earthy-crunchy appearance, is a bit of a control freak herself, but it didn't seem like the right moment to bring this up. "Don't worry. I'll stake my claim on the guest room and make sure she can't move in."

Hannah laughed, probably because she knew I didn't mean it. Jonathan and I had barely managed to get through my first two weeks in Vermont without coming to blows. She pushed at my arm. "Now go back to your side and eat your French fries. I'm about to pounce on them and I'm trying not to gain too much weight."

I moved back to my side of the table. When I looked at the bar, Martin's spot had been filled by the round slope of a thick-framed man. "So," I shouted across the table, "what are you and Jonathan up to this weekend? Nest building? Picking out bassinettes? What is a bassinette, anyway?"

"We're carving pumpkins," she shouted back. "Mr. Darling, who owns the funeral parlor, is trying to beat the Guinness world record for number of lit jack-o'-lanterns. Want to come?"

I had already spent enough hours that week digging into raw squash. "I need furniture."

"There's an estate sale tomorrow morning. An old patient of Jonathan's. He thinks she might have had some good stuff."

It seemed wildly disturbing for your family doctor to be sizing up how good a yard sale there would be when you kicked the bucket, but I kept my mouth closed. I needed a dresser. The band started in on a new tune — could that really be "Life in the Fast Lane"?

"I'd love to go."

Hannah stabbed at the romaine lettuce with her fork. "Has this been enough local color for you, Livvy? That mandolin is giving me a migraine. Let's go back to my house."

"All right. Just let me pee first." I knocked back the rest of my beer and stood up. As I weaved my way through the crowd, one thing became very clear: I was smashed. I gripped the shoulders of the bar patrons standing around me as I pushed my way toward the bathroom. After I peed, I splashed cold water on my face to fend off a slight edge of nausea. Refreshed, I stepped out of the ladies' room, tripped over the foot of the growling black bear, and slammed into a tall, heavyset man in front of me, causing his beer to shoot up like a fountain before it crashed to the floor.

"Oh my God, I'm so sorry!" I shouted

into the man's flannel chest. His expression went from surprise to anger to a cold curiosity.

"I know you," he said, his voice low and level. It sounded like an accusation.

"You don't," I said, grabbing a towel off the bar and swabbing beer off of his chest.

"You're that bitch who took Bonnie's job!" Flannel man's face was getting redder. I stopped dabbing.

"I'm sorry about the drink and your shirt, but I have no idea who Bonnie is and I haven't taken anything."

I reached into my back pocket, searching for cash so I could replace his beer.

"Where'd you come from, anyway?"

I fished out a five and slapped it on the bar, waving at the bartender and pointing a finger at Flannel. "Boston."

"Fucking figures." His eyes shrank into slits. "Think you're so great, don't you, slumming it up here with your purple hair."

"Electric Amethyst," I said, the room getting warmer. I leaned against the bar.

"She worked like a dog for that woman." He leaned in closer, towering over me, his breath hot and boozy on my face. "Stupid. City. Bitch," he spat. "So full of yourself. You think you can do any better?"

"Stupid. Redneck. Loudmouth," I spat

back. "I bet I can." Have I mentioned that I shouldn't drink whiskey? It makes me belligerent. A hand reached over and pulled Flannel back upright.

"Hey, Frank."

It was Martin. His voice was steady but his jaw was clenched.

"Figures you're out with this trash."

"Not now, Frank."

Martin put a hand gently on my back and turned me toward the door. Frank shouldered between us and leaned toward him.

"Girls around here still not good enough for you?"

I should have been worried about Frank, but I was too busy noticing that Martin's eyes were the same color as his sweater.

I felt a hand grip my elbow, and suddenly I was being led through the bar and out the front door. The night air soothed my burning cheeks. Martin sat down on the front steps, pulled out a sack of tobacco, and began to hand-roll a cigarette. I sat down next to him and leaned my throbbing head against the cool metal railing.

"Would you roll one of those for me?"

"Does Margaret know you smoke?" he asked as he licked the thin white paper.

"How do you know that I know Margaret?"

"My mother mentioned you. I'm Martin. Dotty's youngest."

I thought of Dotty's plump figure and loose braid. He must take after his father.

"I only smoke on special occasions."

"She wouldn't approve." He handed me a book of matches and began to roll another.

I lit the cigarette and took a small, tentative puff. "She doesn't seem to approve of me much anyway, so this will just confirm her general feelings. Anyway, do you have any idea what that was about?" I pointed to the bar behind us.

"You don't know?" Martin struck a match and drew in a long stream of smoke.

"Apparently not."

"Welcome to Guthrie."

"What do you mean?" I asked.

"Where everybody knows everything but no one says a word."

We both sat staring out into the parking lot, the muffled noise of the bar escaping as a group of boys stumbled out the side door.

"Well. Here's your chance to break tradition."

"Margaret has won the Coventry County Fair apple pie contest every year since I can remember. That and every other baking contest. Mom says her family has always won. There are pictures of them hanging in the Grange Hall."

"The ribbons," I said under my breath.

"Blue ribbons? She must have hundreds of them."

"And three red ones," I added, uneasily.

"Couple years back she took second place. She's been hiring and firing bakers ever since. At least that's how Mom tells it. I haven't been around. I think you might be number four."

"A baking contest."

"Yup."

"At the county fair?"

"The Coventry County Fair. Oldest fair in the U.S. It's a big deal around here."

I had been to the fair every year with Hannah. It had always been one of my favorite weekends — a perfect New England autumn getaway — apple picking, a drive farther north to see the first leaves change color, then a night of fried dough and riding the Zipper at the county fair. We had just been there a few weeks earlier.

"God, here you are." Hannah poked her head out the door, looking relieved. "I went looking for you in the ladies'. I thought you'd been abducted." Hannah walked down the steps and handed me my bag. She smiled at Martin and extended her hand. "Hi, I'm Hannah Doyle, Dr. Doyle's wife."

68

"Martin McCracken."

"Oh, you must be Dotty's son!" Hannah beamed, happy to know a little something about him.

Martin stood and ground the little stump of his cigarette under his scuffed black boot. "Well." He turned away from us, giving a tiny wave of his hand.

"Hey," I called. Martin turned back half-way, his profile sharp and pale against the night sky. "Thanks."

He grinned at me then. It was a sort of partial grin that involved only half of his face. I've heard experts talk about how what makes a person beautiful is symmetry, but I had a thing for odd numbers and funny angles.

"See you around," he mumbled over his shoulder.

I watched him disappear into the parking lot.

"What were you doing out here with Martin McCracken?" Hannah whispered.

"Not getting accosted by some thick-necked giant seeking revenge. Did you see that guy in the bar? I thought he was going to burst a blood vessel. Apparently his wife, Bonnie, used to bake at the Sugar Maple." I grabbed the metal railing and pulled myself up.

"Oh, yes, Bonnie. She's a nice girl, not half as talented as you." Hannah started walking ahead, digging into her purse for her keys.

"Hannah."

"That was fun, wasn't it?" Hannah busied herself with the lock on the car door.

"Why didn't you tell me about the apple-pie contest?" I asked over the roof of the car. "Don't try and fake it. You know everything that goes on in this town."

"Look, Margaret really needs your help. She keeps losing. Everyone in town is gossiping about it, saying she's lost her touch."

"Apparently she has."

"Well, she's been through a lot, the past couple of years."

"Is that when her husband died?" I remembered how crazy my grandmother had gone when my grandfather passed away. Nana had set a place for him at the dinner table every night until the day she finally joined him.

"Yeah. It was really sad. They married late and didn't have any kids, so now she's all alone. And then these terrible rumors started spreading that he gave away all of her family baking secrets to Jane White before he died." Hannah looked guilty for a second, like maybe she had had a part in

70

the rumor spreading. "I'll talk to you tomorrow." She slammed the car door shut and turned on the ignition before I could ask any more questions.

The red taillights of Hannah's Volvo were just out of sight when I realized I was still too tipsy to drive. I tossed my bag onto the bench seat. My cell phone slid out, its face lit, glowing angrily up at me. Seven missed calls. I slid into the car, leaned the seat back as far as it would go, and hit Play.

Livvy, It's Glen. Listen. The board met today, and they were thinking it might be a good idea if you take a break, just until the fiscal new year, when the executive committee has their new budget in place. Give me a call.

Ms. Rawlings, It's Joseph Harmon from Federal Student Loan Services. We haven't received a payment from you in three months. It really is in your best interest to call us. Our number here is 1-800-

Livvy, It's Dee Dee. Listen, I hate to ask this, but that money you borrowed a couple of months ago? I really need it. Jake and I are getting married, and we

need to scrape everything we have together. I feel weird asking, but . . . could
you give me a call? I dropped by the Emerson but they said you were on a break?

I pressed End.
At least I was now sober enough to drive.

CHAPTER THREE
NOVEMBER

Although we had exchanged many kind notes in my first few weeks at the Sugar Maple — his complimenting me on a huckleberry clafouti, mine thanking him for the delicious plates of leftovers he had left me for lunch — I didn't actually meet Chef Alfred until the week after Halloween, when we scheduled a time to sit down and plan the menu for the annual Harvest Dinner.

I had learned about the Harvest Dinner not from Margaret but from a block-print poster hanging on the White Market bulletin board, between flyers advertising free bark mulch and an autumn equinox moonlight drum circle. The poster promised "Old-fashioned New England Family Fun!" It was then that I noticed the whole town was already swaddled in bales of hay and dried corn husks. I had thought that things would quiet down in Guthrie now that the only leaves left to peep at were the stubborn crumpled-grocery-bag brown leaves on the oaks. But apparently the Guthrie Harvest Festival — capped off by the Harvest Dinner — was the social highlight of the season.

An older man in a tie-dyed T-shirt sat alone in the parlor, sipping coffee out of one of the gold-trimmed peony-patterned teacups. His large hand dwarfed the cup. He looked like he was drinking from his daughter's tea set.

"Chef?"

"Livvy, great to meet you." Alfred stood up and, after a moment's hesitation, pulled me into a great bear hug. The top of my head came up only to the middle of his chest. He smelled good, like a grandfather — Irish Spring and Right Guard. "Sit, sit. So, you have to tell me what was in that buttermilk custard you made the other day. We sold out by seven o'clock. I didn't even get to try it."

"Gosh, I didn't know if that one would go over well. I'll have to make it again this week."

"Do, but be sure to hide a cup of it for me." Alfred smiled through a thick nest of gray whiskers. "Settling in okay?"

"Everything's good on my end. But Margaret hasn't said much — or anything —

since I started."

"She's been preoccupied. I can tell you that the desserts are phenomenal. And the bread — God, that sourdough." Al rubbed a reddened palm across his belly. "I've put on five pounds since you started."

I beamed at him. There is no better compliment you can pay a baker than to tell her she has made you gain weight. "Would you mind saying some of those nice things to Margaret? I'm afraid she's going to boot me before my trial period is even over."

"I don't think she's thinking about making any staff changes now that the place is officially on the market."

"The inn is *for sale*?"

"She didn't tell you when you interviewed?"

"Um, no. She didn't mention it." I felt equal parts irritation and relief. If the place changed hands, I would have an easy excuse to leave without hurting Hannah's feelings.

"She's turned down offers in the past. I think she wants to make sure it will stay exactly the same. The sale could take awhile."

Oh, Margaret was looking for another *Margaret.* Good luck with that. "So, are we serving the Harvest Dinner in the barn?" I had seen a couple of high school boys dragging tables in there earlier that week. "Do we ever get busted by the health department?"

"No, no. Our Harvest Dinner is one of the town manager's favorite events. If he shuts us down, he can't come."

"Then I won't worry so much about the dog." I tilted my head toward Salty, who had somehow broken out of the sugarhouse and was now sitting on a worn velvet couch scratching an ear with a hind foot.

"Quite beautiful," Alfred said, "the dinner, I mean. I think you're gonna love it. Very Martha Stewart. We serve all the courses family style, on big platters. It's mostly locals that attend — we can only seat one hundred in the barn, and most of the tickets are sold by the beginning of the summer. All the guests who are staying at the inn can come, of course, since the dining room is closed that night." Alfred leaned back in his chair, arms folded loosely across his tie-dyed chest.

Whether it was served in the barn or in the walk-in refrigerator, I didn't care. Making desserts for a big, fancy dinner put me back in my element, and I was ready to shine.

"So, I have a couple of ideas." I dug my spiral-ringed notebook out of my canvas bag and flipped to the right page. Alfred and I got to work, heads down, leaning over our notes — his shiny with grease stains, mine streaked with chocolate.

"First course is a corn consommé," Alfred said.

"That's brilliant. Can you do that?"

"Just the pure essence of corn."

My mouth began to water. "Then a salad?" I asked.

"Baby red oak greens with toasted black walnuts and a maple vinaigrette."

"With goat cheese?" I licked my lips.

Alfred smiled and ran his fingers up and down his hairy arm. "An excellent idea."

"I could make croutons out of a dried-apple spice bread."

Alfred leaned in a little closer. "Or maybe just a thin slice of the apple bread with the goat cheese spread on it."

"Yum." We weren't even to the main course yet. "What's next?"

"Prime rib, with a cipollini au jus. We get the beef from the Haskell farm."

"Not Snowball," I gasped. I had spent the better part of Tuesday afternoon letting the cow gum at my coat sleeve.

Alfred laughed. "You'll get used to it. And, no, not Snowball. She's a heifer, for one thing. She's used for milk and breeding."

I let out a long breath. Only a couple of weeks in the country and I was getting dangerously close to becoming what all chefs loathed — a vegetarian. "So what's the wraparound?"

"Wild mushroom risotto and roasted Brussels sprouts."

"I could make popovers," I offered.

Alfred closed his eyes. "With chives?"

I smiled. "Done."

A cheese course would follow. Vermont cheddar with quince paste, fresh chèvre with homemade blackberry preserves, and a sheep's-milk blue cheese with pears poached in port. And then dessert. Pumpkin crème brûlée baked in hollowed-out miniature pumpkins. Apple galettes with frangipane in puff pastry. Pears stuffed with cognac-soaked figs and wrapped in phyllo, baked to a crispy golden brown, the fruit inside tender and succulent. And thin chocolate shells, filled with a thick amber caramel, studded with toasted pecans and a layer of dark chocolate ganache just barely sweetened.

Alfred and I leaned back in our chairs and smiled at each other, our foreheads glistening with sweat. All we needed was a couple of cigarettes.

"It's going to be a meal to remember,

Livvy. If she does sell, it will be a great meal to go out on."

"Fantastic." I raised my arm in the air, like I was standing in front of a roaring crowd, about to take a bow. "It could be my debut and grand finale, all in one."

Alfred laughed. "You know, you are nothing like I thought you'd be."

"What did you think I would be like?"

Alfred rubbed his fingers in his beard, considering. "Intimidating?"

"How intimidating can a baker be?" I asked. "We make brownies all day. Besides, my hair is purple. Nothing says 'easygoing' like purple hair."

"I love it. My mother was a hairdresser right up until the day she died. She made the ladies' hair blue — although I don't think it was on purpose."

"And she let you go gray?"

"Oh, she tried, believe me."

Margaret walked into the parlor. She looked at me and at Alfred, then over at Salty asleep on the sofa. "In the kitchen, please, Ms. Rawlings. When you are done." She nodded at Alfred before disappearing into the back of the house.

I rolled my eyes. "I'm settling right in." Alfred laughed as we headed back to the kitchen.

■ ■ ■ ■

My last task for the day was to put together a poaching liquid, which I wanted to steep overnight. Margaret came out of her office just as the port was coming to a simmer and, to my surprise, sat down on the stool that Tom used on the mornings he delivered the milk. Silently, she watched me scrape a finger of fresh ginger with the edge of a tarnished silver teaspoon.

"I've never seen ginger peeled that way," she commented.

"I picked it up from one of the prep cooks at the club — he was from India." I placed the piece of ginger in the center of a square of cheesecloth that lay flat on the table before me. I had already piled a small mound of spices there — cinnamon sticks, cloves, a piece of star anise, pink peppercorns. I reached for an orange and dug into its skin with a zester, stripping it of its brightly colored flesh and releasing a burst of orange oil into the air.

Margaret closed her eyes and inhaled deeply. Her face softened for a moment before she pursed her lips. Her back straightened. "Is this for the Harvest Dinner?" she asked.

"Yes," I said as I gathered the edges of the cheesecloth into a tiny bundle, which always reminded me of a hobo's pouch, and secured the top with twine. "I'm making batches of all the desserts for you and Chef Al to taste, in case you want to make any changes."

Margaret looked surprised.

"This" — I held up the cheesecloth bundle before dropping it into a pot of simmering port — "is to flavor the pears." Poised at the stove, spoon in hand, I stared into the pot, stirring occasionally, trying to look professional. Margaret sat and watched.

"So . . . ," I asked after what felt like hours of silence. "Is there something you wanted to talk about?" I hated being observed. During my practical exams at cooking school I had managed to both burn all the hair off my hands and slice off the tip of my thumb. And judging by the deep channel that appeared between her eyes, it looked like Margaret had something on her mind.

"Can't I take a minute in my own kitchen?" she clucked. "You don't mind Tom Carrigan sitting here all morning long."

Why was I always saying the wrong thing? I grabbed my knife and cut a slender slice of the apple tart. I slid it over to her, hoping she would accept the gesture of apology. Margaret stared down at the tart for a moment.

"A civilized person would eat this with a fork," she said before raising it to her lips and taking a tiny bite. I watched her expression out of the corner of my eye as she chewed. Nothing.

I gathered up my courage. "Margaret, I wanted to ask if I could get a telephone line put into the cabin. I don't have any cell reception up here." Not that I was burning to have access to my cell phone. But it would be nice if Hannah could call me at the sugarhouse.

"You can use the telephone here at the inn."

"But what if there were a family of bears keeping me trapped in the cabin? I couldn't call for help."

Margaret broke an edge of crust off the tart. "Why would a family of bears trap you in your cabin?"

"For dinner?"

"Black bears are mostly vegetarian."

Just my luck. Hippie bears.

"Well — let's see how you do during your trial. I don't want to pay out the expense until I know for sure that you're the right person for the job." Margaret pushed the tart aside and folded her arms in front of her. "There is one matter I would like to discuss. There's a fund-raiser during the Harvest Festival to raise money for the public library. It's a bake sale."

"Seriously?" I bit the inside of my cheek to keep from saying anything snarkier. The last fund-raiser I had baked for had been a five-hundred-dollar-a-plate black-tie gala.

"This year it's cookies. They did cupcakes last year. Every year it's different." Margaret wiped her hands with a dish towel. "The best bakers in the county donate several dozen cookies. It would be a chance for the people in the town to try something you've made. And it's for a good cause." Without another word she hopped off the stool and walked toward her office. "I'd rather you not wear that jacket in the parlor. It's a tad ratty."

I looked down. Most of the last batch of raspberry coulis had ended up on my chest instead of in the squeeze bottle I was trying to pour it into. I only had one jacket. Normally, kitchens supplied coats for the chefs and sent them out to be laundered. I popped the coat open with a flick of my wrist, tossed it onto the counter, and tied the gingham apron with the dancing sheep around my waist.

"I'd be happy to make something," I called, my face bathing in the steam of boiling port.

"All right, then," she said, and slipped back into her office.

"You're not going to buy that," Hannah said the following Saturday morning as she unfolded a lace-trimmed tablecloth and spread it across a table in the church hall thrift shop.

"Why not?" I gave the multicolored afghan I was holding a little squeeze.

"It's awful."

"You mean awfully beautiful, right?" I wrapped it around my shoulders like a cape. The scent of mothballs filled the air. "Besides, someone's granny crocheted her poor arthritic fingers down to the bone making this thing. I can't let it fester in the basement of a church hall for the rest of its life."

"Well, if you're going for that seventies-rec-room look."

"Hann, I live in a one-room shack made for boiling tree sap."

"You live in a sugarhouse, not a shack. And besides, it's your *home.* We want it to look inviting."

Hannah was a ruthless bargain shopper with an amazing eye. Even though Jonathan's salary would have allowed her to furnish her whole house from the antiques shops on Newbury Street, she loved the hunt. We had spent part of every one of my visits to Vermont scouring yard sales and thrift stores, then heading to the Miss Guthrie diner to eat tall stacks of blueberry pancakes while Hannah gave me the dirt on everyone we'd run into that morning. It was our ritual.

With her help, the sugarhouse had already begun to look more cheerful. We had replaced the old workbench with a sparkling turquoise Formica table, complete with two matching chairs, only slightly ripped and discreetly mended with clear packing tape. The previous week Walt, the elderly man who ran the recycling center at the town dump with the strictness of a nun at an all-girls Catholic school, had called me at the inn to tell me one of the summer people had dropped off a perfectly good couch. I didn't need to ask how he knew I was looking for one. Hannah had even managed to get Walt to make his grandsons deliver it for free. It was a puffy, overstuffed sofa covered in spotless canvas, like something you would see in a catalog. We positioned the couch against the wall near the front door, facing the woodstove and the kitchen. Two upturned wooden crates that served as end tables held lamps of bottle green glass with cream linen shades. I loved to sit on that couch in the afternoon, reading and looking out the windows into the sugar bush, stark except for the carpet of fallen cardinal red leaves.

"What do you think about this, Livvy?" Hannah called from across the room. She was standing beside a hand-carved coffee table.

"It looks heavy."

"I saw one of the butcher's sons over by the paperbacks. I'm sure he would be willing to carry it to the car."

"Do you really think I should be investing in any more furniture, Hann? Alfred told me about the inn being for sale."

Hannah flapped open a hand-stitched quilt. The squares were ripping apart at the seams. "Really, don't people know they have to use a front-loading washer to clean these?" She tutted and left the quilt in a heap on the table.

"Did you know about it?"

"She's been talking about selling for years."

"Alfred made it sound like it was more than just talk."

Hannah looked over both shoulders. "As

far as I know, the only offer she's ever had was from the Bradford family," she said in a fast whisper, "and she would never sell to them."

"Why does that name sound familiar?"

Hannah gathered up the cotton curtains she had found. "Remember what I said the other night, about Margaret's recipes? Jane White? She used to be Jane Bradford."

So Margaret had an arch enemy. Somehow I wasn't surprised. But that didn't explain why the name *Bradford* rang a bell.

Salty brushed by my shins as we unloaded all of our treasures from Hannah's Volvo. Along with the afghan, which I promptly spread over the back of the sofa just to make Hannah's nose twitch, I had found two pillows, embroidered with the faces of hunting dogs (obviously a labor of love by some farmer's wife). Hannah had picked up white cotton curtains with scalloped edges and all the hardware, but our biggest score of the day had been two screens made of rice paper, which we used to hide the bathtub that sat in the middle of the cabin, right behind the woodstove.

"This looks much better," Hannah said, nodding in approval. She had been obsessing over the exposed bathtub. I've never been able to get her to skinny-dip. And don't ask about the time I brought her to the hot-tub place in college. She wouldn't speak to me for a month.

"Hmmm," I agreed as I fed one of the metal rods into a curtain. "It's starting to look like I live here." This was the most furniture I had ever owned. It made me feel a little itchy knowing I couldn't move in one trip.

"You do live here," Hannah agreed as she straightened the last curtain. "In fact, I know you are officially part of the town, because when I was at the pharmacy I heard two members of the Friends of the Guthrie Library talking about you."

"Was it about Jeff Rutland?" I began to crumple up newspaper and stuff it into the mouth of the woodstove.

"Jeff Rutland from Lyndonville?" Hannah stepped down from the stepladder, hands on her hips, surveying her work.

"Never mind."

"Why would they be talking about — Livvy, you haven't . . ."

"Jesus, Hannah! No. I've never met the guy. Tom the dairy farmer said something about him to me my first day."

"It's just that — Liv, you can't just, you know . . ." Hannah picked up her purse and

88

rooted around inside. As if she didn't know exactly what side pocket she kept her lip balm in.

"Sleep around? Become the town home wrecker?" I went back to the woodstove, layered in kindling, and threw in a lit match.

"Listen, my first month in Guthrie I had a third glass of wine at book group. They were *small glasses.* It's been ten years, and every single time someone mentions book club one of the women will say, 'We better get more wine if Hannah is coming.' "

"You do love your Chardonnay."

"And you love your trysts. Just be discreet, okay? You'll like it here more if you don't ruffle a bunch of feathers."

"I'll try," I mumbled as I jabbed a too-big log into the stove, but I had serious doubts about my ability to please anyone.

Hannah opened her mouth to say something, then closed it. "Anyway, the two ladies from Friends of the Guthrie Library were talking about the bake sale. They were wondering what you were going to make."

I watched as the log sparked and started to burn. "I was thinking macaroons."

"The ones that were featured in *Cookie Connoisseur?*"

"Yup," I said, closing the door to the woodstove.

"Perfect." Hannah grabbed her coat and draped it over her arm. "You'll be the talk of the town," she said as she leaned over and kissed my cheek. "In a good way."

I grabbed my banjo by the neck and headed out onto the porch, wanting to take advantage of the precious few hours of afternoon light. I sat down on the rocking chair, leaned back and propped my feet up on the porch railing, and, with the banjo balanced between my knees, twisted the pearly pegs until the strings began to talk to one another. My banjo leans toward the lazy, letting its strings wander and go slack at their own will. And on a humid day, well, forget it; it sounds like Salty howling after I have tethered him to a parking meter. But this afternoon was dry and warm and made for playing. I started with "Cluck Old Hen," and then came "My Pretty Crowing Chicken," old-time standards that keep your feet tapping. Before I knew it I had frailed a full hour of tunes named after poultry.

"The Cuckoo" required me to adjust the strings to a minor tuning. These modal tunes are my true love. Play me something in double C and I feel like someone has cracked me open. It's like those odd little notes are the voice of some truth I can't name. I let my mind wander as I played. The sun, now waning, still warmed my cheeks.

Hannah was right about one thing. It was peaceful here. I couldn't remember the last time I had spent a lazy afternoon playing. In Boston, when I wasn't at work, there always seemed to be something to do — laundry to schlep to the cleaners, checks to be deposited, Jamie to bed. My heart stilled. I guessed I should have told him I was leaving, even if our relationship wasn't exactly based on what people call feelings. Now that I was no longer distracted by the thrill of meeting him in bedroom 8, when I thought of him, I also couldn't help but think of his wife. Not talking to him seemed like the best thing for everyone.

I focused on my fingers. Without my meaning them to, my hands had settled into the tune that I had heard in the woods with Salty. It was the saddest melody I had ever heard — a last waltz of unwelcome good-byes and a desire I couldn't name. I played it over and over, a little surer of the notes with each round. I was lost in the rhythm, how it held both longing and joy.

"You can't play that."

My feet slipped off the railing and I was flung forward, the banjo losing its place between my knees and landing on the porch floor with a loud twang. I picked it up and whirled around. Martin McCracken was standing at the bottom of my porch steps, fists clenched.

"I didn't hear you walk up."

Martin crossed his arms against his chest. "You can't play it."

"I thought I was doing pretty well."

"It's not yours."

I could feel my eyebrows involuntarily pinching together. "Well, 'Whiskey Before Breakfast' isn't mine either, but I play it." I leaned my banjo against the wall of the cabin and stood up.

Martin paced in front of the porch, his eyes to the ground. "Where did you hear it, anyway?" I could barely hear his mumble over the crunch of his boots on leaves.

"I don't know," I lied. "I must have heard someone play it in a jam." I walked to the edge of the porch, looking down at him.

"That's impossible," he said under his breath. "You shouldn't go around just picking up people's tunes."

I threw my arms up in the air. "That's how music has been passed down for centuries!"

Martin turned his back to me. I heard him let out a puff of air.

"I know that, but —"

"What are you doing here, anyway?" I had been having a perfectly peaceful afternoon. Now I felt like I was back in Boston, being lectured by one of my neighbors on the proper placement of the recycling bins on trash day.

Martin's back straightened. "Is this your dog?" He pointed down at Salty, who was sitting politely next to him. Salty panted and gave his tail a thump. Traitor.

"Hi, Salty," I said. I hadn't noticed that he wasn't on the porch while I played. "He is. What are you doing with him?"

"Me?" Martin turned away from me again. He walked a couple of paces, then turned back. "I came home today to find your dog and one of the goats lying on my mother's sofa."

"Were they asleep?"

Martin gaped at me. "Uh, no." He put his hands in his pockets.

"What were they doing?" I had no problem picturing Salty lying on someone's sofa. I just thought he would be too excited to sleep next to a goat.

"Apparently they were watching TV," Martin said in a tight voice.

"What were they watching?" I asked.

Duck Soup.

"God, I love that movie," I said, laughing.

"Me too." Martin sat down on the bottom step and leaned his head against the railing. I tucked my skirt around my knees and sat on the top step. "My mother was in the La-Z-Boy, snoring away, with Mabel and your dog on the sectional. I managed to get them both out without waking her."

I pressed my lips together, picturing Martin whispering and gesturing wildly. "Well, I'm sorry if Salty had anything to do with liberating your goat. The vet said he has separation anxiety. He's pretty good with doorknobs and latches."

Martin reached down and stroked Salty's head behind his ears. Salty let out a low groan and rolled onto his back. Martin laughed and rubbed Salty's belly.

"Well," he said to the ground, and then stood. He glanced up at me, his mouth open as if to speak, then turned and began walking into the sugar bush behind the cabin.

Salty stood and watched him as he disappeared into the trees, then padded up the steps, brushing past me, and into the cabin, no doubt ready for his supper.

CHAPTER FOUR

The next morning I made a test batch of pumpkin crème brûlée. While the milk scalded on the stove, I whisked together egg yolks and pureed pumpkin, the bright orange mixture brilliant against the blue bowl. As I poured the milk slowly into the bowl, whisking all the while, a cloud of cinnamon and ginger wafted up, filling the kitchen with the scent of fall.

"Smells good," said Tom as he walked by, carrying a crate of heavy cream into the refrigerator. I sliced a piece of frangipane tart for him.

"You've been holding out on me," Tom said, mouth full. Flakes of puff pastry flew into the air.

"How so?" I transferred the custard into a glass pitcher and poured the mixture into the tiny pumpkins I had hollowed out the day before, lined up in a roasting pan.

"Here I am, having breakfast every other

day with a banjo picker, and I didn't even know it."

I put down the pitcher. "How did you . . . ?"

"And here I am, in need of a banjo picker." Tom took a long sip of his coffee.

"Tom, I hate to break it to you, but I hate the Eagles." I wiped my hands on my apron, then cut myself a piece of the tart. "I just don't see myself as a Beagle. Besides, I *frail,* I don't pick. Now, what do you think of the tart? Too almondy?"

"How can you not like the Eagles?"

"I've got two words for you. Hotel Cali—"

"You're losing the taste of the apple."

I nodded, taking another bite. I had been thinking the same thing.

"Now, it's not the Beagles that need a banjo player. It's the Hungry Mountaineers."

"The who?"

"My contra-dance band." Tom looked longingly at my plate.

"Take it," I said, pushing it toward him. "Are there a lot of dances around here?"

"Ten or so a year. Next one's during the festival." Tom popped the last bit of my tart into his mouth, reached into his back pocket, and pulled out a clean cotton handkerchief to wipe his lips.

"I've never played in a contra-dance band before." I dampened a dish towel and wiped down the table.

"Have you ever been to a contra dance?"

I laughed. "I took my first steps on a contra-dance floor."

Tom raised his eyebrows. "Really?"

I leaned my elbows on the table. "My dad was a frailer too. He played in a dance band when I was a kid."

The door to the dining room swung open, and Margaret marched in. I straightened. "I'm surprised you don't have more deliveries this morning, Tom," Margaret said as she walked past us and into her office. "I can see by the crumbs in your beard that you haven't given up the pastries despite what Dr. Doyle told you."

Tom ran his fingers through his beard. "Darn wife tells everybody everything," he mumbled under his breath. "Well," he said, slapping his hand against the counter, "rehearsal's at eight tomorrow night in my barn. I'll see you then."

"But I —"

"Bye, Margaret!" Tom called over his shoulder. "I'll be sure to tell Marcie you say hello!"

I took out a fresh eleven-pound block of chocolate and a cleaver. Play with a dance band? I had to admit, it sounded like fun. I had complained endlessly when my dad dragged me off to folk festivals in the summers growing up, wanting to spend my afternoons with my girlfriends in the air-conditioned paradise of the mall. But I secretly loved the dancing. The sweaty scent of the grange hall on a hot summer night. The flashes of color when the women twirled in their full skirts. And the music! Tunes with silly names like "Kitten on a Black Dog's Tail" and rhythms so uplifting that you couldn't help but get up and join in. The best part was always the last waltz, when we paired off with whomever we had been crushing on to sway together for those few moments before the hall lights went up and we all went giggling into the darkness of the night.

The Carrigan place was on the outskirts of Guthrie, where farmland stretched far on both sides of the road. I turned into the driveway, tires crunching on gravel, past a peeling white farmhouse and down a long hill toward the cattle barn, a yellow rectangle of light marking the open door. I pulled my station wagon in between two pickup trucks. Salty leaped out over my lap and sauntered straight into the barn. I stood up and stretched, taking in the wide expanse of stars in the moonless sky. I grabbed my banjo from the backseat and headed into the light.

"Hey." Three men sat in a circle on folding chairs. Tom stood up from behind a small upright piano and slapped me on the back. He was wearing a pressed shirt tucked neatly into his jeans. Even in his barn Tom looked like he was on his way to church.

"Glad you could make it, Livvy. Come meet the band." The men looked up shyly. "This here is Arthur on bass." I recognized him as the Beagles' bass player as well. He grinned and took a long swig from a green bottle. "That's Gene on rhythm guitar." He was older than Tom, at least sixty, slender with wavy silver hair and pink cheeks. "And on fiddle we have Martin McCracken." Martin looked up at me and nodded. Salty, who had chosen to lie down on a patch of hay beside Martin, rolled over onto his back. Martin stretched down and scratched his stomach.

"We've met." Though I'd suspected it was Martin who'd told Tom I played, it hadn't occurred to me that he might be in the band. He didn't seem like the joining type. Tom opened another folding chair and placed it next to Salty.

The cows radiated heat, and the barn was cozy despite the open door. I unzipped my fleece and settled in as Tom handed me a beer without asking. I took a long swig while Martin raised his fiddle and drew out a long G for me to tune to. I folded over, my ear to the drum, twisting the tuning pegs that tightened the strings, listening for the match.

"I thought we'd just run through our set, Livvy, so you could get to know how we play," Tom said. "Join in anytime you like."

I sat back, my arms relaxing.

"Ready?" he asked. Arthur stood with a groan and picked up the bass. Tom sat on the piano bench and tapped his brown work boot on the dirt floor. "One, two, three, and . . ." The barn leaped alive with music. My feet kept time with the rhythm Tom pounded out on the piano keys. Arthur rocked his bass in his arms like a dance partner, while Gene arched his whole body over his guitar, his silver hair hiding his face. I couldn't keep my head from nodding to the beat. Even the cows in the barn had turned to face us.

I sneaked a look at Martin from the corner of my eye. He sat on the edge of the folding chair, leaning forward. The fiddle was pressed into a spot under his collarbone, as if he were pressing it into his heart. His eyes were closed. He moved the bow effortlessly across the strings, as if it were an extension of his hand. His knee bounced up as if his boots were spring-loaded. The folding chair threatened to collapse beneath him. If I had been deaf, I could have heard this tune by his gestures alone.

It was as if I were watching another person entirely. He played with the grace and strength of a long-distance runner. I had never seen his face look so unguarded. When his lips curled up as he leaned into a double stop, I found myself wishing he would smile like that for me.

At the end of the third round Tom stuck out his foot and everyone ended on the same note. Without realizing it, while watching Martin I had turned in my seat to face him directly. When he opened his eyes, I swiveled back to face the center of the room, dabbing with the back of my hand at the sweat that had beaded along my hairline.

"So, Livvy. Think you can keep up?" Tom asked with a grin.

I braced my banjo squarely between my knees and strummed an open chord, my thumb plucking the fifth string with a bright twang. "Let's give it a whirl." And with my foot tapping in time to Tom's whispered countdown, I frailed my first chords with the Hungry Mountaineers.

When I stepped out of the barn, the droplets of sweat instantly froze on my skin. Reluctantly I zipped up my fleece and made my way to the station wagon in the dark. Light pooled from the car when I opened the door.

"Come on now, Salt." I scanned the darkness, straining my ears to hear the jingle of his tags.

"He's right here." Martin appeared on the other side of the pickup next to mine.

"He likes you," I said. I patted my thigh and whistled a short loop. "Come here."

Salty walked around the truck and leaped onto my backseat. I closed the door and opened the driver's side.

"Have you played with them long?" I asked, leaning my arms on the roof of the car.

"I used to — back in high school. Now I'm just sitting in."

"They're all older than you, aren't they?" I guessed that Martin was only in his late thirties at best. "Was that strange?"

"I think Tom's around fifty, so yeah. Not a lot of options in a town like this."

I tried to imagine being a teenager without

record stores or coffee shops or the sweaty crush of strangers in the mosh pit, and failed.

"So why Salty?" Martin asked, leaning against his truck, still clutching his hard, black fiddle case.

"It's short for Old Salt. Doesn't he look like the Gorton's Fisherman?"

Martin raised his eyebrows.

"You know." I took a deep breath, then sang, "Trust the Gorton's Fisherman."

"The fish sticks commercial?"

"Exactly!"

Martin peered into the backseat of the station wagon. "I guess a little around the eyes."

I laughed. "It probably helps that I found him in Gloucester. Right by the Fisherman's Memorial statue, in fact." I gazed through the fogging windows at Salty's long frame. "I never really wanted a dog. I sat by the statue for hours waiting for someone to come looking for him, but no one ever did."

"You don't like dogs?"

"No, I love dogs. It's just . . . too much responsibility. Anyway, he looked so pathetic, all alone."

Martin took a sudden interest in something on the ground. "You play beautifully."

"You're not bad either," I said. In fact, he

was the most remarkable fiddle player I had ever seen.

Martin barked out a laugh. "Thanks a lot."

"Thanks for getting Tom to invite me," I said shyly.

"It seemed like a good fit." He slid into the driver's seat. "I'll see you tomorrow for practice."

"See you." Waving, I ducked into my own car.

Martin started the truck's engine, stretching his arm around the bench of the cab as he backed up. I watched his taillights snake up the hill and turn onto the main road, disappearing into the dark night.

I stopped at the inn to make a phone call before feeling my way back to the sugar-house. Raphael was my old specialty-foods rep, and he owed me a favor because I'd introduced him to his now-husband, Charles. Margaret hadn't said another word about the bake sale, but I knew that it wasn't just a casual charity event. And I had to admit that there was a grain of truth in what Hannah had said: I needed to make a good impression. Every private club from Boston to DC had almond macaroons on its dessert menu, but mine were legendary. Crisp on the outside, fragrant with the scent of bitter almond, the center tender with just enough chewiness. They were sweet without being cloying, rich without being heavy. My first magazine write-up had been about my macaroons. They had established me as a notable chef and given me job security at the Emerson; in situations like this one, they were my secret weapon.

When I told him I had a special event a week away, Raphael agreed to overnight me a can of my favorite almond paste and a pound of Belgian cocoa powder, extra dark. I was not going to take any chances with ingredients. I could make macaroons blindfolded, but the key to perfection lay in the oven being precisely 325 degrees, and I just hadn't developed that kind of trust with the oven at the Sugar Maple. When my package arrived, I stayed late in the kitchen. I measured the almond paste, sugar, and cocoa powder into the bowl of the stand mixer and set it in motion. The mixture began to make a swish-swish sound like maracas being shaken. The inside of the bowl sparkled like a black-sand beach as the tide went out, the almond paste perfectly cut by the sugar and cocoa. After adding egg whites that had been whisked together with instant espresso powder and a drop of rum, I stopped the mixer, pinched off a piece of raw dough, and popped it in my mouth — the mixture melted on my tongue. *All right, Guthrie bakers. Bring it on.*

CHAPTER FIVE

"You have to try this."

All of my favorite conversations began this way. Chef Al handed me a small wedge of a dark orange cheese. I took a bite and purred. The nutty flavor spread across my tongue in salty waves. "What is it?"

"It's an aged Gouda that Betsy has been fooling with. She gave us the first wheel."

All the ingredients for the harvest dinner were locally sourced. Betsy, an amateur cheese maker from a neighboring farm, was one of our purveyors. "I hope she kept better track of how she made it than the Camembert."

Chef Al chortled. "That was a shame, wasn't it? That first taste was a revelation, then . . ."

"Every wheel after was a complete disaster." I shuddered as my tongue remembered the sour bite and mealy texture. "She has to keep better notes."

"We can only hope." Al wrapped the chunk of Gouda in a sheet of waxed paper and headed to the sink to wash his hands.

I popped the rest of the wedge into my mouth and turned my attention back to brushing a sheet of phyllo dough with clarified butter. You could tell by the length of my daily prep list that the festival was two days away. All week my workdays had started and ended in complete darkness. I juggled making desserts for the dining room with preparing for both the harvest dinner and the bake sale. The list was only half crossed off when the night crew began to trickle in. I hadn't realized how lonely I had been in the mornings until I found myself in the middle of the dinner rush, squeezing past the dishwasher to grab a clean spatula, shouting, "Behind you!" to the waitstaff as I raced from the stove to the sink with a smoldering pot of molten caramel. Suzanne and Helen, who waited tables in the evening, were warm, full of gossip, and always willing to try a bite of whatever I was working on. In the back, Chef Al had an easy grace, and we fell into a comfortable rhythm. He could perfectly flip an omelet while giving relationship advice to the hostess. He had a way of looking like he wasn't doing anything but chatting, but at the end of the night hundreds of ears of corn had been husked, bushels of Brussels sprouts had been trimmed, and the kitchen was spotless, even though the dining room had been full just hours earlier.

After the third time Salty showed up, whining, at the back door of the kitchen, Margaret relented and allowed him to hang out in the front sitting room while I worked, saving me from having to feel my way through the orchard to collect him for his evening walk. I occasionally caught her talking to him in the foyer, and one afternoon I found them both dozing on the same love seat.

"I hope I made enough," I said for the hundredth time on the morning of the dinner.

"You did," said Al as he rubbed olive oil onto the small bodies of cipollini onions. He spread them onto a sheet pan with his slick hands and slid the tray into the oven.

"But what if I didn't?"

"Stop worrying. It's a five-course meal. We don't want them stuffed with bread." Al turned his attention to his corn consommé, gently simmering on the back of the stove. "Now, what we *should* be worrying about is this soup — does it have any flavor at all?"

Al ladled a small portion into a coffee cup and handed it to me. I blew on the soup lightly and took a sip.

"Alfred," I sighed, "it's like drinking a summer picnic."

Al beamed. "Does it need salt?"

"Nope." I took another swallow and gave him back the cup. He refilled it and handed it back to me.

"Too much butter?" he asked.

I licked my lips. "Well, now that you ask, I do feel like I need to wipe my chin."

Al snapped his dish towel at my hip. I shrieked and began to pelt him with the bits of bread dough that I had been scraping off my fingers. "It's perfect and you know it."

"So, Livvy," Alfred began, his voice suddenly formal, like he was going to make a speech. "Are you going to the contra dance tomorrow evening?" He had removed the red bandana that he wore to keep his gray curls from getting into the food and was twisting it in his hands. His hair was a shaggy mess, like he had just rolled out of bed.

Heat rose up my neck. I turned my attention to the bread dough in my hands. "I'm playing in the band."

"Oh, I didn't know that."

"I just joined a week ago."

110

Alfred still stood by my table. "I thought maybe I could accompany you."

I had never seen him look so awkward. *Go chop something,* I silently pleaded as I pressed my palms into the dough. "Like a date?" I asked.

Margaret walked into the kitchen through the back door, accompanied by two men in suits. She waved her hand and said, "This is the kitchen," without acknowledging either Alfred or me, then led the men into the dining room.

"If you are saying yes, then yes. If not, then no, strictly a professional invitation."

I laughed. "Alfred, under different circumstances I would say yes," I answered truthfully. "But I just got out of a relationship with someone I worked with, and it didn't end well." *And by "not well," I thought, I mean in flames.*

"That's the problem with being a chef," Alfred lamented. "The only people who can understand your life are the people who won't date you. Maybe I'll get lucky and you'll get fired."

I sank the edge of a serrated knife into the crust of a loaf of apple bread, trying to saw away the uncomfortable realization that, actually, I didn't want to get fired. I wanted to stay.

■ ■ ■ ■

There is a moment after the prep is done and before the theater of the dinner service begins when I love to escape the kitchen. Dusk had fallen, and when I stepped outside, I was drawn to the light spilling from the barn, golden and inviting. I poked my head in. Margaret had outdone herself. The long tables were covered in cream linen. Squash-colored tapers stood tall in sparkling silver candelabras. Fat bouquets of sunflowers, goldenrod, and black-eyed Susans stuffed into mason jars were surrounded by tiny pumpkins and crab apples. I looked up to see a thousand white Christmas lights hanging from the rafters. The whole room glowed. I pictured Martin sitting at the table, the lights reflecting off his eyeglasses.

"Not as nice as that fancy club of yours, I imagine." Margaret's voice brought me back to reality.

"It's stunning."

"Well. It's an important night. I expect everything will go smoothly?"

"Of course it will," I said, running my prep through my mind for the millionth time.

"Good. I have some important guests

coming. Remember, you are representing the inn, not just yourself." She looked me up and down for a long minute. "Come into the kitchen. I have something for you and Alfred."

Margaret led me back into the inn, which had been decorated to match the barn and smelled like wood smoke. I lingered in the doorway for a moment, watching the guests sip brandy and chat by the fireplace, before making my way to the back of the house. Alfred had the waitstaff slicing the loaves of peasant bread and stuffing them into baskets. The dishwasher was feverishly trying to keep up as Chef Al tossed him pan after pan. I tied an apron around my waist and walked toward my workbench. Margaret came out of her office with a large plastic bag and handed it to me.

"I thought you would want something special to wear tonight." She looked strangely uncertain.

I unwrapped the plastic. It was a cream-colored chef's jacket with the Sugar Maple's logo stitched onto the right lapel and my name embroidered over the left breast. I hugged the jacket, then dropped it on my table and wrapped my arms around Margaret.

"I love it!" I shouted, squeezing her. It

was like hugging a day-old baguette.

"There's one for Alfred as well," she said as she pried herself out of my embrace. She removed the other jacket from the bag and handed it to Alfred. "I expect you can keep your expressions of gratitude to yourself."

Alfred untied his apron and slipped the jacket over his concert T-shirt. "Thank you very much, Margaret." Alfred bowed. "It's sharp."

"Keep it clean. We can't afford to buy you both a week's worth."

With one hand I tugged my old coat open, popping off a button, which shot across the kitchen.

Chef Al watched, blushing.

"Good Lord, child!" Margaret exclaimed, turning away.

"I'm wearing a tank top!" I laughed as I slipped my arms into the new coat and buttoned it up. Suddenly, I felt like a real pastry chef again. "Tonight is going to be perfect!" I called over my shoulder as I made my way to the walk-in to check on the pumpkin crème brûlées.

The large white tent from which we would serve the dinner had been set up behind the barn. Steaming chafing dishes sat on top of one of our improvised tables made of wooden doors balanced on sawhorses. The servers for the event, all kids from the high school, giggled with one another in the corners. They looked cute in rented tuxedo pants and white button-down shirts. Sarah paced the edge of the room, trying to keep them together like a border collie herding a field full of sheep.

Margaret poked her head into the tent promptly at ten past seven. "Everyone's seated."

"Okay, people. We're on the fire," Chef Al called.

Al lined up the trays of soup cups that were being kept warm in a rented proof box. I spooned kernels of roasted corn into each cup as Al poured the corn consommé from a giant steel pitcher. The waitstaff were right behind us, grabbing each cup as it was filled.

"Remember, kids, serve from the left!" Sarah called as the first tray of soup was carried out of the tent.

Al and I kept our heads down in concentration until the last cup was taken. I ran my sleeve across my forehead and blew out a breath.

"One down, four to go." Al smiled down at me.

From the rented refrigerator we wheeled out a stainless-steel rack with trays of salads.

115

With latex-gloved hands I fluffed up the red oak leaves, which had flattened under their blanket of plastic wrap.

"They love the soup, and it's going fast," Sarah called as she bustled into the tent. "I'll start clearing in two minutes."

"You dress and I'll put on the croutons?" I asked Al. He nodded, already shaking a squeeze bottle of maple vinaigrette back and forth. I carefully laid a crouton on each plate of greens. The goat cheese was soft from the heat, barely holding its shape on top of the slice of apple bread. The waitstaff hurried into the tent, chatting in pairs, gossiping about who was sitting with whom at the table.

Margaret appeared a few minutes after the last salad was served. She looked elegant in a coal gray dress and black stockings. A sterling silver brooch with tiny diamonds in the shape of a maple leaf sparkled at her throat. "So far, so good," she said, nodding. "How are things going in here?"

"Smooth sailing, thanks to Livvy here," said Al. "It's nice to have an experienced pair of hands to work with."

I beamed. "They're having a good time?"

"I expect so." Margaret smoothed her skirt. "About five minutes to the main course."

I rolled the rack of cheese plates out of the refrigerator as Al gave a final polish to the silver platters that would hold the prime rib, roasted Brussels sprouts, and mushroom risotto.

Sarah came bustling back into the tent. "They're clearing the salad plates. We'll pour more wine before serving, so you still have a couple minutes."

I smiled over at her. "How's it going?"

"Great. The plates are clean, and everyone is chatting up a storm."

I looked over at Al. "Clean plates."

He shook his hands over his head in a silent cheer. "Halfway there."

Al began to slice the roast. The main course was being served tableside. Since Al didn't need my help plating, I focused my attention on the cheese course that would follow. I spooned dollops of my blackberry preserves onto the coins of chèvre. Tiny cubes of homemade quince paste sat next to the traditional Vermont cheddar. Next to each small wedge of sheep's-milk blue cheese I carefully draped a succulent slice of ripe pear.

"Those look amazing," Al said as he wiped his hands on his apron.

"Thanks. The whole meal looks great so far." I twisted one of the strings of my apron around my hand, feeling a familiar mid-event anxiety. Dessert was coming up quickly.

"If you want to go freshen up, now would be the best time."

I gave Al a long look. "Freshen up? Why?"

"When it's time to serve dessert, we'll go out into the barn and be introduced."

I swallowed. "Introduced?"

"To the guests. They like to be able to ask questions about the meal. Margaret will introduce me, and then I'll introduce you. It's a chance for everyone to meet you."

"Margaret didn't say anything." I frowned and began to pick invisible lint off my skirt.

"You've got nothing to worry about. Your desserts are outstanding. Everyone is going to love you." Al's cheeks reddened like apples. He looked down. "But you might want to do something about your hair."

I reached up to feel a halo of frizz surrounding my face. "The cheese plates are ready to go. I'll be right back."

The cool evening air felt fresh against my skin. I walked quickly to the front door of the inn, resisting the temptation to peek in at the dinner guests. The inn was quiet, the only sounds the ticking of the grandfather clock and Salty panting from one of the love

118

seats near the fireplace. I went into the ladies' room. When I looked at my reflection in the mirror, I was surprised by what I saw. Sure, my face was glossy with sweat, and my hair had liberated itself from most of its bobby pins, but I looked happy. Content, even. I couldn't remember the last time I had felt so at ease. I pinned back my curls, wiped my face with a paper towel, and walked back out into the evening.

The tent smelled like the home of someone who loved you. Like Sunday dinner at my Nana's house, rich with the aromas of roasted meat, dark and crisp at the edges but tender and pink inside, of caramelized onions and woodsy mushrooms. My stomach grumbled.

"You held back enough for staff meal, didn't you?" I asked Al.

"Not to worry. There's a whole extra roast."

"Are they slowing down?" I asked as I eyed the cheese plates.

"Want a hand with dessert?"

I exhaled. "Yes, please."

We began with the chocolate shells. I topped the ganache with a rosette of freshly whipped cream and crowned each tartlet with a tiny half-dome of spun sugar, its amber color hinting at the caramel inside. The apple galettes were cut into wedges. I brushed the edges of the puff pastry with apricot glaze and sprinkled them with toasted slivered almonds. I was worried that the phyllo-wrapped pears would not have weathered well, but the pastry was still crisp and golden and the cognac-stuffed pears still looked moist and tender. The crème brûlées were last. I arranged the tiny orange pumpkins on the tray. Without having to be asked, Al spread a thin layer of sugar on each. I lit the blowtorch and waved the flame across the custards; the scent of caramelizing sugar filled the tent.

Margaret came in as the last wisps of smoke from the burning sugar dissolved into the air. "It's time. Follow me."

Al handed me a tray of the custards. "Margaret will say a few words, then I'll follow. When you hear me say, 'And now for dessert,' let the servers go out first with the other platters, and then you follow holding the brûlées. I'll introduce you. Just say whatever you like. Okay?"

"All right." I hovered by the door as Margaret and Al disappeared into the barn. From outside I could hear the pleasant hum of the crowd, as though I were standing close to a beehive. Sarah peeked out from the doorway and gave me a thumbs-up. I followed the servers in. At the head of the tables stood Al, with Margaret standing a few steps behind him, her arms folded across her chest. I looked over at her and shrugged. She nodded her head toward Al.

When I reached his side, Al placed a comforting hand on the middle of my back. He turned his attention back to the room. "We've had a wonderful new addition to the Sugar Maple staff this year, as you all are about to discover. It's with deep pleasure that I introduce you to our new pastry chef, Olivia Rawlings."

The sound of clapping filled the room. I was happy to have the tray of crème brûlées in my hands to steady me. To my left sat the town manager and his wife. To Alfred's right was Dotty. The seat next to Dotty was empty. The applause died down as the servers worked their way through the crowd, but the clap of a single guest's hands continued with gusto. I scanned the barn. A chair in the back scraped the dirt floor, and a figure stood up. I squinted across the room to see who it was. All I could see was that he was wearing plaid patchwork pants. My hands began to tremble. The tiny pumpkins started to vibrate, marching toward the edge of the tray. The tray itself grew heavy and slick as my palms started to sweat. A pumpkin teetered off the edge and landed in the town manager's lap.

"Are you all right?" Al whispered as he grabbed the tray.

"I'd like to propose a toast," Jameson said from across the room. He raised his martini glass. I didn't even think the inn *had* martini glasses. He probably traveled with his own. "Miss Rawlings was the pastry chef at the Emerson Club, of which I am president, for more than two years. She is a treasure, an absolute delight, a gift from the heavens. . . ."

My face and neck burned hotter than caramelized sugar. I clenched my hands into tight fists at my sides.

Beside him, Jameson's wife glowered. I imagined her hands mirroring mine.

"I just hope you all appreciate what a wonderful person you have here, because sometimes we do not really appreciate what we have until it's gone."

Al coughed. "Yes, well said. Let's all —"

"To Olivia!" Jameson shouted. His wife grabbed him by the elbow. He shooed her away as if she were one of his hunting dogs.

"Yes," Al interjected, "let's all raise a glass to Ms. Rawlings, to welcome her, although I am sure she would agree that the best show of appreciation would be your enjoying the amazing desserts she has prepared for all of you." Al passed the tray of custards to one of the waitstaff. The crowd began to clap politely as the servers offered the desserts. Jameson remained standing.

"To Olivia!" He raised his glass in the air. His wife stood up and walked out the back door of the barn. Jameson swayed. "Olivia. Livvy." He took a long swallow from the glass he was holding. He drained it and let it slip from his fingers. "Livvy, what are you doing here?"

Chef Al looked down at my frozen expression, took me by the arm, and led me out of the barn.

The fact of Jameson Whitaker, drunk at the harvest dinner, began to settle in my spine. Pressure built up behind my eyes.

"Livvy, was that . . . ?"

I pulled my arm out of his grip. "Please," I said as I pushed past Alfred and headed back toward the inn.

"Livvy?"

"I'll be back to clean up in a minute, okay?" I called as I slipped into the building.

I marched into the darkened kitchen and grabbed by the neck the bottle of bourbon I kept for flavoring pecan pies. I poured a shot into a juice glass and knocked it back. Salty pushed open the swinging door and pattered in.

"Just this once," I told him as I sank down into one of Margaret's rocking chairs, bottle in hand.

I was on my fifth shot when Al came in looking for me. He sat next to me in the other rocker and reached for the bottle.

"So, that was your old boss?"

"Yup." I reached down and stroked Salty's fur, avoiding Al's eyes. "Did he do anything else? Pass out? Sing? Start tipping the staff with fifty-dollar bills?"

Al laughed. "No, I'm pretty sure he just sat down and ate dessert. The folks next to him probably got an earful."

I groaned. Pushing off the ground with my feet, I rocked for a few moments. Al took a swig from the bottle.

"When I mentioned I was involved with someone at work . . . Jamie wasn't just my boss, exactly."

"You don't say." Chef Al stood and held his hand out to me. "When was the last time you ate?"

I rocked furiously. "I had that piece of spice bread this morning."

"Come on, you need to get some food into you."

"I can't go back in there."

"Sure you can." Al reached down and pulled me out of the rocker. "The table is all set for staff meal. Let's not keep them waiting." Al tucked my arm into his to steady me and led me out of the inn.

"Livvy!" Sarah called when we ducked our heads into the tent. "I saved you a seat."

Platters of prime rib, Brussels sprouts, and risotto were making their way around the table. Al placed a bowl of end cuts of beef on the ground for Salty.

"Great meal, everybody," he said as he opened a bottle of wine.

"The whole thing was a big hit," Sarah said, tearing open a popover. They were still steaming.

"Did they like dessert?" I asked, fixing my eyes on Salty.

"They loved every bite," Al said from across the table.

"Well, I feel very appreciated right now," I said with a grin.

"We treasure you, Livvy," said Sarah.

"You're an absolute delight," Al said, laughing so hard be began to choke on a Brussels sprout. One of the high school kids pounded hard on his back.

"To Livvy," Sarah said as she held up her

wineglass.

"To Livvy," chorused the high school kids.

I cracked the burned-sugar topping of a pumpkin crème brûlée with my teaspoon, revealing a smooth orange layer of spicy cooked cream.

"To all of you," I said, lifting up the bottle of whiskey.

Margaret walked in and joined us at the table. "Please tell me that dog was not in here the whole time you were serving dinner."

"Of course not. Just for the after-party," I said.

Margaret poured herself a glass of wine. "Excellent job, Alfred. The guests certainly seemed to enjoy everything." She looked about the table. "The service went smoothly, Sarah. And you kids did a good job. I'm proud of you." Margaret finally turned to face me. "You certainly made an impression, Miss Rawlings."

I rolled my eyes and poured a finger of whiskey into my water glass. "Did your friends have a good time?"

"They did," she said, standing. "I'm going to retire. Alfred, the rental company is going to be here to pick up the equipment first thing. Can you manage that?"

"No problem. I'll have it all packed up

and ready."

"Okay, then." Margaret stood up. "Don't raise too much of a ruckus out here. I've got an inn full of guests."

I didn't return to the sugarhouse until one a.m. My mind raced as I shuffled through the darkness, guided by the crunch of Salty's paws on fallen leaves. Margaret hadn't seemed too upset, and maybe that speech of Jamie's hadn't been as bad as I thought. I mean, no one here knew about our relationship. Maybe they thought that I really was just a beloved employee? My thoughts drifted to the empty seat beside Dotty. If Henry hadn't been able to make it, why wasn't Martin there? I was simultaneously relieved and disappointed. Thank God he hadn't witnessed Jamie's toast. But I had wanted him to try my desserts. I bit my bottom lip. It was never a good sign when I was trying to impress some man with how succulent my poached pears were.

I fumbled with the doorknob and let Salty and myself in. It was a relief to be alone. I carefully unbuttoned my new coat and pulled my tights off with a grateful sigh, then tugged on a faded pair of yoga pants. I was wrestling with the elastic snarled in my hair when someone knocked. Salty's head shot up, his ears pricked. My heart leaped. I stood up and opened the door.

Standing in the light of my cabin was Jameson Whitaker IV.

"You've got to be kidding me." I leaned against the doorframe.

"Livvy." Jamie's voice had the breathless quality that told me he had been drinking gin. I'm pretty sure he did it on purpose because he thought it was sexy. To me it sounded more like he had just been jogging up Beacon Hill.

"What are you doing here?"

"You live here."

"Yes, I know. What are *you* doing here?" My shoulders were bare and I wasn't wearing any socks, but I didn't want to take a step back into the cabin for fear he would take it as an invitation.

Jamie reached out and wrapped his arms around me. I had forgotten how tall he was. I stood still as he held me tighter and tighter.

"Jamie, you're squishing me. Seriously. I can't breathe."

He loosened his grip and leaned in to try to kiss me. I pressed my hands against his chest and pushed.

"Not going to happen."

"But darling, I —"

I pushed him over to the bench on the

porch. "Sit there. Stay."

I ducked back into the cabin to grab a cardigan and rifle through my underwear drawer in search of a pair of wool socks. Salty let out a long growl.

"Don't worry about it, Salt. I'll be right back."

Jamie was leaning back with his head against the side of the house. I tiptoed over to see if he was still awake and pressed my toe into his thigh. He started and sat up. "Livvy."

"How did you find me?" I leaned against the porch railing.

"Glen gave me your forwarding address." Jamie looked around at the trees. "Does the post office even deliver here?"

"Jamie." I made a mental note to cross Glen off of my list of people to send toffee to at Christmas.

"What are you doing here, Livvy? This is a big step down for you."

"All sorts of chefs are moving to the country. That chef from the Top of the Tower moved to rural Maine last year, remember?"

Jamie shook his head slowly from side to side. "No one could cook a steak better than his."

"See?"

"You can't be making enough money to survive."

I waved my hand at the cabin. "It comes with free rent!"

"And what about your other expenses? Your landlord called the club looking for you."

I winced. "Did Glen tell you that? What did he say?"

"That we don't give out private information about our employees."

"Former employees."

"Everyone knew it was an accident, Liv. You didn't have to leave."

"That's not what the executive committee said." I turned and looked out into the dark orchard. "I would have left anyway," I said quietly.

"You didn't call. I was worried. You didn't want to see me?" Jamie asked.

I let out a long breath. "It's not that I didn't want to see you, but — I needed to go."

"I meant everything I said tonight. We miss you at the Emerson. *I* miss you."

I slid my back down the railing and sat on the floor of the porch.

"You could have your old job back."

I pressed my palms to my eyes.

"The new chef knows the position is only

temporary. A trial run. It would be so simple for you to slip right back in."

"That's the thing. I don't know if I *want* my old life back. Working eighty hours a week at the Emerson? Spending every night alone in my crappy apartment unless your wife has a Friends of the Public Garden meeting?"

"Don't be like that." Jamie reached over and grabbed my foot. I pulled it out of reach.

"Be like what? Jamie, we had a good time together, but . . ."

"A very good time." Jamie reached for my foot again. I let him hold it.

"But it's not like we were planning to run off together." The more I characterized our relationship to him, the worse I felt. It had been such a risk to be with him, and for what? A few wasted hours every week in an Emerson bedroom? "And besides, I think I might have the chance to . . . I don't know." *Or had the chance to . . . until your toast.* The look of humiliation on Mrs. Whitaker's face flashed across my memory. "Jesus, what were you thinking? I can't believe you brought your wife here. You don't think she knows?"

Jamie leaned an elbow on his patchwork-plaid thighs.

"When she heard about the dinner, she wanted to come. I didn't want to miss the chance to see you."

"Not your smartest move." I stood up. "Go on back to the inn. Forget that I'm here and get into bed with your wife."

Jamie stood up slowly and faced me. "I mean it, Livvy. You could come back anytime."

He leaned over and kissed me gently. I leaned into him an inch. It felt so good to be kissed. Familiar. I pulled away when his tongue pushed past my lips. He traced his hand down my back, resting it on my butt. I ducked out of his embrace, grabbed the flashlight I kept on the porch for outhouse runs, and pressed it to his chest. "Take this or you'll get lost and eaten by bears."

He flashed the light into the orchard before him and then took slow, careful steps down the stairs.

"Hey," I called after him. "How did you know where to find me?"

"I told you, Glen —"

"No, I mean here, at the cabin?" I hugged my elbows.

Jamie paused for a moment, thinking. "A young man I met when I first arrived. Tall, glasses. He was at the dinner with his mother."

"Oh," I said, and walked back into the cabin, closing the door behind me before Jamie could see the disappointment on my face.

CHAPTER SIX

The parking lot was packed by the time I arrived at the grange hall the night of the Harvest Festival's "Frost on the Pumpkin" contra dance. I had spent all day hiding in my cabin. Hannah had been expecting me to stop by the children's festival on the town green, where she manned the first-aid station, but every time I tried to muster up the energy to put on my boots, Jamie's drunken toast would play in my head, and I would flop back down on the couch. The idea of running into Jamie or, even worse, Mrs. Whitaker, in front of the citizens of Guthrie made me feel like I had been pushed into a blast freezer. Instead, I spent the day stripping the purple out of my hair and redyeing it — Manic Panic Electric Tiger Lily. The jar promised it would glow under a black light, but somehow I didn't think the grange hall was going to turn the lights off and get funky.

By the time I left the cabin, a persistent cold rain was falling. Tom had asked that we all wear white shirts and black bottoms to look "professional," but beyond that it was up to us. I chose a full black skirt that came down to my knees, long enough that I would show nothing but my skill on the banjo to the dancers down below. A white cotton wrap shirt did its best to send the message of curvy rather than chunky. My orange red curls were loose and wiry. It was pouring when I opened the car door. I pressed my banjo case close to my body, wrapped us both in my yellow slicker, and ran for the hall. In the grange folks were already gathered by the refreshment table, and there was a line at the check-in desk. The rest of the Hungry Mountaineers were sitting on stools onstage tuning their instruments. I ducked into the cloakroom and shrugged off my slicker, shook the water out of my hair like Salty would, and strode across the hall and up onto the stage.

Martin gave me a quick glance before returning his attention to tuning his fiddle. Tom clasped my shoulder and leaned down to whisper in my ear.

"Glad you made it." Tom looked sharp in black slacks and a white oxford, a silver string tie at his throat.

"Sorry," I whispered back. "Traffic."

Tom snorted. "That thing going to stay in tune in this weather?"

I brushed the strings with my right index finger. It sounded like a wounded cat. "Not likely. I'll just play quietly."

"Don't sweat it. Just do your best." He stood up and walked over to a tall, slender woman wearing a white blouse and floor-length skirt.

I leaned over to Martin. "Is that the caller?"

Martin looked toward the microphone stand. "Yes. Her name is Kate. She comes over from New Hampshire."

She looked lithe and elegant. I smoothed down my skirt and reached up to pat my hair. I had accepted a long time ago that I was cute at best, interesting-looking most days. Elegant wasn't in my body's vocabulary.

I leaned back over to Martin. "I didn't see you last night."

"No." Martin plucked at the strings of his fiddle with his thumb.

I twisted the tuning peg of my fifth string, trying to match it with the first. Martin stood up abruptly and walked off the stage. I watched him as he marched across the grange hall, black Converse high-tops peeking out and squeaking on the waxed floor. I turned and gave a weak little wave to Gene and Arthur. Tom raised his eyebrows at me questioningly. I whispered across the stage, "Can anyone play me a G?"

The hall grew warm as it filled with dancers. It smelled of mulled cider, rubber wellies, and rain-soaked oak leaves. I spotted the stocky figure of Frank, the man I'd gotten into a tussle with at the Black Bear tavern, in the crowd next to a tiny blonde. He leaned over and spoke into her ear. She whipped around and glared at me from the dance floor. Martin returned to his seat, his face damp around the hairline. He pressed the bottom of his fiddle into his chest, bow alert in his right hand. Tom stepped up to the microphone.

"Welcome, everyone, to the Guthrie Harvest Festival's annual 'Frost on the Pumpkin' contra dance. We're the Hungry Mountaineers, and we are pleased to introduce our guest caller from Franconia, New Hampshire, Kate Conroy!"

The crowd applauded as Kate stepped up to the microphone. Tom took his place at the piano, eyes on Kate.

"Okay, dancers, let's get in line."

The crowd scuttled to form four stripes

running from the stage to the back of the hall.

I turned my attention to Tom's right foot. As he began to tap it, I tucked the banjo head between my knees and brought my left hand to rest lightly on the neck, ready to play.

"This is the walk-through," Martin whispered.

I hadn't been to a contra dance in years. I'd forgotten that they teach the dances at the beginning. I gave Martin a small smile, grateful not to have started playing a solo. He looked at the floor.

"Take four hands from the top," Kate called. The lines formed into squares, two couples each, all holding hands. It reminded me of the playground game foursquare.

"Allemande your neighbor right once and a half." The couples across from each other touched each other's right hands, held them up in the air, and walked in circles, looking into each other's eyes. My mind flashed on a drunken evening I had spent on a culinary conference dance floor, rubbing my booty up against some sous chef. This was sexier.

"Same neighbor, balance and swing." The couples stepped toward each other, then away, then the men caught the women in an embrace and swung them around in circles, making their skirts twirl.

"Circle left three places," Kate called, "partner swing."

I glanced at Martin. His mouth tightened slightly when our eyes met. I was relieved that Jamie's big, blond head was nowhere to be seen. I did spot Alfred, who was dancing with Sarah. Her face lit up as he swung her around.

"Ladies chain across. Left hand star." The couples all put their left hands in the center and walked around in a circle.

Martin raised his fiddle and tucked it under his collarbone, in the spot where my cheek would rest if we were dancing. He cleared his throat and nodded his head toward the piano.

Tom played the first three notes of the tune.

"And turn to the right."

I grabbed my banjo and began to strum, missing only the first chord.

With the music playing, the room began to swell with a feeling of joy that was irresistible. My feet tapped out the rhythm along with Tom's piano. From the stage you could see the lattice pattern the dances made, the couples weaving in and out like fluted strips of piecrust. With each swing bursts of giggling could be heard from the less experienced dancers when they fell out of step. I closed my eyes and let myself get lost in the music. When the last note ended, the crowd burst into cheers. I turned to look at Martin, whose sweaty face broke into a broad smile. I felt like I had won a blue ribbon. It was the first time I had ever seen his teeth. They were crooked but bright. I beamed back at him.

At intermission Martin sprang up and walked off the stage before I had a chance to speak. Tom took his stool and wrapped his arm around my shoulder.

"Having a good time?" he asked.

"Yes," I said breathlessly. "I'd forgotten how much fun this is."

Tom chuckled. "I think it's more fun to play up here than it is to dance down there, but let me know if you want to sit one out and take a turn."

"Oh, no, I'm much happier up here."

"Go get yourself something to drink before the next set begins. These folks are serious dancers. They don't like to dillydally too long."

A crowd had gathered around the refreshment table. I elbowed my way around a group of women who had formed a huddle worthy of a football team at the Super Bowl.

"I mean, of course she needs the help —

she's getting too old to run that place on her own," said one of them.

"My cousins have been trying to buy that place for years," said a heavyset woman, probably in her late sixties. She talked a little louder than the rest.

"Why couldn't she hire someone local? It's not like there aren't plenty of people around here looking for work," replied another.

"It just figures she hired someone like that." The stout woman — the quarterback of the group — looked over her glasses at her team. "I mean, who else would work for her?"

The women around her jutted their heads like hens, hanging on her every word. I grabbed a cup of apple cider, wishing I had something to spike it with, and turned back around.

"I mean, it was obvious he's been sleeping with her. The way he kept drawing out her name. Ollivvviiaa," the quarterback said in a mocking slur. She raised her gaze and looked me square in the eye.

I froze in my tracks.

"I'd keep an eye on your husbands, ladies."

Tom played a couple of notes on the piano to get everyone's attention. I placed my cup back on the table and climbed up on the stage. I felt like every single person in the grange hall was staring at me, with the exception of Martin, who was directing all of his focus at the white rubber toes of his high-tops. I shifted in my seat, fussing with the tuning pegs of my banjo, wishing the stage would open up and swallow me whole.

As the evening progressed and the dances became more complex, I kept my eyes on my banjo and tried to think only of the next note. Among the couples still dancing was Jack the coffee roaster and his partner, Peter. No one seemed to bat an eye. I wondered how long it had taken for them to be accepted in this town. So far the Harvest Festival had left me feeling chafed, and I was grateful when Kate announced the last dance before the ending waltz — a duet between Martin and Tom. I placed my banjo down on the stage floor.

"Livvy," I heard someone say from the bottom of the stage. It was Chef Al. He offered his bent arm. "Care to dance?"

I glanced at Martin. He stood and walked over to the piano.

Gene, the guitar player, gave me a smile and a wave. "Go on, now."

I walked down the steps and took Alfred's

arm in mine. "I thought for sure you would show up in one of those T-shirts with a tuxedo printed on the front," I said as Al placed a hand gently on my waist and the waltz began.

"I thought about it." Al laughed. "But it seemed like a special occasion."

"Sure you want to be seen dancing with me? I might ruin your reputation."

Alfred's grip tightened on my waist. "Too late for that," he whispered.

Martin played standing next to the piano. The waltz held the feeling you get when you finish a well-loved book. It left me longing for something I couldn't name.

Al sighed and leaned his cheek against my hair. "You're a good dancer too."

"Hmmm?" I asked, watching Martin draw out a note with a long pull of his bow.

"Nothing," said Al. "Just plotting how to get you fired."

Margaret arrived at the sugarhouse at eleven on the dot the morning of the bake sale, her sharp knuckles rapping against the window by the door. "Wanted to make sure you were up after gallivanting all night," she said, as if my playing an acoustic instrument until ten in the evening would make it impossible for me to get out of bed the next day. Margaret paced about the cabin as I got dressed, straightening pillows and turning the faucet on and off to see if she could keep it from dripping.

"Ready," I said as I grabbed my car keys.

She looked me up and down. "I'm driving."

Margaret sped into the parking lot behind the old white church and came to a grinding halt.

"Now, when we get in there, let me do all the talking."

My seat belt retracted with a sigh. Were we going to a fund-raiser or to see a man about a truck? "Oookay," I said. "You know, there isn't that much I could do in a church basement to embarrass you."

"If there's a way, Ms. Rawlings, I'm sure you'll find it. Just remember, you are here with those cookies to represent the inn. And to help out the library."

I looked down at the cookies through one of the clear plastic Tupperware lids. There were four containers in all — eight dozen cookies — stacked up to my chin. I had been tempted to embellish — at least to garnish the cookies with a little confectioners' sugar and some fresh raspberries — but she had insisted on leaving them plain.

Anyway, I wasn't worried. These macaroons had once won the heart of the French ambassador. He had told me so over champagne in room 10 of the Emerson.

"Fine."

Margaret opened the car door, and before my boots were on the pavement, the straight tweed line of her back had already disappeared into the church. I clutched the boxes of cookies close to my chest and pulled open the heavy wooden door. It took a minute for my eyes to adjust to the dim light of the chapel. Weak afternoon sun filtered through the wavy glass windows.

"Ms. Rawlings!" Margaret's voice cut through the silence. I followed the dull hum of muffled voices down the back stairs and into the church basement.

A card table had been set up at the bottom of the stairs. I found Margaret standing with a hand on one hip. A woman with curly frosted hair sat behind the table, clutching a clipboard.

"Here I am," I said to no one in particular.

"Melissa, have you met my new pastry chef?"

Melissa peered up at me from behind red plastic reading glasses. "I haven't had the pleasure."

"Melissa is this year's Mrs. Coventry

County." Margaret drew out each word.

"A pleasure." I extended my hand. "Olivia Rawlings."

"Olivia just came to us from the Emerson Club in Boston."

"On Beacon Hill?" Melissa asked.

My eyebrows shot up. "Yes. Do you know it?"

"I have family in Boston. Cousins."

I looked over at Margaret. She was bent over, furiously filling out a form.

"How lovely. Do you visit them often?"

"Usually just at Christmastime. I'm not much of a city person. But I love shopping on Charles Street and seeing the lights in the park."

"On the Common." My heart sank a little as I thought about the draped lights in the trees that I used to gaze at through the Emerson's kitchen window. You could see the ice skaters on the Frog Pond from the chef's office on the sixth floor.

"Okay, ladies, you're all set. You're in your usual spot over by the windows, Margaret. The sale begins in an hour. Thanks for donating!"

Margaret took me by the elbow and led me into the coatroom.

"We've got an hour to kill. Now what do we do?" I asked, leaning against the wall, overwhelmed by the smell of mothballs.

"We go check out the competition."

"But it's a bake sale, not a contest. Isn't it?"

Margaret straightened her coat on a hanger. "That doesn't mean there isn't a winner at the end."

The church hall was filled mostly with women huddled in groups of two or three. There were a few men, standing on the edges of the hall, drinking black coffee out of small Styrofoam cups. They all looked like they were still dressed for church. Long tables covered by paper tablecloths filled the center of the room. I followed Margaret to the corner near the coffee urn, where a little natural light filtered in from the windows at the top of the wall. She arranged the macaroons on a silver platter she had stashed in the church kitchen, hiding the plastic tubs under the table.

After we had set up the hand-lettered signs that Sarah had made, Margaret led me to the front of the hall, where she walked us slowly down the aisle, considering each platter one by one. Golden brandy snaps looked dressed up next to a plate of plump butter cookies studded with dried cranberries and mini marshmallows. Peanut-butter cookies with the classic fork-pressed lattice rested next to carefully rolled rugelach. There were more than seventy plates, and there was still a line at the card table where Melissa sat. These people took their baking seriously. The pie contest I had been hired to win no longer sounded like a charming small-town tradition. I had real competition.

"Those look pretty good," I said, admiring the dainty shell shape of a madeleine.

"She uses imitation vanilla," Margaret said under her breath.

"Gross." I approached a plate of sugar cookies buried under blobs of neon green icing. "What do you think of those?"

"They look like they could break teeth."

I snorted. Margaret walked briskly down the aisles, examining each plate as if she were looking for something. Some of the bakers sat behind their tables, ready for business. Margaret said quick hellos, skipping introductions, and worked her way down to the last table.

At the end of the row was an unmanned plate of pecan sandies. Margaret turned to face me and leaned in close.

"When I walk away, grab one of those."

"There's no one here to pay yet."

"Exactly." She handed me an embroidered handkerchief. "Just snatch one and meet

148

me at the car." Margaret marched down the hall and disappeared behind the ladies'-room door.

Bakers were filing into the room and setting up their tables. I looked over both shoulders to make sure no one was close and plopped my courier bag on the table, pretending to look for something. My hankie-lined hand darted out and grabbed a cookie. When it was stashed in my bag, I crossed the room in long, purposeful strides, not looking back.

I found Margaret sitting in the backseat of her car with the door still open. I slid in on the other side.

"Did anyone see you?"

I placed the cookie and handkerchief in her hand. "I'm ninety-nine percent sure no."

Margaret unwrapped the small package, then broke the cookie in half. It fell into crumbly pieces all over her lap. She handed me two of the larger crumbs. "What do you think?"

"Dry. Coarse. Too sweet. In other words, your typical pecan sandy."

Margaret gave me a satisfied smile. She looked so pleased that I didn't want to break the spell by asking her why she'd had me commit a petty crime.

"My thoughts exactly. Let's get in there and raise some money."

By twelve thirty the church hall was filled with festival-goers armed with plastic baggies and dollar bills. Margaret and I had argued over the price of the macaroons. I had wanted to charge three dollars and she had suggested twenty-five cents. We settled on a dollar each. Margaret handled the money while I sat next to her and answered questions about ingredients and calorie count.

"You know, this really is a one-woman job," I said. "Don't you think it would be better if I went back to the inn and begin working on —"

"No," Margaret said sharply. "I need you here."

"But —"

"Margaret." A woman about Margaret's age — seventy? seventy-five? — appeared in front of us. "How nice to see you here."

"Jane." Why did that name sound familiar? I froze in my seat. I didn't recognize her at first — her hair was up, she wasn't wearing her glasses, and she had on slacks and a turtleneck instead of a dress — but I would never forget that voice trash-talking me at the contra dance. Jane looked from Margaret to me and then back again. "I'm surprised to see you this year."

Margaret pressed her nails into the flesh beneath her thumb. "I always pitch in. You know that, Jane."

I cleared my throat.

"And who is this?" Jane smiled down at me. I swear she had fangs.

"My pastry chef."

"Another one?"

Margaret leaned forward. I stood up and stuck out my hand.

"Yes, Olivia Rawlings. Nice to meet you." I put on my most saccharine smile. "Margaret was so generous about making room for me at the Sugar Maple. I really needed a change of scenery after the feature in *Food & Wine*. God, people treat chefs like rock stars these days, you know?" I shook my head. "There are only so many benefit dinners and interviews a girl can do. And most of those chefs you see on TV — they don't even cook anymore! Can you imagine? I just wanted to get real. Back to the *food*. So when my best friend, Hannah Doyle, Dr. Doyle's wife, told me about the Sugar Maple, I knew I had to work there. And here I am!" I sat down, exhausted. Margaret rolled her eyes.

Jane looked at me evenly, smiling with her

lips firmly clamped over her false teeth. She picked up a macaroon, turned it over to inspect the bottom, then put it back on the plate, rubbing her fingertips together.

"Well, good luck," she said as she worked her way down the row.

"Who the hell is that?" I whispered into Margaret's ear.

"Nobody," she whispered back.

"Well, that nobody was spreading lies about me last night at the —"

"Hello, my dears." I recognized Dotty's warm voice. When I looked up, I saw that Martin was standing behind her. Dotty popped a whole macaroon into her mouth.

"Oh, Livvy, these are divine!" She handed one to Martin. "I'll take a dozen."

Margaret grabbed the handle of her handbag. "We'll be right back," she said to me. "Keep an eye on the cashbox." She and Dotty walked off, their heads bent together.

"They look like they're plotting something," Martin said.

"I think that might be closer to the truth than you think." I handed him a plastic bin of macaroons. "Here to buy treats?"

"Mom needed a ride."

Martin looked awkward, standing there holding the box of cookies. It was painful to look at him. I patted Margaret's empty chair. "Want to keep me company for a bit?"

Martin squeezed between the tables and sat beside me, stretching his long legs. I slid the cashbox toward him. "You're in charge of the money."

We waited on customers. All the nontourists told Martin how glad they were to see him after all this time and asked after his father. His responses were polite and vague. He was the most laconic person I had ever met, and it made me edgy. I craned my neck to look for Margaret and Dotty, but they were nowhere to be seen.

"So," I said when I could no longer bear the silence. "I thought the dance went well."

"Yeah." He paused for a moment. "You're a good player."

"You play like it's easier than breathing."

Martin laughed, then coughed. "It feels that way sometimes." He opened up the cashbox and started turning all of the bills to face the same direction. "So how was your visit with your friend?"

"Who?"

"Your friend, the man from Boston. Big guy, kind of loud. Spectacular pants."

"Oh. Fine." Great. "How did you know I had a friend?"

"I met him at the dinner."

"You weren't at the dinner," I pointed out.

"How do you know?"

I looked down at my boots. "You weren't at Dotty's table."

"I was. Then I left."

"You missed the dinner part of dinner."

"I'm sure it was good."

"It *was* good." I tucked my fingers under my thighs. "You should have stayed."

"I gave him directions."

"Who?" I asked, avoiding the obvious.

"Your friend." Martin zipped the gray wool sweater he was wearing up to his Adam's apple.

"He's not my friend." I swallowed. "He's just my old boss."

"Why did he need directions to your cabin?"

"He offered me my old job back, at the Emerson. He probably didn't want to ask me someplace where Margaret could walk in."

I swear the corners of Martin's lips moved up a quarter of an inch. He straightened in his seat. "Would you like to . . ."

Just then Melissa, Mrs. Coventry County, stopped by the table. "Hello there, Martin. I haven't seen you since we graduated."

"Hey, Melissa." He pointed to her rhinestone crown. "Congratulations."

Melissa blushed and handed me an envelope with "The Sugar Maple" written across the front in script. "Livvy, just put the money you raised in this envelope and write the total on the front. I'll be by to collect it in a bit."

"She's the same age as you?" I whispered as Melissa walked over to the next row.

"We were in the same class, so yeah. She's around forty."

"She looks so much like an *adult*." I grabbed the cashbox and opened it. It was stuffed full of dollar bills.

"Some might consider forty to be an adult, I guess." Martin ran his hands through his hair. "That's what my dad keeps telling me. Anyway, Melissa has four kids, I think, maybe five. That might have something to do with it."

I finished separating the money into piles. "What were you going to ask me?"

"Would you like to come to dinner? Tonight? Just over at the house. My father would like to meet you."

"Sure, thanks. I'd love to. What time? What can I bring?" Some people get quiet when they're nervous. I talk.

"My folks eat early." Martin nodded his head toward the back of the hall, where Dotty and Margaret stood chatting with the pharmacist. "Around six?"

"Okay."

Martin stood, reached into his pocket, and handed me a twenty-dollar bill, waving the box of macaroons. He gave me a lopsided grin. "I'll see you then."

I had to count the money in the cashbox six times before I got it right.

By the time Margaret made her way back to the table, I had already packed up the remaining cookies and returned the silver tray to the kitchen. She had both of our coats draped over her arm.

Melissa came to the front of the room. "Gather round, everybody!"

Margaret grabbed my elbow and ushered us to the front row.

Melissa adjusted her red reading glasses and cleared her throat. "Thank you so much for donating to the Harvest Festival annual fund-raiser bake sale! It looks like we broke a record this year. The folks over at the library are going to be thrilled. I want to express my deepest thanks to Bonnie Fraser, who did such a wonderful job decorating the hall this year. Let's give her a hand."

A slight woman with bone-straight blond hair and bright red lipstick stood and bowed.

"That's my girl, Bonnie!" shouted a man

from the back of the room. It was Frank, the drunk guy from the Black Bear Tavern. So this was the former Sugar Maple baker.

"Bonnie!" the man shouted again. The crowd clapped politely.

"Thanks again, Bonnie." Melissa cleared her throat and held up a white envelope. "The Miss Guthrie Diner generously donated a gift certificate to use as a token of appreciation for our top baker. This year the person who raised the most money — a record-making one hundred and twenty-two dollars — for the Guthrie Library is . . . Jane White! For her pecan sandies!"

Margaret stared straight ahead, her gaze so fixed I thought that whatever she was looking at was going to burst into flames.

Light applause was quickly followed by the hum of gossip. Jane gracefully walked up and took her envelope from Melissa, peering at Margaret the whole time.

Melissa clapped her hands together. "Well done, everyone."

I leaned my head toward Margaret's ear. "I can't believe those pecan sandies did better than —"

"You'll do better next year," said Margaret, although she looked doubtful — about whether I would do better or whether

I would be there next year, I didn't know which.

"Better luck next year," Jane said as she breezed past us.

"I'm sure we won't have to wait a whole year to compete, will we?" I called.

Jane stopped in her tracks. She turned to face us.

"I heard something about an apple pie contest?"

Jane's lips curled into a smirk. "Perhaps. If she keeps you that long." She tucked the envelope into her handbag and walked away.

"What a bitch," I said under my breath. I looked over at Margaret. Her fingers were entangled in her pearls.

"We'd better get back so you have time to get yourself cleaned up before we head over to Dotty's," she said.

"We?"

"Yes, for supper. Dinner will be on the table at six. I'll drive."

My cheeks reddened.

"What?" Margaret put her arms on her hips.

"Nothing."

"And leave the dog at home."

CHAPTER SEVEN

When we arrived, Margaret walked ahead and up onto the porch. I lingered behind, still feeling embarrassed and slightly over-dressed in the 1950s cocktail number I had bought at the church thrift store when Hannah and I had been out furniture hunting. It was the only thing I had that wasn't covered in flour or dog hair. Margaret had on her standard uniform of cardigan, wool skirt, and pearls. She knocked once on the door and let herself in.

"Well, hello there!" a gravelly voice called out. I entered the front hall and was greeted by an elderly man standing up straight with the help of a wooden cane. He offered me his free hand. "You must be Olivia. I'm Henry McCracken."

"Pleased to meet you," I said, clasping his hand in mine. It was bony but strong underneath, with skin that felt like washed canvas. He was almost an exact replica of

Martin, only twice as old and half as big, with shaggy gray hair instead of brown.

"Marty, come on down here and take the girl's coat," Henry shouted, and then turned to me. "It takes me a little while to get around. I better get a head start."

Henry turned and shuffled toward the living room door. Martin was slight but sturdy; Henry looked like a just-birthed fawn.

Martin clomped down the stairs like a teenager called to supper.

"Hey." I slid out of my wool coat and handed it to him. He looked down at my dress and grinned slightly before turning his attention to a coat hanger. I blushed. Why on earth had I gone for the polka dots? Martin looked more scrubbed than usual. He was wearing a blue cotton dress shirt with his usual jeans and black Converse sneakers. I wondered if Dotty had made him get cleaned up.

"Hey." Martin led me down the hall into the living room where Margaret, Henry, and Dotty were all sitting, holding glasses of wine. Margaret was leaning over the armrest of the couch, talking to Henry.

"You should have seen the look on her face when they called her name."

"Livvy!" Dotty looked up and smiled. "Have a seat, dear. Martin, get the poor girl something to drink."

Martin disappeared, returning moments later with two glasses of white.

"Now we can have a proper celebration." Dotty raised her glass. "To the Sugar Maple and its new pastry chef, Livvy."

"To Livvy," the rest of the room chimed, and we all reached to clink. Martin sat next to me on the sofa. He smelled of Ivory soap and something greener, like moss by a brook.

"We're all so happy you could pitch in today. Everyone loved those macaroons, and —"

"It was good for the library," Margaret interjected, and gave Dotty a long look.

"Margaret, why don't you help me get supper on the table?" Dotty pressed her palms onto the sides of her chair and hefted herself up to standing. Margaret silently followed her.

"Can I help?" I called.

"Best leave the two of them to squawk," Henry said. "So where's this dog I hear has been hanging around the goats?"

"Margaret told me not to bring him."

"She's like most older folks. She believes that animals belong outside."

You would never think that if you saw her with Salty in the parlor. "Did you have pets

161

growing up?"

Henry nodded. "Had a pet squirrel when I was a kid. Used to sneak him up to my room. I thought my mom didn't know about him, then I found out his favorite game was to ride on the mop while she washed the floors."

I laughed. "Did you name him?"

"Sure." He paused for a few moments. "Cricket. I don't remember why, though."

"I always wanted a pet raccoon," Martin said quietly. "They advertised them in the back of *Field & Stream*."

"Oh, yes, I remember you crying one Christmas after the gifts were unwrapped and there was no raccoon among them." Henry leaned toward me. "He was the sensitive one," he said, pointing a long finger toward his son.

"Dad."

"So, young lady. Marty tells me you are an excellent frailer."

"He exaggerates." I winked at Henry. "I'm okay. But I'm not nearly as good as *Marty* is on the fiddle."

"Don't even think about it," Martin whispered to me. "That's strictly for family use."

"What's that, Marty?"

"Did you bring it with you?" Henry asked. "We could have a tune after supper."

"Oh, I wish I had. Do you play? I could go back and get it . . ."

Martin rested a hand briefly on my forearm.

"Not the banjo, though I love the sound of one. No, fiddle's my instrument. And Dotty plays the dulcimer, or she used to. I made her one when we were courting."

"I had no idea," Martin said under his breath.

"That's wonderful," I said. "I've always wanted to learn."

"Well, maybe Marty can dig it out of the attic for you. It's just gathering dust up there."

I glanced quickly up at Martin. His eyes were fixed on his father.

"So, who taught you how to play?" Henry asked.

"My dad did, when I was a kid. I didn't really take to it until I was older." The banjo had seemed hopelessly lame to my young, rebellious self. It had become something to treasure only after he died.

"Good thing to hand down to a child, the old songs. Course, you have to settle down and have a family before you can pass them down to anyone, but I'm sure your father is after you about that."

"He passed," I said.

163

Henry leaned over and patted my forearm. "I'm very sorry to hear that."

Dotty bustled into the room. "Supper's ready. Come on in."

Dinner was spread out on a large Formica table in the kitchen. It was a traditional bean supper with all the fixings — a ceramic crock filled with steaming baked beans flavored with molasses, bowls of potato salad and coleslaw, and a plate of sour pickles. And, to my delight, there were thick round slabs of brown bread that had clearly been baked in an old coffee can.

Henry reached out to either side of him. "Let's join hands and give thanks."

Margaret took my left hand in hers. It felt dainty and smooth. Martin's arm reached across the table and wrapped his hand around mine. My palms began to sweat. Margaret pinched her eyebrows together.

"Dear Lord, thank you for the many blessings you have given us, today and every day. May we always strive to be deserving of your gifts. Amen."

"Amen." Margaret dropped my hand and wiped hers on her napkin. Was it just me or had Martin's hand lingered for a second before retreating? I reached for a slice of brown bread and focused all my attention on spackling it with butter.

"I ran into Jessie when we were at Dr. Doyle's yesterday," Dotty said.

"Jessie is my brother Ethan's wife," Martin explained.

Henry said as he served himself seconds of coleslaw, "I didn't see Jessie."

"You were in with the doctor." Dotty smiled at me. "He doesn't like me to come in with him. Says I interrupt too much."

Henry shook his head and kept eating.

"Is she all right?" Margaret asked.

"Well, remember when she started volunteering at the dog warden's?"

"When her youngest married."

"That's right. Well, last week one of the dogs that came in had parvovirus. Had to shut the whole place down to do some special sanitation treatment."

Martin put his fork down. "What did they do with all of the dogs?" He looked like a worried little kid. I could picture him asking for the raccoon.

"Notice how he hasn't asked about his sister-in-law," Henry teased.

"That's the thing," Dotty said as she stacked Henry's empty plate on top of her own. "She took every single last one of those dogs home to be quarantined. She said there were twenty-seven of them."

Margaret shuddered.

"That sounds like fun," Martin said as he reached between Margaret and me and collected our plates.

"So why the doctor visit?" I asked, delighted by Dotty's roundabout way of story-telling.

"She was covered head to toe in flea bites," Dotty said over her shoulder as she headed into the kitchen. "She couldn't stop scratching."

I scooped vanilla ice cream into glass sundae cups, thinking about how much more at ease Martin seemed when he was around his family, while Margaret arranged the macaroons on a small silver tray and Dotty poured boiling water over loose tea leaves. In the other room Henry dozed in his chair. Once we were all seated again, Dotty cleared her throat and began pouring the tea.

"Tea, dear?"

Henry straightened, looking confused for a moment. "Lovely," he said, fumbling for the cup.

Dotty smiled and passed the tray of maca-roons to Margaret. I spooned vanilla ice cream into my mouth and let it melt on my tongue.

"So," I said as I swallowed. "What's up

with Jane White?"

Margaret's tea immediately went down the wrong pipe. Dotty thumped her back as she coughed.

Martin shoved a whole macaroon in his mouth and Dotty studied her cup of tea with the attention of a fortune-teller.

"That old bat," Henry said.

I turned my attention to Henry.

"I bet she cheated."

"Henry," Dotty said.

"Dad, how could someone cheat at a fund-raiser?" Martin asked.

Margaret remained silent, but her face looked tight and colorless.

Henry reached for a cookie. "By putting her own money in the pot."

"Martin, why don't you take Livvy out to do the evening chores?" Dotty interjected. I looked down at my half-eaten bowl of ice cream. I guessed dessert was over.

The night had turned cold, and white stars shone brightly against the inky October sky. My breath came out in little puffs as we walked the short distance between the house and the barn. Martin shut the barn door behind me and gestured to a wooden bench. The goats were sleeping, resting their necks on one another in a bed of hay.

"I guess I shouldn't have asked about Jane White," I said. "Your dad seemed a little riled up."

"Nah, it's fine. My folks are just really protective of Margaret." Martin reached under a milking bench and removed an earthenware jug. He poured golden liquid into two speckled tin cups. "She and Mrs. White have always had a thing between them. I'm not sure what."

Martin sat next to me on the small bench, his thigh and arm and shoulder touching mine. I felt acutely aware of every inch where our bodies met.

"So what are the evening chores?" I rubbed my hands together and placed them on my cheeks.

"There aren't any, really." He handed me a cup and placed the jug on the ground.

I took a long sip. "Hard cider?"

Martin drank his in one swallow. "My dad makes it from the windfalls. *Evening chores* has always been Dad's excuse to have a little nip in the evenings. Mom will have a glass of wine on a special occasion, but she doesn't like to keep alcohol in the house. Her dad was a drinker."

"Does she really not know?" I asked, taking another sip. They seemed too close a couple to keep secrets from each other.

"I think she knows but likes to pretend she doesn't so Dad can save face. That's why she sends me out to do chores every evening. It's basically so I have an excuse to come get Dad a cup of cider, even though he's not supposed to drink."

"So." I paused to take a long swallow. "How long has he been sick?"

Martin bounced his heel off the leg of the bench. "He was diagnosed about six months ago."

"Is it cancer?" I asked tentatively.

"Yes, colon."

"Did he have surgery?"

He nodded. "Radiation first. They couldn't get it all out. Now it's chemo. Did your dad have cancer?"

"Heart attack. It was sudden." I poured myself another cup, offering the jug back to Martin.

"Careful. It tastes like apple juice but it'll creep up on you."

Straw crackled under the twitching foot of a dreaming goat.

"So when that Frank guy said that thing in the bar — about your coming back — did you come home to take care of your dad?"

"Mom takes care of him, and a nurse comes in in the mornings to help. I came back to help with the farm."

"Where do you live, usually?"

"Seattle."

"You're not a farmer, then?"

Martin huffed. "I couldn't get out of here fast enough."

"Was it hard to come back — I mean, with work and all?"

"I teach. I came up as soon as the semester ended. I'm on family leave now."

"What do you teach?"

"Industrial arts."

"Ahh, the troublemakers."

Martin laughed. "Some of them, yes. They're good kids, though."

I stretched my legs out in front of me and watched the silver sparkles on my flats glint in the dim light. "So you're sticking around, then?"

Martin scuffed at the ground, making a circle in the dirt with his toe. "We'll see," he said, and stood. He bent to pick the jug up off the floor and poured some of the cider into a red plaid thermos that was stationed on a shelf. "I think the chores are done."

"We don't have to milk the goats?" I asked.

"Mabel stopped giving milk a long time ago. And Crabapple is a billy goat. They're just pets now."

Margaret met us on the porch in her coat. "Your folks have already gone up to bed, dear," she said to Martin. Turning to me, she said, "Grab that potato sack you call a purse and let's get going."

Margaret walked past us. I heard the car engine ignite and begin to hum.

"Thanks for the invitation," I said, looking up at him. I tried to read his expression, but in the darkness I couldn't see his eyes behind his thick glasses. "It was great to meet Henry, and Dotty is amazing."

"They like you."

"It's mutual."

I stood awkwardly for a minute, fighting the urge to hug him. "Night."

"Get in the car, young lady. Are you trying to freeze me to death?" Margaret scolded from the open car window. I rolled my eyes and climbed in.

I dipped the end of a French fry into my chocolate frappe and swirled it around while watching the waitress glide from table to table as if she were on roller skates: pouring coffee, taking orders, wiping spills, all the while keeping up a flirty conversation with a logger sitting on one of the stools at the counter.

"That's so disgusting," Hannah said as she slid into the booth.

"The fries or the waitress pinching butts?" I popped the fry into my mouth and reached down for another.

"Both."

I pointed a French fry at Hannah. "What makes a complex dessert," I said in my best French accent, "ees contrast. Say it with me, chefs. Contrast. Salty and sweet, hot and cold, soft and crunchy, light and dark. Your desserts must balance all of zee senses." I popped the fry into my mouth and grinned. "It's much better with pommes frites. These steak fries have a little too much potato and not enough fry for my liking, but they're better than nothing."

Hannah shook her head and scanned the menu.

The waitress glided over. "Can I get you anything, Hannah?" Even her voice was smooth.

"Just a decaf, thanks, Liz." Hannah smiled up at her and placed the menu back behind the napkin dispenser.

"It still boggles my mind that you know everyone," I whispered. "Don't you ever miss being . . . nobody?"

Hannah shrugged. "Sometimes I drive a couple towns over to go to a matinee, just so I don't have to hear from the woman at the concession stand how surprised she is that a doctor's wife would take butter on her popcorn."

"Or what they think of the movie you're seeing," I said, thinking about Hannah's weird obsession with horror films.

"Exactly." She nodded toward my French fries. "You know, for a chef you really eat like crap."

"A chef's favorite meal is the one cooked by someone else."

Liz placed a cup of coffee in front of Hannah. I bit my straw.

"Excellent, excellent job at the festival dinner." Hannah beamed. "The head of the board of directors at the hospital has already asked if you would make the dessert for their next fund-raising dinner."

I rolled my eyes. Ever since Hannah had become Mrs. Doyle, it'd been one fundraiser after the next.

"What? It's for a good cause . . ."

"We'll see, Hann." After the contest and the dinner, I felt superstitious about making any future commitments in Guthrie. For all I knew, Margaret had already placed an ad for a new baker in the *PennySaver.*

Hannah leaned back, her hands neatly folded in front of her. "Everyone's talking about you, you know."

"You know I had nothing to do with Jamie coming up here."

"I meant about your food, Livvy. The desserts. Everyone's raving about them. Molly over at the pharmacy asked if you would be willing to share the chocolate tartlet recipe."

I let out a long breath.

"But since you brought it up," Hannah leaned forward. "So . . . that was Jamie."

"Yup, in the flesh." I unwrapped a fresh straw and jammed it into the frappe.

"He was quite . . . talkative."

"He was quite drunk."

Hannah sat a little straighter in her seat. "Are you okay?"

"I'm fine. It was . . . surprising. He just showed up. There wasn't anything I could do about it."

"You never mentioned he was married."

I sucked on my frappe. Loudly. "It's not something I'm super proud of."

Hannah smoothed out a paper napkin and folded it into a perfect square. "Did you see him over the weekend?"

"He stopped by the cabin that night, but no, I think they might have left the next day. So, what can you tell me about the pecan sandy queen?"

"Jane White?"

"Yeah. She 'won' the bake sale. If I don't up my game, I'm going to be out of a job *and* homeless. I tried asking about her at the McCrackens', but . . ."

"When were you at the McCrackens'?"

"Sunday. For dinner."

I watched several unrecognizable thoughts pass across Hannah's face. "Do you want the facts or the gossip?"

"Both, in that order."

"Well, Jane grew up a few towns over, in the next county. She married John White, whose family owns a small chain of grocery stores, including the one here in Guthrie. They had four children who all live in the area and manage the stores."

I made a rolling gesture in the air. "Get to the good stuff."

"Well, Jane's husband passed away four years ago. Had a stroke, right in the middle of the produce aisle."

"That's not gossip."

"It's what happened afterward. A couple of months after Mr. White died, Margaret's husband had a heart attack. It was shortly after that that Jane took an interest in baking. Margaret lost her first contest a month later."

"There is a disturbing amount of heart disease in this town."

Hannah eyed the three stray fries left on my plate. "Smoking and a poor diet, both of them, but you didn't hear that from me."

"So Jane poured her grief into a new hobby. What's the problem?"

Hannah stole a quick glance around the diner and leaned in close. "Well, there's talk that there had been something between Jane White and Margaret's husband, Mr. Hurley."

"No way."

Hannah shrugged. "It's probably just a rumor. But it might explain why Margaret started losing and Jane started winning. Was Margaret upset about the fund-raiser?"

"Let's see, at first she just stared straight ahead like she was in a coma. Back at the inn she was cold. She warmed up at the Mc-Crackens', but —"

"Margaret was at the McCrackens'?"

"Yes."

"So it wasn't a date?" Hannah looked oddly relieved.

"I don't know. It was just, like, family dinner." I raised my hands so they would cover my face. "I wore a dress."

Hannah snorted. "Which one?"

"The polka-dot one." I leaned forward

and rested my face on the Formica.

Hannah peeled back the paper lid off a creamer and poured it into her cup. "So what was he like?"

"Martin?" I shrugged. "Shy. But nice. He seems younger at home." I realized I was twisting my napkin into a tight ball. "I don't know. He smelled good. Like a campfire."

"You were close enough to smell him." It wasn't a question.

"Just for a moment." I had thought about the feeling of his arm pressed against mine more than once that day already. "I wish you had seen him play fiddle at the dance. He's incredible. I could watch him play all night."

"You like him," Hannah said, her voice incredulous, as if she had just discovered that aliens were real. I ground the last cold fry into a pile of salt on my plate and shoved it into my mouth.

"Did you meet Henry?"

"Yes." I smiled. "He's amazing."

"You know I can't reveal anything," Hannah whispered, "but did Martin tell you about Henry's condition?"

"I know it's colon cancer, that they couldn't remove it all, which sounds bad. Martin says he's doing chemo now."

Hannah nodded and looked down. "Well,

I'm glad he told you. It wouldn't be good to get too attached."

I frowned. "To Henry or to Martin?"

"Either." Hannah twisted around and waved at the waitress. "Just a refill, when you get a chance, Liz."

"Why?" I tried to keep my voice even. "I mean, it's obvious Henry isn't doing well. I could carry him and a fifty-pound bag of flour up a flight of stairs, but —"

"He probably won't stick around. I heard he left the day after he graduated from high school and went as far away as he could. I'd just hate to see you get hurt, Liv."

"Since when do we worry about my getting attached?" I asked, even though my stomach was churning. Martin made living in Guthrie feel possible. I didn't want to think about his leaving when we had only just met. "I'm the queen of casual. Right?"

CHAPTER EIGHT

I took the back roads to the Sugar Maple. The inn was closed, dinner service long past. The kitchen was dark except for the small table lamp. Margaret was sitting in one of the rocking chairs, her feet firmly planted on the ground, looking out into the darkness.

"Oh," I said. "I didn't think anyone would be here."

Margaret reached for her wine and leaned back. Finding the open bottle on my workbench, I poured myself a glass and sat down in the other rocker.

"I hope you don't mind. Quiet night?"

"As expected."

"I just came in to pull out my cinnamon roll dough so it can rise overnight."

"Hmm."

The joints squeaked as I rocked back.

"I'm sorry about the cookies," I said quietly. "Honestly, they've never let me down before."

Margaret nodded her head a fraction.

"I won't be so cocky next time."

She leaned back in her chair and began to rock, her feet just leaving the ground.

"They tasted good."

"What's that?"

"The macaroons. They were good cookies. I thought they were the best."

"Really?"

"They were certainly better than any pecan sandy," Margaret mumbled into her wineglass.

"I know, right?" My shoulders dropped down an inch or two away from my ears. Without the hum of the exhaust fan and the rhythmic beating of the mixer, it felt like we were sitting in any farmhouse kitchen. Warm and safe.

Margaret drained her glass. She stood, tucking the red ribbon she'd been winding between her fingers into the pocket of her skirt, pulled out a folded piece of stationery, and handed it to me. "Dotty was by earlier to drop off some plates. She left you this."

"Olivia" was written across the page in a scratchy cursive.

I raised my eyebrows.

"I didn't read it. Turn the light out when you're done," Margaret said as she walked toward the parlor. "And don't stay too late; you have to be in by six tomorrow. The Rotary Club breakfast meeting is at seven thirty sharp."

I leaned toward the table lamp and unfolded the letter.

Dear Olivia,
Marty has restrung the dulcimer and she is waiting for your first lesson. Are you free Saturday afternoon around one? Bring the dog.

Sincerely,
Henry McCracken

A wave of warmth washed over me, like I had just opened the door to a bread oven. I tucked the note into the pocket of my fleece and went in search of my cinnamon roll dough.

The apple pie in my lap felt toasty against my legs on the short drive from the inn to the McCracken farm. Margaret had insisted that I bring along one of the new test pies for Dotty to try. I had spent the week after the fund-raiser channeling all of my frustration into perfecting my apple pie. Nutmeg, allspice, and cardamom were added and subtracted by the eighth of a teaspoon.

Crates of apples from the McCracken farm were peeled, cored, and sliced into several pies, each with a different combination of fruit. Chef Al and I spent an afternoon discussing the benefits and drawbacks of cornstarch versus arrowroot. By the end of the week I was left feeling like a deranged mix of Sherlock Holmes and Christopher Kimball, my palate completely numb.

Salty sat up straight in the back and looked out the window that I had cracked open for him. Margaret glared at me from the driver's seat.

"Henry requested that he come along."

"He's getting slobber all over my clean window."

"You didn't have to drive." Margaret had insisted we take one car to the McCrackens'. Hers.

Salty hopped over the seat onto my lap, his tail brushing Margaret's face, his paws just barely missing the pie box, and leaped out of the car as soon as I opened the door. He trotted over to the empty goat pen. I held the untrampled pie up in the air in triumph.

The scent of roasting chicken and pearl onions greeted us in the foyer. "We're here," Margaret called.

"Come on in," came a muffled cry from

the kitchen. Dotty emerged, gingham apron wrapped around her thick waist. "The bird is just about done," she said to Margaret. "I wanted to get everything ready for supper so we wouldn't have to rush back." She turned her attention to me. "Hello, Olivia. How thoughtful," she said, taking the pie out of my hands. "Henry's been looking forward to your visit all week. He's in the sitting room." She and Margaret disappeared into the kitchen.

A wave of shyness washed over me as I stood alone in the hallway. I knocked lightly on the door before poking my head in.

"Hello," I called.

"Come in, come in," Henry said. He sat on the coach, wearing a robin's-egg blue sweater that made his shock of white hair glow. A bright red afghan lay across his lap. Underneath, two shearling-slippered feet poked out. "Sorry not to get up. Not as easy as it used to be."

"No need."

Henry tilted to the side to look behind me. "So, no dog?"

"Crap!" I ran back to the front door. I returned with Salty at my heels. "Here he is. Where would you like us?"

Henry patted the couch. "Come sit beside me. It'll be easier to show you what to do."

Salty walked straight to Henry and wagged his tail, sniffing Henry's outstretched hand. He gave it one lick, then lay down on the braided rug beside him.

The dulcimer sat on the coffee table in front of us. It was a beautiful instrument, its hourglass shape cut from pale polished maple, with four tiny hearts carved out in pairs at either end.

"You made this for Dotty?"

"Back when we were courting."

"May I?" I reached for the dulcimer.

"Of course."

I placed it on my thighs. The wood on the bottom was worn, and it rested on my lap like it belonged there.

Henry leaned over and spun it around. "Now, the tuning pegs are always on the left, and the area where you strum the strings is on the right. Just like a banjo, really, except on your lap."

"How old were you when you made it?"

"Sixteen, I'd guess."

My index finger tugged at the first string. "She must have been thrilled."

"More like irritated. She was a feisty girl." He grunted. "Dotty had been insisting that she didn't have a musical note in her body, and I was determined to prove her wrong. Now," he held up a small wooden dowel, "this is your noter." He leaned toward me and took my left hand in his. He smelled like bay rum and those soft pastel wintergreen candies. "Hold it like this. Now press down on the third fret." Henry slipped his hand into the pocket of his sweater and produced a brown plastic guitar pick. With a quick flick of his wrist, he strummed all four of the strings. The room filled with a satisfying chord. "See, the reason I chose the dulcimer for her was because it's so easy to learn. You only use the noter on the first string, the one closest to you — all the other strings are drones. Let me show you." Henry pulled the instrument onto his lap and with knotted fingers he began to play "Go Tell Aunt Rhodie."

"Did she?"

"What's that?"

"Have a musical note in her body?"

"No." The corners of Henry's mouth twitched upward at the memory. "Not a single one. Now you give it a try."

He slid the instrument back onto my lap.

Following Henry's gentle instructions, I took a deep breath and plunged in, finding the notes with ease and allowing myself to get lost in the melody. The sound of clapping broke in from across the room. Dotty stood in the doorway, beaming, Margaret a shadow behind her, buttoning her coat.

"That's lovely, Livvy! I'm so pleased to hear my dulcimer being played again."

"She's a natural," Henry said.

I looked down at the dulcimer, trying to hide the fact that Henry's compliment made me feel like I was eight and had just been given a gold star.

"We'll be expecting a concert this afternoon," Dotty said. "We're just going out shopping for a bit. We'll be back soon." She blew Henry a kiss and ducked into the hallway.

When the front door clicked shut, Henry sat back, leaning into the couch. He pressed his palms to his face, covering his eyes. When he removed his hands, his face looked older, weathered, worn. We sat and listened to the growl of the car engine coming to life and the crunch of pebbles beneath the tires. When the room finally fell silent, Henry turned to me.

"Would you mind doing me a favor?"

"Sure," I said, standing.

"In the barn, underneath a wooden bench, there is —"

"The cider?"

Henry laughed. "Marty gave away my secret to you already, did he?"

"We shared some of your secret last

Sunday night," I said, smiling down at him. "It's delicious. I'll be right back."

The crisp air was a surprise in the abundant sunlight. Salty found his goat friends and gave them an affectionate sniff. I took down the red plaid thermos from the shelf and poured the cider in.

Henry was sleeping when I returned. I tiptoed out of the sitting room and made my way down the hall to the kitchen in search of glasses. The walls were covered with photographs hung randomly and with no regard for chronology. A black-and-white picture of Henry and Dotty dancing in the grange hall sat next to a faded color Instamatic of three skinny boys, shirtless and grinning, each holding up a fish the length of his arm. I recognized the smallest one. Even as a young boy, Martin's face had had a look of seriousness and determination. I had known that Martin had brothers, and there was no denying the family resemblance, although the older two took more after Dotty than their father. At the center of the wall was a formal wedding picture of Henry and Dotty, with the wedding party lined up on a staircase. Behind Dotty stood her maid of honor. It took me a moment to realize it was Margaret. She looked like *Gilda*-era Rita Hayworth's brunette twin, her long locks falling down her back in a loose wave, a short string of pearls around her neck. How she had remained unmarried until she was older I couldn't fathom.

I grabbed two jelly jars that were drying on the enameled counter next to the sink and walked back into the sitting room. Henry blinked up at me, looking confused for a moment before jutting his chin toward me in greeting. Salty had taken my spot on the couch, and Henry reached over to rub his belly. I sat in a chair across from him, placed the two glasses on the table, and poured them half full from the thermos.

"No need to be polite."

I hesitated, then unscrewed the cap of the thermos, topped off both glasses, and handed one to him.

"That's better."

The cider was cool and tart. "Martin told me you make it?"

"Marty made this batch. Not bad. But yes, I taught all my sons. My father taught me. Makes good use of the bad apples."

"Very good use," I said, taking another long sip.

Henry drained his glass and placed it on the coffee table. I reached down for the thermos and refilled them both.

"Dotty didn't like it. The boys would get

188

into it from time to time when they were growing up, but they were just being boys. I always said it was better for them to get into trouble here than out in the town."

"Well, at least now the boys are old enough for her to worry less about them."

"You must not have children." Henry tapped a fingernail on the side of the jelly jar. "Marty may be on his way to forty, but that doesn't mean we don't worry about him, Dotty and me both."

"Martin? Why?" I asked. I drained my glass and busied myself with the thermos lid, not wanting to seem too curious. I leaned over to refresh Henry's glass, hoping to distract him from my nosiness.

"I have no idea what that boy is doing in the city."

"He's teaching, right? What's wrong with that?" I offered.

"When Marty was a boy we couldn't keep him indoors long enough to bathe and feed him. He spent more hours in the woods or in the fields than he ever did in the house."

I leaned forward, wanting more.

"All my sons work well with their hands, mind you. Mark has a small dairy over in Shelburne." Henry tilted his glass back. "Ethan took over the apples and the Christmas trees and grows vegetables for some sort of co-op — what do they call it now? Folks give him money up front and collect vegetables every week? But Marty" — he wiped his lips with the sleeve of his sweater — "he was a natural. Gentle with the horses. Could make anything grow in any weather." Henry looked out the window through the lace curtains. "I thought he'd be the one."

I looked down at my glass. "The one?" I asked gently.

"Don't be shy, girl. Have another. I would but they've got me on all sorts of medication."

I emptied the thermos into my glass.

"So, why did *you* leave?" Henry asked.

"Leave?" I asked, confused. "Home? It was just me and my dad. When he died I was the only one left. And we didn't have a house or anything, we just rented an apartment, so it didn't really feel like leaving."

"How old were you?" he asked.

"Sixteen."

Henry looked as if he was deciding among a hundred questions, but he settled on a simple one. "What brought you here to Guthrie?"

"Oh." The room suddenly felt warm. "I was just looking for a change of scenery."

"Well, this must be quite a change."

"You could say that," I said, smiling.

"You had to have left a lot of friends behind."

"Not really." I picked at a patch of pills on my sweater. "So, I thought Martin was here to help on the farm, but it sounds like Ethan took over."

Henry tilted his head. "Yes, well."

I kept picking.

"So no friends?"

"I didn't really have time for them. Just coworkers. I worked all the time."

"Any special coworker?"

"Nope." The cider had warmed a little, but it still went down easy.

Henry leaned forward. "Not even a special coworker with plaid pants?"

"Aha!" I shouted, pointing my finger. "Henry McCracken, have you been gossiping?"

"Young lady, all town gossip gets filtered through this sitting room. I couldn't avoid it if I tried."

"I'll keep that in mind," I mumbled into the jelly jar.

"Well?"

"Well, what?"

"The special coworker?"

"Nope." I stood up and walked across the room to the fireplace. My head spun for a moment, and I grabbed the edge of the mantel to steady myself. "No special anything. It makes it easier to leave that way." I walked over to the window and peeked out.

Salty stood up on the couch, circled three times, and lay back down, this time with his head in Henry's lap. Henry stroked the velvety fur behind his ears. "Sit down, dear. You're making me nervous."

My head felt thick with cider. "I kinda had to leave," I mumbled.

Henry looked into my eyes, waiting.

"My last night at the Emerson — my old job — there was a big gala, and I had been asked to present a baked Alaska in the traditional way, which means on fire. I was standing in this banquet room, with hundreds of guests — people whose birthdays and weddings and christenings and anniversaries I had helped celebrate — and it just hit me." I placed my head in my hands, leaning forward. "Standing there all I could think was *This isn't my life.* And Jamie — that's Mr. Plaid Pants — was there with his . . ." My voice trailed off. I looked down at the ground.

"With his family?" Henry offered.

I looked out the window, avoiding Henry's gaze. "I felt like such an idiot. Like, of course, this was *his* real life, and I was just

192

some foreign country he visited from time to time." I pressed my palms into my eyes. "Everything became clear to me all of a sudden." I looked up at him. "Do you know that scene from Dickens, where the kid has got his face plastered to a bakery shop window, looking in?"

"Oliver Twist."

"Exactly. And he's just burning to eat one of those cakes. He'd do anything. That's how I've felt since my dad died."

"Like you wanted cake?" Henry asked. "Is that why you became a baker?"

"Like I'm on the outside — of everything. Being at the Emerson just made me feel more like that. I wanted out."

"Sounds like a good reason to leave."

"Yeah, well. Tell that to the fire department."

Henry tugged at the afghan on his lap, pulling it higher. "Do you think you belong in Guthrie?"

I blew out my breath. "I don't know. You'll have to ask Margaret. Seems like she's the one who will be deciding that one."

"You have a say, young lady. Don't you forget it. And don't wait too long to decide. Not making a decision *is* making a decision. Besides, you'll be surprised at how much can happen once you settle down."

The front door opened, startling us both.

"Hey, Dad," Martin called. He walked in, carrying a tall wooden pole that was marked with faded painted stripes — one green, one yellow, one blue, and one red. "I finished tagging all the trees." He eyed Salty, who was still resting his head in Henry's lap. "Dad, did you find him with the goats?"

"Were there enough twelve-footers?"

"At least four dozen. That dog —"

"You're sure you measured them right? You're out of practice. We don't want people saying we're overpriced."

"I used the stick, Dad. It's not —"

"I've been giving Olivia here a dulcimer lesson."

Martin scanned the room, and found me sitting in the corner. I gave him a weak wave. "Hey."

Having Martin in the room woke me up to the fact that I had just been spilling my secrets to his father. And that maybe his father wouldn't be thrilled with his — friendship? — with a pyromaniac adulteress, no matter how many stringed instruments I played.

Martin's gaze fell on the empty jelly jars and the thermos that sat on the floor beside my feet. "Dulcimer lesson. Right. I can see that." He turned to his father. "How'd it go?"

Henry smiled at me. "She's a natural. Livvy, take her home and practice. Next time we can work on the strumming." He stretched his back a bit and turned to Martin. "I think I'm ready to lie down for a spell before supper. Would you see Olivia back?"

"Of course." Martin reached down for the jelly jars.

"Let me do that," I said, jumping up. I bent down and gave Henry a small kiss on the cheek. "Thanks so much for the lesson."

"Thanks for the good company." He grasped my arm and squeezed. "Come by anytime."

"I will," I promised.

"And bring the dog."

Dotty arrived as I was rinsing out the glasses. She sat me down at the kitchen table, peppering me with questions. By the time Martin came back downstairs, I was drinking my third cup of coffee and eating my second piece of apple pie.

"So, Livvy, is your mother down in Boston?" Dotty asked.

"No," I said. "She died a couple of years ago."

Martin poured himself a cup of coffee and

sat down next to me at the kitchen table.

"The thermos?" he whispered.

"Back in the barn."

Dotty cut a thick slab of pie and placed it in front of Martin. "I'm sorry about your parents," she said. "Any relatives?"

I watched Martin carefully as he took his first bite. His eyes closed as he chewed, and a small sigh of pleasure escaped his lips as he swallowed.

"Nope, it's just me."

"Well, that settles it. You'll spend Thanksgiving with us."

"Um . . ." I said as I watched Martin take another large forkful. "I'm not really a family holiday kind of person." I had spent last Thanksgiving sitting on a bench next to Plymouth Rock, eating a turkey sandwich.

Martin pierced a piece of apple that had slipped off his fork.

"Too much nutmeg?"

His eyes met mine for a brief moment. "No."

"Nonsense," Dotty said over her shoulder as she walked out of the kitchen.

The corners of my lips lifted. "How's the crust?"

Martin rubbed at his lip with the back of his hand. "You people are crazy. You know that, don't you?"

"What people?"

"Bakers," he said as he forked the last piece of pie into his mouth. "I can drive you home after we're finished."

"You don't have to."

"Are you sure you should drive?"

"My car's at the inn anyway. I was thinking I'd walk. Salty needs the exercise."

"I'll walk with you."

I brought my coffee cup and plate to the sink, trying to hide the grin I couldn't keep from spreading across my face.

Salty ran ahead of us through the open field as we walked toward the sugar bush that separated the inn from the McCracken farm. Patches of Queen Anne's lace had dried into tight fists. Their stiff edges tickled as I ran my palms gently over their frozen faces. Martin's hands were jammed into his jacket pockets. We walked beside each other as the afternoon sun warmed the backs of our necks. Martin shortened his stride to keep in time with mine. We walked in silence, listening to the sound of crows cawing to one another as they flew overhead.

"So how was the lesson?" Martin asked.

"Great. I can't believe your dad made that dulcimer. It has a beautiful tone."

"I didn't know he made it until he mentioned it to you."

"Seriously? That's crazy. It's amazing. Have you played it?" I stole a sideways glance. His hair was in his eyes, as always, and he looked like he hadn't shaved in a couple of days.

"I fooled around with it when I was a kid, before I took up the fiddle." He picked a stalk of Queen Anne's lace as we walked by, tracing the edge of its dried face with his thumb. "So when did he break out the cider?"

"Right after your mom left to go shopping with Margaret."

"What did you two talk about?" Martin's voice was so low I almost didn't hear him.

I smiled up at him. "He told me about him and Dotty courting. I can't believe how long they've known each other."

"They all have — Margaret was her maid of honor."

"I saw a picture of the wedding party in your hallway. God, she was gorgeous."

Martin nodded. "John White is also in that picture — you'd know his kids, they run the grocery store. He married Jane White."

"Jane White, Margaret's nemesis?"

Martin laughed. "The one and only. Bonnie's grandfather Burt was my dad's best man. And Tom's uncle was the priest who married them."

"I've never stayed anywhere longer than three years. I can't imagine spending my entire life with the same people."

"Yeah. I couldn't either."

"Is that why you left?" I asked.

"You sound like my dad."

"Why *did* you leave Guthrie?"

Martin tossed the flower onto the ground. "One of my brothers got his girlfriend pregnant when they were in high school. He skipped college and went straight to work for my dad. Then my buddy Frank — from the bar — got into the same situation with Bonnie. It just seemed like everyone around me got stuck somehow. Wife, kids, animals, house, farm. I didn't want to get saddled with a bunch of responsibilities before I had a chance to travel, play music, you know."

"That makes sense," I said, feeling a confusing mix of relating to his not wanting to feel trapped and at the same time burning to know how he felt on all the same subjects now. I stopped walking for a moment and pulled a tattered purple knit cap over my curls. "Henry talked about you. And your brothers. But mostly about you."

Martin turned to face me, his lips slightly parted. He looked so vulnerable.

"He's worried about you. He wants you

to be happy."

"He wants me to be here."

"Could you be happy here?" I had been asking myself the very same question.

Martin reached down to pick up a handful of rocks and pitched them one by one into the tree line.

"My dad is a stubborn old man. He decided how my life should be when I was eleven and hasn't changed his mind since, no matter what I say or do."

"Well, he did tell me he thought you didn't fit in the city. That you belonged someplace else."

"Exactly. Here."

I shrugged. "If it makes you feel any better, he also gave me a good talking to. That man doesn't hold back, does he?"

Martin laughed, his expression softening. "No, when he wants to say something, he says it. I hope he didn't give you too hard a time."

"Oh, no. Just wanted to know what I was doing here and when was I going to settle down."

"Then you do know what I mean."

I laughed. "You came in the nick of time. I'm not used to having anyone that interested in my future."

"That can't be true." Martin wound a

piece of hay that he had plucked around two fingers.

"Um. My dad was a day-to-day kind of guy. Not very future oriented. And my mom . . . didn't exactly take to motherhood. She took off when I was around nine months old. I was raised by my father."

"Was that tough?"

"For him — I can't imagine being on my own and having a toddler. I mean, I'm thirty-two, and I can barely take care of myself."

"Around here you'd be a grandmother by now," Martin muttered.

"He was a really good dad. And I had Judy Blume to fill in the gaps."

"Deenie?" he asked.

"Of course, and *Are You There God? It's Me, Margaret.* And don't forget *Forever.*"

Martin blushed. "I grew up with a lot of cousins."

"That must have been nice."

"How about you?"

Until this moment I had never felt so acutely alone. "Nope — both my folks were only children."

Martin's smile slipped, and he was quiet for a minute before asking, "Can I ask how old he was? Your dad?"

"Only fifty-three."

Martin kicked a rock, sending it flying into the tall grass. "And how old were you?"

"Sixteen. As of September I've officially been on the planet without him longer than I was with him."

Martin blew out a breath. "That sucks."

"It does. For the first couple of years, all I could think about was how he wouldn't be there for all of the big life things. He wouldn't see me graduate from high school, wouldn't walk me down the aisle. Wouldn't hold his grandchild." I shrugged. "I didn't end up doing any of those things, so I guess it didn't really matter in the end."

"Do you think you didn't do them because he died?" Martin asked.

"I don't know. Maybe. For a long time nothing really seemed worth doing if he wasn't going to be there to share it with."

Martin's mouth tightened, and he turned his face away.

"Oh, gosh. I'm so sorry." I stopped and reached for his arm to stop him. "Here I am going on about my dad and —"

"It's okay."

"It's not okay." I tried to catch his eye but failed. "I was young, and it was sudden. He had a heart attack. It's really different. Your dad is getting treatment."

"Yeah." Martin turned back to face the

hill, and we started to climb. "So you didn't graduate from high school?"

"It was a little hard to stay motivated."

"How did your mom deal with that?"

I stuffed my hands into my jacket pockets. "She didn't."

Martin stopped for a moment, looking puzzled. "She didn't come back after your dad died?"

I shook my head.

"Then who took care of you?"

"I was sixteen. I could drive a car and make my own snacks. Mom said it would be good for me — a 'growth experience' I think is how she put it. She was living somewhere at the time where the girls had their first baby by thirteen."

"I couldn't ditch a class without someone seeing me and telling my folks." Martin looked over at me, his face full of questions. "How did you get by? I mean, did you have to work?"

"My dad had life insurance. And besides, I was much too busy to hold onto a job."

"Doing what?"

"What every teenage girl would do with an apartment in the city and no parents."

I walked ahead for a minute and then turned to face him. "So tell me what you do with that big stick of yours," I said, wanting to change the subject.

Martin coughed. "I'm sorry?"

"The one you carried into the house, with the stripes."

"Oh." Martin looked relieved. "It's for measuring the Christmas trees." He pushed his hair out of his face. "When we were kids, my dad would measure us boys with the stick, then assign us the color that was closest to our height. We had a contest to see who had the most trees our size." He smiled. "I think that stick was his father's before him."

"I know this will shock a farmer like you," I said, "but we had a fake tree growing up. I remember sitting at the top of the staircase watching my father smoke and curse while he screwed the branches into the trunk. That was always the first sign of Christmas."

Martin laughed. "My dad used to hang strings of lights on the hut where we sold the trees. Every year, the day after Thanksgiving, drinking cider and cursing while he twisted and untwisted all the bulbs."

When we reached the top of the hill, Martin sat down on the ground, arms around his knees, his face toward the farm. Salty came bounding out of the woods and lay down next to him. The shadows of the Christmas trees stretched long over the field in the afternoon sun. A host of barn swallows swooped through the sky as if they were stitched together with an invisible thread.

"This is where I first heard you play, you know."

Martin's face glowed in the orange light. "What do you mean?"

"The weekend I moved in, Salty and I walked through the woods up to this spot. I heard the fiddle playing. It's where I picked up that tune."

"Oh." Martin lay down, one arm folded underneath his head. He stretched out his legs. "That must have been my dad playing, not me."

"Really?" Their bowing was as similar as their sharp noses.

"It's his tune. That's why it was odd to hear you playing it. He wrote it for my mom."

"It's beautiful." My eyes teared up suddenly, thinking of Henry carving the hearts into the dulcimer's soundboard and sanding the wood until it was soft and smooth. I might have escaped the pressures of growing up in a large family, but I suspected that there were some things you could learn only from living with parents whose love was an active, living thing.

"You know how, growing up, your family's house always smells the same?" Martin asked.

"Newsprint, pipe tobacco, and egg rolls. We lived upstairs from a Chinese take-out place."

"That's what hearing that tune is like for me."

My hand worked through Salty's fur, worrying out stickers. "It must have been strange hearing it from my porch."

Martin rolled over onto his side. From the corner of my eye I could see that he was studying my face. "We better get going or we won't make it out of the woods before the sun sets."

The forest floor was thick with a golden carpet of spent leaves. We shuffled ankle deep through them as they crunched under our feet, the damp, earthy scent of fresh soil wafting up with every step. The orange light raked across the ground, making it glow as if on fire, and the black trunks stood stark in contrast. There was a peacefulness to being in the woods that made talking unnecessary. Even as it grew darker I felt safe trailing Martin, who looked even more comfortable here than behind his fiddle. Halfway up the carriage path Martin's steps slowed and then stopped. He reached over and grabbed my hand, squeezing it gently as he whispered, "Shhh."

Martin gently raised our clasped hands to shoulder height and pointed his index finger up into the trees. "Look," he whispered into my ear. I followed his gaze, distracted by the warmth of his hand and the scent of balsam and woodsmoke that clung to his jacket. As my eyes adjusted to the darkness, I caught a flash of white stripe. A plump shape emerged against the night sky. A pair of yellow eyes blinked. I gasped. Martin lowered our arms, keeping my hand in his.

"It's a great horned owl," he whispered. "Look at his ears." Two pointed tufts poked up into the night. We watched the owl until the last lingering light dissolved, leaving us in darkness. The whoosh of wings pushing against the air announced that the owl had moved on to more interesting pursuits.

Martin squeezed my hand. "We're not far from your cabin," he said, his breath soft against my ear, and he tugged me forward. Our footsteps seemed louder in the dark, but I was grateful, hoping the sound was drowning out my racing heartbeat. The carriage path bent in a familiar curve, and the woods opened up to the clearing where my little cabin stood, bathed in light. Salty was waiting on top of the woodpile, tail wagging. Martin led me to the porch but stopped at the bottom step.

"I could give you a ride," I offered.

Martin laughed. "I was taking *you* home."

"It's dark." I pointed toward the clearing. A lone star sparkled low in the sky above the tree line.

"I'll be fine. I've been stomping around these woods since I was a kid."

I looked toward the trees. I stood beside him for a moment, not wanting to go inside.

"Would you like some coffee?" I asked his chest, not daring to look into his face.

Martin hesitated. "I better not."

In the soft porch light I could see his breath escape in a small frosty stream from his rosy lips. I longed to touch his stubble with my fingertips.

Salty let out a soft woof.

Martin tightened his grip for a moment before letting go, shoving his hand into his jacket pocket. "Night, Olivia."

"Night." I walked up the porch steps, wondering how I had never noticed how empty a hand could feel by itself. Hugging myself, I turned and watched him melt into the darkness.

CHAPTER NINE

Miss Rawlings. I'll need you to make several additional desserts to be served at lunch this afternoon. I will be in early this morning to discuss. — M

I stuck my finger into the croissant dough to see if it was soft enough to roll. It bounced back, releasing a yeasty scent that lingered in the air. Perfect. Taking my rolling pin, I pounded the dough until it covered the entire surface of the workbench.

"Hey, missy," Tom said as he walked in carrying a case of buttermilk.

"Hey, yourself," I said, pressing the rolling pin into the dough to thin one of the edges. "There's fresh coffee."

I handed him a pear and ginger scone and got back to work, slicing the dough into long strips with the help of a rotary cutter and a yardstick.

"It's freezing out there," he said, holding

the cup up to his face to let the steam warm his pink cheeks.

"I know. I woke up with Salty under the covers with me. I forgot to build the fire up before bed."

"You should get an electric heater for that cabin."

"I like the woodstove. It smells good." My mind conjured the woodsy scent of Martin's jacket.

"Well, tell me how much you like it in the middle of a February ice storm." Tom bit into the scone, dropping crumbs onto his quilted flannel shirt. "So, the boys were thinking of getting together next week to go over some new tunes. You in?"

I rolled my cutter crosswise, making perfect little rectangles. "Is there another dance coming up?"

"New Year's Eve."

The door to the dining room swung open. "Good morning, folks." Chef Al's warm, booming voice filled the kitchen.

"Ha," I said. "This is a sight I never thought I'd see — I didn't think you were familiar with this side of seven o'clock."

Al wrapped his arms around my shoulders in a sideways hug, leaving behind the faint scent of Old Spice. He was letting his beard come in. It was stark white and threatened to make him look like Santa. "It's true — if I'm up this early it's usually because I haven't gone to bed yet. But Margaret asked me to come in — something about a lunch?" Al pulled off his wool hat and made his way over to the coffee pot.

"Mystery. Who do you think is coming in? The pope? The president of Talbots? Ooh, maybe it's that silver fox she waltzed with at the dance." I squished two batons of dark chocolate into the edge of one of the rectangles of dough and gently rolled it into a tiny loaf.

Al reached into the box of chocolate.

"Hands off," I said, giving him a light slap. "It's imported and costs a fortune. I'm afraid Margaret won't reorder when she sees the invoice."

"Hear you're getting into some cheese making," said Tom to Al. I handed them each a cranberry muffin.

"Livvy here inspired me. She insists on making everything from scratch."

I smiled at him. "Well, we're chefs, aren't we? I think everything should be handmade if we have the time."

"If you want to get away from the goat's milk, we could do a trade," Tom offered. "Fresh cow's milk for a few wheels of cheddar?" Tom took a long sip of coffee. "Oh,

211

hey, Marty."

I spun around. Martin stood in the door of the kitchen, his cheeks flushed from the cold. He was holding a black cardboard instrument case.

"Hey," I said.

"Hey." Martin placed the case on the floor, took off his fogged glasses, and wiped the lenses with a white handkerchief. I had never seen him without his glasses on. His face looked unprotected.

"Can I get you anything, Martin?" Al offered, a bit formally I thought.

The croissant dough on my table had begun to rise, the rectangles puffed and billowy. I wanted to take Martin's hand in mine, pick up where we had left off last night, and see what would happen next. I felt heat creep up my neck like someone had turned the flame up under a simmering pot. I turned my attention back to the croissant dough and chocolate batons.

"I was just telling Livvy about practice next week, for the New Year's dance. You up for it?" Tom asked.

Martin was watching my fingers. "I brought the dulcimer," he said, his voice low in a way that made me want to lean in toward him. "My dad said he expects you to practice every day before your next lesson."

"Well, I had better, then," I said, my voice just as low. "I wouldn't want another lecture from Henry."

The dining room door opened and Margaret marched in. "I pay you to work, not stand in my kitchen, flirting with every man in town, Miss Rawlings." She glared at me as she walked straight into her office and slammed the door.

Mortified, I bit my bottom lip to hold back the tears that were threatening to spill. Al placed a big pot under the faucet and turned on the water. Tom stood, brushing the crumbs off of his shirtfront. "Well, that's a sign to get going if I ever saw one. See you kids at my place next Wednesday?"

"Sure," Martin and I said in unison.

I wiped the flour from my hands with the edge of my apron. Martin cradled the dulcimer in both hands, as if it were a child. "Where should I put this?"

I walked with Martin to the rocking chair at the other end of the kitchen, where he placed it gently. Frost still trimmed the grass across the field and into the apple orchard, making everything sparkle.

"Thanks for coming by," I said. "With the dulcimer, I mean."

"I thought you'd want to practice."

"Yes, definitely. Did Henry mention when our next lesson will be?"

Martin leaned against the doorjamb. "He said you should come around every Monday afternoon." He looked out across the field. "Does Salty stay in the cabin all day?" he asked.

"Usually."

Martin rested his hand on the doorknob. He hesitated, glancing back over his shoulder at Alfred before opening the door. A gust of cold air rushed in. "Guess I'll see you soon."

"Yes," I said, clasping my arms behind my back to keep from touching him.

I lingered by the back door and watched as Martin walked through the apple orchard.

"So what was that about?" asked Al, startling me back into the present.

"What?"

He nodded toward the closed office door. "That."

"I guess one of us should find out."

"It's too early in the day for that much negative energy. She's all yours."

I straightened my apron and knocked on the office door.

"Come in."

Margaret sat at her desk, head down, a stack of invoices piled high beside her. "What was Martin McCracken doing here so early?"

"Martin?" I asked, surprised at the question.

"You can do what you want in that cabin, but I'd appreciate it if you didn't bring your personal life to work. It's a small town. People talk."

"He was just dropping something off."

"At seven in the morning." It was a statement, not a question.

"Yes, at seven in the morning." I ripped my ponytail holder out and began twisting my hair into a knot at the back of my head. "Not that it's any of your business."

"Martin McCracken is the son of my best friend and certainly is my business."

"Then you'd know that he was dropping off Dotty's dulcimer so I can practice between lessons."

Margaret leafed through the pile of invoices, uncovering a legal pad at the bottom of the pile. I sat down in the chair opposite her desk. "So what's up?" I asked.

Margaret adjusted her eyeglasses and leaned back. "It looks like we might have a wedding booked for June. The clients are coming today to walk through the inn and to talk about the menu. I want you and Alfred to make them lunch — something summery. It's not an official tasting — I just want you to give them some ideas."

June. One of a baker's favorite months. Strawberries would be available, and sour cherries. Rhubarb, of course. And lavender would be blooming. I could feel the sun on my cheeks and smell the green scent of cut grass.

"Olivia."

I opened my eyes. "Sorry. But wait — we aren't open for lunch."

"Miss Rawlings."

"How about an orange Chiboust with strawberry rhubarb compote? Or I could do my sour cherry napoleon. Ooh, or how about lavender honey Bavarian torte? With a blueberry coulis?"

"That sounds fine," Margaret said.

"Fine? That sounds fabulous! But I'll have to stick to just the napoleon. I could have done more with, you know, some *notice.*"

"That will do," Margaret said, distracted by the invoice in front of her. "Tell Alfred I'll be in to discuss the menu in a few minutes."

"What's all this fuss about, anyway? We had a couple come in to check out the place last week and you had them order off the menu. At dinner."

Margaret didn't say anything.

"Who's coming in?" I prodded.

"Jane White," Margaret said to her pile of paperwork. "It's her granddaughter Emily who's getting married."

I sat back down. "Seriously?"

"At one o'clock."

"But — she's *Jane White.*"

"Yes, and?"

"You're the owner. You can do whatever you want. Just tell her —"

"That may be the way you did things down in Boston, Ms. Rawlings, but that's not how we conduct business here. You should keep that in mind. Now —"

"Is this like a 'keep your friends close, your enemies closer' kind of thing?"

"You only have a couple of hours, Ms. Rawlings. Shouldn't you be getting to work?"

I kept my seat. I could hear the clang of a heavy metal pot being placed on the stovetop, Alfred's smooth cadence, and Sarah's laughter through the wall.

"Bring me to the meeting."

Margaret eyed me over her reading glasses. "Excuse me?"

"Bring me to the meeting. Brides love me. I'll do the walk-through with you, sit down with them at lunch, talk menu. You can just say you're showing me the ropes, since I'm new, which would be true. I've got lots of experience with brides-to-be and their families, trust me. Besides." My eyes fixed on the red ribbons in the case behind her head. "It will level the playing field. Two Sugar Maples against two Whites. No one should have to spend all afternoon with two Whites alone."

Margaret eyed me with suspicion. "One o'clock. Be sure to give yourself some time to get cleaned up. They'll be prompt."

"No problem. I'll tell Al you'll be right out." I walked straight from the office into the walk-in freezer, praying the chef had frozen some of last year's cherries.

I stepped into the foyer, buttoning the chef's coat that Margaret had bought for me. Margaret was pacing around the sitting room with a clipboard clenched in her hand. The front door opened, and a young woman with loose blond curls walked in, followed by the thick form of Jane White swaddled in a red wool cape.

"Hi, Mrs. Hurley," the young woman said.

"Hello, Emily." Margaret walked into the foyer to greet them. "Jane."

Jane regarded the sitting room, frowning.

"The light in here isn't very good, is it?"

Margaret looked like she was ready to throw the first punch.

I stuck my hand out to the young woman. "Olivia Rawlings, the inn's pastry chef. Congratulations on your engagement." The young girl beamed.

"You're supposed to congratulate the groom," Jane said.

I smiled at her warmly. "May I take your coats?"

Jane and Emily peeled their coats off and handed them to me. I draped them over the edge of one of the love seats, not knowing what else to do with them.

Margaret cleared her throat. "You've been here plenty of times, Jane. What do you need to see?"

"Well, there are going to be at least seventy-five guests. All of Emily's cousins will be coming; she has dozens of cousins from the Bradford side of the family. And her friends from college." Jane was puffed up with pride. "Did you know Emily graduated with honors from UVM? And of course, all of John's family will be there." Jane turned to me. "John is my late husband. He came from a large family."

"Our dining room only seats forty, so it looks like we won't be able to help you,"

Margaret said, turning away from the group.

I grabbed her elbow. "Unless you were planning on having the reception outside, where we could set up tents. It's a June wedding, isn't it?"

"Yes," Emily gushed. "That's what I've been picturing since I was a girl."

"It will be lovely," I said. "A warm breeze, fireflies blinking at the edges of the field."

"Mosquitoes biting the grandmother of the bride," Margaret murmured.

"The wedding is at noon," Jane interjected.

"I'm sure the guests will be dancing until dawn. And before the fireflies light their tails in celebration, the guests will enjoy gazing down at the beautiful view of the valley."

Emily sighed. Jane coughed. "What if it rains?" she asked.

"We'll have tents over the dining area and over the dance floor. And your guests could come in here as well to have drinks and to relax." I waved my arm around the sitting room. "We have twelve guest rooms, so some of your bridesmaids could stay right here. You could even reserve a room for yourself to get ready in."

Margaret rolled her eyes.

"Why don't we talk about this over lunch? Chef Alfred and I have made some summery dishes for you to try."

We made our way through the inn into the dining room. Margaret and Jane ignored each other as Emily described the color scheme of the flower arrangements in breathless detail.

Sarah arrived a few moments later carrying a tray of arugula salad with fresh burrata and cherry tomatoes, drizzled with a basil vinaigrette. I ran my tongue over my lip. Al's burrata was the creamiest I had ever tasted. Margaret waved her salad away when Sarah tried to serve her. "None for us, Sarah."

"You're not eating?" asked Emily.

I looked at Margaret with questioning eyes.

"No, we've already had lunch."

My stomach rumbled in protest. I straightened in my chair and looked at my legal pad, trying to stay professional. "These are just ideas for an early-summer menu. When you've had a chance to look at the banquet menu, we can arrange a formal tasting."

Emily took delicate bites of her salad. Jane speared a cherry tomato into her mouth and pushed the cheese around the plate with her fork.

"This is delicious," said Emily. She was a polite girl. It was hard not to like her, even if she was a White.

"Your grandfather would have loved this." Jane smoothed Emily's blond curls out of her face. "I wish he were here to see you getting married."

Margaret shifted in her chair. Sarah cleared the salad plates and served two small cups of vichyssoise. "The price includes soup or salad. You'll have to choose."

"Unless you want to go with four or five courses," I added.

"For an additional price," Margaret said.

"Price isn't an issue," Jane said, dabbing at the corner of her lip with the cloth napkin. "John set up a trust for precisely this occasion. He wanted the best of everything for Emily."

Even I was getting tired of hearing about John. Margaret's face was inscrutable, but I could see that under the table she had twisted her handkerchief into a tight knot.

"I do have one important question," Jane said, looking directly at Margaret. "Are you sure the inn will still be under the same management? We wouldn't want to commit if there's a chance that strangers will be running the place. Unless, of course —"

"I honor my commitments." Margaret looked like she was ten seconds away from stabbing Jane with the salad fork. She needed help.

"Margaret, do you know where I left my cake portfolio?" I asked lightly.

Margaret's chair scraped loudly against the floor. "I'll get it." She walked quickly through the swinging doors and into the kitchen. She didn't return with the leatherbound binder until Sarah was clearing the entree.

"Now, I know you'll want to have cake, but most weddings in Boston also feature a plated dessert, and the cake cutting takes place later in the evening."

Sarah served the napoleon I had prepared, along with several other desserts I had whipped up. A tall wineglass held fresh berries bathing in a champagne sabayon. A crepe stuffed with white chocolate and mascarpone mousse was topped with strawberry and rhubarb compote. I sat back, pleased with what I had accomplished in late November with only a few hours' notice. Jane took small bites of everything without comment. Emily licked the spoon clean after each taste. When she pressed her fork into the crepe for a third bite, Jane patted her wrist and said, "Don't forget about your dress, dear. You'll want to fit into it."

Emily put down her fork.

Margaret stood up. "Miss Rawlings, I trust

you can manage to talk about the cakes without me?"

"Of course," I said brightly.

"We won't hold the reservation until we have received a fifty percent deposit. I'll send over an estimate." Without even a good-bye nod, Margaret walked purposefully out of the room.

I picked up the portfolio and stood. "Let's have coffee in the sitting room and look over the options for the cake."

Emily and I sat by the fireplace paging through my portfolio while Jane walked around the room, picking up the small statues that perched on mantels, flipping them over to see what was underneath, and peering at the paintings, photographs, and decorative plates that hung on the walls, as if she were searching for clues.

"Look at this one, Granny." Emily held up the binder, open to a photograph of a three-tiered cake wrapped in fondant, the surface worked with quilting tools to make it look as if it were sewn. "It reminds me of the quilts in your house."

Jane was standing by the wall of photographs, her head leaning forward, peering at one over the rims of her glasses.

"Do you sew as well as bake, Mrs. White?" I asked sweetly. "I'm surprised you would trust anyone else with your granddaughter's cake, you being such an accomplished baker yourself."

"I'm not much of a cake decorator," Jane said, her voice distant and faltering. She eyed me cautiously. "Pie is my specialty. Apple pie."

"We have that in common," I said.

Jane gave me a level look. "All right, Emily, I think we've seen enough. We'd better be on our way."

As Jane and Emily buttoned their coats, I planted myself where Jane had been standing, taking quick glances at the photograph she had been studying. It was one from Dotty and Henry's wedding, a candid of the wedding party coupled off on the dance floor. "Let us know if you have any questions," I said, smiling brightly. "Chef Alfred is looking forward to hearing your menu ideas."

Jane walked past me and into the front yard. Emily stopped and shook my hand. "It was nice to meet you," she said.

I gave her hand a small squeeze. "You too. And congratulations. Or whatever I'm supposed to say to the bride."

Emily laughed. "I like being congratulated. I'm getting what I've always wanted."

"What is that?" I asked. When I was her

age all I wanted was to score some pot.

"My own family." Her eyes softened, and she looked shy all of a sudden.

I pictured myself sitting at the McCrackens' kitchen table, Dotty and Margaret gossiping about the people in the church basement while Henry and Martin talked about the Christmas-tree crop. That led to thoughts of Martin's breath on my cheek that night in the woods, and how natural his hand felt in mine. I looked over at fresh-faced Emily, who looked like she was born to be a bride, and pushed the thoughts aside.

"Well, congratulations, then," I said as I closed the door behind them.

I walked back to my cabin after the Whites left. I needed a break from the tension that was radiating from the closed door of Margaret's office. Expecting a chilly cabin and an anxious dog, I was surprised to find Salty sleeping heavily by the woodstove, which held a roaring fire. A small pile of wood was neatly arranged beside it. When I peeked out the back door, the cord of wood that had been a sprawling mess was stacked under the eaves and tucked under a blue plastic tarp. On the kitchen table was a note.

Salty was on the porch with the door open when I walked by. Noticed the woodpile. Let him play while I stacked it. Hope you don't mind. Martin

I kicked off my boots and put the kettle on to boil, humming an old tune whose name I couldn't remember.

Hannah arrived at the sugarhouse a couple of hours later, a large pizza box balanced in one hand, a sonogram clutched in the other. She pushed the box at me and collapsed onto the couch. "Twins," she said, waving the sonogram in the air. "I'm having twins. I just found out."

I dropped the pizza box onto the counter. "Seriously?" One baby seemed impossible. Two babies — at once — seemed catastrophic.

"Can you heat that up? I drove all the way to Littleton to get it. I've been dreaming about that pizza for days."

I turned on the oven and flipped open the box. It was just a cheese pizza. "What makes this so special?" I asked.

"I have no idea, but it's all I want to eat. That pizza from that shop. Jonathan won't eat it, so I don't feel right asking him to go." Hannah kicked off her shoes and put

227

her feet up on the couch.

"I'd have gone," I said, pouring bubbly water into two cups.

"You've been busy."

I could hear the note of hurt in her voice. It had been two weeks since I had seen Hannah at the diner. Between baking, practicing dulcimer, and having lessons with Henry — which always led to visiting with the McCrackens — I hadn't had much time to do anything other than take Salty out for walks.

I handed her a warm slice and a glass of water and then plopped down on the couch beside her. She had taken off her coat and her belly was noticeably rounded.

"So, how do you feel?"

"Terrified."

"And what did Jonathan say?"

"He was thrilled. He always wanted a big family, and we got a late start, as you know."

Twins. Hannah's and my friendship had weathered the changes of her marrying Jonathan and moving up to Vermont with little conflict, most likely because I had convinced myself they were temporary. Some part of me still believed that Hannah and I would always be partners in crime. You could still be a partner in crime with one baby, but with two? Now I couldn't avoid the truth that things would never be the same.

"That's great, sweetie," I said, grasping her foot and giving it a little shake. "I'm so happy for you guys."

"I just wish we could keep it to ourselves a little longer, but with my belly . . . Jonathan wants to announce it to his family on Thanksgiving. Thank God you're going to be there."

I stood up and went back to the stove to refill our plates. "Um, Hann, about that. I've been invited to the McCrackens' for Thanksgiving."

"But I assumed you'd be coming to my house. I need you as a buffer."

I leaned against the kitchen counter. "I'd like to, but Henry is . . ." *Like a father to me,* I couldn't say. And I was going to lose him too. "I just couldn't say no to them."

"But you can to me?" Hannah put her plate down. "Is there something going on between you and Martin that you haven't told me about?"

"I honestly don't know."

"How can you not know?"

Because he hasn't tried to get down my pants, like every other man I have ever been involved with. "Look — we're just friends. But I've been spending a lot of time with

229

him and his family, and . . ."

"I need you there, Livvy. The doctor is threatening bed rest. And Jonathan was talking about his mother *moving in.*"

"I'm sorry. I just feel like I need to be there." I turned to face the sink and stuck my hands under the hot water.

"I thought that you moving up here meant that we'd see more of each other, not less. You can be so frustrating sometimes." Hannah appeared beside me. She dropped her plate on the counter with a loud clang. "You know what's going to happen. Henry is going to die, and Martin is going to go back west. And then you'll be back on my doorstep, just like you are every time you get hurt, and —"

"Hannah, you don't need to tell me that everyone leaves," I said quietly.

"I never leave," she said, her hand on the doorknob, "I just wish you would appreciate that."

CHAPTER TEN

Thanksgiving had never meant Indians and Pilgrims, or football, or even turkey to me. For twelve years it had equaled long days and cramped fingers. The day before Thanksgiving was always a marathon — twenty-four hours of pie baking — and I spent the morning of Thanksgiving boxing them for pickup. By the afternoon I was capable only of icing down my forearms, trying to ease the pain of rolling out hundreds of piecrusts. When Margaret informed me that the Sugar Maple was closed for the holiday, I should have felt elated. Instead I was surprised to find that I was nervous instead of relieved. Hannah and I hadn't spoken since our argument, and it left me feeling deeply unsettled.

I tried to find a way to decline Dotty's invitation, but excuses are hard to come by in such a small place. The closer we came to the day, the more I found myself with an anxious energy that could be released only by baking pies. I began with the basics — double-crust apple, sweet potato, bourbon pecan. A friend from the Cape had just sent me a crate of fresh cranberries, so I added a cranberry with crumb. Then an old-fashioned custard pie that I thought Margaret would enjoy. The custard reminded me of an old recipe for chess pie that I'd saved. I added a key lime and a lemon meringue after I woke up in the middle of the night thinking that all the flavors were too heavy. Then I started to worry that the pies were all too adult somehow. I knew that Martin's nieces and nephews were coming, and children like chocolate, so I filled a cookie crust with pudding made from cornstarch and cocoa and piled it high with mounds and mounds of whipped cream and ribbons of milk chocolate. Everything would need to be accompanied by ice cream — vanilla. I spent an afternoon scraping the tiny black seeds out of fresh vanilla beans with the edge of a paring knife. I couldn't help but make Parker House rolls when I had the original recipe — not the one found in magazines but truly the original, which I had teased out of the chef at the hotel while we drank sidecars in the very room where Jack proposed to Jackie. I was determined to dazzle the McCrackens with baked goods so that they wouldn't notice that I lacked experience in the family department.

By Thanksgiving morning I had run out of pies to bake, so I dyed my hair. I must have been thinking about my walk in the woods when I chose the color — Enchanted Forest. It looked like the dark green balsams that lined the McCracken fields. When I was dressed, I grabbed my banjo and Dotty's dulcimer and marched down the hill. By the time I arrived at the inn, Margaret had already loaded the pies into the trunk of her car and was waiting by the door.

"Green, Olivia? I thought crimson might have been a more festive choice."

"Did you remember the ice cream?" I asked, ignoring her comment.

She nodded.

"And the pumpkin and the cream pies? Some of them were in the back of the walk-in."

Margaret let out a breath. "Yes, Miss Rawlings. Now stop fussing. It's a holiday."

We pulled onto the dirt road that led to the McCracken farm. Cars were lined up along the road, and the parking area was full.

"That's a lot of cars." I knew from dinner conversations at the McCrackens' that the extended family was large, but seeing it live and up close made my stomach churn.

"It's usually just the kids and their families," Margaret replied. "A stray friend or two."

Three boys who looked about nine or ten ran by the car holding sticks in the air and shouting. Margaret stepped out of the car and called them over.

"Hi, Auntie Margaret," said the tallest boy, stopping to kiss her cheek.

"Hi, Auntie Margaret," said the smaller two.

"You boys drop those sticks for a minute and give us a hand." Margaret popped open the trunk and handed each boy a tower of pie boxes. "Now, be careful. Go straight into the kitchen and give them to your great-grandmother."

The boys held the boxes in front of them and walked as if they were carrying gifts for a king.

I carried the ice cream, leaving Margaret with just the apple pies. We were met on the porch by a handsome man with salt-and-pepper hair and Dotty's hazel eyes. He wrapped his arm around Margaret's shoulder and gave her a tight squeeze.

"Great to see you," he said, kissing her on the cheek. "Mom's in the kitchen. Tim!" he shouted into the open door. "Get your brothers and come out here."

Three young men, all in their late twenties or early thirties, slipped through the door.

"I'm Mark," said the salt-and-peppered man. He held out his hand. I balanced the ice cream awkwardly on one hip and shook his hand with the other.

"Olivia Rawlings." I didn't know how to introduce myself. "I work at the Sugar Maple."

"Do you go by 'Livvy'?" Mark asked. "Henry mentioned you. Hope you brought your banjo."

I nodded. "It's in the car. Your mom's dulcimer too."

Mark handed the ice cream to one of the young men and took the box from Margaret and passed it to another. "Good, let's go get them. Maybe we can have a tune before supper."

The once-peaceful McCracken homestead was buoyant with sound. I put the instrument cases on the floor and wrestled out of my coat. I could hear Dotty and Margaret talking in the kitchen, as well as some younger female voices. In the sitting room someone tuned a guitar string while a couple of men laughed. Three boys stood in a cluster unarmed but arguing. From some-where deep inside the house, a baby cried. All I could think was *Thank God I didn't bring Salty.* I stood still in the foyer, not knowing where I belonged.

"I'll bring the instruments into the sitting room — it's where we usually play," Mark explained, and disappeared into the room. Not sure if I should follow, I waited in the hallway. When he didn't emerge, I walked toward the room I had the highest chance of feeling comfortable in — the kitchen. It was as steamy as a sauna and every flat surface was covered with pans and dishes. Dotty stood at the center of it all, her face serene.

"Livvy, dear, glad you could make it." She leaned over and kissed my cheek. "I thought I saw a custard in one of your boxes," she whispered. "I might have to hide that for myself. Now, I put the ice cream in the freezer downstairs, and all the pies are on the back porch — it's cool enough out there, don't you think?"

"That's perfect." I rolled up my sleeves. "What can I do?"

A young redhead in her early twenties walked through the kitchen and handed me a baby. "Thank God. Could you take Dotty? I'm dying for a nap." Without waiting for an introduction or an answer, she walked out of the room.

"That was my granddaughter, Nicole," explained Dotty, reaching over to stroke the downy hair on the baby's head, "and this fine young woman is my great-granddaughter and namesake, Dorothy."

Dorothy let out a cry and all the women laughed. I looked down at the baby in panic.

"You know, I'd probably be a lot more useful helping in the kitchen," I hinted.

"Nonsense," replied Dotty. "She's just like me — she likes to move. Just walk her around a bit and she'll be fine."

All the other women in the kitchen turned back to their tasks. Feeling out of place, I tucked young Dorothy's butt under my arm and walked through the door. The baby radiated heat like a little furnace. I bounced her gently up and down as I walked her back and forth in the foyer, wondering where Martin was but feeling too weird to go in search of him. Dorothy reached behind me, grabbed my ponytail, stuck a curl in her mouth, and began to suck. A deep voice chuckled from down the hall.

"I see Nicole has already found someone to babysit my granddaughter." I turned to see the perfect combination of Henry and Dotty at the end of the hall. He had Henry's sharp nose and Dotty's sweet smile. "Ethan," he said, offering his hand.

"Livvy."

"I figured. Marty told me about you." Ethan tilted his head toward the sitting room. "Want to play? The boys are just tuning up."

I held up the baby in *Lion King* fashion. Dorothy kept a tight grip on my hair, and a stream of drool escaped from her lips. "I've got my hands full."

Ethan reached toward the baby. "I can take her."

The baby felt like a security blanket — she was comforting and didn't expect me to talk much. I felt shy playing music with all of these strangers. "I'll just listen for this round," I said, smiling. "But I'm sure I'll get the urge to play as soon as this one starts howling."

Ethan chuckled and held open the door.

"There you are," Henry called out. He was sitting on the couch, fiddle in hand, flanked by two of the younger boys. His sweater hung off his frame loosely, but his eyes looked bright, and he looked happy being surrounded by so many generations. "Everyone, this is Olivia."

I waved hello, noticing that one of them had my banjo on his lap.

"I hope you don't mind," he said, his fingers already twisting the tuning pegs.

"Not at all. Warm her up," I replied as I settled into an armchair. The baby nestled her head into my shoulder and grew a tiny bit heavier as she sucked on my lock of hair. I rubbed my nose across her head.

Henry pressed his fiddle into the flesh beneath his collarbone, the same way Martin held his, and raised his bow. Counting under his breath, "One, two, three," Henry began a slow version of the Shaker hymn "Simple Gifts." Tim and Charlie, two of Henry's grandsons, followed in time. I tapped my foot, singing the words softly into the baby's hair.

'Tis the gift to be simple, 'tis the gift to be
    free
'Tis the gift to come down where we ought
    to be,
And when we find ourselves in the place
    just right,
'Twill be in the valley of love and delight.

I looked up to see Martin leaning against the doorframe, looking at me, his expression unreadable. I waved. He tilted his chin in a single nod. The tune wound around three times before Henry stuck his toe out from under the red afghan on his lap. After the last verse, the room felt silent. Baby Dorothy let out a piercing roar.

"You better keep playing." I laughed as I soothed the baby's back. One of her uncles strummed a chord on his guitar and the baby responded with a thundering "Ga," waving a chunk of my hair in the air. The front door opened and a male voice called hello. Martin stepped back into the hallway. The house seemed to expand with the addition of each new guest. Ethan walked in and placed a glass of wine on the table next to me. The baby reached her hands out to him and squeaked.

"Ready for a break?" Ethan offered.

"Livvy, where's that dulcimer?" Henry asked. "Come show me how you're doing."

I handed Ethan his granddaughter prying my hair from her tight grip. I grabbed the glass of wine and settled myself beside Henry on the sofa.

"Have you been practicing?"

"Of course," I said as I removed the dulcimer from its case. "Will you play with me?"

Henry tucked the fiddle into his chest. "How about 'Shady Grove'?"

I tucked the noter under my left finger and strummed the strings with the pick in my right.

"You start." I closed my eyes and sang along to the sweet notes of Henry's fiddle. The difference in his and Martin's playing was slight but palpable. Henry had a way of teasing out the notes, almost as if he were lazily waiting for them to find him. When Martin played, I could feel his urgency deep in my belly, the feeling that each note was almost out of reach. I pressed the noter behind the second fret and joined in on the chorus. A low mumble that sounded more like a harmonium than a voice sang the next verse. I opened my eyes and found Martin sitting across from me with the guitar in his lap. I beamed at him. His face broke into an unguarded smile. We played until Henry stuck out his slippered foot, ending with a whoop and a shout.

"Dinner is ready," Dotty called. "We've been blessed with a good crowd this year. If you could all join us in the dining room for grace, then we'll find everyone a place to sit down and eat."

Martin and Charlie hung back to help Henry up off the couch. When Henry took his seat at the head of the table, the family gathered around. "Now, if you could all join hands," Henry said as he reached over and took his wife's in his, smiling up at her. She kissed the top of his head and reached over for Margaret's hand beside her. Martin slipped in quietly behind me and took my hand in his. My heart sped up as his fingers wove themselves through mine. I could have sworn Margaret was staring at us from across the room. She seemed to be looking at our hands. "Now, I hate to put you on the spot, Livvy," Henry said, and a few people tittered. "But it's custom in this house to have our newest guest offer the blessing."

"Wouldn't that be little Dorothy?" I asked.

Henry laughed. "No — it's your first Thanksgiving with the McCracken brood, not hers."

"Well, then." I thought for a moment. "I don't know many prayers. But I do know a poem. It's Emerson.

For each new morning with its light,
For rest and shelter of the night,
For health and food,
For love and friends
For everything Thy goodness sends."

"Amen," Henry said, his eyes warm.
"Amen."
"The food is laid out in the kitchen." Dotty announced. "Adults in the dining

room, everyone under thirty in the living room."

"Ha. You're still stuck in the kids' room," Charlie said to his cousin, who rolled his eyes.

"It's easier to wait," Martin said into my ear, eyeing the crush of children trying to push their way into the kitchen. "Come with me." I followed him through the room and out the front door onto the porch. Ethan was already out there on the swing with his arm around a tiny woman with a dark brown bob, a cooler at their feet. Martin grabbed two beers and handed one to me.

"Hi," I said, giving a half wave to the woman on the swing. "I'm Livvy."

"Jessie," she said, placing her palm on Ethan's thigh. "Ethan's wife."

"Good to meet you." I sat down next to Martin on the steps. He reached over and popped the top off my beer bottle with an opener.

"Glad you could make it, Martin," Jessie said. "Not spending the holiday with — what's her name? Sylvie?"

Martin looked up at her. I looked from Martin to Jessie and back as the silence stretched.

Who was Sylvie? A girlfriend? *A lot can change in a year,* I reminded myself.

"He's here now," Ethan said. "That's all that matters."

I couldn't imagine ever missing this cheerful gathering. This time last year, I had been in the kitchen at the Emerson while Jamie hosted his family five floors down. I leaned back on my elbows so I could see Jessie. "Is Dorothy your granddaughter?"

"It still gives me the chills to hear that word, but yes."

"She's adorable," I said.

"Our grandson, Eli, is here too," Ethan added. "I think he's been down for a nap since you got here — I'm sure he'll be up soon."

"You'll know it when he's up," Jessie reassured me. "He's two. Do you have children, Livvy?"

"No, not yet."

"What are you, in your late twenties?"

"Jessie!" Ethan said.

"I'm thirty-two."

"Our oldest was fifteen when we were your age." Jessie patted Ethan's leg, as if to remind him he had something to do with it. "You should have them when you're young enough to keep up with them."

Martin tilted his beer back, drinking the last bit. "We should go down to the tree hut later," he said to Ethan.

"Where you sell the trees?" I asked.

Martin nodded.

"That's a good idea. We can get Luke and Mark's boys to help clean it out. It shouldn't take them more than an hour. I've got the baler all set up. We can start cutting in the morning."

"What about Henry, and the lights?" I asked.

Ethan looked at Martin with his eyebrows raised. "We'll get all the heavy lifting done, then take Henry down later in the day to torture us with the lights. He'll be exhausted after this."

"He looks good today," Martin said.

"He does." Ethan stood up. "Ready for supper, lady?"

Jessie stood up with a little groan and took his hand.

Martin stood, reaching down his hand to me. "We should head in too."

"There's plenty of food, kids," Dotty called. "Help yourselves."

When we sat down with our plates, I was introduced to Tim's and Charlie's wives. It was difficult for me to understand how they could be Martin's nieces and nephews, when they looked like people I would go have drinks with. There was an eleven-year age difference between Mark and Martin. I wondered if Martin had been a surprise.

"So Livvy," Mark began, "I know you're new to the area. Where's your family?"

"Livvy's parents have passed away, dear," Dotty said gently.

"Not recently, I hope?" asked Susan, Mark's wife.

"No. My father died when I was a teenager. My mother a couple of years ago."

"You must miss her," Susan said.

"Um, I was actually raised by my father," I began. "My mother was the cofounder of a theater troupe. She traveled a lot." I speared a huge bite of stuffing and shoved it into my mouth.

"Didn't your father mind her being away so much?" Tim asked.

"Well, they sort of broke up when she started doing the theater thing."

"Sorry," Martin whispered.

"Life on the road with a theater company sounds exciting," said Charlie. "Did he ever consider going with her?"

"No," I said. "The name of the theater was the Women's Liberation Puppet Collective. It was a lesbian separatist group. They made giant vulvas —"

White wine shot out of Charlie's wife's mouth.

"— out of papier-mâché and performed street theater in countries where women were fighting for equal rights. She never stopped performing. She died doing what she loved, I guess." I peeked over at Dotty, who looked amused. "These are the best sweet potatoes I have ever had," I said, forking them into my mouth.

"Thank you, dear. You know, I think I may have seen one of your mother's performances, over at Bread and Puppet."

I didn't think it was possible to love Dotty any more than I already did, but my heart stretched an extra inch. "She met her partner while doing an internship there."

"Interesting people. Excellent sourdough."

"What got you into baking, Olivia?" asked one of the wives.

"I had an elderly neighbor who used to babysit me when I was little — her name was Mary. She had all these wonderful family recipes, and every afternoon she would bake something from her cookbook. And I'd help." I shrugged. "She never married. I think in a way she wanted to hand her recipes down to someone. I still make a lot of them. The custard pie is hers." I felt a wave of sadness thinking of Mary, alone in her little dark kitchen — a loneliness no one in this room would ever know. "Every time we would bake something together, she would say, 'You should always do what you can to make life sweeter.' "

"Amen to that," said Henry.

Dotty handed me an apron and put me in front of the sink to wash while Susan dried and one of the boys' wives whose names I couldn't keep straight put away the dishes. Margaret was put in charge of coffee and tea while Dotty and Jessie made use of a tower of Tupperware and an industrial-sized roll of plastic wrap. Nicole, the redheaded mother of Dorothy, wandered in with the baby on her arm but slipped out when she saw all the work to be done.

I couldn't decide whether my mother would have approved of us — the power of women working together — or thought we were oppressed as women, slaving away in the kitchen while the men lounged about. Probably a little of both. But I enjoyed the steam rising from the enamel sink, the lemon scent of the soap, and the soft voices around me. When the dishes were done, I began the cheerful work of slicing pies and setting up the table for dessert. Along with my buffet of pies there was a big dish of apple crisp, a cranberry upside-down cake, and a tray of sugar cookies cut into the shape of turkeys.

"What a sight," said Margaret, untying her apron.

"It is," I agreed. "Be sure to try the apple. I added a pinch of mace. I wanted to get your opinion."

Margaret looked pleased. "You're having a good time?"

"Very," I said, realizing that it was true. "I haven't had this day off in a long time."

"Well, you'll be busy soon enough." Margaret poured herself a cup of tea and headed back into the dining room.

A peacefulness had settled over the house, like the feeling I get after I cross the last thing off of my prep list. In the dining room Margaret and Dotty were playing a board game with some of the older children. Henry was asleep in his recliner in the den while Mark and his wife sat on the couch eating pie and watching football. Grabbing my coat from the closet, I wandered out onto the front porch in search of Martin. A tall young man in a fitted black sweater and pointed leather boots that poked out from under dark-washed jeans sat swaying on the porch swing.

"We haven't met yet. In the eyes of my grandmother, I'm still a child at twenty-eight, so I was stuck in the other room." He stuck out his hand. "Samuel. Son of Mark."

I laughed. "That sounds biblical."

"On some days it feels that way. Are you Olivia?"

"I am."

"Uncle Martin told me about you."

I looked around at the empty yard. "Where is Martin?"

"He and Uncle Ethan took my brothers and my cousin down to clean out the shack where they sell the Christmas trees. They should be back soon."

I tucked my hands into my coat pockets. "Have you had dessert yet?"

"I'm waiting for Gregory to come back. He got roped into helping."

"I'm sorry, I'm having trouble keeping up — there are a lot of you."

"No need. Gregory is my partner."

"Oh," I said, a little surprised.

"I know, right? Who would have thought a family dominated by this much testosterone would produce a little gay boy like me." Samuel batted his eyelashes at me.

"Do you still live in Vermont?"

"God, no. I got out as soon as I could. Vermont may have been the first state to pass civil unions, but in this part of the woods, every other house had a big black

Take Back Vermont sign staked in the front yard." He sighed. "But I do miss it. Especially at this time of year. We live in LA."

"That's about as far away from Vermont as you can get."

"In more ways than one." Samuel patted the seat next to him. "Come sit."

We both kicked out and sent the bench swinging. "Do you like it there?"

"The weather is great, and Gregory has an amazing job as an entertainment lawyer. I miss my family, though. I'm always trying to lure Uncle Marty down there, but he won't leave Seattle."

I laughed. "How come?"

"He claims to hate the sunshine."

"He is a little pale," I offered, although he seemed more alive to me when he was out walking in the woods than he ever did indoors. The room he was in always felt too small to contain him.

"He's just a snob. I can't complain, though. I don't think I could have survived my teenage years without him. When I was first coming out, having a hard time at school and fighting with my father all the time, Martin would let me spend the summers with him in Seattle. He'd take me to cafés and sneak me into bars. He even took me to a gay club one night just so I could see what it was like. I think he got hit on more than me!"

I giggled. "He is pretty cute."

Samuel met my eyes for a long second before smiling. "You have no idea. He was even cuter then — all rock and roll, leather jacket, motorcycle boots — the whole thing. I'll send you pictures. Are you on Facebook? Anyway, Uncle Marty was the only person in the family, other than my grandmother, who acted like it wasn't a big deal that I was gay. And he gave me a chance to see the possibility of life beyond all of this." He waved, gesturing at the fields.

"It seems like you and Martin have a lot in common. I mean, wanting a different life."

"It's funny. I used to think so. Now I'm not so sure." Samuel dragged his feet and stopped the swing. "Screw Gregory. Let's go eat tons of carbs."

Samuel and I were playing a cutthroat game of gin rummy with Margaret when the troop of boys came crashing in from the tree hut, tossing their jackets onto the floor and marching straight for the kitchen and hot coffee. Soon the seats at the table were filled with men hunched over plates of pie, grunting compliments between forkfuls. I couldn't help but feel a little proud when I saw that Martin had taken a small slice of each pie, including the chocolate cream.

The sun had set, and with my belly full of pie, I felt my eyelids growing heavy. I wandered into the sitting room, which was blissfully empty. I curled into a chair by the fireplace and felt myself drifting off.

"Livvy, would you like to head back?" I felt a cool hand on my shoulder. It was Margaret. Her coat was on, her purse slung over her forearm.

I blinked. "What time is it?" While I slept someone had lit the fire and tucked an afghan around my legs.

"Eight o'clock."

I threw off the blanket, suddenly overheated, my mouth thick and craving sugar. "Did everyone already leave?"

"Henry went upstairs a while ago. And the children have been sent to bed."

I stood up, disoriented, and followed Margaret into the hallway.

"You're not leaving, are you?" Samuel was standing with a sweet-looking man with green eyes and a shock of red hair. "You haven't even had a chance to talk to Gregory yet."

Gregory smiled. "That would be me."

I glanced over at Margaret.

"Will you bring her back with you?" she asked Samuel.

"Sure."

"You're staying at the inn?" I asked. "Fun."

"Yes, and we heard you make killer muffins, so we better get you back early enough to keep you on your A game."

"I'll stay a bit longer," I said to Margaret. "Night." Without thinking, I reached out and hugged her. Margaret stiffened, but she patted my back before letting go.

"I'll see you tomorrow," Margaret said, stopping to receive a kiss on the cheek from Samuel before leaving.

He closed the front door behind her. "Okay. Now it's time for the real party to begin. Get your coat."

All of the movable instruments had been carried to the barn. Martin's brothers Mark and Ethan sat on the bench, watching two of their sons struggle to tap a keg. Samuel came in through a side door, took the tap out of their hands, and pressed it into the seal.

I sat on the folding chair closest to my banjo and took a long sip from the plastic cup of beer that one of the boys handed me.

Suddenly Salty's long snout stuck through

the barn door. With a bark he pushed his whole head into the room, followed by his long, shaggy, gray body, tail high. Martin came in behind him with a bottle of bourbon in his hand.

"Puppy! How'd you get here?" I asked as I wrapped my arms around Salty's neck and buried my nose in his scruff. His breath smelled like brown sugar. "Have you been eating pie?"

"Your door was unlocked." Martin took off his coat. He had changed into a long-sleeved black T-shirt and a pair of jeans. I felt a little silly in a dress sitting in the barn with the goats. Mark picked up the guitar and began to play something sweet and unfamiliar.

"Not that again," said Tim. "Dad always starts to feel sentimental around the holidays," he explained to me. "Can't we hear anything livelier?"

"Like what?" Mark kept defiantly strumming.

"I can play the whole Sex Pistols album on the banjo," I offered.

Luke laughed. "You can not."

"I can." I picked up the banjo and twisted the tuning pegs into a G tuning.

"I am an Antichrist. I am an anarchist," I sang as I frailed out the melody.

Everyone burst out laughing.

"The banjo is totally punk rock," I mock defended.

"It's kind of like the opposite of Uncle Martin's old band," said Tim.

Ethan groaned. "I forgot about them. What were they called?"

"Wildwood," Mark answered, his voice full of sarcasm.

"We were nineteen," Martin said, his voice a little defensive.

"Yeah, and all you could think about was your hard-ons," said Mark.

"Come on, Dad," said Tim. "If you hadn't been thinking with your hard-on when you were nineteen, I wouldn't be here today."

Martin took the guitar from Mark. "We were called Wildwood," he said, looking at me from the corner of his eye, "because we were a Carter Family cover band." And without further introduction he drove his hands into the guitar, spitting out a speed-metal version of "Will the Circle Be Unbroken."

"Oh my God," I said when the song was finished. "I saw you."

"That's impossible." Martin passed the guitar to Luke and cracked his knuckles.

"You opened for Son Volt in 1999. At T.T.'s in Cambridge."

Martin gaped at me. "You were at that show? How? You would have still been in high school."

"My boyfriend was the bouncer," I said a little shyly. "I bought your record that night. I still have it somewhere."

"How could you bear to be parted from it?" shouted Charlie, laughing.

I leaned toward Martin. "I remember the cover. You were wearing those wolverine masks and sitting on BMX bikes."

We both looked down at the dirt floor then. Had my sixteen-year-old self noticed this serious-looking boy? What would it have been like to know him then?

"I thought Henry was going to have a coronary when we went to see you perform at the fair," said Mark.

"How's Grampy doing?" asked Luke.

"Fine," said Martin.

"Not great," said Ethan at the same time.

"Martin," Ethan said.

"What?" Martin ran his fingers through his hair. "You saw him. He had a great day today."

"He did, Marty. Today was a good day." Ethan pumped the tap of keg. "Today."

"I live with him. He's been doing well."

"He barely got through his last treatment."

"And he bounced back." Martin poured some of the bourbon into a plastic cup. "Jesus, out of all of us, I should know. Unlike you guys, I see him every day."

"And you see what you want to fucking see," Mark said. "Just like always."

"What's that supposed to mean?"

"Exactly what I said. You've got your head up your ass. You don't come home for two years —"

"Mark, give it a rest," said Ethan.

Martin sat, unmoving.

"What? He moves as far away as he could without going to Alaska, then he comes waltzing back here, and suddenly he's the expert on Dad?" Mark stood and turned to Martin. "You weren't here when he felt sick enough to ask for help for the first time in his life, or to take him for tests behind Mom's back, or to hear the diagnosis, or visit him in the hospital after the surgery. And now — Jesus, Martin. Look at Dad tomorrow. Really look at him." Mark walked out the barn door, leaving his jacket behind.

Ethan crossed his arms across his chest and looked at his nephews. "Your grandfather is . . ." The barn was silent. Ethan looked at Martin and said, "Well, we'll see. Henry is a tough old bird. That we all know." He clasped Martin's shoulder. "I'll be by tomorrow around seven and we can get the baler going and fill up that lot." Ethan grabbed his and Mark's coats and walked back toward the house. Martin grabbed the bottle of bourbon and followed him out of the barn.

One of the boys asked for my banjo, and I handed it over.

They played three tunes and Martin still hadn't returned. I buttoned my coat, grabbed Martin's corduroy jacket, and stuck my head out the door. Martin was sitting on a bench just outside the barn. I sat down next to him, draped the jacket over his shoulders, and tucked my hands in my coat pockets. He took off his glasses and leaned forward, cupping his face in his hands. I could hear the boys in the barn singing old songs from the seventies. I thought I heard Samuel joining in, or maybe it was Gregory. One of them had a rich voice.

"How is it we all know these songs?" I asked. "My dad hated any music that came out after 1958. It's not like I heard them in my house — but put on *Frampton Comes Alive!* and I'm singing right along."

"Do you think he's right?"

"Who? Peter Frampton?" I asked, trying to lighten things. I couldn't stand seeing him so vulnerable. "I have to admit I kind of have a soft spot for 'Baby, I Love Your Way' —"

"Mark." Martin leaned back and took a swig of bourbon.

It was the second time I had seen his face without glasses. He looked like a blind pup.

"Right about your dad, or about you?"

"My dad."

"It's hard for me to say," I said gently. "I've never known Henry in full health. But it seems like he has good days and bad days, like you both were saying. What does the doctor think?"

"That the treatment isn't really doing anything." Martin buried his face back in his hands.

"Oh." I felt a pinch in my heart. "I'm so sorry."

"The past couple of years I haven't come back much. I just got caught up with work and the band and — he just made it hard, sometimes, you know? The constant pressure. *What are you doing over there? When are you going to settle down? When are you coming home?* It was easier to stay away. If I had known — but everyone is so fucking secretive."

"No one told you he was sick?"

"Not until after his surgery. Dad didn't want them to."

"That's awful."

"Mark's right. I should have been here. And now today, all day, all I could think was *This will be the last . . .*" Martin's voice broke before he could finish.

I reached tentatively toward him.

"There isn't enough time," he said in a low rasp.

"There's never enough time," I said, stroking his back.

Martin turned to face me, his eyes glassy. "I don't know how to do this."

"It's okay," I said softly. "No one does."

Martin turned to me and buried his face in my neck. I pressed my cheek to the crown of his head. His hair smelled like sweat and sleep and sweet, like bourbon. He wound his arms around my waist, holding me closer. I felt the scrape of his stubble against my collarbone, and the damp warmth of his tear-streaked cheeks. I stroked the hair at the nape of his neck, feeling the weight of him against me. The moon rose. I would have sat there all night, but at the first sounds of the barn door creaking Martin straightened, wiping his face with his shirt-sleeve. Sam and Gregory appeared with Salty at their heels.

"I should take you home," Martin said to me.

"We'll take her," Sam said. "We're staying at the inn."

Martin looked at me for a moment, his expression a mixture of sadness and longing. He cleared his throat and put on his glasses.

"Thank your parents for me," I said.

Martin nodded. He kept his eyes fixed on Salty and reached down to stroke behind his long, curly ears. I took his other hand in mine and, while squeezing it, kissed Martin on the cheek.

Salty whined for a beat before following me down the driveway. When I looked back, Martin was still standing by the barn, watching us leave.

After building a fire in the woodstove, I made myself a cup of tea, too restless to sleep. Salty and I curled up under blankets on the couch and watched *It's a Wonderful Life,* but I was only half paying attention. My mind guiltily traveled to the way the muscles in Martin's back had felt under my fingertips, and the soft heat of his breath on my neck. I thought about how he had sought me out in the dining room before grace to hold my hand, and the way he had let it slip out of his hand after the prayer. Whatever was happening between Martin

McCracken and me was apparently not going to happen in front of his family. But it didn't stop me from staring at the door every time I heard a twig snap in the woods, hoping to hear a knock. When the screen faded to static, I burrowed under the afghan, remembering what it felt like to be in his arms.

CHAPTER ELEVEN
DECEMBER

The first fat flakes of snow fell on the afternoon of December 1. The kitchen was steamy; all of the stovetop burners were blazing under sauté pans, meat searing, greens wilting, garlic browning. The convection oven was stuffed with gingerbread men and women. Margaret had called an all-staff meeting, so the kitchen was filled with waitresses, dishwashers, and prep cooks. She pulled up one of the rocking chairs and sat in front of the crowd, much as she had the day I first interviewed.

"Okay, everyone, find a seat and quiet down for a moment," Margaret called.

I dipped a square of cheesecloth into a bowl of brandy and wrapped it around a loaf of fruitcake like a present. Only ninety-nine more to go.

"Listen up. The dining room is booked solid, as are the bedrooms, from this weekend until Christmas week. Sarah, did you order extra table linen?"

"Done," Sarah said, biting off the head of a gingerbread man.

"Santa's first visit is scheduled for this Saturday, and he will be seeing children from two until six every weekend day until Christmas. Al, did you get the suit back from the cleaners?"

"You're Santa?" I said, laughing.

"Every year," Al said, rubbing his whiskers. "All set," he called over his shoulder.

"Don't forget to give out the ten-percent-off coupons for the McCracken farm when the parents pay for Santa. Miss Rawlings, be prepared to have about thirty dozen cookies per weekend."

"Thirty *dozen*?" I asked.

"That's not a problem, is it?"

"Of course not," I replied. I would have to start sleeping on a cot in the corner of the kitchen, but no problem.

"The hospital's annual dinner for the board is on the eighteenth, and it's the biggest event of the season. I expect everyone to be available at all times during the next four weeks, no exceptions." Margaret looked out the window that faced the orchard. The dark limbs of the apple trees were already trimmed in a thick coating of snow. Together they looked like layers of cake and frosting.

"If this snow keeps up, it looks like we will be hosting a lot of sleigh-ride parties as well." Margaret pressed into her knees and hoisted herself up. "Well, I expect we will have a festive season, and that all of you will do your best work. Now let's get back to it."

The staff were clearing out of the kitchen when the back door opened, and with a rush of cold air, in came a snow-covered Martin McCracken.

"It's snowing," he said, beaming at me from under fogged glasses.

I smiled back and, without thinking, reached over and pulled the blue knit cap off his head, shaking it out on the floor.

"What time do you finish?" he asked.

I looked at the tray of eighty unwrapped fruitcakes. "Maybe five? Six?"

"Are you free this evening?" Martin looked almost giddy. It was adorable.

"I am."

"Pick you up at six thirty at your cabin." He took the cap out of my hands and tugged it back onto his head. "Wear something warm," he called over his shoulder as he slipped back out into the storm. I watched him walk across the snowy field and up into the orchard, his dark silhouette striking against the expanse of pure, glowing white. When I turned, both Al and Margaret were standing perfectly still, watching me. I made my way to the walk-in. After I made sure the door was closed tightly behind me, I hopped up and down as if I were back in a mosh pit, pumping my arms in the air, silently shouting, *Yes.*

I had yet to master the art of dressing for winter and looking cute, but knowing Martin, I decided it was safer to choose function over form that evening. Wool stockings under jeans under knee-high rubber boots. I layered a silk long-sleeved T-shirt and a green cashmere turtleneck sweater I had scored at Filene's Basement (wrestled out of the hands of a very tough old Russian woman). Martin knocked on my door as I was digging around in a basket for a second mitten.

"Come in," I called.

"Hey." Martin's cheeks were red from the cold, but he looked toasty in a down jacket and fleece hat. "Almost ready?"

I held up the missing mitten and said, "Yes! Found it." I pulled on the pair of mittens and zipped up my long wool coat. "Do you think I'll be warm enough?"

Martin looked me over from the pom-pom on top of my head to the tips of my rubber boots. My cheeks flushed. "I think so. Come on."

He stepped out in front, stopping at the bottom of the steps next to two enormous chestnut horses.

"Olivia, I'd like you to meet Rick and Ilsa."

Ilsa flicked her tail and huffed out a strong breath. Steam rose from her nostrils. Attached to the horses was a wooden sleigh, painted cherry red.

"After it snows, we have to take the sleigh out to pack down the trail, so it's easier to take the tourists out," Martin explained. He looked down at his feet. "I thought you might like to come with me." Martin kicked at the snow. One of the horses whinnied.

I ran my palms across Rick and Ilsa's long faces, feeling the strong bones beneath.

"How do we get on?" I asked.

Martin wove his fingers together and leaned down. "I'll give you a lift. Step up."

I held onto his shoulder and climbed onto the sleigh. Martin hoisted himself up and took the reins. The bench was small, and I found myself pressed against his side, his leg warm against my own. Martin reached behind us and tucked a plain red blanket over our laps.

"I didn't know you had horses," I said.

"These are Mark's. We used to keep our own. Dad did, that is. Fred and Ginger."

I laughed. "Did Dotty get to name them?"

"How could you tell? So you've probably guessed that Mark let her name these two as well." Martin tightened the reins. "Rick, Ilsa — walk."

The horses stepped forward. It was slow moving at first, but as they warmed up they picked up speed, and it felt like we were gliding on the snow's surface. As we reached the inn, Martin made a circular path around the building, then turned back toward the cabin. It had stopped snowing. A half-moon peeked out from behind the thin cover of clouds and the ground glowed an icy blue, as if it were lit from within. It was silent except for the breath of the horses, the soft swoosh of their hooves, and the icy chink of the bells that trimmed their harness. When we got to the edge of the woods, Martin pulled on the reins. He reached under the seat and handed me the red plaid thermos. "Here."

"Cider?" I asked, untwisting the top.

"Hot chocolate," he said. "After Thanksgiving, I didn't want you to think I . . . Well, I had a lot to drink."

"We all had a lot to drink in the barn," I said, pouring the steaming liquid into the red plastic lid.

"Yeah. I'm sorry that I —"

I handed him the cup. "Please don't apologize."

"But I broke down. All over you." Martin puckered his lips and blew to cool the cocoa.

"Not a big deal," I said.

"But —"

"Please don't say you're sorry. If you do, it sounds like something you regret, and I'm not sorry. I mean, I'm not glad you broke down, but . . ." I sipped at the cocoa, trying to gather my courage. "I'm glad you could talk to me. I want to be there for you." I busied myself with tightening the thermos cap.

"I'll say thanks, then," Martin said, studying the straps of leather in his gloved hand.

I leaned back, letting my shoulder press against his. The field stretched out in front of us, looking as if it had been covered in a smooth layer of marzipan. "It's so beautiful," I said, smiling up at him.

His face mirrored mine. "It's in moments like these that I can't imagine being anywhere else."

"I can't imagine having grown up here."

"You always lived in a city?"

"Grew up in Boston, and I've lived in Chicago, San Francisco, London, Paris, and

DC. I did go to school in New York State, but I never left the kitchen. How about you?"

"Seattle is the only place other than here." Martin picked up the reins and we started moving again.

"Do you miss it?" I asked.

"Sometimes. Mostly when I want to go eat somewhere other than the Miss Guthrie."

"I dreamed about pita stuffed with falafel and baba ghanoush the other night." I sighed. "Made by a Lebanese man with a little silver cart on a street corner. And those spicy pickles."

Martin laughed. "In Seattle there's a pho shop on every block. That's my dream meal right now — spicy beef broth and noodles."

"I'd love to see Seattle. Or better yet, Vietnam," I said.

"At least you've actually traveled some. I'm dying to go to Japan."

"Me too. And Alaska. A friend went and got to see grizzly bears salmon fishing." I pulled the blanket up higher. "Where else?"

"Anywhere. India. Scotland. Australia."

"Those all sound good."

"You were in Boston last, right? Why there?" Martin asked.

"The Emerson was a good gig — they

gave me full creative control. And there are little things I love about Boston. My old apartment was near Fenway Park, and on game days I could hear the crowd cheering from my living room. Good, strong coffee on every corner. The nut roasters on the Common. The ocean. Sunday afternoons at the bookstore."

"There are some great bookshops in Montreal."

"I've never been."

"Maybe after Christmas?"

"I'd like that," I said, my heart expanding at the idea of time after Christmas, of future plans. A perfect dome of stars capped the field. The horses picked up their pace as we reached level ground. When I closed my eyes, it felt as if we were flying.

We had reached the farmhouse. Martin guided the horses into a turn. "How about we head down to the tree shack, then make a loop back into the woods. Are you warm enough?"

I nodded. Our legs were touching underneath the blanket. Martin's body radiated heat. "It's funny. I think some of the things I loved the most about the city were country things — like going to the farmer's market. I always dreamed about living in the country."

Martin adjusted the reins in his hands. "Could you picture yourself staying here?"

"Yes," I said, surprising myself with the clarity in my voice. "Especially if I get to ride in a horse-drawn sleigh through the woods on the night of the first snowfall."

"You like it?" he asked shyly.

"It's a million times better than anything I could have dreamed up."

The horses trotted at a fast clip, their bells chiming cheerfully in the darkness. When we'd arrived back at my cabin, Martin jumped down, took my hands in his, and helped me off the sleigh.

"I know it's crazy at the inn," he said, "but if you can get away, the film society is showing a double feature next Saturday night at the grange hall — *Swing Time* and *Shall We Dance.* Henry and Dotty are planning on going."

"I'd love to come, if Margaret will let me." I laughed. "I always feel like a teenager around her. A bad one."

"She's always had that effect on me as well. Doesn't matter how old I get."

I pulled off my mittens and stuffed them into my coat pockets. I reached a hand out to Rick and Ilsa, stroking their smooth necks. "Thank you for the sleigh ride," I said.

Rick snorted.

"He says you're welcome." Martin placed a hand next to mine, stroking Rick's neck. "I'd better get the horses back to the barn," he said quietly.

I turned to face him. We were inches apart. I could smell the chocolate on his breath. "You know, I think you like it here more than you let on. Do you ever think about staying?"

He gave me a long look, his expression unreadable, and for a moment I thought he was going to lean in and kiss me. "Sometimes," he said, and climbed back onto the sleigh.

CHAPTER TWELVE

It took thirteen pounds of flour, two quarts of buttermilk, two pounds of butter, four pounds of molasses, forty eggs, ten pounds of confectioners' sugar, more than fifteen pounds of candy, and every second of my free time that week, but I managed to finish my gingerbread house before the children's cookie-decorating party, with an hour to spare. It was an exact replica of the Sugar Maple, including the barn and grounds. I fashioned the iron benches out of black licorice and cats to sleep upon them from softened Tootsie Rolls. Trees of upside-down ice cream cones covered in sliced green gumdrops lined the property. I even made a little sugarhouse, complete with fruit-leather curtains and a stone chimney built from jelly beans. A marzipan Salty stood alert on the porch.

The couches were pushed off to the side of the sitting room, and long tables were set up, covered in small dishes of sprinkles and candy, plates of naked gingerbread people, and piping bags of royal icing. I kept fingering the bags, worried the icing would set up too quickly in the cool room. When I asked to turn the heat up, I got a pained look from Alfred, who was already sweating in his red velvet suit, a child on his lap tugging at his all-too-real beard. Children poured through the door in waves, stuffing fistfuls of candy into their mouths and screaming for their mothers to take them over to see Santa. I directed the exhausted-looking parents to Margaret, who was pouring wine, and joined the children at one of the tables, demonstrating how Red Vines make the best lips while Froot Loops create a convincing head of curly hair. When all the gingerbread people were modestly dressed and I was sticky from head to toe, I went over to join Margaret at the back of the room.

"This is a fun party," I said, picking up a piece of Manchego and topping it with a slice of quince paste. Some of the children were putting on a play with their gingerbread people. Alfred still had a line of children waiting to see him. A group was gathered around Sarah, who sat on one of the couches reading Christmas stories.

"It is," Margaret said. "It's nice to have

the house filled with young people."

"Did you not want to have children?" I asked.

"I didn't marry until I was forty."

"I'm sorry," I said, although I wasn't sure if I was sorry that she hadn't gotten to have children or that I had asked the question. Probably both.

"Wasn't in God's plan." Margaret took a sip of tea. "How about you, Miss Rawlings? Do you want children, or is that giant mutt of yours enough responsibility?"

"I don't know, honestly. I haven't really given it much thought."

"Well, you'd better. You're no spring chicken. You kids think you have all the time in the world, but I'll tell you, it goes by quickly."

"There's just the pesky issue of not having a husband."

Margaret raised her eyebrows. "Doesn't stop most people. What about Alfred?" She waved her hand toward Santa. A child was crawling up his lap and trying to pull off his hat.

"What about him?"

"He's good with children, patient. He has steady employment. I've always found him to be a nice man. Good-natured."

"Margaret."

"They do say the sperm count is low among men who have worked a long time in kitchens." She made a circular gesture below her waist. "The heat."

"Margaret! Stop!" I said, laughing. "I don't want to spend any time today thinking about Alfred's scrotum. He is like an uncle to me."

"He likes you."

"And I like him. As a friend. A good friend." I reached behind my back to untie my apron. "Sarah said she would finish the cleanup. Do you mind if I take off? I'm going to the movies with Martin and the Mc-Crackens, and I want to wash this sticky layer off of me first."

Margaret's eyebrows knit together. "Martin called earlier. He said to tell you that they couldn't make it."

"When did he call?" The lack of cell phone service was beginning to be a problem.

"This afternoon."

"Why didn't you tell me sooner?" I mashed my apron up into a tight ball.

Margaret put down her teacup. "Because I was busy, Miss Rawlings, and so were you."

"Did he say why?" I asked, my voice steady.

"No." Margaret hesitated. "But I spoke to

278

Dotty earlier, and she said Henry was having a bad day. Dr. Doyle was going to drop by this evening."

"Is he okay?"

"I didn't press." Margaret shook her head once. "You shouldn't either."

"It's not pressing if they're your friends."

"The McCrackens," Margaret said, her voice clipped, "have been my best friends for more than sixty years. I think I'll be the judge of what is appropriate."

"They're my friends too. I'm not going to leave them alone because it would be more convenient for you if I were less involved in your life." I tossed the apron onto the dirty cookie table. "And I'd appreciate it if you would give me my messages in a more timely fashion, since this town doesn't have any cell service and you won't let me get my own line in the sugarhouse." And with that I pushed my way into the kitchen.

I thought a long walk with Salty would calm me down, but after he was walked, fed, and sleeping by the woodstove, I still found myself pacing around the cabin. After several failed attempts at reading and watching TV, I put my coat back on and grabbed my car keys. I drove slowly down the road, thinking I would just knock on their door, but the closer I got to the McCracken farm the more right Margaret's words felt. When I reached the cell phone hot spot, I pulled over behind a pickup truck and saw that Martin had left a voice mail. He apologized for canceling at the last minute. I pulled back onto the road and kept driving, not knowing where I was headed until I saw the blue and yellow neon glow of the Black Bear Tavern's sign through the trees.

The tavern was quiet. I plopped down on one of the free stools.

"Bourbon, straight up," I said as I propped my elbows on the bar. The logger sitting next to me pushed a bowl of peanuts in my direction.

"Cheers," I said, holding up my glass. We clinked drinks.

I felt a slap on my back. Tom was standing behind me, white shirt tucked in and string tie clasped at the neck. "Glad to see you here, Liv. Want to sit in?"

"The Beagles are playing tonight?"

"You didn't know? I thought that was why you were here." Tom sounded hurt, but his eyes were crinkled and sparkling.

"Just a quick drink."

"Well, if you change your mind, we'd love to have you. No Martin tonight?"

"No, not tonight."

I was sipping my second bourbon when a man leaned on the barstool next to me. "Didn't think I'd see you in here," he said. I turned to face the familiar flannelled bulk of Frank Fraser.

I held my hand up. "I get it. I'm not from here. I don't belong here. Sorry to crash your bar, but it's not like there are a lot of options."

"What?"

"Not tonight, okay? I just want to have a drink in peace."

"I just meant I didn't think she would let you out of the kitchen this time of year. At least that's how it was when Bonnie worked there. I hardly saw her all Christmas season. Sucked." Frank held two fingers up to the bartender, who opened two Rolling Rocks and placed them on the bar.

"Just part of the glamorous world of baking."

Tom stepped up to the microphone and tapped it with his index finger. "Evening, everyone. Since I know everybody in the room, I don't think I need to mention that we're the Beagles. Let's do it, boys." And with a tap of his foot and the strum of a banjo chord the band broke into "Hotel California," singing in a high, lonesome harmony.

I groaned. Frank slid off the barstool, taking his beers with him.

Cold air hit the back of my neck when the bar door opened. I felt a hand on my shoulder. Martin slid onto the stool next to me and ordered a whiskey.

"Hey."

"Hey," I replied, surprised but pleased.

We drank as we watched Frank and Bonnie press against each other on the dance floor. Frank's hand slipped into the back pocket of Bonnie's jeans. Her arms were wrapped around his neck and her eyes were closed.

Martin leaned over so his lips brushed my hair. "Do you want to get out of here?"

My heart sped up. "Sure."

We drove down the highway in silence for half an hour, but I didn't mind. The bourbon I had drunk at the bar had left my body feeling loose — the tension of my argument with Margaret and the long hours spent in the kitchen were finally lifting. I was blanketed by a feeling of calm that I hadn't felt since the sleigh ride.

A bright yellow glow lit up the fog in the distance. "Almost there," said Martin. He took the next exit, and we pulled into the familiar parking lot of the F&G truck stop.

"How did you know?" I asked. "This is

my favorite place in the world."

"You've been here?"

"It was on my dad's truck route. He'd take me with him every so often."

Martin smiled. "I used to come here all the time once I got my driver's license. It's the only place open past nine that isn't a bar."

We weaved our way through the tractor-trailers and into the brightly lit lobby. The revolving display was jam-packed with pies. The hostess sat us in a corner booth.

A waitress came over with a pot of coffee and filled our cups without asking. "Anything else?"

"Black bottom," I replied.

"Pumpkin for me," said Martin, handing her the menu. He leaned back in the booth. In the bright yellow light of the diner I could see that his eyes were bloodshot. He looked exhausted. "I'm sorry I had to cancel tonight."

"When Margaret gave me the message, she mentioned that Henry wasn't feeling well." I paused. "Is he okay?"

Martin paused. "The doctor suggested it was time to bring in hospice."

My heart clenched. "What does that mean, exactly?"

"More help, mostly. A visiting nurse."

Martin cleared his throat. "The focus will change to just keeping him comfortable."

I reached over and took his free hand in mine.

The waitress wordlessly placed the slices on the table.

"I'm glad I found you."

I wondered if he meant tonight, or in general. I unwrapped the paper loop that held my fork and knife together.

Martin scraped off the whipped cream with his fork. "My brothers were over with their wives and some of the nephews and the doctor. I needed a break."

I tried to spoon a bite of custard that was only vanilla, saving the chocolate part for last. "Too many people?"

"My family can be a little overwhelming at times." Martin ran his fingers through his hair, his gaze focused on something behind me. "I never thought I would feel that way about them."

"What do you mean?"

"When I was a kid, I was really close to my brothers. Now they're just pissed off that I've stayed away for so long." Martin alternated the pink and blue artificial sweetener packets in their plastic holder. "I just wanted to know who I was when I wasn't Mark and Ethan's little brother, or my mom's baby, or my dad's prodigy. I thought I'd join a band, play music, tour some, get to see a little of the world, then come home."

"Why have you stayed in Seattle so long, then?" I asked. No one had ever had expectations of me. I wondered whether it would feel like pressure or a comfort.

"You know how it is — one thing leads to another. Time passes and you have your bandmates and your job, your apartment with the great little coffee shop downstairs and the cool dive bar right around the corner. Good friends. Suddenly your life is someplace else. The funny thing is that when I'm there, I feel like a kid from Vermont, and when I'm here, I feel, or I felt . . ."

I licked the last bit of chocolate custard off my fork. "I've never had any of those things."

"Really?"

"Well — favorite coffee shop, yes. But I've never stayed in one place long enough for the rest. And I work all the time. The kitchen has always been my world."

Martin cleared his throat. "Don't you think it's time to settle down somewhere, young lady?" he said in his best Henry voice.

"Oh my God," I laughed, "you sound just

285

like him." I peeled off the lids of three creamers and dumped them into my coffee cup. "I do, actually. Think about settling down," I said. "But I'll tell you what I told your dad — I think that decision is going to be Margaret Hurley's."

"What did you do now?"

"I'm pretty sure it's somehow your fault," I said, pointing my empty fork at him. "I don't think she's a fan of our friendship."

Martin lined up the ketchup bottle with the salt and pepper shakers. "She means well."

"So do I." I brought my empty coffee cup to my lips and pretended to drink, just to give my face something to do. "What do you think?"

"About Margaret?" Martin asked.

"About our friendship."

"You all set here? Do you need anything else?" asked the waitress with the world's worst timing. If I hadn't worked in food service, I would have stiffed her the tip.

"What kind of pie do your folks like?" I asked Martin. "We should bring them some."

"Two pieces of orange chiffon, to go," he said to the waitress. He stood, reaching into his back pocket for his wallet. "I'll go settle up."

We listened to an old country music station all the way back to Guthrie. I dozed for a while, until I was startled awake by the sensation of the tires crunching on gravel. Martin pulled into the space next to mine in the Black Bear Tavern parking lot.

"What time is it?" I asked.

"Nearly midnight."

"I've been working at least twelve-hour days all week," I said, stifling a yawn. "I never feel it until I slow down."

"Thanks for staying out with me."

"I'm glad you found me," I said. I meant it in all the ways.

"My dad was asking for you." Martin turned to face me and leaned his head back against the seat. "He wanted me to apologize for his missing the movie." Martin closed his eyes for a long moment. "And . . . he asked me to make sure you would come see him this week. With the dulcimer."

I brushed at my eyes with the back of my sleeve. "Of course. I'll come by as soon as I can get away. Should I call first?"

"Just come by anytime. Mom would love the company if Dad's resting."

"When will you be there?" I asked, tugging at the drawstring at the bottom of my fleece jacket.

"If I'm not there, I'm selling trees. You

could come by and see the lights."

"I will."

Martin caught my left hand in his before I made my escape. "Olivia . . ."

I turned back to face him, holding my breath.

"You asked me what I thought about our friendship."

I nodded, wide-eyed.

"It makes me feel like I'm home."

It was as if he had answered a question I hadn't known I was asking. Speechless, I slipped out of the truck, closing the door quietly behind me.

The crush of holiday parties at the Sugar Maple kept me tied to my workbench from dawn until late into the evenings. I practiced deep breathing each morning while making my daily prep list, each day seeming more impossible than the last. We were just as busy as I had been at the Emerson, but at least there I'd had a staff. My arms ached from whisking giant vats of egg yolks for the chestnut buttercream to fill my bûche de Noël, and I had a permanent indentation of a gingerbread man pressed into my left palm from cutting out cookies. Alfred managed to keep his good humor despite his moonlighting as Santa on the weekends, and his relentless teasing made even the most stressful moments feel like we were the hosts of a never-ending party.

One afternoon in the middle of December, Margaret found me lying on my back on the storeroom floor with frozen bags of peas pressed to my forearms.

"What on earth are you doing, Miss Rawlings?"

"Just resting," I answered, twisting my hips from side to side.

"Well, why don't you do that in the cabin, in private?"

"I'm helping with the hors d'oeuvres party." Things between Margaret and me had remained chilly since the cookie-decorating party.

"Sarah can help Alfred tray everything up. Take the night off. I need you fresh for the hospital-board dinner at the end of the week."

I pressed myself up. Standing, I eyed her carefully. "Are you going to use this against me at a later date?"

"Stay if you don't need the break," she said.

"I'm out of here," I called as I struggled to untie my apron strings while walking back to the kitchen.

"Don't forget about the brunch tomorrow

morning. And what about these peas?"

I kept walking before she changed her mind.

By four o'clock I was standing on the Mc-Crackens' front porch, my hair freshly dyed Manic Panic Atomic Turquoise, holding a bowl of homemade caramel corn in one hand and the dulcimer in the other. Dotty answered the door.

"You shouldn't be out in this cold with wet hair," she scolded, ushering me into the foyer and closing the door. "Henry is reading in the sitting room. Go on in."

I knocked lightly on the door before entering, dulcimer first. Henry was dozing, his head back, lips slightly parted. I was grateful he was asleep so I had a moment to compose myself. Henry had looked thin at Thanksgiving. Today he looked almost skeletal, his translucent skin pulled tight across the points of his cheekbones. I blinked back tears and cleared my throat.

"Hey, Henry," I said softly as I clicked open the latches of the dulcimer case.

Henry's head snapped forward. He wiped at the corner of his mouth with a white handkerchief. "I was wondering when you were going to get around to seeing me."

I laughed and bent down to kiss his cheek.

"I was wondering that myself. I didn't think Margaret was ever going to let me out of the kitchen."

"She's a slave driver, that one. Always was. Drove her husband crazy with an endless to-do list." Henry patted the spot next to him on the couch. I sat down. "Now tell me, have you had any time to practice?"

"None at all."

"Well, let's hear, anyway." Henry settled back into the cushions and closed his eyes.

I brushed the pick across the strings mindlessly a few times before I settled on a tune. I played it three times. When I stopped, he opened his eyes and smiled.

" 'Blackberry Buckle'?"

I nodded.

"I haven't heard that one in a long while. We should make a playlist just of songs about sweets."

"Speaking of which" — I grabbed my messenger bag from the floor — "I made you some caramel corn, and I brought over these." From my bag I pulled out two DVDs: *Swing Time* and *Shall We Dance.* "I thought we could watch them here since we couldn't make it the other night."

Henry nodded once, smiling. "We can watch one after supper. You're staying. Now play me something else."

I placed the dulcimer back on my lap, picked up the noter, and began the first phrase of "Kitchen Girl."

Henry took hold of the end of the dulcimer and slid it onto his lap. "You can do a nice slide there in the second part. Blend the notes together." He demonstrated. "Now you try it."

I played the tune from the beginning, adding the slide technique where it worked. I sneaked a look out of the corner of my eye. Henry looked tired, his eyes dark and hollow. He caught me looking and smiled.

"This is a good tune to play with the fiddle. If I weren't so blasted tired, I'd join you. You'll have to teach it to Marty. I'm not sure if he knows this one." Henry placed his hand on my forearm. I stopped playing. "Keep going," he said. I strummed the strings with the pick.

"You, know, Olivia," Henry said softly, "Martin is a good man."

"I know," I said, blushing. "Just like his father."

"Humph. Too much like his father, if you ask me. Now stop your sweet talk and listen." Henry's grip tightened. "Marty is a good man, but like me he's stubborn, and slow to make changes. You'll have to be patient with him."

I looked over at Henry, willing him to say more, but I focused on my fingers working the strings.

"Patient how?" I asked as I practiced his slide technique.

"Like this." Henry covered my hand with his again and slid over the frets, again and again until I got the feel of it. Despite Henry's frail appearance, his grip was strong. "Mark and Ethan too. I've been lucky."

I slid the dowel across the frets. Henry bowed his head in approval.

"You don't have children of your own yet. But when you do, you'll see that all you want is for them to be happy."

I nodded, feeling confused.

"We do our best as parents while we can. But after we're gone, we expect that our children will go on. That they'll keep becoming who we raised them to be."

Henry paused and squeezed my arm. I stared hard at the dulcimer strings, fighting the pressure that was building in my chest.

"I have regrets. I imagine all fathers do. I wish I could live to see Marty settled with a family of his own. But I'm proud of that boy. I raised a good man. I just want you to know you can count on him."

I turned to face him. Henry looked

straight at me, his blue eyes bright against his pale skin. "You'll remember that, right?"

"Sure," I said, putting the dulcimer on the table and tucking the pick into the strings. "He can count on me too," I said quietly.

"I know he can." Henry tucked the dulcimer into its case. "Now, I want you to take good care of this old girl."

"Henry, I couldn't." My heart raced. This sounded too much like good-bye.

"An instrument needs to be played." He snapped the metal clasps shut.

"But you made it for Dotty. You should keep it in the family," I said.

Henry took my hands in his and leaned toward me. "That's what I'm doing."

The door to the sitting room opened and Martin appeared in the doorway, his cheeks red from an afternoon outside. "Hey, Dad." Martin's smile widened when he saw me. "Hey," he said, shoving his hands in his pockets. "Dad, Mom said dinner is ready. Do you want to eat in here?"

Henry pressed into the couch and held himself straight. "No, son. Livvy brought some movies to watch. Why don't we get settled into the living room?"

"I'm just going to run up and change," Martin said as he backed out of the room.

I stood up, brushing my wool skirt down.

"I'll go see if Dotty needs any help."

In the living room Henry settled into an old recliner. Martin looked fresh in a white Irish fisherman's sweater and a pair of jeans. Taking center stage by the bay windows was the most magnificent Christmas tree I had ever seen. Twelve feet tall, the white pine was covered trunk to tip with tiny colored lights, tinsel, garland, and hundreds of ornaments, many of them homemade, which looked to be from at least ten different decades. I stood in front of the tree in awe, wanting to know the story behind every treasure.

"It's a beauty, isn't it?" Henry said.

"It's dazzling."

"We look forward to it every year."

"I can see why. It's like a museum."

Henry smiled. "More like a scrapbook. There are hundreds of memories on those branches."

I sat down next to Martin on the couch. Dotty came in with a basketful of bread and sat on the other side of me. When we were finished eating, I cleared the bowls while Martin set up the movie and Dotty brought out the caramel corn. By the time the RKO signal stopped beeping, Henry was asleep, his breath ragged.

"Should we turn it off?" I asked Dotty.

"No, dear, he'll sleep through it. It's good for him to rest."

Dotty tucked a yellow wool blanket over my lap as Fred Astaire borrowed a dog to have an excuse to walk near Ginger Rogers. I curled up under the blanket and let myself drift.

When I woke up, the room was dim, lit only by the lights of the Christmas tree. Henry and Dotty were gone. And I was lying with my cheek nestled on the chest of Martin McCracken, my arm across his stomach. Martin's arm was around my waist. He was leaning against the edge of the couch, deeply asleep. My cheek felt scratchy against his wool sweater and I realized that I had drooled on him. Horrified, I slid carefully from under Martin's arm and repositioned the blanket to cover him. I tiptoed into the hallway to find my coat and boots. When I was bundled up, I crept back in to peek at Martin one more time.

He looked boyish. His hair was mussed, and his lips were parted slightly. I could picture waking up to this face every day. I leaned over, pressed my lips lightly to his temple, and quietly left the room.

The week before Christmas, when the last dollop of hard sauce had been placed on the final dish of figgy pudding, Alfred let out a loud whoop and wrapped his arms around me, spinning me around the kitchen.

"Put me down," I laughed, batting at his biceps.

Sarah walked into the kitchen with a tray of four champagne glasses, followed by Margaret carrying a bottle of chilled prosecco. Alfred grabbed the bottle and twisted off the cork with a satisfying pop. He poured the wine carelessly into the glasses, letting it bubble over the rims.

"I wanted to say thank you," Margaret said. "You all did an excellent job. We had our best holiday season on record."

"Hear, hear," said Alfred.

"The guests were all so happy," said Sarah. "Especially with the desserts, Livvy."

I raised my glass to the group. "This has been the happiest Christmas season I can remember," I gushed. "Thanks for letting me be a part of it." I took a long sip from my glass, too shy to look at their faces.

"Well," Margaret said, setting her glass down. She reached into the inside pocket of her blazer and retrieved three white envelopes. "I hope this will help with your Christmas shopping, now that you have time to do some." She handed us each an envelope.

I hadn't expected a bonus from such a small business. I reached over and wrapped my arms around Margaret. For the first Christmas in years, I had many presents I actually wanted to buy. "Thanks so much," I said, rocking her back in forth in a tight embrace. Alfred and Sarah looked on, shocked and amused.

Margaret patted at my arms. "That's enough of that, now."

"What do you all do for Christmas, anyway?" I asked. After serving Christmas lunch at the Emerson, I had always spent the day at the movies in Chinatown. You'd be surprised how packed theaters get on Christmas Day.

"My family is just across the border in Littleton," said Sarah.

Alfred scratched his beard. "I'm off to go skiing with a bunch of buddies. You headed down to Boston, Liv?"

"God, no. I hadn't actually thought of it. I'll probably end up —"

"You're expected at the McCrackens'," Margaret interrupted. She leaned toward me. "I saw Dotty embroider your name on a stocking." My heart swelled.

"Well, I'm off to bed," Margaret said firmly. "I'm not planning to be in until after breakfast. Enjoy your evening." Margaret patted Alfred on the shoulder as she walked out of the kitchen.

Alfred pulled another bottle of prosecco out of his reach-in refrigerator. "Another drink?"

I took off my chef's coat and pulled on the old purple cashmere sweater I kept under my station. "Not me. I'm dying to curl up under the covers and drift off *not* making a prep list in my head."

Sarah laughed. "I had nightmares about missing tablecloths all month. I'll stay for one more."

Alfred got to work on the cork. I kissed them each on the cheek and said good night.

It had snowed every third night since Martin had taken me on the sleigh ride. The woods between the inn and the sugarhouse were knee deep in snow, but the sleigh had packed down a path to travel on. I loved to walk the path in the mornings with Salty, who bounded through the fresh snow face-first, leaping like a deer through the high banks.

The moon was hidden behind a thick blanket of clouds, and as I approached the cabin, a layer of tiny flakes covered my shoulders. The snowdrifts that hugged my cabin were bathed in an unusually rosy glow. Salty came to meet me as I opened the door, wagging his tail in greeting. The cabin was warm, a fire in the woodstove blazing. "Oh my God," I gasped. Standing tall and full in the corner of the cabin was a giant tree, its outstretched branches draped with chunky colored lights, each bulb as big as an egg and glimmering softly. The tree shook from side to side as Martin emerged from underneath and brushed his hair out of his eyes.

"The season's winding down, and we had a good number of trees left. It seemed a shame that you didn't have one," he explained, looking at his boots. He glanced over at my bed. "You can see it from anywhere in the cabin," he offered.

"You can," I said, looking around the tiny space, "even the bathtub."

"I didn't know what to do for ornaments." He shrugged, looking lost. "Do you like it?"

"It's perfect. I love it," I said, and without thinking I kissed him.

It was a light kiss. Just a soft brush of my lips against his.

My first thought was *His lips are chapped.*

Then I looked up at his face. He looked wide-eyed and nervous, like an owl.

His back went rigid. My heart sank. My

hands slid down his arms and back to my sides.

"Olivia," he breathed quietly, "We should . . ."

"I'm so sorry," I said, feeling lost. "I shouldn't have."

Martin took a step forward, closing the gap between us. I raised my gaze, daring to look into his eyes. They still held a nervous spark, but his expression had softened. He leaned forward and pressed his forehead into mine. I closed my eyes and breathed him in. He smelled green and new, like the tender grass that sprouts on a muddy riverbank in earliest spring. His hands traveled to my shoulders, and I felt his lips press against my temple. His rough cheek glided against my own, and his lips brushed the tender spot in front of my ear, his nose grazing the delicate outer shell. Then his mouth found mine. A tiny sigh escaped from the back of my throat as his lips moved against mine. He moved slowly, each kiss deliberate. I wrapped my arms around his waist. I could feel the muscles in his back work as he wove his fingers into my hair. One hand moved down to my shoulder blade as his tongue parted my lips. He tasted like cinnamon Tic Tacs and tobacco. I rose up onto my tiptoes, wanting him closer. Martin made a sound like a harmonium and moved his hand down to my lower back, pressing us together.

Someone knocked on the cabin door. Martin drew back and nestled his face into the crook of my neck. I could feel heat radiating from his cheek. I pressed my face to his chest, listening to his heart pound a steady, quick beat.

"One minute," I called.

I felt the cold air on my neck before I heard the door knock against a bookcase. Martin took a quick step away from me, as if we were teenagers caught necking on the couch. Margaret stood in the doorway and looked from me to Martin.

"It's your father."

Martin's face lost all color. He walked past me and began tossing pillows off my couch, looking for his jacket.

"What happened?" he asked, his voice panicked.

"They took him to the hospital. Your mother is with him." Margaret picked Martin's gloves up off the kitchen table. "I have the car running at the bottom of the hill. I'll drive."

I stood in the corner by the Christmas tree, frozen.

"Get your coat, Olivia," Margaret said quietly as Martin pushed past her. "Now."

CHAPTER THIRTEEN

Margaret and I sat in the waiting room outside of the ICU. It had been hours since Martin had disappeared behind the swinging doors through which only immediate family were allowed to pass. I sat feeling helpless as I watched Martin's brothers' wives breeze past us.

"What did Dr. Doyle say, again?" I asked Margaret, who was sitting quietly, her back straight.

"The home-visit nurse couldn't control his pain," she said patiently for the fourth time. "So they brought him in to see if there was anything they could do for him here."

"Have you talked to Dotty?"

"Not since she was trying to track down Martin."

I tossed the catalog I was paging through onto the coffee table and paced around the small room. Memories of sitting in the ER waiting for news of my father flooded me.

"It's driving me crazy not to know what's going on."

"Sit down, Olivia."

I sat, digging my fingernails into my palms.

Margaret reached over and took one of my hands in hers. "When the pain gets to be this hard to manage . . . It might not be long now."

Fat tears spilled from my eyes.

Margaret squeezed my fingers. "You know," she said, her voice sounding tight, "I went on a date or two with Henry before he and Dotty fell for each other."

I looked over at her. She had a sweet smile on her face.

"He was so handsome. He used to play at all the dances, and Dotty and I would go to watch the band. She had a crush on the guitarist. Wouldn't give Henry the time of day. So he asked me out — and when I said yes, he asked if I had a friend who would want to double-date. Said his parents wouldn't let him step out alone with a girl, which was probably true — things were different back then. But I could tell from the moment we sat down at the diner that he only had eyes for her."

"Were you mad?"

"Oh, Lord, no. He was never my type. Too full of mischief. And someone had already captured my heart."

"Your husband?"

"Dotty and Henry were so sweet together." Margaret took a deep breath. "I've been lucky to have such good friends." She looked over at me. "I know you've grown very fond of Martin. You should —"

Dr. Doyle pushed his way through the swinging doors and headed down the corridor.

"Jonathan!" I called, hopping up to chase him. "How is he?" I asked when I reached him.

"Livvy, you know I can't —"

"Jonathan Doyle, you've known me long enough to know how close I am to the McCrackens," Margaret said sternly, crossing her arms.

"Sit down," Jonathan sighed, flipping his white coat out of the way. "Henry's in a coma. The medication put him under." He reached out and took one of Margaret's hands. "I'd start preparing."

Margaret stilled. "We should get going."

"No," I said. "Why?"

"I appreciate it, Jonathan. Have one of the nurses call me if anything changes." Margaret folded her coat over her arm. "Come on, dear. Let's get home."

■ ■ ■ ■

After a long, silent drive, Margaret pulled into the back parking lot behind the inn. She turned off the ignition and sat back in her seat. I stared into what I knew was the orchard as it lay hidden in darkness.

"He's not going to come out of the coma. It's the pain medication. It will keep him under as his body slows down. We should get a good night's sleep. It could be days. And we need to get things ready for the funeral." I wondered if she was saying this more for herself than for me, to try to make it feel a little more real. "I know tomorrow is supposed to be a day off, but could you come to the kitchen around nine? We can go over things then."

I nodded, feeling the tide of grief rising inside me.

"Do you want to stay at the inn tonight?" she asked, placing her hand gently on my shoulder.

I wanted to say yes, to be safe in the inn — warm and comforted by the sound of Margaret's squeaky rocking chair and the scent of vanilla that always dominated the kitchen. But I thought of Martin. He wouldn't be able to find me if I wasn't in the cabin. "No, but thank you."

"I'll come if there is any news."

I didn't start crying until I saw the honey-eyed glow of the Christmas lights through the trees. Though it was cold when I came in, I flushed at the memory of my last moments there with Martin. Even the scent of the cabin reminded me of him: tree sap and cinnamon. Sitting down on the floor near the tree, I hugged Salty's soft body to mine and let my tears soak into his thick ruff.

Three long days had passed. Dotty called Margaret from the hospital every morning and again at suppertime. I wanted to go to the hospital, but Margaret said that with the extended McCracken family gathering there we would only be in the way. I spent the time baking restlessly. The inn was officially closed until New Year's Eve, so I had the kitchen to myself. I baked coffee cakes and tea rings, muffins, scones, and shortbread. I made a special batch of hermits, because Dotty loved molasses. I worked my worry into baguette dough. Margaret came and worked beside me most afternoons, baking casseroles, cutting them into small portions, and freezing them in tiny aluminum tins. Every time I looked at one of those containers I could only think about how alone Dotty would be without Henry.

I spent the evenings wrapped up in an afghan, trying to read, but I couldn't focus on anything more demanding than travel magazines. I went to bed early, snuggled up with Salty, and gazed at the Christmas lights, thinking about Martin — and sometimes, guiltily, about his kiss. But then my thoughts would turn to Henry and the fact that I would never see him again, and I would be lost in grief. I couldn't help but think back to my own father and the days that followed his death. The empty house after the funeral. Sitting in the living room, hugging one of his quilted flannel work shirts. How even now, after so many years, I still felt like something was missing. I didn't want Martin to have to know that the pain never goes away, that it just becomes a part of who you are.

A blizzard was forecast for Thursday, and Margaret sent me home early, telling me she didn't want to have to worry about my getting blinded by the snow and lost in the woods. I walked to the cabin reluctantly, not wanting to spend another evening at the cabin alone, hoping that Martin would come by. But the sky was dim, the smoke from the chimneys at the inn white against the dark clouds, and I knew that even if I had wanted to go out, most of the town would be closing early.

The cabin was dark except for the blue glow of the television when I was awakened by the sound of sharp knocking. I had no idea what time it was. I didn't see anyone when I opened the door. Then I peeked out onto the porch. Martin was standing there, looking out into the orchard, snow clumped in his hair and on his shoulders, his fist wrapped tightly around the handle of his fiddle case.

He turned to face me. His eyes were wide, his mouth slightly open. He wasn't wearing a coat.

"Hey," I said.

Martin held up the fiddle. "I thought you would play with me. Mark and Ethan wouldn't. They said . . ."

"Of course. Come in."

His glasses fogged in the warmth. He placed the case on the coffee table and began to unhitch the latches.

"Martin, you're soaked through. How long have you been outside?"

"I don't know." He began to tighten the horsehair of the bow. His hands were shaking.

"Let's get you warmed up first." I turned

toward the woodstove. It had cooled down as I slept. I grabbed a couple of towels off a shelf and handed them to him. "Take off those wet shoes. I'll get the fire going."

Martin ignored my instructions and drew out a long, slow note on the fiddle, then a double stop, two strings droning together. From his spot by Martin's feet, Salty lifted his snout into the air and let out a low, lonesome howl. I sat down on the floor, biting at the inside of my cheek, and listened to Martin play Henry's tune for Dotty. My stomach hollowed, then filled with wave after wave of grief. When the bow hit the ground, I turned to look up at Martin. He was staring at it as if he had never seen it before, still holding the fiddle pressed into the soft skin below his collarbone. His face crumpled, his open hand trembling. I moved toward him. I took the fiddle out of his hand and gently placed it back in its case. Then I took his hands in mine. They were flaming red and felt like ice.

"It's okay," I said quietly, rubbing his left hand between my palms. "We just need to get you warmed up." I led him to the couch. He sat, his face held so carefully that I thought if I moved him the wrong way he would break. I bent down, carefully untied his laces, and slipped off his sneakers and socks one by one. I held his feet in my hands, drying them with a towel and holding them between my cupped palms. I stood and took off his glasses and rubbed the towel gently over his hair. "You need to take your shirt off, okay? Then we can sit by the fire." Martin sat motionless. I reached behind him and slid the shirt, wet and heavy, up his back and over his shoulders. I let it fall to the ground in a soggy heap. I wrapped the afghan around his back and then took his hand in mine.

He looked so young, and so vulnerable. *His dad is gone.* My mind flooded with images of my own father's passing — the principal standing in the doorway of my classroom. Being led down the hospital hallway by a nun. Not knowing what to say when she asked me about last rites. I tentatively reached up to smooth the hair out of Martin's eyes. My hands lingered on his cheeks. Martin stepped closer and pulled me to him, his coarse chest hair rough against my cheek. He pressed his lips onto my crown. "Olivia," he choked.

I pulled back a fraction, confused, waiting.

His hands twisted in my hair, and he crushed his lips to mine, his tongue searching. My face flushed from the heat of the fire, his mouth on mine, and the feel of his naked chest beneath my palms. I felt his jagged breath in my ear as one hand fumbled with the zipper of my fleece. My mind raced. I had dreamed about this moment for weeks, but it had never been like this. I could feel Martin's despair in this kiss.

But any thoughts of Henry were pushed away as Martin slid the jacket off my shoulders, revealing the thin white camisole underneath. He locked his lips on mine as his hands worked up my back under my shirt. They were still cold. He stroked my shoulder blades and released me just long enough to pull the tank over my head. He held me tightly against him. The sensation of our bare skin pressed together and the need to be closer pushed past the overwhelming feeling of loss. We moved toward the bed. When we were at the foot of the futon, he slipped his hand into the waistband of my pants, his fingers questioning. I reached for the zipper of his brown corduroys in answer, easing them over his narrow hips. On the bed, our bodies tangled. Urgently, we explored each other with hands and lips. Martin hesitated only when he rolled on top of me, pressing his hips, questioning. I reached between us and guided him in.

"Livvy," he breathed into my ear. He nuzzled my hair before bringing his lips back to mine. We stayed like that, joined and kissing. Martin began to move, slowly at first, then pushing deeper and deeper inside me as if he couldn't get close enough. I wrapped my legs around his hips, and as his pace quickened, I felt myself stirring, slick. Martin tilted his hips, and as if he had turned the burner to high, it pushed me over the edge. Martin followed a moment later, and a sob choked out from someplace deep within him. He collapsed, his full weight on me, buried his face in my neck, and wept. I pulled the blankets over us, stroking his hair, finally letting my own tears stream down my cheeks.

I woke up once in the middle of the night. Martin was wrapped tightly around me, legs tangled with mine, one hand cupped around my breast, his breath warm and heavy on my neck.

When the sun beamed through the cabin window, Salty was in bed beside me. The woodstove was blazing, and Martin was gone.

The kettle had just whistled when I heard a knock at my door. Margaret stood on the porch. She looked exhausted, her eyelids heavy.

"Henry," she said.

I nodded.

"Did Martin tell you?" She didn't look surprised.

"Do you want to come in for some tea?" I asked, tilting my head toward the kitchen table.

Margaret surprised me by coming in. Dressed in last night's yoga pants and fleece, I kicked my camisole under the futon.

"Don't bother." Margaret sat down at the kitchen table, leaving her coat on. I threw another log onto the fire. "You did a nice job with the cabin. Brian never would have recognized it."

"I remember you told me he used to hang out here — wood carving?"

"It's good for a man to have a hobby. Keeps him out of your hair."

My laughter somehow brought back the tears, and I quickly brushed them away.

Margaret dug into her handbag and fished out a tissue. "It's a sad day."

"When did you lose Brian?"

"It's been three years."

"Is that why you want to sell this place? Does it remind you too much of him?"

"You can never be reminded too much of someone you love." Margaret traced her pearl necklace with her fingertips. "No, I've been thinking of selling because I'm ready to retire. But now that Henry has passed — I'm glad I went through it before Dotty did. I'll know what she needs."

I poured the tea into pretty china teacups, one of the few things I'd kept from my grandmother's house.

"Milk?" I offered.

"No, thanks." Margaret took a sip as I spooned sugar into my cup.

"Sorry I don't have anything else to offer. I usually eat in the kitchen."

"I barged in on you at six thirty in the morning. I wasn't expecting breakfast."

"Is it that early?" I wondered what time Martin had left.

"The wake has to be tonight so they can hold the funeral tomorrow — otherwise it will have to wait until after Christmas because the church won't have a burial during the holidays. Dotty didn't want to put the family through that."

"Of course not. Will people have time to get here?"

"Most of the folks Henry knew are here in Guthrie. And the family is already here for Christmas." Margaret's eyes glistened.

"You know that man arranged to have his grave dug before the first frost? Can you imagine that? He was always so damn practical." Margaret sat up in her seat and put her hands on her lap. "I'm headed over to the McCrackens' shortly. I was hoping you could box up the food for after the wake. I can have one of the boys come pick it up."

"Sure, anything." I stirred the tea with a spoon, even though it had already cooled. "I could drop it off."

"Let one of the boys come get it. Everyone likes to feel useful in times like these."

"Okay. I'll have everything ready by two?"

"Good. The wake is from four till seven. The funeral will be at nine tomorrow morning." Margaret stood and buttoned her coat.

I stopped her before she reached the door. "Margaret, would you do me a favor?" I handed her the fiddle case. "Martin will want this later."

Margaret gave my shoulder a little squeeze before taking the fiddle in her hands.

I leaned against the doorframe, watching as she stepped carefully into the newly fallen snow.

"Margaret!" I called.

She turned. "Yes?"

I ran down the snowy steps in my wool

stockings. "I'm sorry about Henry."

Her lips turned up in the gentlest of smiles. "You know, Henry was very fond of you." Margaret reached her arms out and pulled me into her embrace. Her lilac scent surrounded me as I let myself rest in her arms. Her eyes were damp when she pulled away.

"I'll have everything ready by two," I said.

"Good girl," she said, and turned toward the inn.

The wake was held at Burke Funeral Home, in the center of town. When I arrived, the parking lot was already full, the line of mourners waiting to pay their respects spilling out onto the front steps. I took my place among them, picking fur off my black coat. I longed to be with Martin, to stand beside him. A wave of nausea flooded me when I stepped into the foyer and through a wall of lilies. I couldn't stand the scent of them since my own father's wake. I held my breath and moved forward. One of the undertakers took my coat and led me to the visiting room. It was a long room, softly lit, with flowers lining the aisle and Carter Family gospel tunes playing quietly in the background. The casket was up front, where Dotty and her three sons stood, receiving visitors. Martin looked different in his black suit — more urbane. His hair had been cut since last night, and he had shaved. For the first time I could picture him in a city. He was leaning down to talk to an elderly woman. Tears threatened at the backs of my eyes. I moved with the crowd into the room.

I stepped out of the receiving line to look at the dozens of framed pictures of Henry that lined a table in the back. Pictures of him as a young man, looking so much like Martin, with his band in the grange hall. His and Dotty's wedding pictures. Holding each of his sons as an infant, his eyes full of wonder. Christmas photos with all of the grandchildren and great-grandchildren. There was even one from this Thanksgiving of Henry, his grandsons, and me, all with stringed instruments in our hands.

"That's a great picture," said a woman beside me. I dabbed at my eyes with a handkerchief before turning to face her. She was striking, and fashionable in an artistic way.

"Thanks," I said. "He was teaching me to play the dulcimer." I could feel Henry's hand on mine, sliding across the strings.

She swept her asymmetrical blond bangs out of her eyes. She wore a vintage black dress and knee-high black leather boots that skimmed her slim calves.

Not from Vermont, I thought to myself.

"Have you signed the guest book?" she asked, gesturing to the podium in the corner of the room. "I'm in charge of it." She glanced back at the family and then at me. "I'm a little nervous about messing it up," she confided, leaning in toward me.

"Don't worry, the McCrackens are sweethearts," I said gently. "No one is going to mind if you miss a few names."

She smiled slightly, but it didn't reach her eyes. "You don't sound like you're from here. Have you known the family a long time?"

"Only since September," I said, looking over at Martin, "But I've grown very attached to them. They've made me feel very welcome." I smiled. "I'm from Boston originally. That's the accent," I clarified. I held out my hand. "Olivia Rawlings."

"Sylvie Ford," she said, her slender hand cool in mine. "From Seattle."

I felt an itch at the back of my memory.

"Martin's fiancée."

The noise of the room grew muffled as if my head had been pushed underwater.

At this time yesterday, he had been in me.

"I'm sorry." I didn't know if I was asking a question or making a statement. My palms

320

began to sweat.

She dropped my hand and rubbed hers together. Her eyebrows pinched slightly. "Martin, the youngest. You must know him if you know Henry."

At that moment I didn't know if I knew Martin at all.

"This is only my second time out here." She smiled apologetically. "I haven't had the chance to get to know the family. That's why I feel so stressed about the guest book."

"The McCrackens are very kind," I said as I turned from her to look up to the front, where Martin was talking to Tom. I was too far away to read his expression. "You have nothing to worry about."

Sylvie swept her hair out of her eyes. "Thanks." Her gaze followed mine toward Martin.

The look of affection in her expression made me blanch. I turned my head away in a lame attempt to hide the fact that my heart was breaking. I felt myself flush and wobbled a bit on my feet.

Sylvie looked at me, her face awash with concern and then confusion.

"Oh, God — I'm being so selfish, blabbing on. I'm so sorry for your loss. Who are you in relation to the family?"

"I'm nobody," I said, turning away from

her. "Please excuse me."

I walked out of the room, cutting through the line of mourners, and pushed my way out the door, gulping for fresh air.

"Livvy?" I heard Hannah's voice through the static buzzing in my ears. She put her hand on my shoulder. "I was hoping to run into you here. I'm sorry I haven't — are you okay?"

I looked up at her, my eyes burning, and shook my head. "Did you know?"

"Did I know what? Look, you're freezing. Let's get you inside." Hannah threaded her arm through mine and led me toward the door, asking a waitress from the diner if we could cut in line. "I've felt terrible since we argued. I —"

"Did you know that Martin was engaged?"

"What? No!" Hannah looked around, smiling apologetically to the people around us. "I mean, there was some talk years ago, but I haven't — who is it? Is she here?"

I couldn't form the words.

"Livvy, you should —"

Hannah's husband stepped up to us, wrapping his arm around Hannah's waist. "What are you doing out here? I dropped you off so you could sit down. You know what the doctor said."

"I'm going to stay here with Livvy for a

minute, sweetheart," she said. I looked down and saw that she had left the bottom three buttons of her coat unbuttoned to accommodate her growing belly.

"I'm okay, Hann. Go on in."

"You sure?"

I nodded but couldn't make eye contact. Her arm slid out of mine just as we reached the door. Jonathan led her down the aisle, his hand on her lower back.

If Hannah hadn't known, it was possible that it wasn't known all over town, either. Yet. By now half the town would be speculating about who the pretty blond woman was by the guest book. And if Sylvie was as candid with everyone else as she had been with me, word that Martin was engaged would be spread before dawn.

With each step toward the open casket I felt as if I were shrinking, my insides growing tighter. Martin's eyes met mine briefly as I moved forward in the line. Soon it was my turn to pay my respects. I reluctantly climbed the three steps up to the stage and dropped slowly to my knees in front of the casket.

He looked gone. Everyone always talks about how good the dead look, what an amazing job the undertakers did. All I could see was Henry and the absence of him, his face hidden under layers of pancake makeup, as if he were onstage. I fingered the white handkerchief in my hand, fighting the temptation to spit into it and wipe his face clean. His suit looked all wrong. I wished they had dressed him in his robin's-egg blue cardigan, let his shock of white hair be windblown, as if he had just stepped in from the fields.

I could feel the push of the people lined up behind me, the McCrackens waiting to receive me ahead. I leaned in toward the casket.

"I'm trying to remember everything you said the other day, but I can't seem to remember any of it. What did you tell me I should do?" I pressed the backs of my hands roughly to the corners of my eyes. "When you said to be patient, I wasn't expecting this."

I imagined Sylvie at the back of the hall, beside the guest book, introducing herself to one of the guests. From behind me I heard someone clear his throat. I stood up, smoothing down the skirt of my dress. I reached into the bodice and extracted the wooden noter I had tucked into my bra strap. I placed it into the pocket of Henry's suit. "If there's a heaven, then there'll be tunes to play," I whispered as I kissed his cool, papery cheek.

It was time to face the family.

When I turned away from the casket, the McCracken family was standing, watching me. Dotty, Mark, Ethan, and Martin. I wrapped my arms around Dotty and pressed my face in her neck.

"I'm so sorry," I whispered.

"I know." Dotty looked down the line of her children at Martin and whispered, "I am too, dear." She took both of my hands in hers and looked at me for a long time. "He thought of you like a long-lost daughter," she said urgently.

I looked down at my shoes. "He was a very special man."

She squeezed my hands before letting them go. I hugged her tightly and moved on to Mark. He clasped my shoulder, his eyes soft. "Thanks, Livvy. You brought Dad a lot of happiness over these past few months."

Ethan threw his arms around me and gave me a bear hug. "You're one of us now, Livvy," he said into my ear, "no matter what happens." He kissed my temple. "Come have a tune with us anytime, you hear me?"

I turned to face Martin.

His arms hung heavily at his sides, as if he didn't know what to do with them.

I folded mine, not trusting that I could

refrain from reaching out to touch him. "I'm so sorry —" my voice broke.

"Livvy —"

It was only the second time he had called me that. I felt my insides crumble and my heart began to race.

Martin drew me into his chest, his cheek resting on the top of my head. I breathed him in, but he smelled different somehow. It might have been just a trace of cologne, but to me it was the scent of Seattle, and of a Martin I didn't know.

"Liv —"

"Not here, okay?" I said, not looking at him.

Martin looked over my head at the long line of well-wishers waiting patiently.

He let me go. I stood still, not wanting to pull away. Martin cupped my cheeks in his hands. "Henry really loved you," he said, his voice strained. "We all do."

I squeezed his arm once and stepped away, biting the insides of my cheeks to keep from crying. With my eyes fixed on the exit sign, I walked straight through the crowd and pushed out the door into the cold, dark night.

I passed Margaret in the driveway, on her way in.

"Olivia," she called.

I turned to face her. "How could you do this to me?" I said. I could feel myself shaking with anger.

Margaret looked taken aback. "What on earth did I do?"

"You knew. You had to. You're Dotty's best friend, for God's sake, which you loved to remind me of all the time. How close you were, how I was just a blip in the McCrackens' life but *you* were family. Well, I might have believed I was just a blip if I'd known that Martin had a fucking fiancée!"

Margaret grabbed me by the elbow and moved us down the path. "Watch your tongue," she snapped.

"Don't you mean hold my tongue? Isn't that what everyone does around here? Everyone talks about everything unless it's to a person's face. Please, just put me out of my misery and tell me how long I've been making a complete ass out of myself. How long have you known? Does everyone in town know? They will by dinnertime, right?"

"Settle down, Olivia. You're making a scene." Margaret stood stiffly, her hands tightly clutching her purse.

"Apparently I've been *making a scene* for some time now, so everyone should be used to it." I threw my arms down. "What's wrong with you people? Why is everything

327

such a big secret around here? I mean, look at *you.* Are you selling the inn or aren't you? And what the hell is the thing between you and Jane White?"

Margaret's face grew pale in the moonlight. "That's enough," she said through clenched teeth.

"You know what, you're right. That *is* enough. *I've* had enough. You don't have to worry about me or my making a scene any longer." I turned and marched toward my car, the tears hot against my cold cheeks, each step fueled by adrenaline and shame.

I made it as far as Concord, New Hampshire, driving as fast as my station wagon would go without shaking, not knowing where I was headed. Then I remembered Salty, who was alone in my dark and chilly cabin, waiting for his supper. *This is precisely why I never wanted a dog,* I groused to myself as I turned onto an exit ramp. I didn't want to go back. I didn't want to see Margaret or risk seeing Martin, although I was sure he was busy with Sylvie and his family. Somewhere along the Connecticut River my anger turned back into tears, and I had to pull over when my vision became too blurred to drive. When I could take a deep breath without choking, I pulled out my cell phone and made a quick call.

"I need a favor. Can you help me?" I asked.

Alfred was standing in the open doorway when I pulled into his driveway, Salty by his side.

"I can't thank you enough. I would have called Hannah, but things have been . . . difficult between us. And I didn't want to make her trudge out to the cabin."

"I'm glad you called. You had a lot of folks worried about you."

I glanced up at him, my eyebrows raised. "I find that hard to believe."

"Hannah called, and Margaret. Sarah was worried." Al led me into his house. It was what is affectionately known as a double-wide, but it had been added onto so many times that it had lost its trailer shape. I flopped down on one end of a well-worn couch and reached for the beer that he set in front of me.

Al handed me a large canvas bag. "Jeans, gray cardigan sweater, yoga pants, a bunch of T-shirts, fleece jacket, rubber boots, Salty's leash. I added a bunch of socks and underwear, in case you forgot." Al sat cross-legged at the other end of the couch. "And I found the stuff you asked for, although

I'm not sure if it'll work. It's from the eighties."

"I don't think those chemicals go bad," I said, turning the package of hair dye in my hands. Chestnut brown. "Thanks, Alfred."

Alfred looked down at the canvas bag. "So, are you going to tell me where you're going?"

"Just away," I said, avoiding his gaze. "I've got to get out of here."

Alfred sat back, taking a long draw off his bottle. "And what will you do for Christmas?"

"Anything but watch Martin and Sylvie exchange stocking stuffers."

Alfred stretched his leg out, poking my thigh with a gray-wool-covered toe. "You want to talk about it?" he asked gently.

"Can we not?"

"It might make you feel better."

"Or it might make solid this feeling of total humiliation and I'll be scarred for life." I drained the bottle. "More alcohol, please." Alfred shook his head but came back from the kitchen with a bottle of Maker's Mark and two glasses full of ice.

"You are a true friend," I said, pouring the whiskey. "To Henry," I said with my glass raised.

"To Henry," Alfred said, and clinked his

glass against mine.

After a few drinks, my curiosity got the best of me. "So, did you know? About Syllll-viiiiie?" I drew the word out. I was trying to get used to saying it without feeling like someone had sucker-punched me.

"I knew that Martin had a girlfriend awhile back. I knew that Henry wasn't crazy about the match — I think because she grew up on the West Coast. Henry kept hoping Martin would come home." Alfred took a drink. "I only know all of that because Dotty and Margaret would talk in the kitchen. You know how those two are."

I nodded, thinking about them, sitting in the rockers. It had been a long time since Dotty had paid us a visit.

"There was a little gossip around the farmer's market last fall. Martin had missed a few holidays, and folks were speculating that some girl had finally pinned him down. It was big news until the owner of the feed store got arrested for selling pot. When Martin showed up here last summer without her, I think everyone assumed she was out of the picture."

"But there she was, in charge of the guest book." I poured myself another glass and pulled the blanket Al had draped over my legs up higher.

"That must have come as quite a shock." Al pulled my foot into his lap and gave it a little squeeze.

I held up the whiskey bottle. "This is helping."

Alfred bowed his head. "Anything you need, Liv. So, how long are you going to be gone?"

"Don't know."

"But you're coming back."

I drained the last drops of bourbon from my glass, reached down into my purse and pulled out a white envelope. "Can you give this to Margaret after the funeral?"

"What is it?"

"It's just a quick note." It was actually instructions on how to dip the chocolate truffles and garnish the petits fours for New Year's Eve, and where to find the cranberry loaves and date nut bread I had made for the New Year's Day brunch baskets. Someone else would have to make the muffins. I felt sick about abandoning her during the holidays. I needed her to know that at least she wouldn't have to start from scratch.

Alfred gave me a long, appraising look. "Make me a promise. Don't make any sudden moves."

"What do you mean?" I asked, hiding my face behind the glass.

"You've got the energy of a fawn about to leap into the woods."

I laughed. "With my fluffy white tail."

"And your big, brown eyes, yes." Alfred stood up. He tucked the blanket around my legs. "Are you going to be warm enough?"

I waved my hand. "I'll be fine."

"I'll bring you coffee by seven thirty. The funeral's at nine." Alfred leaned down and kissed my cheek. He smelled like whiskey and Old Spice. It was comforting.

"Livvy, there are a lot of folks around here who care about you, not just the McCrackens," he said from the doorway.

Eternal rest give to thee, O Lord: and let perpetual light shine upon them.

I slipped through the side door and into the back of the church while the priest sprinkled the casket with holy water. He swung the censer in the sign of the cross, filling the air with frankincense and myrrh. The pews were tightly packed; the mourners huddled together in their winter coats, as if to protect themselves from death. I stood in the back, leaning against the wall. The casket — *Henry,* I reminded myself — was in the center, close to the sanctuary. I could see the straight back and dark brown hair of Martin seated in the front row, Sylvie's blond head beside him. I wondered if they were holding hands.

Mark and Ethan gave the readings. When the priest finished reciting the Gospel passage, he invited the brothers up to say a few words about their father.

Mark stood at the podium, flanked by Ethan and Martin. Martin held his fiddle, the bow swinging off his pinkie. My heart ached when I saw his face. He looked stunned and sad. I wrestled with my longing to be up there with him, and the fact that it wasn't my place.

"One of the many gifts that Dad gave us was the love of music, and all the old songs." Mark nodded to his brothers. "This was one of his favorites."

Martin pressed the fiddle into that spot under his collarbone, and Ethan began to sing.

I'm just a poor wayfaring stranger
I'm traveling through this world alone
Yet there's no sickness, toil nor danger
In that bright land to which I go.

I pulled the handkerchief from my coat pocket and wiped at my cheeks. I hadn't bothered with makeup. Ethan's voice was rich, like a cello, and held as much grief as the notes pouring from Martin's fiddle. Martin leaned over the fiddle, his waist bowed, hair swept over his glasses. He looked broken.

I'm going home to see my Savior
I'm going home, no more to roam
I am just going over Jordan
I am just going over home.

When the last note of the fiddle rang through the silent church, Martin followed his brother back to the pew.

The priest continued the Mass, preparing the Host for the parishioners.

The family knelt and bowed their heads in prayer. They filled up eight pews on both sides of the church. Four generations at least, stitched together like a sweater knit in the round, with Henry's casket in the center. I let my gaze settle on Martin, the sandy brown hair that tapered into a *V* at the back of his neck. My mind drifted to how soft it had felt against my cheek, how sweet it had smelled. *Not for you,* I reminded myself. I pushed my back against the church door, taking one last look before I slipped out quietly and into the bright morning sunlight.

■ ■ ■ ■

The ring of the bell at King's Chapel woke me from my nap with a start. I had been sleeping almost nonstop since I had arrived in Boston the day before. Jamie had put me up at the Parker House, saying it would be "safer" than staying at the Emerson during the holidays. I knew that meant that Mrs. Whitaker was probably hosting the Christmas Eve dinner or Christmas Day brunch and would be spending a lot of time at the club. To assuage his guilt, he booked me the Harvey Parker Suite. It had its own dining room, along with a butler's pantry and kitchen. I should have refused, but it was on the fourteenth floor and had the prettiest view of the white steeple of Park Street Church. The Hancock Buildings, both old and new, shined brightly in the distance.

Promptly at three there was a knock on the door. Jamie was standing in a three-piece tuxedo, complete with black silk bow tie, holding a bottle of chilled champagne.

"Merry Christmas, darling," he said as I stepped aside to let him in. He bent down and placed a lingering kiss on my cheek before making his way into the pantry. I felt underdressed in my yoga pants and white

T-shirt. I followed him, hugging my gray cardigan to my chest.

Jamie popped the cork and filled two champagne glasses.

"It's so good to see you," he said warmly. "I'm sorry I couldn't get away last night. It's a difficult time of year."

I took a long swallow of champagne and walked toward the seating area.

"I have to admit, I'm surprised you're here. Christmas in Vermont sounds lovely." Jamie put his glass down and slipped out of his coat, laying it carefully across the back of an armchair. "Aren't you happy there?" he asked as he sat down.

I ignored his question and climbed onto his lap, straddling his legs. I undid his cuff links. They clinked against the glass table-top. I pulled at the end of the bow tie, unknotting it and sliding it slowly from around his neck.

Jamie fumbled with the buttons of his vest. "Because if you're unhappy, Livvy . . ."

I unbuttoned the top two buttons of his starched white shirt and licked his neck.

"Oh dear God," he gasped. "My offer still stands."

I popped the last button open and slid my hands across his chest, against his white undershirt. With Jameson it always took a long time to get to skin. "Not happy with the new chef?" I asked, breathing into his ear.

"I missed this," he said, cupping my breasts. He moved to kiss me, but I turned my face away, offering him my neck instead. His hair smelled expensive.

"So you want me back in your kitchen?" I teased, as I sucked at the skin where his neck met his shoulder.

"Their bûche de Noël has nothing on yours."

"So how long was she at the Emerson before you tasted her bûche?" I asked innocently as I took his hand and pressed it between my thighs.

"It's a he," he moaned, wrapping his free hand around me and clutching my butt. "The bedroom?"

"About four miles from here, to the left."

Jamie took my hand and I grabbed the bottle of champagne on the way, drinking from the bottle, the bubbles harsh against my throat. "I don't have much time," he breathed, a cool, smooth hand snaking under my shirt and stroking my belly.

I leaned into him, trying to block out the memory of Martin's hands. I reached down and pulled off my own shirt. Jameson unzipped the fly of his tuxedo pants. I crawled onto the bed so I didn't have to watch him take off his shoes and socks.

Jameson lay down, his face hovering over mine, and kissed me.

I started to cry. I rolled him onto his back and a fat teardrop landed on his throat.

Jamie stroked my hair. "Darling, what's wrong?"

"It's nothing," I choked, burying my face in his shoulder, unable to stop the flow of tears once they had started.

Jamie rolled me off of him. "Sweetheart?"

I faced the window. The lights on a building across the way blinked red.

Jamie turned me around to face him, his expression full of concern.

"I'm so sorry," I said, rubbing my nose with my bare forearm. "I shouldn't have called you."

Jamie looked at me, his pleasant club-president smile almost masking the disappointment in his eyes. "I was glad you called. You can call on me for anything. You know that, right? Now talk to me."

I sat up, my arms crossed over my breasts. Jamie retreated into the bathroom, emerging with a cream-colored bathrobe. He handed it to me and stepped into his tuxedo pants. Grabbing his discarded clothes, he led me to the other room.

We curled up on the couch by the fire-place, and I told him everything — about the Sugar Maple, Margaret and the pie contest, meeting Martin and getting to know Henry. About Henry dying, and about learning of Sylvie.

"I feel like such an idiot," I said, wiping my face on the sleeve of the bathrobe. "I should have known. I should have assumed he wasn't available in some way. Those are the only men I'm ever drawn to." I grabbed the angora throw on the back of the couch and hugged it to my chest. "All those times I thought something might happen between us, I thought he was just being a gentle-man."

"It sounds like he was," Jamie offered.

"Yeah, but now I don't know what to think. Maybe he never liked me at all. Maybe I was just a comfort, something to take his mind off everything. Wasn't that what I was to you?"

"Not quite," Jamie said, his ears turning pink. "You never exactly made me feel comfortable, Livvy." He stroked the back of my neck lightly with his fingertips. "I'd say you kept me on my toes."

"Or on your back," I said, squirming out of his embrace and hopping off the couch. "But you never loved me in that way people

340

sing about."

"I'm very fond of you; you know that."

I paced the long length of the sitting room. "Do you think she knows? Your wife? Or is she really dumb?"

"Hush, now," he said, scowling. "Agatha is a brilliant woman."

"So how on earth could she not know that her husband was banging the help? I mean, seriously, Jamie, we had a good time together. You couldn't have been up for much when you got back to the mansion."

"We did have a good time, didn't we?" The corners of Jamie's lips lifted a fraction, and his eyes lost their focus. "To answer your question, Agatha's and my relationship is . . . complicated. I think she sees what she wants to see and ignores what's inconvenient for her."

"I wish I could do that," I said, collapsing back on the couch.

"Wish you could do what?"

"Pick and choose what I see. Because all I can think about right now is Martin crawling into bed with his fiancée, and it's . . ." I was crying again.

"Come here," Jameson said, and scooted over to sit next to me. He rested a warm arm over my shoulder. "You like this man."

The church bells rang. Jamie glanced at

his watch. He took back his arm and stood. "I'm sorry, Livvy. I really am. And I'm sorry I have to leave you like this."

He stood and pulled on his shirt, buttoning it quickly. I sat watching him, knowing it would be the last time. I scooped up his cuff links from the coffee table and slid them into his cuffs.

"I am sorry I called you. I didn't mean to be a tease," I said as I buttoned his vest, smoothing my hands over his chest.

"Stay as long as you like. I mean it. Order anything in the dining room. The manager knows it's on my tab."

I walked Jamie to the door. "I meant what I said, Liv — the door is always open at the Emerson."

"Thanks. I'm afraid it would feel like taking a step backward."

"Well, that's probably the best perspective, at least for my marriage's sake." He cleared his throat. "Let me know. I could make a few calls. Perhaps the St. Botolph Club?"

"I doubt I'll be in Boston for long," I said, although the idea of moving even from the hallway back to the living room was exhausting.

Jamie hesitated in the doorway.

I gave him a small nudge. "Don't worry about me. I'll be fine."

CHAPTER FOURTEEN
FEBRUARY

I woke up from my nap to the sound of a fiddle being tuned. As a child I often drifted off to sleep under my Wonder Woman comforter, tapping my feet to the jaunty sound of my dad and his friends jamming in the living room. I knew in the morning I would find a stray musician asleep on the sofa and the scent of pipe smoke and whiskey lingering in the air. That meant cartoons all morning and a late breakfast at the diner — two of my favorite things. Now the sound of a bow drawing across open strings dug into a place inside of me I had been fighting hard to keep blocked off. I pulled my pillow out from under my head and squashed it to my ear.

Salty, who had been lying next to me on the cot, sat up, stuck his muzzle into the air, and let out a long, low howl — a perfect D. I threw the blanket over his head to shush him, but he was determined to match the fiddle note for note. I pulled on a sweater, zipped up my boots, and grabbed his leash.

"Come on, pup." I crept through the storeroom, trying not to trip over the pizza boxes strewn all over the floor, and out the back door into the alley. I didn't want to be spotted by the music-shop guys. It wouldn't seem unusual for me to be working into the night at the Friendly Eating Place — the neighbors knew a baker was using the space until the pizza shop was sold — but a giant Irish wolfhound mix emerging from a commercial kitchen was a little harder to explain. There was no getting around the fact that it was illegal to keep a dog in a pizza shop, just as it was illegal for a baker to be living in one. We needed to keep a low profile.

The day after I had cried all over his tuxedo, Jamie — my knight in shining Brooks Brothers — had insisted that I spend Christmas week at the Parker House. I passed the first few days sleepwalking from room to room, my heart swinging wildly from numbness to panic. On New Year's Eve I dyed my hair Manic Panic Electric Banana. People say happiness starts from within, but I'm a firm believer in "fake it till you make it." Desperate for distraction and something other than hotel food, on New Year's Day I took the train across the Charles into Cambridge. I had lunch at Café Pamplona and ran into Richard, my favorite friend from culinary school. When I told him I was taking a sabbatical from the high-stress world of fine dining, he asked me if I was interested in freelancing for him, testing recipes from his new cookbook. I almost broke down. If there were a patron saint of wealthy, gay chefs, I would burn incense in front of a statue of him every day and drape him in marigolds. It wasn't a glamorous job — Richard looked a little embarrassed to be suggesting it to me — but the money bought me some more time in Boston. I knew in my heart that it would be a while before I could let go of Guthrie and start someplace new. Now I just needed a place to live and a kitchen to bake in.

I did then what I always do when I am looking for something out of reach. I called my specialty-foods purveyor, Raphael. His exceptional ability to hunt down ingredients like the world's thinnest phyllo dough, hand-rolled by elderly Greek grandmothers, made him privy to every piece of culinary gossip on the eastern seaboard: which bartenders were sleeping with which hostesses, which chefs were snorting up their profits, and who hadn't met payroll the week before. Despite having been in Miami Beach for the winter, he had heard that the owner of the Friendly Eating Place had closed its doors without warning and that the landlord was looking for someone to fill the space while he fought with the bank. The Friendly Eating Place was about the size of a train car — no seating up front, just a counter with an empty cash register and a straw dispenser. The kitchen doubled as an overflow storeroom, with open metal shelving crowded with cans of roasted tomatoes and rows of refrigerators that, thankfully, had been emptied of their old mozzarella and pepperoni slices. It was perfect for my needs — a large convection oven, an even bigger brick oven for bread baking, and just enough room to set up the cot from Goodwill in the corner. I papered over the storefront windows and got to work.

Richard's book was a treasury of American home desserts, each recipe rustic and comforting. Weeks passed as I let myself get lost in the dependability of baking. Measure correctly, use proper technique, and everything always comes out exactly how you planned. I took immaculate notes, washed the dishes in water hot enough to scald my skin, and tried to think only of noodle kugel or pear pandowdy. Martin, the McCrackens, the Sugar Maple — I felt their absence like a phantom limb.

One afternoon at the end of January, I returned home late from walking Salty with ten pounds of apples and a pound of butter, feeling crabby. It was sleeting, and my mittenless hands were raw from lugging grocery bags. I had been avoiding the pies and tarts chapter of Richard's book the entire month, but I knew I had to face it sometime.

Peeling apples always calms me. It's satisfying, almost meditative, to run the paring knife right under the surface of the skin. I worked through the whole bag even though Richard's recipe called for only three pounds. When it was time to add the spices, I ignored his instructions altogether. I put what I was certain was a blue-ribbon apple pie in the oven and shut the door.

From the music shop I could hear the faint strains of a guitar being tuned. Perfect. Every Monday night — regardless of the weather, or if there was a broken-hearted pastry chef squatting next door — a group of old-time players gathered after closing to trade tunes. I turned the volume on the abandoned radio to ten, rolled up my sleeves, and clanged the metal bowls against the sink wall as I did the dishes. If I'd had to, I would've run the empty stand mixer on high. Anything to block out those dear old songs.

The oven timer had just buzzed when someone tapped on the front door.

"We're closed," I shouted as I pulled the pie out of the oven, the filling bubbling out of the air vents and onto the floor. The tapping grew more aggressive — whoever it was had switched to keys against the glass. The sound plucked at the nerves in the back of my neck. I fumbled with the sticky dead bolts and whipped open the door. There, on the sidewalk, stood Hannah.

"You are going to tell me where your bathroom is," she said, pushing past me, "and then you are going to get a piece of my mind."

"In back to the left," I said, locking the door behind her.

I waited for Hannah in the storeroom. When she squeezed her way out of my tiny water closet and I got a look at how big her belly had grown, it hit me how much I had been missing in Guthrie.

"Livvy," Hannah said, throwing her arms around me and hugging me as tightly as the babies would allow. "God, I can't believe I found you."

I couldn't either. "I can't believe how fast the babies are growing," I said. "How do you feel? Do you want to sit down?" I looked around the room. The cot was the only place to sit. I shooed Salty off and ushered Hannah over.

"My back hurts like crazy, and I live on Tums, but that's the worst of it so far." She put her hand on her belly. "We can talk about the babies later. What I want to know is *where* are we? And what are you doing here?"

"It's temporary" was all I could think to say.

Salty climbed back on the cot and proceeded to lick Hannah's hand. I felt a wave of shame wash over me, seeing the room through her eyes — the torn pizza boxes I hadn't bothered to clean up stacked into a life-sized game of Jenga, the fifty-pound bags of flour leaning against one another, the yellowed walls of the windowless room, the dog hair–covered sleeping bag that I had been crawling into every night.

"How did you find me?" Other than going to the grocery store and walking Salty, I barely left the pizza shop.

"I called Raphael. Margaret gave me his

phone number off an old invoice. I figured no matter where you were, you'd be ordering from him."

Raphael. Why is it that when someone lets me have all the dirt, I never think that they would also spill about me?

The sound of men's laughter filtered in through the wall, along with the cat cry of instruments being tuned. I winced.

"Let's get out of here," I said, extending my hand to help her up.

We passed several taverns serving more familiar fare before Hannah chose a Tibetan restaurant. We sipped masala tea, studying the menu, avoiding each other's eyes.

"I hear the yak is good," I offered.

"We've all been worried sick, Livvy. You shouldn't have just left like that. Alfred has been threatening to hire a private investigator."

That might cure him of his crush on me in a hurry. "What about Margaret?"

Hannah unfolded her napkin and draped it across her belly. "Margaret's pissed, of course. You can't really blame her. You bailed out on her in the middle of the holidays."

My belly churned as if I had drunk the buttered tea the restaurant was known for.

Walking out on a job during the holidays was breaking serious culinary code, and I still felt deeply guilty.

"And Martin?" I tried sounding nonchalant and failed.

"He's gone, honey."

It wasn't a surprise. Martin and I were alike in that way. But that didn't stop the tears from spilling down my face and onto the tablecloth.

"I should have called. I'm really sorry, Hannah. I just needed . . ." To let the skin form over my pudding-soft heart. "I just needed to get out of there."

Hannah reached across the table and took one of my hands in hers. "I'm sorry. We got into that argument before Thanksgiving, and we hadn't talked. I had no idea things had gotten serious between the two of you."

"It wasn't serious, exactly." I traced the mandala pattern of the tablecloth with my index finger. "But it felt like it could be. It was like he saw me differently than other men. And when I was with him, I saw myself differently. I liked who I was when I was with him." I shrugged. "I should have listened to you. You were right. Henry has died and Martin is gone and here I am." I took the cloth napkin off my lap and pressed it to my face, trying to dam the tears I couldn't control.

Hannah got up and took the seat beside me. "I hate seeing you like this. And I can't bear the thought of you living in the back of that kitchen."

"It's fine, really," I said, giving my eyes a final wipe. "It's just a place to land while I weigh my options. I have a freelance gig that's keeping me busy. You know me, Hann," I said, giving her a weak grin, "onward and upward."

When I had regained my composure, the waiter came over and took our order. Hannah told me all of the gory details about being pregnant and about how insufferable her mother-in-law had become.

"The worst part is that I'm so tired all the time. And you can't drink coffee! Every day my to-do list gets longer and longer, and all I want to do is lie on the couch and watch *Real Housewives* reruns."

I had been feeling tired too. Like, someone-pulled-the-plug exhausted. I chalked it up to heartbreak. After my dad had died, I had been able to fall asleep wherever I could be semihorizontal, and at any time.

"So far the only good thing I can think of, other than the babies, of course, is not getting my period. I'm not missing that *at all.*"

A chill passed through me, as though the restaurant door had blown open. I searched my memory for some detail — a day baking, bent over with cramps, needing to run to the pharmacy down the street — and came up with nothing.

"So, speaking of babies, Livvy, I have something important I want to ask you."

I quickly did the math in my head. It had been five weeks since Martin and I were together. Maybe I was just late.

"I want you to be the boys' godmother."

"Boys?"

Hannah patted her belly. "Yup. Two of them. It's going to be the house of testosterone."

"Do you really think I'm the best person to be left in charge of their religious education?"

Hannah laughed. "Better than Jonathan's cousin, the Scientologist."

"Of course I'll be the babies' godmother. I'd be honored." I put my credit card on top of the check. "Can you come back for some pie? I just made an apple."

"I would have thought you'd have made a vow to never bake a pie again."

"It's a hard habit to break."

Hannah glanced at her watch. "I wish I could. Jonathan is going to pick me up in a few minutes. You'll have to bring me a piece when you come to the shower. Although you know key lime is my favorite," she said in a singsong voice.

The baby shower. Blue crepe paper and silly games and every woman in the town of Guthrie knowing I'd been played by the town fiddler.

"Oh, Hannah, please don't ask me to come to Guthrie." I pushed the leftover rice around my plate with a fork. "It's too soon."

"You're my family. I need you there so I can feel like something other than an heir-bearing vessel for the Doyle clan."

I would rather have hiked up Mount Washington in the middle of January, in flip-flops, than go back to Guthrie, but Hannah had always had my back. "Just for the afternoon. No overnights. I'm going to your house, then back home."

Hannah's eyes held a million thoughts, but she gave me no argument. "March twenty-eighth, one p.m."

I locked myself in one of the graffiti-covered stalls of the Skull's ladies' room and sat on the toilet with my pants still up, pregnancy test in hand. Guitars shrieked and drums thrashed through the walls while a man shouted into the mic. I had spent the week since seeing Hannah in a state of denial, convinced I was just late, until the nausea kicked in, and even then I had carried the pregnancy test around for days, unable to settle on the right place to take it. The Friendly Eating Place had seemed too small, somehow, as though Salty, the results, and I couldn't all fit in the crowded space. Two girls came into the bathroom. I listened to them gossip about the bass player while spraying each other's hair with what, judging by the smell, could only be Aqua Net Extra Super Hold. "Suck it up, Livvy," I muttered as I pushed my jeans down to my ankles.

It would be pretty after-school-special of me to get knocked up after having sex one time *with a man,* I said to myself as the three minutes it would take to reveal my fate eternally dragged on. Besides, I had had a lot of sex with a good number of men, and I had never gotten pregnant. I tried to push aside the fact that I had run out of pills sometime around Halloween and hadn't seen the point in refilling the prescription. A group of girls came in, and one pounded on the stall door.

"I have to pee so badly," she wailed.

I dropped the test into my purse, opened the door, and pushed past her.

"Thank you," she whimpered, slamming the door behind her, her friends laughing behind the other stall doors.

The club was dark and cool. When their set ended, the kids with egg-whited Mohawks packed up their gear while a boy in tight black jeans and an ironic Christmas sweater said, "Check, check," into the mic. I sat down on a barstool. Jimmy, the bartender, reached out a tattooed arm and patted me on the shoulder.

"Haven't seen you in ages. How've you been, kid?"

"Can you do me a favor?"

"If it's legal." He shot me a grin that sparkled with two gold teeth.

I slapped the pregnancy test onto the bar in front of him. "Just tell me what you see — one stripe or two."

Jimmy squinted at it. He reached into his pocket, retrieved his iPhone, and shined the light on the plastic wand. He looked at me for a second, his expression soft, before saying, "It's two, kid."

I grabbed the test, trading it for a couple of singles. "Thanks, Jimmy."

Feedback screeched through the mic as a young man grabbed the stand. "We are the Fetuses and we are here to fuck. You. Up." A grinding guitar riff and throbbing drums played me out as I stomped down the long cement hallway to the door.

The walls of the clinic exam room were covered with brightly colored posters with cheerful fonts, warning of the dangers of domestic abuse, alcoholism, and unprotected sex. I sat on the exam table in a blue paper gown, angrily contemplating the heart-shaped doilies and paper Cupid on the door. There was a brisk knock, and an impossibly young female doctor came in and sat down.

"All right, Ms. Rawlings. Your urine test came out positive, but the blood test will take a day or two to confirm. Let's take a look, shall we?"

I scooted my butt down to the end of the table, placed my feet in the stirrups, and thought about all the ways in which I would be a terrible mother:

1. I didn't really have a mother, so I would have no example to follow other than "Don't abandon your kid."

2. I couldn't stand the sight of creamed vegetables. Even mashed potatoes gave me the shudders, so basically until it could chew, the

358

baby would starve.

3. The last two places I'd lived were a shack made for boiling tree sap and a gutted pizza shop. Where would I end up next, an abandoned wine cellar?

4. Babies are fragile — and ugh, that whole soft-spot-on-the-skull thing — and I was super clumsy.

5. —

"Okay, Ms. Rawlings, all set. You can sit up." The doctor pulled off her disposable gloves and tossed them in the hazardous-waste bucket. It felt like my insides were dangerous material right now. "We can unofficially say you are definitely pregnant. If you like, we could do an ultrasound right now to estimate the date of conception."

"December twenty-first," I mumbled, wrapping the paper gown tightly closed.

"What's that?"

"December twenty-first is the date of conception. We only had sex once."

"That's all it takes," she said with a warm smile. "Now, have you made any decisions?"

"I'm pregnant. I'm really pregnant?"

"You're pregnant."

"But I'm too young to be pregnant." I was speaking of my mental age, of course.

The doctor looked at my crow's feet, then at my chart. "You're thirty-two. In a few years your fertility will actually start to decline." This made me feel as if I had just eaten a dozen fried cider doughnuts. "Let's go over your options. You're still in the first trimester. If you choose abortion, I would wait one more week — it's best to perform the procedure between weeks eight and twelve. We don't recommend you wait any longer. If you choose adoption or to keep the baby, I can give you a referral to a low-cost OB-GYN clinic nearby."

"You know, I've always made fun of the girls on TV that got knocked up after just one time."

"All it takes is healthy sperm and a mature egg. It's not that unusual." She placed a pile of pamphlets next to my hip and patted my hand. "I'm going to pop into the exam room next door and check in on my next patient. Take a minute to see if any questions come up that we can answer today. You don't have to make a decision right away."

Not making a decision is *making a decision.* Henry's words seemed to float by like a banner behind an airplane. I ripped the paper gown off, dressed as quickly as I could, and sprinted out of the clinic, ignoring the call of the receptionist asking if I needed a follow-up appointment.

I'll get an abortion, I said to myself for the millionth time that week. Every time I said it, I believed it less. Every time I considered my options, the thought ended with the words *Martin's baby.* Not just *a* baby — that would be hard enough — but his. A tiny little brooding creature with thick black glasses. Martin's, and mine. Then I would say to myself, *I'm keeping the baby.* And that seemed just as impossible. How could I do the one thing Martin had devoted his life to avoiding? It was bad enough having lost him. To have him and have him resent me seemed a thousand times worse. No matter which way I looked at things, all I could see was disaster.

CHAPTER FIFTEEN
MARCH

The hopeful signs of spring that had shown their faces in Boston — the witch hazel blossoms, the greening of the willow trees — disappeared one by one as I drove north. Guthrie was still in winter's grip.

Hannah greeted me at the door, her belly round and heavy-looking, but she waited until I was in her living room to tell me that the baby shower had been moved to the Sugar Maple. "Mrs. Doyle invited practically the whole town," she explained. This did not make me feel any better. I handed her the little blue gift box and made my way into the bathroom to make sure I was ready for public viewing after the long drive.

I had freshly Manic-Panicked my hair — Electric Lava — so the curls were the color of candied apples, and I had pulled them into a tight bun on top of my head. I had been switching the color every time I changed my mind about what my next move would be. The loose-fitting black tunic and pair of black leggings I wore didn't exactly scream baby shower, but the tunic hid the roundedness of my own belly. My boobs were another story. They had grown two cup sizes. No one knew about the baby yet — not even Hannah. I was hoping everyone would assume I was just eating my way through the cookbook I was working on. I made a brave face in the mirror, but I wasn't fooling myself. With every exit off Interstate 93 had come the temptation to turn around. I hadn't factored in that my best friend still lived in the town as I had slipped out of the back of the church three months earlier. In my mind Guthrie was frozen exactly how I had left it — Henry in a casket, Martin next to Sylvie. The arrival of a single slim blonde in beautiful leather boots had turned the town into enemy territory. And I had just crossed the border.

"There's my girl," Alfred whooped when I pushed through the swinging door to the Sugar Maple kitchen. The scent of garlic and browned butter enveloped me. Walking into the kitchen felt like zipping up my favorite fleece jacket. Alfred pulled me into a tight bear hug, swinging me around in a circle.

"There is a really good chance I'm going to vomit on you," I giggled into his ear, although my stomach had made a remarkable recovery in the past week. I had moved from the nauseated not-wanting-to-eat-at-all stage to the wanting-to-eat-everything-all-the-time one.

Alfred put me back on the floor but kept an arm firmly around my shoulder. "You are a sight for sore eyes."

I punched him on the bicep. "And you are a scent for sore stomachs. Whatever you're making smells delicious."

Alfred beamed. "You'll have to stay for dinner, then. The shower is just hors d'oeuvres."

"I can't stay — it's a long drive back. I don't want to drive through Franconia Notch in the dark."

"Nonsense. You'll stay. The dance is to-night."

I crossed my arms over my stomach. "I can't."

The door to the office opened. Two men in suits emerged, followed by Margaret, who ushered them toward the door to the dining room without even a nod in my direction.

I waited until the door stopped swinging. "What's up with that?"

"She was pretty upset when you left."

"That much I figured. I meant the suits." They looked different from any visitor Margaret had ever had.

Alfred poured a heap of salt into the palm of his hand and sprinkled it by the pinch into the saucepot. "Not sure exactly. But they aren't the first."

I made my way over to my old workbench, hit by a wave of longing at the sight of the Nancy Drew books still piled underneath the legs, and pulled up the stool that Tom used to occupy in the mornings. "So where's my replacement?"

Alfred looked surprised and handed me a teacup of the soup he was making.

"She didn't replace you." He turned back to his pot. "So, how about it? It's the Maple Sugaring Festival weekend. The Sugar on Snow contra dance is tonight in the grange hall. Be my date."

"Who's playing?" I tried to sound casual. Maybe he had come back after all.

"I think it's just Tom on the piano and a fiddle player over from Montpelier. I'm sure they'd let you sit in if you'd rather play than dance with me. But I've been taking lessons."

I laughed as he promenaded an invisible partner.

"Stay, Livvy. It will give us a chance to

catch up."

"I don't know. Salty is in Boston, and Hannah's place is full of the Doyle family. I don't have a place to crash."

"Well, you can't stay here," Margaret said as she walked past us carrying an empty silver tray. "The sugarhouse is busy with what it was intended for, and the inn is all booked up."

"What did you do with all of my stuff?"

Margaret held the tray up in front of her. "Alfred, they already went through the cheese."

"Alfred is here, you're here — who's sugaring, anyway?" I said in the same dismissive tone she had used with me.

Margaret put the tray down on the table in front of me. "Not your concern. Are you coming into the party or are you planning on hiding in the kitchen all afternoon?"

The kitchen was warm and familiar, and Alfred's eyes were always kind. Hiding in here sounded like a very good plan.

"Hannah is asking for you. She wants you to keep track of the gifts for the thank-you notes."

I rolled my eyes and slid off the stool, stopping to kiss Alfred on the cheek. "I'll see if I can find someone to take care of Salty."

"And you'll stay with me," Alfred said over his shoulder.

Margaret raised her eyebrows at me. I ignored her and walked straight out of the kitchen.

Hannah was seated in one of the wing-backed chairs, flanked by two enormous papier-mâché storks, the babies in their beaks suspended over her head like anvils. Seated next to her was her mother-in-law, Mrs. Doyle, looking regal in her cornflower blue suit with matching shoes. I was pretty sure she had the same outfit in pink for the arrival of granddaughters, and another in black for funerals. The room was packed shoulder to shoulder with women. A giant mound of presents was piled up at Hannah's feet.

"Livvy!" she called, patting the chair on her other side. I wound through the crowd, nodding and returning smiles, trying to ignore the rising hum of hushed voices. "Did you try the punch? Chef Alfred made it up — he's calling it the Doyle Twins. It has twin rums — light and dark."

I shook my head. "I have a long drive ahead of me."

"I actually miss drinking. I didn't think I would." Hannah eyed her mother-in-law.

"But it helps with stress relief."

I looked toward the back of the room, where Margaret was standing. "I can't believe you didn't tell me the shower was going to be here."

"You wouldn't have come." Hannah leaned toward me. "Are you okay?"

"Yeah."

"I'm so not believing you."

"Open your present," I said. My blue box had made it to the top of the pile.

Hannah grinned and leaned down to grab the box. She undid the white ribbon with a single pull and popped open the lid. Inside was a silver locket in the shape of a heart.

"Two pictures will fit in it," I said shyly. I leaned and whispered into her ear, "I figured you were going to have enough Diaper Genies after this."

"It's perfect," she said, her eyes welling up.

"You need to push those babies out so I can have my pragmatic best friend back. The tears are killing me," I said, wiping my own.

Mrs. Doyle called everyone to attention, and Hannah unwrapped the rest of her gifts, cooing appropriately over each tiny sock and onesie. I studiously recorded the gifts, happy to have something to focus on. Hannah tore the wrapping off a rectangular box to reveal a hand-crocheted afghan in yellow and pale green. "Dotty McCracken," she whispered. My eyes scanned the room. I found Dotty sitting in a rocking chair toward the back, next to Margaret. She gave me a warm smile when our eyes met. I waved to her with both hands. Her gray hair was loose around her shoulders, and she looked smaller than I remembered, swallowed by the chair. Memories of gray afternoons drinking tea and playing music flooded my thoughts.

When the gifts were unwrapped and Hannah was making the rounds with her thank-yous, I elbowed my way over to Dotty.

"Hello, my dear girl," she said, kissing my cheek as I leaned down to greet her.

She smelled like maple candy. I bit the inside of my cheek. "Hey, Dotty."

"It's been quiet without you and your dog around the house. Have you been keeping up with the dulcimer?"

I hadn't had the heart to open the dulcimer case since Henry died. I attempted a weak grin. "How are the boys?" I hadn't meant it to be the first question I asked, but it was impossible to look into Dotty's blue eyes and make small talk as if we were strangers.

"Mark and Ethan are good — busy with their families and their farms. I think they keep a schedule so one of the grandchildren is always at the house," she confided. Tilting her head, she kept her eyes trained on mine. "I'm sure you heard Marty is back in Seattle."

I held her gaze, holding my breath.

"He calls on Sundays. He seems busy with school, so that's good." Dotty leaned toward me, her face near my ear. "He took his father's death the hardest, I'm afraid. I wish he hadn't left."

"Me too," I said quietly.

"You could call him. It would do him good to hear from you."

My eyes reflexively looked down at the braided rug.

Dotty reached for my hand and gave it a squeeze. "How about brunch with an old woman tomorrow? Tom gave me a jug of fresh syrup just this morning. Come over to the house for pancakes, won't you? We have a lot to catch up on."

I smiled as I stood. "Ten o'clock too late?"

"Mass ends around ten. Let's make it eleven."

Margaret stood. "Will you come into the kitchen with me for a minute, Miss Rawlings?"

I looked over at her, but she was already halfway to the kitchen. I shrugged at Dotty and made a face. Dotty laughed and waved me off.

The kitchen was quiet, Alfred nowhere to be seen. I found Margaret sitting at her desk in the office. From the case on the back wall, the three red ribbons from the failed pie contests glowed like warning lights.

"Close the door behind you."

"So what's up?" I asked, plopping into the chair opposite her.

Margaret frowned. "Mrs. White took the time to remind me that when she paid the deposit on her granddaughter's wedding it was with the expectation that you would be baking the cake."

"God, what is up that woman's butt?"

"Diamonds from the White family fortune, or so she'd like everyone to think. I need you to fulfill that commitment."

"I'm committed elsewhere."

"I'm told you're freelancing, so your schedule must have some flexibility. It's only one day."

"Wedding cakes take a week to make. Besides, I'm not sure what I'll be doing then. I could find someone to make it for you."

371

"They're expecting you. Mrs. White made that quite clear this afternoon."

"Since when do you do what Jane White says?"

"Since you raised the girl's expectations with that quilted cake pattern. And you did make me a commitment of one year, which I let you out of without a single complaint."

I winced. I still felt bad about New Year's. "Did she decide on a flavor?"

"She wants three different layers."

"Of course she does."

"The coconut with the passion-fruit curd, the devil's food with a rum ganache, and the lemon with the fresh raspberries and white chocolate cream."

I grimaced. That was a week's worth of work, minimum. "What's the date?"

"June twenty-fifth." I'd be six months pregnant. There would be no hiding it then. I huffed out a breath. "Is there even going to be a Sugar Maple in June?"

Margaret gathered some papers on her desk and patted them into a neat pile. "Of course there will be. Why would you ask that?"

"I know investors when I see them."

"I don't see how who I meet with in private is any of your concern."

"I don't want to commit myself in June if

you might close the place."

"Believe me, Miss Rawlings, come hell or high water, Jane White's granddaughter will be married here in June. Now, are you going to be fit to make a wedding cake in June?"

"Of course, why wouldn't I be?" I said, having no idea if I would or wouldn't. I didn't have anyone to ask. "I'll do the baking from wherever I am and do the finishing work here. You'll cover the cost of ingredients?"

"Of course. Do I need to draw up a contract?"

"For a wedding cake?"

"You broke the last verbal agreement we had."

"Fine," I said, suddenly feeling exhausted. "Whatever. I'll sign whatever you want."

Margaret looked me up and down, her face first a question, then a confirmation. "Have you made a decision?"

"I said I'll do it."

"I meant about the baby," she said evenly, eyeing the hand resting on my belly. Stupid hand. Apparently some part of me thought the baby was going to pop right out if I didn't hold it in place.

"How did you know?" I asked, my voice not entirely free of accusation, although I couldn't blame anybody for this one. No one knew.

Margaret looked at me, not unkindly. "Your face looks softer. And I haven't seen you take a drink since I arrived."

I laughed. Great, it was my being on the wagon that had given me away. "You should see my nipples."

Margaret ignored this. "Is it Martin's?"

I fought the urge to say something snarky. "Yes."

She nodded slowly, lost in thought. "So, three months, then." Margaret took a deep breath and leaned toward me. "There are things — herbs — you can take, if you decide you don't want to follow through with it."

I stared at her, unblinking.

"They won't hurt the baby if they don't work. They just encourage your body to — let go. It doesn't always work. The sooner the better, first trimester for sure, but you're — it would have to be in the next week or so."

I sat, stunned. "How do you know . . . ?" I whispered.

"My aunt." Margaret looked far away.

I thought of the young Margaret pictured on the McCrackens' wall, that beautiful young woman, in trouble. She must have been so frightened. I fought the urge to ask her a million questions.

"I've given it a lot of thought," I said, meeting her gaze. "Honestly, I have no idea what I'm doing, but whatever it is, it's going to be with a baby." I shrugged. "It just already feels, I don't know. Like mine. Like my baby."

Margaret's face looked solemn. "Are you going to tell him?"

I slid down in my seat, looking up at the ribbons hanging from the ceiling. "Yes? No? I don't know. We haven't spoken since Henry's wake."

"It's his responsibility." Margaret wove her fingers together and rested them on the desk. "Shouldn't you give him the chance?"

"One man's responsibility is another man's cage." I sighed.

"What do you mean?"

"I just don't want to be that girl. Even if he did the right thing, whatever that means, he'd hate me for it."

Margaret leaned back. "You're going to have to tell him sometime. You can't keep it a secret forever."

"I could if I didn't have to come back here. In June."

"Olivia."

"What? *I* was raised by a single parent. I

came out just fine."

"That child will have a family that loves her, regardless of what Martin wants. She'll have a grandmother and aunts and uncles, cousins. Surely you wouldn't want to keep her from that?"

"You think it's a girl?" I asked, rubbing my belly.

"You ate cookies at the party, not chips." I had to admit she was right. I hadn't craved a French fry in weeks.

A girl. I could picture Martin with a little girl. God, he'd be overprotective. I shook my head. "Look, I'm just getting used to the idea myself. I'm not ready to face all of that."

Margaret leaned over, tucking a stack of envelopes into her leather handbag. "Well, you're going to have to face it soon enough."

"Tell me about it." I figured I only had another month or so before I stopped looking like I'd been drowning my sorrows in ice cream and started looking truly preggers. I grabbed my purse and stood. "I'm afraid the cat's going to be out of the bag when I come back in June. I'm just hoping that I'll have been gone long enough that people won't stop to do the math."

"Humph. That's wishful thinking."

She was right again.

"You should get back to Hannah."

I leaned on the doorframe, looking at her birdlike shoulders draped in green wool. "Margaret, can I ask you for one favor before I go?"

She looked up, her face open.

"Could you not tell Dotty? Not just yet. I know she's your best friend, and it's a lot to ask. She's had enough heartache. I'd hate to disappoint her." My cheeks flushed, and a wave of fatigue swept over me.

"I don't think Dotty would ever feel disappointed about another grandchild, especially one of Martin's," she said. "But it's your news to tell, when you choose to."

It felt good not to be keeping the secret on my own. I lingered in the doorway. "Thanks, Margaret. For not judging me."

Margaret looked up at me, her face suspended in surprise. "You're welcome, Olivia." She hesitated, her eyes on a pile of papers before her. "You know, I'm here if you need me."

With those six words, I felt six thousand pounds lighter. "Thanks," I said with a grin, and slipped out the door before she could see that I was crying. Again.

After the shower, Hannah and I lay on opposite ends of the couch, our feet pressed against each other's thighs. Her belly rose up under the camel-colored throw like a giant chocolate truffle. I wondered how big I would be in my seventh month.

"You'd think that she would want me to be happy — I mean, those storks could have raised my blood pressure to a dangerous level and harmed her grandchildren. But no, she insisted."

I grabbed one of Hannah's swollen feet in my hands and pressed into the bottom.

"Oh my good Lord," Hannah moaned, snuggling into the couch cushion. "You have no idea how good that feels." She pressed her other foot into my leg. "You know, I was pretty pissed at you."

"I figured."

"I've been really worried. And I was surprised to find you in Boston. I never pictured you back there. You're not back with Jamie, are you?"

"No. God, no." I pressed my foot into her thigh. "I shouldn't have just taken off. I didn't mean to put you through that, Hann. You're always looking out for me. I just —"

"I wish you knew you could lean on me."

I squeezed her feet with my hands. "I know I can. When I found out, the only thing I could think of was leaving. I wasn't thinking of anyone else. I'm really sorry."

"Shush." Hannah placed a hand on my kneecap and gave it a little shake. "Thanks for coming up for this, Liv. It meant a lot to me."

"And miss getting a picture of you cowering under two storks? I've already posted it on Instagram."

"I mean it. I know it wasn't easy for you." Hannah's expression softened. "I'm sorry about Martin."

"Did you really not know?" I asked, surprising myself. "You know everything that happens in this town."

"I didn't. I'm so sorry. I asked around when it seemed like the two of you were getting close. There was an old rumor, but no one seemed to know much about him now." Hannah paused. "And you looked so happy. I've never seen you like that. I wanted everything to be good."

"It's just — he felt like he was *mine*. Do you know what I mean? I've never felt that way before. The sound of his voice and the way he smelled, the way he moved when he played the fiddle — he felt so familiar, somehow. And his family — God, at Thanksgiving, I just felt like I could belong there. With them. That they could belong to me." I rested a hand on my belly, thinking about my dad. It hadn't been so bad, our little family of two. Dad didn't exactly know a lot about raising a little girl, but he figured out the important stuff.

"You're a part of my family, Livvy. Like a sister. And you'll be an auntie to these boys."

"Yes," I said, smiling for her benefit.

"I know this must have been hard for you. But it meant the world to me, really. You'll see when your time comes. It feels really important to have the people you love and trust around you."

"Um, Hann?" I switched feet, digging my thumb into her arch.

"Mmmmmm?" she said dreamily.

"I may be finding out how important that is a little sooner than you think."

Hannah bolted upright, leaning toward me as far as her belly would allow, which is to say an inch. "Livvy?"

I smiled my best Liza Minnelli smile. "I'm knocked up!"

"Are you serious? Jesus Christ! I thought you looked a little chunky! Is that why you didn't drink the punch? Do you know what this fucking means?"

I hadn't seen Hannah this excited since she won a box lot of Bakelite bracelets.

"Our kids are going to be practically siblings! It's fantastic! They're going to grow up together!" And with that, Hannah wrapped her arms around my neck and burst into tears.

The doorbell rang, startling us both.

"That's probably Alfred," I said, wiping her eyes with the sleeve of my shirt. "Listen, Hann— you can't tell anyone. Not even your husband. No one knows except you and Margaret."

"You told Margaret?"

The doorbell rang twice.

"It's a long story. But I've only just decided to have it, and I'm not ready for anyone to know, okay?"

Hannah blew me a kiss from the couch. "Of course I won't tell anyone."

Alfred had arrived at Hannah's at seven on the dot, freshly scrubbed and wearing a soft blue sweater under a suit jacket and slacks. He handed me a bouquet of pink carnations wrapped in cellophane. To my surprise, he had trimmed his beard short, and his usual oniony scent was gone, replaced by something musky. "Ready to see my moves?" he asked, a little nervously, I thought. I linked my arm through his and together we marched down Hannah's walkway as if we were going to the prom.

"How are things in Boston, Liv?" Alfred

asked on the drive over.

"Lonely," I admitted, braiding the tassels of my scarf. It was harder to be back in Guthrie than I expected, and not just because of Martin.

"Any chance you'll come back?"

I looked out the window as we drove down Main Street. Pharmacy, hardware store, knitting shop, the White Market — each with its lights off, done for the day. The sidewalks were shoveled clean, not a dirty ice mountain to be seen. The diner parking lot was full of pickup trucks bearing bright yellow plows. "Maybe a small one."

The parking lot of the grange hall was packed by the time we pulled into the dirt lot, and when I stepped out, I could hear the beat of the piano and the stomp of dancers in leather-soled shoes on the old wooden floor. The hall was a wall of bodies. Hundreds of paper snowflakes covered in silver glitter hung from the ceiling. We hurried into the coatroom and peeled off our coats.

The concession tables were covered with evergreen cloths. Bonnie manned a cotton-candy machine that spun maple syrup into billowy clouds. Corn popped in time with the piano, filling the glass case with pale puffs. A pack of Girl Scouts sold lemonade and cold cider.

There were four lines of dancers, and the room was a cheerful swirl of movement. You could feel everyone's happiness at just being out of the house. We lingered at the back of the hall, watching the men twirl their partners. I smiled up at Alfred. "Thanks for convincing me to stay tonight."

The music ended, and the dancers drifted over to the refreshment table or switched partners for the next dance. Tom stood up from the piano and stretched. I waved up at him.

"Dancers, line up," the caller said into the microphone.

Alfred took me by the elbow. "Ready, Livvy?" he asked with a determined look in his eye.

"Ready," I said, grinning.

Tom played the first bars on the piano, then the fiddle player joined in. The tune was so bouncy it would have been impossible to stay still.

"Four hands around," the caller said, and we joined hands with another couple, walking in a circle.

Alfred's hand felt solid in mine.

"Now swing the opposite," the caller instructed, and the man from the other couple took my hands. I looked up to smile at my new partner. He was one of the suits who had come out of Margaret's office that morning.

"Now swing your own." Alfred wrapped an arm around my waist, his hand in my hand. "Stop trying to figure out what's next and come back," he said into my ear as he swung me with strength and grace.

"Four hands around," said the caller. I absently placed my hand in my neighbor's and walked around in a circle.

"I saw you at the Sugar Maple this morning," the stranger said.

"You did. You had a meeting with Margaret?" I asked innocently.

"The other way back," the caller said.

"You wouldn't be Olivia Rawlings, would you?" His grip tightened on my hand slightly.

I let my hand go slack, but he held his firm. "I would be. Have we met?"

"Now swing the opposite."

The man took my hands in his and swung me in a circle. "No. Charles Bradford. I'm in the hospitality business. I'm familiar with your work. I was disappointed to hear you're no longer baking for the Sugar Maple."

"Change partners." Alfred wrapped his arm around my waist. As he swung me around in a graceful circle, I closed my eyes, trying to remember where I had heard the name Charles Bradford before.

"Four hands around," said the caller. Alfred grabbed one hand while Charles took the other.

"Have you left the Sugar Maple permanently?"

"The other way back."

I felt dizzy as we switched directions. Charles Bradford. Bradford.

"Swing the opposite."

Charles Bradford watched me with interest as he swung me around. His suit looked expensive. "What does *permanent* mean, really?" I asked him, plastering a smile on my face. "No one really knows what's going to happen in the future, do they?"

"Now swing your own."

I slumped gratefully onto Alfred's shoulder. Something didn't feel right. And then it hit me. The Bradford Group. My knees locked, and as Alfred tried to swing me, he tripped, bashing into the couple beside us. I stepped away from the fray and out of the line.

"Four hands round."

"I'm sorry, I'm so sorry," I shouted as I pushed through the crowd. The line broke and crumbled, the dancers squawking in confusion like disturbed hens. Alfred followed me as I marched to the coatroom.

"Livvy, what just happened?"

I rummaged through coats, aggressively pushing hanger after hanger to the side, looking for my own. "She's going to sell it."

"What are you talking about?" Alfred stood in the doorway, looking nervous.

"Margaret — the inn. She's really going to do it. The people she met with today? They're from the Bradford Group — that's a hotel investment group."

"Yes. Jane's cousins."

"Seriously? Of course they are. Did you know that they love to buy up little mom-and-pop places and make them depressing corporate tourist traps?"

"It makes sense that she would want to sell."

I whipped around. "What are you talking about? That doesn't make any sense at all. She can't sell it."

"She's in her seventies, Livvy," Alfred said gently. "She might be getting tired."

"Margaret doesn't get tired. Besides, it's her home. Where is she going to go?"

"Someplace warm, maybe."

"God, I can't believe you're being so philosophical about this."

"And I'm a little surprised at how selfish you're being."

It felt as if he had slapped me. "How am I being selfish? It's her. What are you going to do if she sells? And Sarah? And the rest of the waitstaff? It's not like this goddamned town is full of job opportunities."

"Did you ever stop and think about what she has here?"

She has everything, I wanted to say.

Alfred stepped closer until he stood behind me, and he placed his hands on my shoulders. "I'm sorry. I know you're upset. But you left. You can't expect to have a say in what happens here when you're two hundred miles south of us."

I pulled on my coat, buttoning it up to the top button. "I need the Sugar Maple to stay the Sugar Maple."

Alfred smiled at me kindly as he zipped up his parka. "Things change, Livvy. Sometimes for the better."

CHAPTER SIXTEEN

I snuck out of Alfred's trailer the next morning, partly because I wanted to go for a walk before I headed to Dotty's, partly because I didn't want to say good-bye. I pulled my car into a space at the far end of the inn's parking lot, not wanting to be caught by Margaret.

I traded my clogs for a pair of green rubber boots I had never removed from my trunk, zipped my purple fleece over my tunic, and trudged through the apple orchard. The sleigh path through the orchard was thick with mud under the slushy snow, and the walking was slow going. Off in the distance steam was rising out of the open windows of the sugarhouse. The front door was wide open, and the voices of men carried over the field.

Home, I thought, my heart reaching toward the cabin.

I stomped the mud off my boots on the

front porch and shouted hello. Tom's familiar red and black plaid back was leaning
over the evaporating pan attached to the
woodstove. He lifted up a ladleful of syrup
and poured it back into the vat.

"It's not aproning yet," he said to the
young man beside him. Then he looked up
at me and smiled.

"Sap's almost done with its run, Livvy.
You'll have to wait a couple more days, but
then the cabin is all yours."

I hugged my waist, feeling the moisture
on my skin. The cabin, with the exception
of the evaporator, the steam, and all the
young men, looked as I had left it. Someone
had put clean linen on the futon and covered it with a pretty chenille bedspread the
color of fresh egg yolks. The Christmas tree
had been removed, the needles swept. I felt
both grateful and sad that it was gone. I
flopped onto the couch and smiled up at
Tom. "So how did she rope you into sugaring this year?"

"No roping involved," Tom said. "I offered
to do the work and share the profit with
her." He tilted his head to the three teenage
boys who were carrying in more logs for the
fire. "I wanted the grandkids to know how
to do more than play Xbox."

The syrup in the pan began to boil vigorously and rise to the edge. Tom tossed in a pat of butter, and the syrup settled back down. "This is the end of the run. We're getting mostly grade B now. It doesn't get the best price, but it's the most delicious." He ladled the syrup again, and it poured down in a thick sheet. Tom poured some of the syrup into a bucket and plopped in a glass tube. "All right, boys, we're ready to draw off. Bring me the buckets."

The boys lined up with metal buckets. Tom filled each one from a spigot at the base of the pan. The boys poured the syrup through a sieve lined with cheesecloth into clean buckets. Tom filled the evaporator with a new batch of sap. He poured some of it into a Dixie cup and handed it to me. It tasted like spring — green, cold, and alive.

"Have a good time last night?" Tom joined me on the couch.

"I did. Not as fun as playing onstage, of course."

"Next time." Tom scratched at his whiskers. "I saw you broke out of one of the lines toward the end."

"I did." I watched two of the boys as they bottled the syrup on my kitchen counter. "She's really going to sell, huh?"

"It's looking that way. In the past she only entertained offers from locals, but I've seen a lot of out-of-state plates in the parking lot lately. Odd for this time of year." Tom looked over at the boys. "Sean, pour some of that syrup into a pot and bring it to a boil." He leaned over to me. "You've never had sugar on snow, I'm guessing?"

I shook my head.

"Well, you're in for a treat."

I followed Tom out into the yard, where he mounded some fresh snow into a pile. The sun felt warm on my neck, but the wind coming down the hill through the woods behind the cabin was cold on my skin.

"Careful," Tom said to the boy with a saucepan between two pot-holdered hands. Tom took the pot and poured the syrup in a steady stream, making roping patterns in the snow. The syrup grew waxy. Tom held up a piece and handed it to me. I put it in my mouth. It was chewy, like taffy. I sighed in delight.

"We used to eat this with powdered doughnuts and pickles when we were kids," Tom explained. The boys came out one by one to grab a piece, then returned to their jobs.

"That sounds like something from a picture book," I said fondly, watching the long-limbed boys push one another around.

I hadn't given much thought to how I'd raise the baby — would I give her a childhood like mine in the city, growing up in bookstores, subways, and cafés? Memories of Thanksgiving at the McCrackens' flooded my mind, the cozy feeling of being surrounded by family, the children wandering from room to room, woods to fields, always with someone to play with.

Tom clamped my shoulder. "When are you coming back, Liv? We got used to you being around. And I've lost five pounds!" Tom rubbed his belly.

"June. Can't miss the White wedding," I said, looking out toward the pines. "I was thinking of walking to Dotty's. Is it passable?"

"Once you get under the evergreens, the carriage path isn't too muddy. You might make it all the way to the farm. Careful, though," he warned, turning back to the evaporator.

I zipped up my jacket. "Thanks, Tom."

"All right, then." Tom tipped his baseball hat to me and set back to work, skimming the surface of the sap.

The air felt cold after the steam of the sugarhouse, and the damp on my cheeks stung. Tom was right — once I crossed into the evergreens the walking was easy. Someone — most likely Mark or Ethan — had kept the sleigh rides going on the carriage trail, so the snow was packed down smooth and hard. Clear white light filtered softly through the pines. The whole world looked white and gray and green. In the quiet I felt my whole body loosen. Martin was everywhere in these woods. For the first time in months, I allowed myself to feel the loss of him. There was something so comforting about his physical presence, something that I hadn't recognized until he had gone. When I was with him, I had felt tucked in, in place. I walked faster, trying to stomp out the thoughts with my boot steps. I knew where they would lead me, and it was just going to make lunch with Dotty more difficult to get through.

Under the tree in the little clearing where Martin had stopped to show me the great horned owl were bits of fur, blood, and bones. I looked up. There she was, as if she had been waiting for me. Her yellow eyes blinked down at me. Beside her sat what looked like two downy footballs.

"You too?" I asked her. The owlets stared down at me with the same steady gaze as their mother. They were covered in gray curls, as though they were draped in sheepskin. One of them yawned and stretched its wings, and the other did the same. The mother's head whipped around. I turned to see what had caused her alarm.

There on the carriage path stood Martin McCracken.

I looked away and then back, expecting him to disappear like a ghost. He looked thinner than before, his black jeans hanging loose, his torso hidden underneath the Irish knit sweater I had fallen asleep on only months earlier.

"Livvy." His voice shook me out of the sensation that this was all a dream.

"What are you doing here?" I asked unsteadily.

"I took the red-eye when I heard you were in town." Martin stood awkwardly for a moment, then took three long strides and pulled me into his arms. I nuzzled into his armpit, breathing him in.

"I'm so sorry," he said in his drone-string voice.

My mind raced, counting the things Martin could regret. I didn't want to be one of them. I loosened my grip and took a step back.

"For everything. For not telling you about Sylvie. I tried — I tried to keep my distance from you. I wanted to tell you the night I brought over the Christmas tree, but . . .”

“But Henry went into the hospital,” I said, remembering his hesitation when I kissed him.

Martin nodded. “I came looking for you to talk after the funeral, but you had left.”

“Is it true, then? You and Sylvie, you’re —”

Martin shook his head. “I told her about you when we got back home. I’d wanted to tell her right away, but my father . . . And then it was Christmas, and I didn’t want to tell her when she was so far away from home.” Martin let his breath out in a steady stream. “She had guessed. She slept in one of the guest rooms while she was here. She said it was out of respect for my mother, but —”

“You’re not together anymore?” My head spun.

“We split up. We just sold the condo. The closing is at the end of April. Listen.” Martin looked like a kid at five o’clock on a Christmas morning — wild hair and tired eyes, barely able to contain his excitement. “I’ve just been hired to play fiddle for the Darnielle Brothers. The Darnielle Brothers!”

They were the biggest name in alt-country.

“The tour starts in Japan! A thirty-city

tour here in the States, then we're going to be in Europe all summer." Martin pulled me back into his embrace. "Come with me," he said into my hair. "You'd have a blast playing in all the jams at the festivals, traveling to all those different places." Martin pulled just far enough away so he could cup my cheeks in his hands. "And we could be together."

He leaned down and kissed me then.

There are only a few moments in my life that I have ever wanted to bask in — driving up the coast of Maine beside my father on an autumn afternoon, when I pulled my first chocolate soufflé out of the oven, the first time Salty rested his muzzle on my lap and sighed. And now this. I would have given anything to pause time right there.

I pushed my palms against his chest and stepped back. "I can't."

"What? Why?" Martin's expression held a mixture of confusion and hurt.

"Because of the pie contest," I blurted.

He took a step back to get a full look at me. "Livvy, if it's really that important, you can come back for the pie contest."

I wanted to say yes. A few months earlier I would have already been digging through my drawers for my passport. "It's not just that. Hannah is going to give birth soon, and Margaret needs me to make a wedding cake in June. I have to stay."

"You're not even living here," he said, exasperated. It was as though I could see his plans dripping off him one by one like slowly melting icicles. "Come on, Liv. This is our chance."

Through my fleece pocket, I pressed my hand onto my belly. Margaret was right — Martin deserved to know. But I knew that what Henry had said was also true — Martin would do the right thing. He would give up his dreams and move back to Guthrie. I couldn't be the reason he stayed.

"Couldn't our chance wait until you come back?" I asked.

Martin looked deflated.

"Listen," I said, grabbing the fabric of his jacket. "Your dad just died. And you ended a long relationship, you sold your house. I'm assuming that you quit your teaching job too?" I leaned my head against him and spoke into his chest. "This isn't the time for any more big decisions. Think about what you really want when you're on the road. Call me when you get back."

I stood up on my tiptoes and kissed him firmly on the lips, then turned away, walking as fast as I could down the snowy path before I changed my mind.

"Apologize to your mom for me," I called, not looking back.

CHAPTER SEVENTEEN
MAY

April did its usual showers-to-May-flowers thing, but the lilacs that hugged the Friendly Eating Place's back alley were cloying, and I kept the back door off the storeroom closed despite the growing warmth. Ever since I had returned from Guthrie, I had felt stuck. Every sign of spring fed my irritation. The daffodils' cheerful faces mocked me. The birdsong at dawn sounded more like a lament. I knew saying no to Martin had been the right decision, but I hadn't given much thought to what would happen next. When I tried to fantasize about the future, the daydream would always end in Guthrie, but with Martin gone and Margaret selling the Sugar Maple it didn't make much sense. It was as if Guthrie, with all its past possibilities, were being eaten piece by piece until there were only crumbs. I tried to keep thoughts of Martin at bay, but my swelling breasts and nightly leg cramps were a constant reminder that a part of him would always be with me. I pushed through each day like it was just something to get through, napping during the daylight, folding my way through the "Creams, Fools, and Jellies" chapter of Richard's cookbook each night.

I was lying on my cot after my OB/GYN appointment, reading a magazine article debating nail art — yea or nay — when I heard the familiar Monday-night sounds of folding chairs squeaking open and stringed instruments being tightened into life.

It was a hot night, sticky for spring, and the heavy feeling of the baby was making me restless. I poked my head into the alley. The music shop's back door was propped open, and without the walls between us the music sounded sweet. I leaned on the doorframe, willing myself to turn around and go back in, when I heard the first notes of "I'll Fly Away," an old gospel tune my father had loved to play.

Some bright morning when this life is over,
    I'll fly away

For a song about dying, it had a joyful lightness to it. It was hard to resist. I stepped quietly into the back of the shop.

The familiar scents of old cigarette smoke and whiskey reminded me of an old-man bar. I eased through a tunnel of instrument cases stacked waist high against the walls, making my way toward the music.

To a land on God's celestial shore, I'll fly
  away

Through the doorway to the front of the shop I could see a couple of the players. Wide men, pants held up by suspenders, faces covered in gray whiskers. Young bearded men playing confidently next to the old-timers. I slipped into the packed room, taking a seat in the corner between the door and a pile of fake books. A middle-aged man with a stumpy little banjo called a banjo-uke in his lap smiled at me and nodded his head. The jam reminded me of ones that my father had taken me to, and sitting among the players felt akin to church, tunes in place of prayers. I settled back into my chair and closed my eyes.

I'll fly away, oh glory, I'll fly away
When I die, hallelujah by and by, I'll fly
  away

I felt it between "Black Cat in the Briar Patch" and "Cumberland Gap." Right where my arm rested against the side of my belly. A little nudge, from the inside out, like she was trying to get my attention.

"Holy crap," I said. I pressed my hand into my side. She nudged again.

"You all right?" the man next to me asked.

"Yes — it's just, it's the baby," I said, blushing, like it was a secret I was keeping.

"You haven't felt it before?"

I shook my head, pressing my hand into my side, just wanting to feel her again. I rested my hands on my belly where I had felt the jab. Nothing. A couple of the players picked the first phrase of "Jennie Jenkins," a silly song sung to teach little kids their colors. When the tune ended, I felt a tumbling inside. "Hey there, baby," I sang. "I think she likes the music," I said to the man, feeling like I was meeting her for the first time.

"We better keep playing, then," he said, and called to the jam leader to play some old children's tunes. The fiddler led "Skip to My Lou" followed by "Polly Wolly Doodle." I placed my hands on my belly and focused my attention inward. I felt as if we were listening together.

The leader stuck his foot out, and the last tune ended with a whoop from the players. One by one instrument cases were latched, mandolins and guitars put to bed for the night.

"Do you mind, just for a second?" I asked the man next to me, reaching toward him. I wanted to test out a theory. He handed me his stubby banjo. I sat up and strummed out a few chords. Another little flutter, and then a sharper nudge. "Okay, kiddo," I whispered as my fingers fell into Henry's tune. "I'll keep playing."

Hannah called a week later to tell me her doctor had put her on mandatory bed rest for the remainder of her pregnancy. The first thing I did when I hung up the phone was dye my hair — Cotton Candy Pink — after I had double-checked to make sure the dye was nontoxic and vegan and wouldn't turn my baby into a woolly mammoth. Then I shoved everything I had into a garbage bag, left the keys to the Friendly Eating Place on the pizza counter, and drove straight to Guthrie, not even stopping at the F&G for pie.

Hannah's house, which was normally decorator-magazine clean, was a mess of unfinished baby projects. I became Hannah's partner in nesting for as long as my body would allow each day, assembling strollers and hanging mobiles. Then we would both cuddle up on the bed and nap or watch talk shows.

I emptied Hannah's laundry basket onto the foot of her king-sized bed. A multicolored mountain of onesies, diaper covers, and spit-up blankets tumbled across the duvet. "Should I sort these by category?" I asked, folding a tiny light green T-shirt into quarters. There were hundreds of pieces of clothing, all adorable. The only thing I had purchased for my baby so far was a black onesie with the Ramones' logo in white.

"Could you keep the long-sleeve and short-sleeve shirts separate?" Hannah asked from under the covers. She was lying on her side, a pillow propped under her stomach, which I could have sworn had grown in the past hour. "I can't thank you enough for doing this," she said for the millionth time.

"You don't have to thank me. Just give me all of the boys' hand-me downs," I said as I folded a baby blue sweater.

"So, Liv — where is Martin now?" she asked, keeping her voice light. Hannah hadn't been too happy when I told her I had sent Martin away.

"LA, maybe?" I replied, but I knew from my daily checks of the band's Twitter feed that they were playing at the El Ray in LA that night, in San Francisco the following night, then up in Portland and Seattle. Martin e-mailed me weekly with details of the tour. I responded only in emojis and pictures of Salty, worried that if I used words I'd let something slip.

"You're going to have to tell him soon, Liv. Before someone sees you in town and tells him themselves."

She was right, of course. My own baby bump had emerged, and I looked undeniably pregnant. I kept to Hannah's house most of the time, and I would travel two, three, or five towns over if there were errands to be run. I figured I was only one or two ice cream runs away from being the hottest piece of gossip at the farmer's market.

"I was thinking of e-mailing him as soon as he lands in Helsinki."

The oven timer went off in the kitchen. From around the corner I could hear the splatter of bubbling pie filling hitting the cookie sheet. The room was heavily scented with browning butter and caramelized sugar. I had finished my work for Richard, but I had told Hannah I was still working on the pies and tarts chapter. She didn't seem to notice that every pie I made was apple.

When I returned, Hannah was sitting upright with her legs dangling over the side of the bed.

"Do you need help?" I asked, assuming she was on her way to the bathroom.

"I think my water just broke."

I stopped in the middle of the room. "Are you sure? What do we do? Should I call an ambulance? Boil water? Tear up sheets?"

Hannah laughed. "No to all of those things. I'm not even in labor, at least I don't think so." She scooted off the bed. "Jonathan is at the hospital anyway. Let's go over and find him. Help me get dressed."

The television in the waiting room of the maternity ward was set to a marathon of *The Bachelor,* which I thought was an odd choice, but by the time Jonathan came out of the delivery room, blurry-eyed and happy, I had watched the whole first season.

"Everybody okay?" I asked, but you could see from the joy in his face that mother and babies were just fine.

To my surprise, Jonathan wrapped me in a bear hug. "Thank you for being here for us, Livvy. You've been a great friend." I wanted to make a joke about how this was the first time we had ever touched, but instead I burst into tears. Once I had entered into my second trimester, I had become a serious weeper. When Jonathan pulled away I could see that he was crying too. "Come see my sons."

Hannah looked exhausted but serene, a white-capped, swaddled bundle in each arm.

"Hey there, babies," I said, rubbing a freshly sanitized finger across one of the twin's cheeks. "They're so little."

Jonathan sat next to Hannah, and a nurse placed one of his sons in his arms. The baby's mouth stretched into a yawn.

"You holding up okay?" I asked Hannah. "Did the drugs work?" I was terrified of giving birth. Hell, I was terrified of the whole thing, from birth through high school diploma. Hannah looked so natural holding the babies, as if she were a nurse or a midwife. I couldn't help but wonder if I would ever look like that.

Hannah beamed up at me. "Aren't they beautiful?"

"They really are, Hann."

Another nurse came in and checked Hannah's chart. "Mom needs her rest now."

"Can I do anything before I go?" I asked, buttoning up my sweater.

Hannah shook her head, not taking her eyes off the babies.

"I'll be back in the morning."

I lingered by the door for a moment watching Hannah and Jonathan, gazing down at their sons, laughing quietly about some little expression one of the boys made. I wanted my baby to know that closeness too. And I knew I had some decisions to make.

It was two in the morning when I left the hospital, but by the time I got back to Hannah's house I felt wired. I swung by the house to pick up Salty and hopped back into the car.

The inn's windows were dark, but I drove around and parked in the back. There was still a light on in the kitchen. I let myself in the back door, the way I had so many times before. Margaret was sitting in one of the rocking chairs, a paperback half read in her hand.

"Miss Rawlings," she said, as if she expected me. I set the pie on the counter and sat down in the rocker beside her. "You're looking well," she said.

"Thanks." I rocked back, not sure if she was being nice or sarcastic. "I brought you something."

"All the way from Boston?"

"Just from Hannah's. I've been here for a while, helping. She had the babies tonight.

Two boys." I jutted my chin over toward the counter. "It's a pie."

Margaret walked over to the counter and opened the Tupperware bin I had stored the pie in. "Everyone doing well, I expect."

"Yeah. They're super cute. You'll have to come by when she's back from the hospital."

Margaret handed me a plate and fork along with a napkin and a glass of water. She settled back into her chair and took a dainty bite.

I studied her as she chewed, looking for a reaction. She really did have the best poker face.

"Now that the babies have arrived, will you be staying long?"

"Indefinitely." I stopped rocking and leaned forward. "Listen, I came by because I wanted to apologize. I've felt terrible about the way I left here. It wasn't fair to you."

"I understood why you were upset," she said carefully, "but many people before you have weathered more embarrassment than a broken heart." I wondered if she was speaking from experience. "You didn't need to leave."

I carefully unfolded the napkin and lay it across my lap. "Leaving just always seems like the best option."

"The world is full of heartbreak, Miss

Rawlings. Might be a good idea to try something different next time." Margaret took another bite of the pie, chewing it slowly. "It's going to be fairly crowded over there when the babies come home."

"Tell me about it. Mrs. Doyle is coming to stay for the month of June, and Jonathan has hired both a day nurse and a house-keeper to come in."

"You know I'm selling the inn, correct?"

"I do." I dug my fork into the pointed tip of my pie slice. It sank easily through the crust, down into the tender apple slices. "Are the papers signed?"

"Not till the end of the summer. They wanted to see how the staff handled a func-tion like the White wedding before they made any final decisions about who stays and who goes. And they want to see the profits, of course."

I hated those corporate hospitality groups. Profit was all they really cared about. "And what will you do?"

"Haven't decided. Something new." Mar-garet scraped the last flake of pastry off the plate with her fork. "I can only guarantee you through the summer, but if you make a good impression, maybe we can get you a contract with the new owners."

"Margaret, I didn't come over here expecting —"

"Sap's stopped running, of course, so the cabin's free." She pointed at my bulging tunic. "But sooner than later you'll want to be close to indoor plumbing. You can have the baker's quarters. The dog can sleep in the living room unless someone complains."

My body suddenly felt buoyant, as if I were floating in Lake Willoughby. "If I stay for the summer, do you know what that means?"

"That you will irritate me for months with these impossible questions?" Margaret collected our plates and brought them over to the sink.

I rocked myself out of the chair. "No, it means I'll be here in July. For the contest." I stood in the middle of the kitchen, beaming. "What did you think of the pie?"

Margaret brushed her fingers across her pearls just once. "Good. Not as sweet."

"Right?" I asked. "I backed way off on the sugar. Now you can taste the sweetness of the fruit itself." I hugged my shoulders, trying to contain my excitement. "If this ends up being your last baking contest, wouldn't it be great to go out with a blue?"

The room was dark, but I swear I saw a hint of a smile cross Margaret's face. "Good night, Miss Rawlings. Let me know what your plans are so I can alert the staff."

CHAPTER EIGHTEEN
JUNE

Vermont in June is like Oz. The mud-caked slush of spring gives way to green fields dotted with yellow dandelions and black and white cows. On the road to the Sugar Maple I rolled down the windows to drink in the aromas of fresh dirt and cut grass. I felt full to bursting, like an overripe tomato, and connected to every living thing.

This was partly due to pregnancy hormones, I'm sure. I had passed into my third trimester with an inexplicable sense of relief. Every part of my life was in transition. It was like the turning of the seasons, when you can feel change hovering beneath the surface. The period between letting go of the old and diving into the new usually makes me restless and prone to terrible decisions, like the time I had a whisk and spatula tattooed on my butt. This time I felt happy to be returning to the inn and my little cabin between the orchard and the forest.

I don't know how long I sat in the Sugar Maple parking lot trying to work up the nerve to get out of the car. I had stayed on at Hannah's for a couple more weeks, wanting to make sure she had everything she needed, and getting a preview of what life was like with a newborn (or two). It was like attending baby boot camp. But when Hannah's mother-in-law arrived, I knew it was time to go. Once I entered the inn, the news that I was going to be a mom would be all over town by nightfall. I leaned back in my seat, stroking Salty's fur, wishing I could just take a small nap and wake up after the baby was born.

Margaret and Alfred appeared in the parking lot. Alfred gaped when I hoisted myself out of the car, but he quickly recovered and grabbed all the heavy boxes of cake-decorating supplies I had ordered from Raphael. Margaret scolded me for spending so much money on a cake wheel but didn't say a word when Salty waltzed through her flower bed.

The kitchen was already bustling when I shuffled in, looking for decaf, the day before the wedding. I had filled and frosted the cakes the previous day, but they still needed to be covered in fondant, decorated, and assembled.

Alfred worked beside me, his long prep table covered with plates on which he artfully placed handfuls of baby arugula. "You know, Livvy, you really shouldn't have left the Maple Sugaring Festival so early."

It was comforting to be back in the kitchen with Alfred. I hadn't seen him since I had arrived, and I'd been worried that he was avoiding me.

I rolled out a thin layer of fondant, a healthy dusting of confectioners' sugar on the table to keep it from sticking. "How come?" I said absently.

"You missed the talent show," he said, suppressing a laugh.

I slid the layer of fondant over one of the cake layers, carefully tucking in the edges so the cake appeared to be completely wrapped in fabric. When the edges were straight and smooth, I pressed a silicone mat with the raised double-wedding-ring quilt pattern into the fondant, then followed the lines of the impression with a spiked embossing wheel so that the fondant looked like it had been stitched.

"Did I?"

"They sang 'Let the Sunshine In,' " he said, a small nest of arugula cradled in his hand. "You know. From *Hair*?"

With tweezers I carefully tucked tiny sugar pearls into the spaces where the stitches met. "Oh my God, they weren't naked, were they?" I dropped the tweezers.

"Yes, they were. You should have seen the postmistress."

"No! Enough! No more visuals!" I said, laughing.

"Good afternoon, Miss Rawlings," Margaret said as she walked through the kitchen and into the dining room, the door swinging in her wake.

"I know about the sale," I said quietly to Alfred, pressing the rolling pin into a fresh piece of fondant. "Although I still can't believe she's selling to anyone connected with Jane. What are you going to do?"

Alfred's expression sobered. "I'm hoping to stay, but if they decide to change things up, I'll find another place. Don't worry about me."

Alfred finished the salads and turned his attention to the stovetop, where he started sautéing something with leeks that made my mouth water. I covered the final layer of the cake. It was time for my least-favorite part: assembly. Each cake layer was already supported by stiff cardboard. I pressed several wide plastic straws through the layers for stability, trimmed them with scissors, then held my breath as I carefully set the chocolate layer on the coconut with passionfruit curd, the lemon-raspberry on top.

"It's stunning, Livvy," Alfred said behind me.

I turned to face him, smiling. "Now the hard part — getting it into the walk-in." At the suggestion of motion, the baby flipped over. "Stop squirming."

"What's that? Are you all right?" Alfred looked alarmed. "Do you need to sit down?"

"I'm fine," I said, rubbing my side. "It's just the baby. She's squirmy this morning."

"She?"

"That's what Margaret said. I'm going with it."

Alfred came to stand beside me. "May I?" he asked before he set his hand on my belly. He started when he felt her move. "Wow. She's strong, like her mother."

"Either that or grouchy like her mother," I mumbled.

"Livvy," he said quietly, "I could make an honest woman out of you."

"I think it's a little too late for that," I said, laughing.

Alfred removed his hand. He looked hurt.

"Alfred?" I asked tentatively.

"I know you probably still have feelings for Martin — it's Martin's baby, isn't it? —

but we're a good team, Liv. And I've always wanted children. I'd treat her like she was my own." Alfred kept his gaze steady. He was serious.

I grabbed his wrist. "That is pretty much the kindest thing anyone has ever offered me."

Alfred's eyes moved from mine to the floor. "That sounds like a no."

"I still can't wrap my mind around the fact that I'm going to be a mother. I can't think about being a wife now. It *is* marriage you're talking about, right?"

"I'm more of a traditional guy than I look," he said. "You don't have to do this alone."

"That's not a good reason for marriage, Al," I said softly.

"I don't think it's so bad."

Margaret walked back in, her arms full of white lilies, gripping a pile of papers. "Lilies for a wedding," she scoffed, plopping them down on a table. "It smells like a funeral parlor out there."

My stomach roiled. Alfred turned back to the stove, but not before I saw the crestfallen look on his face.

Margaret came and stood behind me, assessing the cake.

"All three flavors?" she asked.

"Three flavors? I thought she wanted all chocolate," I said, throwing my hands up in mock horror.

She smacked my hands with the seating chart. "Now, how are we going to move that thing?"

"I'll do it," said Alfred, and effortlessly, he picked up the three-tiered cake and carried it into the walk-in.

"You could do worse," I heard Margaret mutter behind me.

The day of the wedding was bright and sunny, as if Jane White had made arrangements with God himself. Puffy clouds dotted a sky so blue it looked spray-painted on. The white tents were set up in the field overlooking the valley below. I spent the morning helping Sarah and Margaret tie white tulle onto the backs of the chairs in the dining area while a team of men laid down the dance floor under the adjacent tent. It was only eleven in the morning but the sun was blazing, and a fine sheet of sweat had formed on my forehead.

The women of the wedding party were giggling in the sitting room in their matching pink gowns, bouquets of miniature lilies clutched in their hands. They were all in their early twenties, fresh-faced and hopeful. I heard a gasp from the group, then a squeal, followed by a chorus of sighs. I looked at the top of the stairs to see Emily White standing in her wedding gown, white lace dotted with tiny crystals. She looked like a confection. Jane White stood behind her in a suit made of teal silk, a choker of pearls tight at her throat, fussing at the back of Emily's gown and frowning. She looked down at me, her eyes trailing from my face to my belly. My hand protectively cradled my bump. I turned and scuttled back into the safety of the kitchen.

Margaret stood leaning over her checklist and drinking a cup of tea. Alfred was giving directions to a couple of young new dishwashers while Sarah poured iced tea into glass pitchers. There is nothing worse than feeling idle in a busy kitchen. I waddled up to Alfred. "Give me a job. I feel useless and in the way."

Alfred's lips attempted a grin, but his eyes told another story. "Everything is under control here, Livvy. Why don't you get off those feet for a little while," he said, tilting his head toward the rocking chairs.

I did as he said. It actually felt good to sit down. Alfred sang along to Frank Sinatra on the radio as he sliced the fingerling potatoes. Margaret was right. I could do worse, a lot worse. He'd make an excellent, doting father. Husband too. I shook my head. Someone opened the back door, and a warm breeze filtered through the kitchen. I was surprised when Dotty appeared, her gray hair piled high in a loose bun on top of her head. My eyes immediately filled with tears. I pressed my hands into the armrests of the rocking chair and tried to hoist myself up. Dotty made a clucking sound and shook her head. She leaned over and kissed me on the cheek.

"I'm pregnant," I blurted. My cheeks blazed and I began to cry in earnest.

"I can see that," Dotty said, laughing. "That's wonderful."

"Kinda," I said, rubbing at my eyes with my forearm. Dotty dug around in her handbag and handed me a packet of tissues.

"You'll be a good mother. I always thought so."

I blew my nose loudly into the paper tissue. "I'm so sorry I didn't tell you." *That I'm carrying your grandchild.* "I haven't really known what to do. Did Margaret say anything?"

Dotty rocked back in her chair. "She mentioned it a couple of days ago. But don't be cross with her. She was just sparing me hearing it at the grocery store."

I leaned back into my chair. "Did she tell you who the father is?" I asked quietly as I watched my feet leave the floor.

"She didn't have to." Dotty reached over and took my hand in hers. "Now," she said, looking serious. "Martin hasn't mentioned it. He's always been a private boy, but I'm pretty sure he wouldn't have kept this from me."

"I haven't told him yet."

"What on earth are you waiting for?"

"I don't know. I don't want to be the reason he gives up his dream. He's out there on the road. I figure the baby is going to come whether or not he's on tour."

"People can have more than one dream, dear," she said. "And it's not for you to decide which one they should follow. Tell the truth and step aside, I always say. But I won't mention it. Just do an old woman a favor and tell him soon, before someone like Frank Fraser does. If he asks me, I won't be able to lie."

"Thanks, Dotty," I said, suddenly feeling shy. Dotty and I would be bound by this newest member of her family growing inside of me.

"I wish Henry could have been here to meet her," Dotty said, her face softening.

I squeezed her hand. "Me too. Although

don't you think he would have been angry?"

"Oh, he'd be angry at Martin for not marrying you yet. But he already saw you as family, dear. I think he would have been very happy."

Margaret came over and handed us each a glass of iced tea. She looked down at her watch. "I'm looking forward to twelve hours from now, when the entire White family is off my land."

Dotty raised her glass in the air and said, "Amen."

I clinked glasses with her and took a long sip, trying to quench the burning urge to point out that this wouldn't be *her land* if she went through with the sale.

Sarah pushed in through the swinging doors. "The first group has arrived. Can someone bring some more ice out to the bar?"

I hoisted myself up out of the chair and pulled one of my old chef's coats over the Clash T-shirt I was wearing. "I'll start traying up the canapés."

The staff moved smoothly from hors d'oeuvres to the first course, and the entrées were served on schedule. We were just wiping down the tables when Sarah came rushing back in.

"Alfred, two of the dishwashers are having

a fistfight out back — can you deal with them before they bleed on a bridesmaid?" Alfred dashed out the back door. "Oh," Sarah added as she reached for the silver coffee pots, "Mrs. White is demanding the cake." It had been too humid earlier in the day for us to set out the cake for display. I looked over at Margaret. I hadn't known it was possible for her back to get any stiffer. She marched into the pantry and returned pushing a large steel cart on wheels. "We can wheel the cake down to the tent on this."

"Shouldn't we wait for Alfred?"

"Nonsense," she said, disappearing into the walk-in. I dashed in behind her to keep her from trying to lift the cake by herself.

It was a stunning evening. The sun was low in the sky, and the white steeples of the churches in the valley glowed. The guests were mingling and refreshing their drinks at the bar. The bride and groom moved from table to table, receiving kisses, congratulations, and not a few white envelopes. The DJ was playing Glenn Miller, and the dance floor was already packed, mostly with the silver-haired crowd. Margaret and I carefully wheeled the cake over to the dance tent. The dance floor was raised off the ground.

"We'll have to carry it from here," I said, a little nervous about the distance between the cake table and us.

I had decorated the cake on a thick wooden base covered in gold foil. Margaret and I each took hold of a side and carefully lifted it off the cart. It must have weighed fifty pounds.

We were clutching the base of the cake, one foot each on the dance floor, when a voice behind us said, "The two of you could be mistaken for mother and daughter." I didn't need to turn around to know it was Jane White. I felt Margaret pause, and I gripped my edge tighter, as if that would help.

"Just lift up your other foot," I instructed, but Margaret remained in place.

"But that's impossible, isn't it? Since you never had any children." The song ended, and the stage fell silent as the DJ furiously pushed a button on his laptop, trying to get the next track to play.

I craned my neck to see Jane leaning against the cake table, which was inching away from us.

"It's funny, I never thought about it before," Jane said, her voice at full volume. "She's just about the age your daughter would have been, isn't she?" Jane paused, looking around the dance floor. "Well, we mustn't question God's plan."

The only sound under the tent was the click of high heels against the floor.

Louis Armstrong's gravelly voice broke the silence.

I gripped the edge of the cake base and looked at Margaret. All the blood had drained from her face and her bottom lip quivered. Sweat gathered at her brow line.

The cake began to wobble.

"Margaret?" I felt the cake slipping from her hands.

My hands gripped the cake base. At least it wasn't *on fire.* I tried to reach around to take Margaret's edge, but my belly got in the way. *I will not drop this cake, I will not drop this cake,* I murmured to myself. The baby chose this moment to practice mixed martial arts in my womb. "Oh," I gasped.

The photographer, who had been capturing the bride and groom's first dance, dropped his camera and raced over, grabbed the cake from Margaret's hands, and together we placed it carefully on the table. I spun around. Jane White was dancing with a silver-haired gentleman whose resemblance to John White was so striking it startled even me, who had never met the man. Jane gazed up at him, a smug look on her face. Margaret stood at the edge of the floor, frozen.

I climbed down, took her by the elbow, and led her back toward the inn, abandoning the cart near the tents. "That bitch," I said under my breath as we weaved our way through the crowd. When we reached the sitting area, I brought Margaret to one of the couches in the back and sat down beside her.

"My God. What is up with her? What does she want?"

"Something that she can never have," Margaret said, her hands folded neatly in her lap. She sat as still as an ice carving, her eyes unfocused and glassy. "And I'll tell you something, Olivia," she said in a flat tone that frightened me. "I'm tired of it. Tired of running this inn by myself. Tired of being alone. Tired of Jane White. Tired of that goddamned pie contest." She rubbed her hands on her thighs, rocking slightly. "What's the point of it anyway? I don't have anyone to hand the tradition down to. Foolish."

Two young women with champagne glasses came giggling into the foyer.

"Margaret," I asked before I could put all the pieces together, "your daughter?"

Margaret's composure crumpled. She

pressed her hands to her face so that I wouldn't see her crying, but her slender shoulders shook.

I ran over Jane White's words in my head. I thought of Margaret's reaction to my pregnancy. My assumptions had been right. "Oh, Margaret." I placed a tentative hand on her knee. "Did you — I mean, it was you that your aunt helped?"

Margaret brushed my hand away, stood, and walked briskly toward the kitchen. Dotty stepped through the swinging door.

Dotty came into the room. She took in Margaret's expression and quickly stepped aside to let her by. "Livvy, what just happened?"

"I'm not exactly sure," I said, toying with the cloth buttons of my coat. "Jane White — she said some awful things."

Dotty looked down at my belly, where my hands reflexively rested. "Come out back with me."

Salty, lying in a patch of shade behind the inn, thumped his tail against the grass when he saw me come around the corner. Dotty and I sat on a bench facing the apple orchard as strains of music and laughter drifted over from the party.

"You must know what's up between Margaret and Jane," I said.

Dotty nodded, but she remained silent.

"You're her best friend. I'd understand if you don't want to tell me."

Dotty settled back and took a deep breath. "When we were girls, Margaret fell in love with a man named John White. He was nineteen at the time; we were only fifteen or sixteen."

I thought back to my sixteen-year-old self, parentless and alone. It was the age when you thought you were all grown up but were actually still just a kid.

"He worked in his father's grocery store. They were the only market in town in those days. If you needed flour, that's where you went. Margaret's mother had a bad hip and relied on her to go into town and run her errands, so Margaret saw him often enough."

"He must have been smitten. Margaret was gorgeous."

"She was a beauty. Still is, if you ask an old lady like me. Well, John asked her to the fair the summer we turned sixteen. Her father wouldn't let her date, and his family wanted him to marry into one of the more established families. They were snobbish like that. So she and John had to hide that they were together."

"It sounds like a movie."

"It did seem exciting at the time. She told her parents that she was going to the fair with Henry and me, but she slipped off as soon as we arrived. Her first kiss was at the top of the Ferris wheel." Dotty looked out toward the apple trees. "From that night on, they would meet up in barns or in the woods or at dances after her parents had left. They were serious about each other from the start. When she got pregnant, John gave her a string of pearls his grandmother had left him, as a promise."

My heart sank. Margaret wore those pearls every single day.

"He went to his family to tell them he was going to marry her. Of course, his father put his foot down. They were pushing him toward a girl in the next county."

"What do you mean?" I asked.

"John had gone out a few times with a girl his parents had set him up with, just to appease them."

"You mean Jane?"

"Yes It didn't bother Margaret at the time — she knew he loved her and it was all for show. I worried, naturally. I wanted her to be as happy as I was with Henry. It was tough on them, sneaking around." Dotty smiled and took my hand in hers. "Martin always complains about what a small town Guthrie is. Well, he should have seen it back then."

"I can't imagine."

"You couldn't get away with anything. When Jane found out about Margaret, she lied to her parents and said John had taken her virginity. Her parents insisted that he make it right with her, and his agreed."

"But Margaret was *pregnant*. What about making it right with *her*? What about *her* parents?"

Dotty hesitated. "Margaret thinks John's parents might have given her father money to keep quiet. They'd barely been scraping by. Then, shortly after Jane's engagement was announced, Margaret's father bought this house and turned it into an inn."

"What about John?" I asked, furious on behalf of Margaret's teenage self.

"His family eventually wore him down."

"And then Margaret's aunt — ?"

"Her aunt came, and they took care of things. John married Jane and moved her here to Guthrie." Dotty pulled a handkerchief from her skirt pocket and dabbed at her eyes. "But he still loved Margaret, and Jane knew it. Thanks to her, it wasn't long before people in town caught wind that Margaret had been pregnant. No one would have her then. But she refused to leave Guthrie. Folks here have long memories." She looked me in the eye. "You keep that in mind."

I nodded, not wanting to interrupt.

"Margaret met Brian Hurley when he came to stay at the inn. They married soon after. Margaret was forty then. She got pregnant right away, but she miscarried. They stopped trying after awhile."

I swore under my breath. No wonder Margaret wanted to sell the inn and finally get out of here. I thought of the many generations of Whites out in the field, that big extended family that could have been hers. "That's so unfair."

Dotty patted my leg. "A lot of things in life are." She looked down at my bulging belly. "Henry always used to say, 'It's not what happens to you but how you respond to it that matters.' I've never seen anyone handle hard times more gracefully than Margaret."

A mixture of sadness and anger washed over me. I wanted to do something for Margaret, to let her know she was worth a million Jane Whites, but the only thing that felt big enough was to win the damned pie contest.

"What about Margaret and John? They

must have seen each other. It's a small town."

Dotty smiled a shy smile. "They met on the Ferris wheel every year until he died. Just to talk, of course," she added, but her lips curled up into a little grin. "He passed away four years ago."

I leaned back on the bench, trying subtly to scratch my belly. Salty kicked his legs as if he were chasing rabbits in his dream. "Does anyone else know all of this?"

"Oh, people know bits and pieces. But I'm pretty sure it's just you, me, and Margaret who know the whole story."

"Why are you telling me? You're her best friend. Aren't you breaking some sacred code?"

Dotty took my hand back in hers and squeezed. "Because we need each other, dear. You don't have to do everything on your own. That's something you and Margaret both need to keep in mind."

CHAPTER NINETEEN
JULY

Pour-through, crumb crust, Dutch, and dried apple — I made them all. Hazelnuts in the crumb, in the crust, then pecans. I changed the spices, tried every variety of apple I could get my hands on, but in the end I couldn't improve on what Margaret and I both loved best — Cortland and McIntosh, sautéed in butter and lightly sweetened with good old white sugar, with a half teaspoon of cinnamon and a pinch of nutmeg, piled high and tucked in with a top crust. No bells and whistles. Perfect in its simplicity.

The month leading up to the fair drifted by like a dream. A record-breaking heat wave hit the mountains and I would rise early and test-bake a pie before the kitchen grew too hot. The rest of the morning was spent baking desserts for the inn. As soon as lunch service was over, Sarah and I would change into bikinis and drive over to

Lake Willoughby, where I would float on my back, my bulging tummy glowing brightly against the dark glacial water, a giant marshmallow in a deep vat of hot chocolate.

I did end up moving into the Sugar Maple, purely for the indoor plumbing, but I liked to go back to the sugarhouse in the afternoons and sit in one of the rockers on the front porch, watching the bees float through the orchard, daydreaming about the baby, until I was dragged down by the undertow of sleepiness and had to curl up on the futon to rest until sunset. In the evenings, Margaret and I joined Dotty for dinner, and we would try the test pie afterward. Sometimes one of Martin's brothers and his family would join us, but no one mentioned the baby. I felt suspended — as if the baby would live inside me forever, the fair would never come, Margaret would always own the Sugar Maple, and summer would never end.

The first sign that the fair was coming was the traffic. Margaret kept sending me into town on small errands, insisting that the cinnamon wasn't fresh enough, or the butter was too salty, and on each trip I would be gone for hours, stuck behind the trucks that towed the stands from which teenagers would soon be hawking French fries and funnel cakes. Then came the midway crew. The carnival rides seemed to arrive overnight, and with them a rough group of men who filled up the booths of the Black Bear and the Miss Guthrie. The RVs came next, driven by the farmers and their families ready to spend their one yearly vacation camping in style.

I decided to take the back roads up to the inn one afternoon, after finally tracking down the brand of all-purpose flour that Margaret remembered her mother using. I drove slowly by the McCracken land, passing the field of Christmas trees, then the apple orchard, before reaching the driveway to the farmhouse. Mabel and Crabapple looked over the car with their blank almond-shaped eyes. Henry's tune played in my mind, and I tapped the rhythm of it on the steering wheel. With a sudden, sharp turn of the wheel I drove back down the hill, pulled over onto the shoulder where it widened, and pulled out my cell phone.

It rang once before I heard his recorded voice.

"Hey, it's me," I said lamely. "Um. Livvy. I forgot about the time difference. It says on the band's Facebook page that you're in

Berlin. What time is it in Berlin?" I leaned back heavily in the car seat, my heart racing. "I'm here. In Guthrie, and I wanted to say hey. Hey. Also, I'm pregnant. Since December pregnant. You don't have to do anything. Just call me at the end of the tour." I pressed the red dot, tossed the phone into the backseat, and pushed my foot onto the gas pedal, kicking back rocks as I sped back to the inn.

The Coventry County Fair was always held on the last weekend of July. Members of the high school marching band played on the backs of tractors decorated with yellow and orange ribbons, parading down Main Street to the fairground. Margaret had pressed me to go with her and Dotty on opening night — "It's tradition," she insisted — but she relented after I showed her my ankles, which after a morning on my feet looked like overproofed croissants. I waved to Margaret and Dotty from the porch as they climbed into Margaret's station wagon, dolled up in cotton sundresses with cardigans draped over their shoulders, looking like schoolgirls off to see which of the farm boys had started shaving over the growing season.

I made three pies Friday night: one for the

judges, one for us to taste, and one, at Margaret's insistence, for good measure. I knew the extra pie was really in case I dropped one on the floor, which, given that the baby seemed to be draining all of my hand-eye coordination, was fine by me. When I pulled the last pie out of the oven, golden brown and bubbling, Margaret popped the top off a bottle of sparkling apple juice and poured us each a glass.

"Here's to the pies," Margaret said.

"Here's to the winning pies," I offered, clinking our glasses.

Margaret held her glass up. "Here's to an honorable contest. Let the best pie win."

"Here's to destroying Jane White."

Margaret actually laughed. She refilled our glasses. "Well. Here's to friendship." She put her glass down and looked at me. "Thank you for coming back. Olivia . . ." She paused, as if she were searching for the right words. "Guthrie is a good place to raise a child. And Dotty would help you with the baby. As would I. I hope you know you always have a home here."

"But you're selling the inn." Margaret had told the staff the week before that she had verbally accepted the Bradford offer and would be signing the papers at the end of August.

"I'll still be here. I'm going to stay with Dotty for a spell until I decide what I want to do."

"What if we lose tomorrow?" I teased. "Will you still want me around then?"

Margaret looked at me kindly. "Well, I hope we won't have to find that out. This seems like a Jane White–crushing pie to me."

"Me too." I pulled off my apron. "Margaret, can I ask you something?"

"Go right ahead."

"Why did you start losing after all those years?"

Margaret sighed. I thought she was going to tell me to mind my own business. She straightened her back and looked over both shoulders to make sure we were alone.

"My husband did all the baking."

Apple juice shot out my nose. "What?"

"The pie contest was a tradition in my family. The eldest daughter took over the baking when she married. My mother knew I was terrible at it, so she kept entering her pies, just under my name."

It was really hard not to laugh, but I kept it together.

"Thankfully, she taught my Brian before she passed." A tender expression settled on Margaret's face. "That man took home twenty blue ribbons, just for me."

439

I smiled, thinking of the elegant Irish man I had seen in photographs and trying to picture him in the apron with the leaping sheep, crimping piecrusts.

"So where does Jane come in?"

"Dotty told me what she shared with you; you don't need to hide it." Margaret looked out the back windows into the orchard. "For as long as I can remember, Jane has always wanted whatever I had. Altar-guild shift, seat on the gardening committee, first prize at the fair. You'd think she'd be content with her big family and her land and the business. She has everything." Margaret picked up the two empty glasses. "I know it's silly to care so much about a blue ribbon — but it felt good to have that one thing that was mine."

"Well, I think we have the pie to put her in her place." I wrapped my arms around Margaret's neck. She smelled like lilac perfume.

"You get some rest now," Margaret said, pulling back, her voice sounding a little tight. "Tomorrow is going to be a long day."

The kitchen was warm when I walked in the next morning. Margaret had already boxed up the two better-looking pies for judging and was cutting into the third, lamb apron tied around her waist.

Alfred walked in, wearing his summer uniform of a tie-dyed T-shirt and a pair of cargo shorts.

"Pie for breakfast? My favorite."

Sarah appeared with a tray of coffee cups, milk, and sugar. "Decaf is on the right," she said to me.

Margaret handed us each a slice of pie and a fork. I stood motionless, watching their expressions, as Sarah, Al, and Margaret took their first bites.

"Mmm," Alfred hummed. "This is so good. Did you change the spices?"

"I took away a tiny bit — maybe a quarter teaspoon of cinnamon. Do you like it?"

Alfred nodded. "You get a cleaner apple taste."

I looked at Sarah. "How's the crust?"

Sarah covered her mouth with her hand. "Fraky," she mumbled through a mouthful.

"The bottom's not soggy?" I asked, closing my eyes.

"Crisp and brown," said Alfred.

I looked at Margaret. "Okay, what do you think?"

"Very good," she said. "Now drink your coffee before it gets cold, and we can head down to the fairgrounds."

The road to the Coventry County Fair was jammed with a line of brightly painted cars headed for the demolition derby that would follow the pie judging. I had followed Margaret's style advice and put on a pink linen tunic I had inherited from Hannah and a clean pair of black leggings. Silver glitter sandals, the only shoes I could cram my swollen feet into, completed the look. I was ready for my close-up in the *Guthrie Town Crier*. I shifted my weight from hip to hip, trying to find a comfortable way to sit, but it was no use.

"When's the cutoff time for drop-offs?" I asked.

"We have plenty of time."

"Yes, but what time do we actually need to be there?" I scooted my butt toward the edge of the seat and leaned back.

"Entries are submitted between nine and eleven." Margaret looked at me. "Will you stop fidgeting? You're making me nervous."

"Okay, Zen master Margaret! How is it that you're so calm?"

"The pies are baked; we're on time; so long as we can manage to carry ourselves and them across the fairgrounds in one piece, there's nothing more to be done. Once we put the pie down on the table, it's up to the judges."

"Very philosophical," I mumbled under my breath.

Screams rained down from the roller coaster as Margaret pulled into the freshly hayed field that was serving as a parking lot. I stepped out onto the uneven ground and was hit with the pungent mixture of smells that can be found only at a country fair — frying onions, horse manure, cut grass, and apple cider. Margaret took out the two pie boxes.

"Are you sure we need to bring both? Shouldn't we leave the backup in the car?" I asked.

"They can keep the extra in the kitchen. This way we won't have to make a second trip."

"We'd better each carry one," I said, offering both hands. "It's like when parents don't take the same flight. This way at least one of the pies will make it to the grange." Margaret handed over the top box. The judges had given strict instructions — plain white box, disposable metal pie tin. Nothing decorative, nothing to tip off the judges to our identity.

From every angle I could see folks headed

toward the grange hall, clutching white boxes. Margaret and I got in the line, which already stretched the length of the hall and then some. Melissa, wearing her Mrs. Coventry County sash, was overseeing all the baking contests. She walked around with a clipboard, handing out entry forms. Margaret held the pies as I filled out the form. I looked behind us. There were at least twenty bakers lined up, and another thirty or so in front.

The grange was also where all of the arts and crafts were exhibited. Quilts hung from the high ceiling. Photographs lined the walls, and knitted and crocheted pieces were displayed on long tables. Margaret paid no attention to the exhibits, keeping her eyes trained on the back of the hall as we inched closer to a large glassed-in kitchen. She looked at her watch. "Dotty is expecting me to meet her in the flower hall. Will you go over there and tell her I'm running late?"

"Don't I have to drop the pie off myself? Isn't it a rule or something?" I wanted to size up the competition.

Margaret gave me a look that said, *I think I can manage.*

I sighed. "Where's the flower hall?"

"On the other side of the fairgrounds. Bring her back here."

■ ■ ■ ■

Dotty stopped to admire the lace doily display while I ducked back into the ladies' room for the zillionth time that day. When I returned, I found she and Margaret had already settled in amid the rows of folding chairs set up in front of the glass.

"What's our number?" I asked, taking a seat beside her.

Margaret looked down at a slip of paper. "Fifty-seven."

Through the huge window I watched the bakers cross the kitchen, boxes in hand. "Good Lord. Do they cut it off, ever?"

"Not in my time. This certainly is a good turnout."

I eyed the white boxes warily, wishing I had X-ray vision.

"Most get disqualified for having a soggy bottom crust," Margaret offered.

Dotty rummaged in her large canvas bag. "I brought provisions. It looks like it's going to be a long one." She pulled out a thermos and handed Margaret a cup.

The edge of someone's large purse bumped the side of my head. I looked up to see Jane White looming over us, the pink and yellow flowers of her blouse fighting to soften her hard face.

"You really are a glutton for punishment, aren't you?" Jane asked, crossing her fleshy arms.

"Ladies and gentlemen, the president of the Coventry County Fair welcoming committee has arrived," I said. "Feeling a little uncertain, Jane? There's a lot of competition this year." I was in a fighting mood.

Margaret laid a hand on my arm. "Good morning, Jane. How did your pie come out?"

Jane pursed her lips. "Just fine, as always." She hesitated before asking, "And how is yours?"

"Just fine," Margaret replied. "Oh, look, they've handed out the last number."

"Okay, bakers. We've got a record number of entries this year — eighty-two. It's going to be a long judging. Go stretch your legs." Melissa walked into the glass room and locked the door behind her.

I turned to see that all of the folding chairs had been claimed and a standing-room crowd had formed all the way to the back wall. Someone had dimmed the lights, and the glassed-off kitchen glowed like a fish tank in a dark apartment. Behind the glass sat the three judges, two women and a man, each grasping a fork, with scorecards in front of them. Melissa served the judges small glasses of water and then carefully sliced the first pie. The male judge wedged his fork under a slice and tilted it into the air. He peeked at its bottom, then pushed the plate away without even taking a bite. A woman at the end of the row stood and walked out of the hall, sobbing.

"Ouch," I said. "That was harsh."

"Shhhh," Margaret said, scribbling a series of numbers on a yellow legal pad. From our side of the glass you couldn't hear a word of the judges' discussion.

One of the female judges, a horsey-looking woman wearing slacks and a T-shirt that read, "Good apple pies are a considerable part of our domestic happiness," took a bite of the next pie and tossed her fork onto the table. The third judge, a chubby redhead in a beautiful green cotton dress, discreetly spit her bite of the same pie into a paper napkin.

"God, these judges are rough."

"They're being particularly ruthless this year," Dotty whispered. "I think it's because there are so many entries."

"What's our number again?"

"Fifty-seven."

"And what number are we on?"

"Three," Dotty replied, and handed me a bag of kettle corn.

I looked over at the legal pad Margaret had balanced on her lap. On the left were the numbers one through eighty-two, followed by a series of figures. It looked like she had been writing down the lucky lottery picks. I reached over and pulled a slip of white paper, worn from years of folding and unfolding, from between the pages of the pad.

Coventry County Fair Apple Pie Contest

Judge's Score Sheet

External

Shape	10 points	Score_____
Color	5 points	Score_____

Internal

Crust

Texture	15 points	Score_____
Flavor	10 points	Score_____
Doneness	15 points	Score_____

Filling

Fruit	10 points	Score_____
Overall flavor	10 points	Score_____
Texture	10 points	Score_____
Mouth feel	10 points	Score_____

Overall Impression

Judge's final thoughts	Up to 5 points	Score_____

*Total Score*_____

"Where did you get this?"

"Hush now," Margaret said, studying a judge as she slowly chewed a forkful. "And keep that out of sight. Don't want to start a riot."

It was difficult to take your eyes off the judges, who chewed, sniffed, and swallowed bite after bite, their expressions moving from curiosity to delight to disgust. It was like watching silent-movie actors eat.

I turned and scanned the crowd, looking into all of those hopeful faces like sunflowers turned toward the sun, and realized that I was one of them. I had been so focused on how much I wanted Jane White to lose, but in truth all this time I had wanted to win. I wanted to win for the Sugar Maple and its long-standing legacy. For Margaret, who deserved every ounce of pride and admiration that the blue ribbon stood for, whether she had baked the pie or not. And I wanted to win for me, because Margaret was my family, and I hoped to carry the Hurley family torch for years to come and, someday, to hand it down to my daughter.

"The next one is ours," Margaret whispered, and with her strong, thin hand she gripped my arm.

"Margaret, I need to tell you something."

"Not now, Olivia," she said, craning forward.

I placed my hand over hers and squeezed. "I want to stay. And I think you should stay too."

"Miss Rawlings, that's our pie." Margaret pointed to the kitchen. Melissa brought the whole pie to the table. It looked as good as I remembered. Around pie forty-six I had begun to worry about the color. But here was ours, golden brown, with a slight sheen from the watered-down egg wash. Edges perfectly crimped. No visible filling spill-over. Plump, even body. The judges hunched over their score sheets, faces serious.

"Don't sell the inn," I whispered into Margaret's ear.

"Look," said Dotty. Melissa cut into the pie with a chef's knife.

"I can help you," I said to Margaret.

"This is it," Margaret said. "They each have a slice."

I leaned forward. "The filling is nice and thick."

Margaret leaned toward me. Her fingers dug into my arm a little deeper. "And it didn't shrink. It reaches all the way to the top of the crust."

I reached over and took Dotty's hand.

The judges each took a bite. The male

judge closed his eyes and leaned back, chewing slowly.

I fought the urge to jump up and scream, *Yes!*

The judge in the T-shirt took dainty bites while jotting down numbers. The redhead picked her piece apart with the tines of her fork before tasting it. She looked thoughtful as she filled out her form. When Melissa reached down to take her plate, the judge grabbed her wrist and said something.

"What's happening?"

Margaret didn't answer me. All of her focus remained on the judge, who was picking her fork back up. With the edge of the fork, she broke off one more bite. She raised it to her nose first, breathing it in, before popping it in her mouth. Margaret, Dotty, and I leaned forward in our seats.

The judge reached for her pencil and, with long vertical strokes, erased all of her numbers. She took her time refilling in the form. A murmur like a hundred violins being tuned at once rose up from the crowd behind us. I looked over at Margaret. "That was good, right?" I asked, standing up and pressing my fists into my lower back.

"We'll see," said Margaret, but she looked hopeful.

"I need a bathroom break." I stepped

around Dotty's feet, making my way down the aisle.

"You're going to miss the next pie," Margaret said.

The truth was I needed a break from the tension. "Fill me in. I'll be right back."

When the last plate was cleared, the judges stood and shook one another's hands. Melissa opened the glass door and stepped outside. "Phew, that was a long one, wasn't it?" she said warmly to the crowd. "It's going to take some time to tally all the scores, but the awards ceremony should start right on time. I'll see you all at the grandstand at five. Now go get something to eat and enjoy the fair."

The crowd seemed to stand up as one, and the room teemed like a beehive in summer. "Lunch?" Dotty asked.

"I'm too nervous to eat," I said.

Alfred joined us from the back of the room.

"I kind of just want a maple creemee," I said.

"You had pie for breakfast."

"And now ice cream for lunch. Maybe after the contest we could all go for a slice of cake at the diner."

"I'm with Margaret," said Dotty. "Please

452

go feed my grandchild some vegetables."

"I'll make sure she eats something healthy," said Alfred.

"Fine. But I'm having ice cream afterward."

"Be careful," said Margaret.

I raised my eyebrows at her.

"It's crowded. And you've been a little less than graceful the past couple of days."

I thought about the open sack of flour I had managed to drop to the floor the other morning. "I'll be fine. I just want to pet the piglets."

"Don't forget to use hand sanitizer afterward." Margaret had become the baby's guardian, which would have been adorable, except that she kept feeling the need to protect the baby from *me.* "Be back by four thirty. I'll save you a seat. Try not to get too wrinkled. You'll be representing the inn if you win."

I rolled my eyes as I grabbed the map. "Yes, boss."

"Want to take a turn in the goat barn?" Alfred asked.

"I'd love to," I said, linking my arm in his.

The sun warmed the paved road of the fairground, and the warm smell of popcorn and candied apples hung in the air. Children walked by clutching newly won stuffed pandas with their sticky fingers. The mothers all smiled at us when they noticed my swollen belly. I let myself pretend that Alfred was my husband, that this baby was just another step in our carefully laid-out lives.

In the center of the poultry barn, among the many stacked cages, was a glass-domed incubator where chicks were hatching. I walked over and pressed my cheek against the glass. Every few minutes an egg would move and a tiny beak would appear, only to retreat, tired from all the pecking.

"Sometimes I wish the baby would come like this."

"Pecking its way out?" Alfred asked.

"No," I said, laughing, "outside of me. Then I could watch it happen without all the pain."

"Starting to worry, Liv?" Alfred asked gently.

I leaned into him. "A little. Sometimes, like when I wake up with leg cramps, or my back aches, this voice inside my head says, *You don't even know the meaning of the word* pain *yet.*"

"Well, every mother seems to forget all about it once the baby is born."

"Not me. I'm a total lightweight when it comes to pain. I'm planning on holding a grudge."

Alfred and I left the barn and found the maple creemee hut. I bought two cones and handed one to him. A young couple gave up their shady bench to us — one of the excellent fringe benefits of pregnancy, I was fast learning — and we sat down, licking away happily.

"Have you given any more thought to my offer, Livvy?" Alfred asked, as if he were asking me if he needed to order more lemons.

I blushed and took a deep breath. "I haven't talked to Martin about the baby yet." He had called several times, leaving panicked-sounding messages from all over Europe. "And I just think — I think the next thing I should do is talk to Martin."

"Martin is an idiot if he doesn't come back for you."

"True." I smiled up at him. "See, it's a mess. You don't want to get yourself stuck in the middle of all of this." I took my napkin and wiped some ice cream out of Alfred's beard. "You're stuck with me, though. I've decided to hang around." It felt good to say it out loud. Blue ribbon or red, with Martin or without, Guthrie had become what I'd always been looking for: home.

"What about the inn?"

"I have a little money stashed from the cookbook job, but I need to start making calls as soon as the inn changes hands. I'm going to need an income, especially after the baby comes. I can't see Jane White's cousins hiring me."

Alfred leaned over and kissed the top of my head. "Well, it's happy news. You belong here." He smiled. "Besides, it gives me the opportunity to wear you down."

I laughed and tried to stand but failed. Alfred stood and hoisted me up. "I've got to head back and get dinner prep started. You knocked it out of the park, Liv. It's yours to lose." I gave Alfred's hand a thankful squeeze and watched him get swallowed by the crowd.

I lingered on the midway, watching the families. A father soothed a red-cheeked girl who sat crying on the back of a carousel horse while a pair of brothers egged each other on as they whipped baseballs at glass bottles lined up on a shelf. A young couple, still maybe in their teens, walked hand in hand, the girl with a newborn strapped to her chest. They were probably making out on top of the Ferris wheel this time last year, I mused. I tried to picture myself last summer, working long hours in the hot kitchen of the Emerson. It felt like a lifetime ago. The baby did a little somersault. "A lot can happen in a year, young lady," I said as I rubbed the spot on my belly where she felt closest. "All sorts of surprises. I'll make sure you're ready for them."

I followed a trail of teenage boys — skinny, greasy frames in baseball caps and black concert T-shirts — over to the arena where the awards ceremony was being held.

"Olivia," I thought I heard someone say as I was making my way to the chairs near the stage.

I turned and looked into the crowd gathered behind the contestants. Sarah waved at me, beckoning me over. "Hey," I called, edging my way toward the front row, where I was sure Margaret was waiting.

"Good luck," Sarah shouted, and I gave her a wide smile in return.

A hand reached out and grabbed my shoulder. I spun around and into a Tom Carrigan bear hug. The rest of the Beagles were standing behind him. "We're playing the grandstand right after the demolition derby. Want to sit in?"

"You know my Eagles rule, Tom," I said, laughing into his shoulder.

Melissa walked onto the stage and removed the mic from the stand. "Greetings, everyone."

"I've got to get up there or Margaret's going to kill me."

Tom patted my arm. "Go, go, before she gets riled."

I passed Dotty in the ninth row, behind the contestants, flanked by at least two generations of McCracken children. She blew me a kiss.

Melissa adjusted her sash. This was her last official act as Mrs. Coventry County before she had to hand over her tiara to this year's winner. "As many of you know, this has been a record-breaking year for entries in the annual Coventry County Fair's apple pie contest. Thank you, everyone, for entering."

I scooted down the first row, carefully stepping over contestants' bags and feet, whispering apologies and pointing to my enormous belly when someone gave me a scowl.

"Do you do this on purpose?" Margaret hissed as I slid into the chair next to her.

"Of course I do. The excitement keeps you young," I whispered back.

I looked up at the judges, sitting behind Melissa. They didn't look too thrilled about the record-breaking number of pies. The horsey one looked a little green.

"Pies are judged based on the following criteria: appearance, crust, flavor, and filling."

I elbowed Margaret in the ribs. "We have it all," I said in a singsong voice.

"Shhh."

"Olivia." I searched the crowd but couldn't pinpoint the voice. Hannah and Jonathan were standing at the edge of the crowd, wearing matching baby carriers. "You made it!" I called, waving. Hannah held a sleeping baby's hands in hers and made him wave back.

"Miss Rawlings," Margaret hissed.

"So, without further ado . . ." Melissa picked up a white ribbon and an envelope from the small table beside her. "In third place, a newcomer to the pie contest" — Margaret grabbed my hand and squeezed — "Ashley Laferrier, age thirteen. Congratulations, Ashley. Come on up here."

A skinny teenager with thin brown hair down to her waist climbed up the steps. Ashley looked overwhelmed as she gazed at the crowd.

"Olivia!"

I stood up and turned around.

Margaret grabbed my wrist. "Will you sit down?"

I plopped back into my chair, annoyed.

"And now for the red ribbon. The judges said it was very difficult to choose between first and second place. The scores were the same, so it came down to the judges' personal taste. Both of you should feel very proud today." Melissa smiled in an apologetic way. She knew the second-place winner was not going to feel proud. "Okay, so our second-place ribbon this year goes to — Olivia Rawlings, baking for the Sugar Maple Inn. Come on up here, Livvy."

I sat motionless and, to my embarrassment, burst into tears.

"Go on up there, dear," Margaret said.

I turned to face her. "I'm so sorry. I thought we had it."

"It's okay. Now go on up and get your ribbon."

I stood on shaky legs. The people in my aisle stood up to let me by, patting my shoulders, uncertain whether to offer sympathy or congratulations. Someone took my arm and led me up to the stage.

"Come on up here, Livvy," said Melissa into the microphone. "Let's give Miss Rawlings a round of applause."

The crowd began to clap. When I reached Melissa, she handed me the red ribbon and then pulled me into a hug. Tears ran down my face like icing over a too-hot cake. I slowly staggered across the stage and stood next to Ashley.

"It's only a pie contest," she offered, and handed me a tissue out of her pocket.

"And now, for our grand-prize winner, I am very pleased to award this to a long-standing member of our community, who is no stranger to this stage . . ."

I groaned out load.

Ashley looked alarmed. "Is it the baby? Do you need me to get someone?"

"Margaret Hurley, also baking for the Sugar Maple Inn."

"What?" I cried.

The crowd let out a roar, and everyone, including contestants and judges, leaped to their feet, clapping.

Margaret stood, smoothing down her skirt. Her hand went to her throat and she touched her string of pearls. A man offered to escort her to the stage, but she patted his arm away. Margaret walked up the stairs to the podium alone, her head held high.

"Congratulations, Margaret. Good to see you up here again," Melissa said, wrapping an arm around Margaret's shoulder. She handed her the blue ribbon. "Would you like to say a few words?"

Margaret stood for a moment, gazing at the ribbon, running it through her fingers.

The crowd continued to clap and whoop. She looked out into the audience and gave a small bow, then took the microphone that Melissa offered.

"I'm not one for speeches, but I would like to say thank you to the judges. I won't lie — it feels good to have this blue ribbon in my hands again." Several people in the crowd chuckled. "Baking pies for this contest has been a tradition in my family for generations. The Sugar Maple has been a place of celebration for many of you, and it's been an honor to serve this community." She paused, looking down the stage at me. "I'm looking forward to many more years of service and celebration, and I'm looking forward to seeing the next generation of blue-ribbon bakers carry on the tradition. Thank you."

I wobbled across the stage and threw my arms around her, squeezing her as tightly as my belly would allow. And in front of all those people, Margaret did the most surprising thing. She hugged me back, just as tightly.

"When?" I asked.

"Early this morning, before you got up. You've been sleeping in lately."

"How?" I asked.

"I've been practicing," she said, pulling

away but taking hold of my hand.

I bit the inside of my cheek. "You really won't sell?"

Margaret smiled. "Not if you'll help."

"Can we get a picture of you ladies for the paper?" asked the town photographer.

I put my arm around Margaret's shoulder and leaned my head against hers. We held our ribbons to our chests and smiled our biggest smiles.

"How about one of just you, Mrs. Hurley? And can we ask you a few questions about how it feels to win again?"

Old friends and well-wishers stormed the stage. I stood back and watched as person after person shook Margaret's hand and patted her shoulder. Margaret stood as tall and graceful as she always did, but she couldn't hold back the joy in her eyes. I stepped out of the crowd that was enveloping Margaret and walked to the edge.

"Woo-hoo! Go, Margaret!" I hollered from the top step. Margaret met my eye. Grinning, she held up the blue ribbon and gave it a little shake. I blew her a kiss.

"Olivia," someone behind me said. I turned and looked down. There, at the bottom of the steps, stood Martin McCracken.

So this is what it feels like, I thought to myself, breathless as my lungs collapsed to make room for my rapidly expanding heart, *to commit.*

"Hey."

Martin held out his arm to help me down and then caught me in a tight embrace.

"Oh, Livvy," he said, resting his cheek against the top of my head. "Seriously? A voice mail?" he asked into my hair, his hand resting gently on my belly.

"I didn't want to tell you," I said into his armpit, burrowing in with my nose. He smelled like an old pillow I slept with every night, mine and no one else's. "And ruin everything."

The baby gave a swift kick.

"Livvy, I knew before they stamped my passport where I really belonged."

I raised my face to look at him. He smiled at me then. Not the lopsided one but the blue-ribbon one. The one that showed both rows of teeth. Martin wound his fingers into my hair, tilted my head back, and kissed me.

"Come on, Liv," Martin whispered into my ear. "Let's go home."

No words had ever sounded so sweet.

CHAPTER TWENTY
JULY, ONE YEAR LATER

I pressed my feet into the floor and rocked back, hoping the gentle sway of the chair would soothe the baby nudging me from within. No luck.

"Start the rolling pin at the center of the dough and roll outward," I said. "Never back and forth."

"That develops the gluten. Makes a tough crust," Margaret added from the chair on my left.

Sarah pressed the wooden pin into the dough and rolled it away from her, brought it back to the center, and rolled it back.

"Perfect. Now just turn the dough a quarter turn."

A little muffled snore escaped from Dotty, who was asleep in the rocking chair to my right.

Margaret stood up to inspect Sarah's work. "Make sure you have enough flour under there so it won't stick. But not too much."

Sarah looked across the table at me, her eyebrows raised, and tentatively dusted the table with more flour.

"That's it," Margaret said, and went to put the kettle on to boil.

Sarah was baking her own entry for the Coventry County Fair apple pie contest. Margaret and I each planned to enter our own pies, and we were harboring a serious fantasy of the Sugar Maple taking all three ribbons. "It would be great advertising," Margaret insisted. Not that we needed it. The Associated Press had somehow picked up the story the *Coventry County Record* ran, and several larger newspapers had published it. By the time the piece in *Food & Wine* came out, Margaret and the Sugar Maple were already all over Facebook and Twitter. Margaret handled herself with grace in every interview that followed and never once mentioned Jane White in the retelling, no matter how tempting it must have been. I'm pretty sure that's why Margaret sent me on an errand every time a reporter came by.

Salty nosed his way into the kitchen, followed by a crawling Maggie, who was never far behind, and then her father. Martin swooped down to pick her up, and she squealed in delight. He stood behind my chair and kissed the top of my head as he deposited Maggie in my lap.

"Not too rough, Mags. Don't hurt your baby brother."

Maggie rested her head on my belly, which had just started to show.

"Hey," I said, looking up and back at Martin's upside-down face. He leaned down farther and kissed me once on the lips.

"Hey," he said, one hand on my head, the other on Maggie's. "I'm on my way to the house. Do you want me to take her with me?"

Margaret reached over and lifted Maggie off my lap and onto hers. "We'll mind her."

After the fair, Martin and I had moved in with Dotty, at her insistence. She acted as if we were doing her a favor, but that couldn't have been more untrue. Dotty taught me how to take care of a baby, which ended up being much scarier, in my opinion, than actually giving birth, and I wasn't alone while Martin finished the U.S. leg of his tour. Margaret joined us for supper most nights, and usually a few members of the extended McCracken family would wander in. Martin and I still slipped away to the sugarhouse from time to time, in search of some privacy, not having had much time for it to be just him and me. That explained Henry Junior, due on Christmas.

"Livvy, what do I do when the dough tears?"

I rocked myself up and sat down on Tom's stool, propping my foot on *Nancy Drew and the Hidden Staircase.* "It's okay, you can patch it, especially if it's the bottom crust. Just try to roll it a little thicker next time."

Sarah carefully folded the dough into quarters and pressed it into the pie tin. She was proving to be an excellent baker. After our double win at the fair, Margaret and I had been discussing the best place to hang our ribbons when she asked if I wanted to be part owner of the Sugar Maple. I said yes without hesitation, complete in the happiness of knowing that I could keep my family — my whole family, Margaret and the McCrackens, and Alfred and Sarah too — close at hand. Margaret taught me how to do the bookkeeping, and I still did almost all of the baking. Margaret took over the pies, of course. We couldn't take her apple off the menu.

Just as Sarah closed the oven door, her pie safe in the oven, Salty gave a deep woof at the back door.

"I should head back. He needs a walk and she'll be waking up soon." Maggie lay sleeping on Margaret's chest. I reached out to pick her up.

Margaret looked over at Dotty. "Why don't you walk him back? I'll run her home when they're both awake."

"Thank you, thank you, thank you," I whisper-sang, kissing Margaret and her namesake on the cheek.

Salty and I burst through the back door and into the apple orchard. The branches were heavy with ripening fruit. Honey-bees flew in lazy patterns among the trees under the warm late-afternoon sun. Salty bounded ahead when the sugarhouse came into view, waiting on the porch for me to catch up and then following me into the maple grove, tail high and wagging. A few leaves had turned a faded yellow, but the canopy above still glowed green. Salty herded the squirrels, which squawked back up into the trees. The air was cooler here and felt fresh against my skin. I ambled along, enjoying the rare moment of being with just Salty. For years I had thought it would always be just the two of us. Wife and mother were two roles I had never thought would be mine, but now I couldn't imagine not being both. Not to mention a business owner, an aunt, and a sister-in-law. But it was being a daughter again that I found the most surprising. Margaret and Dotty teased me and comforted me and pestered me like I was one of their own. I knew both Henry and my dad would have approved. Wherever they were, I hoped that they had found each other and spent their days swapping tunes.

We walked the carriage path up the hill. The maples thinned, replaced by oaks and pines. When we came to the clearing, I sat down on the grass and Salty scratched at the ground, turned three circles, and lay down next to me with a sigh. Puffs of cloud moved across the deepening blue sky overhead. Before us lay the farm, now so familiar, white farmhouse dwarfed by the big red barn where the cider was kept, a shaggy vegetable garden that Martin, Dotty, and I had planted in the spring. Mabel and Crabapple in a pen. *Home,* I said to myself, the word still new on my tongue. I stood and patted my thigh with my palm. "Come on, Salt."

Salty sprang up and brushed past me. I watched as he bounded toward the farmhouse, racing with abandon, his long legs outstretched, ears flying back, nose in the air. I followed him across the green grass and into the field, the hay high and ready for reaping.

BLUE RIBBON APPLE PIE

DOUBLE CRUST PIE DOUGH
Ingredients
3 cups all-purpose flour

1 tablespoon sugar

1 teaspoon salt

12 tablespoons (1 1/2 sticks) unsalted butter

3 tablespoons solid vegetable shortening (like Crisco)

6 (or more!) tablespoons ice water

Instructions
1. In a food processor, pulse together the flour, sugar, salt, butter, and vegetable shortening until the mixture looks golden and resembles coarse cornmeal.
2. Pour the flour mixture into a large bowl. Add the ice water one tablespoon at a time, lightly fluffing the mixture with your fingers. Add ice water to the mixture until the dough just begins to come together. (I

always mix the water by hand so I have more control.) If you are not sure, try squeezing a little of the dough together in your hand. If it clumps, you are done.

3. Gather the dough into a ball, divide it into two pieces, then flatten the pieces into discs. Wrap the discs in plastic and put them in the refrigerator to rest for at least 1 hour.

4. Roll out the two pieces of pie dough. There are two main tricks to rolling out pie dough: One is to not use too much flour — you can always add a bit more if the dough is sticking to the table, but you can't take it away. The other is to never roll the dough out using a back-and-forth motion. Always work from the center and roll out. That will keep you from working the gluten too much. Use one dough disc to line a 9″ deep-dish pie pan. Place the second rolled-out dough on a cookie sheet. Place both discs back in the refrigerator to rest.

NOW ONTO THE FILLING!

Ingredients

2 tablespoons unsalted butter

4 pounds apples, peeled, cored, and sliced into

1/4-inch thick wedges (I like to use a

mixture of mostly Cortland and McIntosh apples, with 1 or 2 Granny Smith thrown in for tartness and texture)

3/4 cup sugar

2 tablespoons cornstarch

1 teaspoon cinnamon

1/2 teaspoon freshly grated nutmeg

1 egg white, for the crust bottom

Instructions

1. Preheat the oven to 400° F. Make sure there is enough room for a tall pie — you may need to remove a rack.

2. Remove the dough discs from the refrigerator and set aside.

3. In a large skillet, melt the butter. When the butter is sizzling, toss in the apples and stir so they are coated in the butter. Cook for about 10 minutes over medium heat, stirring occasionally. If you do not have a pan large enough, you can do this in two batches.

4. Remove the apples from the skillet (but not the liquid from the pan) and put them in a large bowl. Toss the apples in the sugar, cornstarch, cinnamon, and nutmeg. Set aside.

5. Brush the inside of the bottom crust with the beaten egg white. Pile the sautéed apples into the crust, then cover with the

remaining dough disc. Trim the crusts, then pinch them together. Using your thumbs and index fingers, crimp the crust edge into a pretty pattern. Slice air vents into the top crust. I like to leave my crusts plain, but you can brush the crust with an egg wash (if you like it shiny) or milk (if you like it brown and soft).

6. Turn the oven down to 375° F. Place the pie pan on a cookie sheet, and bake until the crust is a deep golden brown and the filling is bubbling, about 50–60 minutes.

7. Let cool completely before serving.

ACKNOWLEDGMENTS

With gratitude and great affection, I would like to thank the following people who made this book possible:

My super hero agent, Alexandra Machinist, who makes the whole process of selling a book and all that follows look effortless. I am so thankful to have her in my corner.

My editor, Pam Dorman, for her brilliant, insightful editing and steadfast support, and for saying keep in touch all those years ago. It was her early encouragement that kept me writing through all the messy revisions and days full of doubt. Never in my wildest daydreams did I imagine that Pam would actually wind up as my editor, and I couldn't be more delighted or grateful that she did.

All the wonderful people at Viking Penguin, who did such a beautiful job ushering this book into the world, including Brian Tart, Andrea Schulz, Lindsay Prevette, Kate

Stark, Carolyn Coleburn, Jeramie Orton, Seema Mahanian, Rebecca Lang, Mary Stone, Roseanne Serra, Hilary Roberts, Jeannette Williams, Tricia Conley, and the sales team at Penguin Random House.

My writing teachers, especially J. G. Hayes, who made it possible to begin, and Michelle Hoover, who saw me through to the end.

All the folks at GrubStreet writing center, who make an education in creative writing accessible to everyone.

The members of the Novel Incubator community, especially Susan Bernhard, Michele Ferrari, Kelly Ford, Lissa Franz, Mark Guerin, Cynthia Johnson, Anjali Mathur, Kelly Robertson, Emily Ross, Patricia Sollner, and Jennie Wood. Thank you so much for your tireless feedback and happy encouragement.

My partners in crime on *The Debutante Ball*: Jennifer S. Brown, Aya de Leon, Abby Fabiaschi, and Heather Young. Thank you for making this nerve-racking year so much fun.

Kate Racculia, mentor and friend, who gave me the greatest revision advice: bring on the dad. I can't imagine what my debut year would have been like without all of your wonderful guidance and good cheer.

Chris O'Connor — incredible writer, astute reader, cofounder of VGAWP and sender of the world's most inspiring (and profanity-laden) text messages — no one could ask for a smarter critique partner, a more enthusiastic champion, or a better friend.

My dear friend Andrea Raynor, who said I should be a writer when I told her I had just dropped out of art school.

Writing pals Margaret Zamos-Monteith and Catherine Elcik, for their friendship and unwavering confidence in this book.

The Albritton family — Bill, June, and Brit — for their love and support.

Bridget Collins for baking, Lorraine Lee Hammond for old-time banjo, and Corey Raynor for Vermont.

The chefs — Luc Robert, Charlie Binda, and Greg Everard — for answering all my savory cooking questions, giving me time off so I could attend workshops and meet deadlines, and the endless teasing.

My mom, Carol Rizzo, and my sisters Lisa Cataldo and Brenda Miller-Holmes, for believing that I could, and for being so excited when I did.

My dad, Douglas Miller, who loved good stories about regular people. Always loved and deeply missed.

And most of all, thanks and love to my Elizabeth Albritton — first reader, first editor, first everything.

ABOUT THE AUTHOR

Louise Miller is a pastry chef who lives and works in Boston. She received a scholarship to attend GrubStreet's Novel Incubator program. *The City Baker's Guide to Country Living* is her debut novel.

The employees of Thorndike Press hope you have enjoyed this Large Print book. All our Thorndike, Wheeler, and Kennebec Large Print titles are designed for easy reading, and all our books are made to last. Other Thorndike Press Large Print books are available at your library, through selected bookstores, or directly from us.

For information about titles, please call:
  (800) 223-1244

or visit our Web site at:
  http://gale.cengage.com/thorndike

To share your comments, please write:
  Publisher
  Thorndike Press
  10 Water St., Suite 310
  Waterville, ME 04901